GATEWAY WEDDINGS

THREE-IN-ONE COLLECTION

MYRA JOHNSON

ISBN 978-1-61626-472-7

Cover design: Kirk DouPonce, DogEared Design

Published by Barbour Publishing, Inc., P.O. Box 719, Uhrichsville, Ohio 44683, www.barbourbooks.com

Our mission is to publish and distribute inspirational products offering exceptional value and biblical encouragement to the masses.

ecpa Member of the Evangelical Christian Publishers Association

Printed in the United States of America.

Dear Reader:

Though I'm a Texas girl by birth, Missouri will always have a special place in my heart as I fondly recall summer trips to visit my grandparents there. Walking along tree-shaded lanes with my grandpa, helping my grandma make a pie with cherries harvested from their own tree, pumping away on the old player piano that always sounded charmingly off-key...memories I'll carry with me all my life.

Writing these three romance novels set in Missouri was almost like a homecoming. For *Autumn Rains* I created the fictional town of Aileen, reminiscent of the area where my grandparents lived that was an hour's drive from St. Louis. Birkenstock, situated between Springfield and Branson, is the fictional setting for *Romance by the Book*. In *Where the Dogwoods Bloom*, the characters meet in a Lake of the Ozarks country inn near the fictional town of Blossom Hills—so named for the profusion of dogwood trees that bloom every spring. (And the flowering dogwood is Missouri's state tree.)

Of course, faith is central to each of these stories. *Autumn Rains* is about casting aside fear and learning to trust again. The theme of *Romance by the Book* is accepting our God-given individuality. *Where the Dogwoods Bloom* focuses on forgiveness and the true meaning of family. I hope you'll be inspired and encouraged in your walk with God as you read the stories in *Gateway Weddings*. As Jesus says in John 10:9 (NIV), "I am the gate; whoever enters through me will be saved. He will come in and go out, and find pasture." Jesus truly is our "Gateway" to the abundant life God has prepared for us.

By the way, I love hearing from my readers. Email me at mj@myrajohnson.com or visit me at www.myrajohnson.com, www.seekerville.net, or www.facebook.com/MyraJohnsonAuthor.

Many blessings,
Myra Johnson

AUTUMN RAINS

Dedication

For my terrific brother-in-law, Pastor James Hinkhouse, whose experience meeting a real-life "Healy Ferguson" inspired this story, and for my Golden Heart "forever friends," Janet Dean, Julie Lessman, and Tina Radcliffe.

Chapter 1

The Greyhound bus lurched to a stop in a swirling cloud of diesel fumes. Healy Ferguson heaved his long legs into the aisle and slung his ragged duffel bag over his shoulder. When he stepped off the bus, the heat slammed into him with the force of a 250-pound linebacker.

"Welcome to St. Louis," he muttered. Still, he hadn't seen so much sunshine in the past sixteen years, and it felt good. Real good.

Inside the ultramodern Gateway Transportation Center, smells from the food court set his stomach rumbling. He plunged his hand into his jeans pocket and fished out his cash. Nine dollars and seventy-three cents. At least he still had another twenty stashed between the pages of the Bible tucked away in his duffel bag.

Pathetic. He might have to choose between a late lunch and taxi fare to Tom's place.

If his best friend even lived in St. Louis anymore.

If, after all this time, Tom still thought of him as a friend.

Healy collapsed onto the nearest empty seat. *Lord, why did I ever come here? Why did I think Tommy would want to see me again?*

He hadn't heard from his friend in over four years. Maybe Tom's silence was his way of separating himself from a guy he should have written off as a loser from day one. Yeah, Ol' Tom must have finally come to his senses.

Awash in discouragement, Healy raked a hand across his forehead. He'd somehow managed to get stuck in a strange city with practically no money and no idea where to turn.

Except to You, Lord, except to You.

His stomach growled again. The bag of chips he'd picked up at the last stop had long since worn off, and the aroma of hamburgers on the grill enticed him like the fabled siren's song. But several other passengers swarmed the counters, and the wait looked to be a long one. He recalled passing some fast-food joints as they drove in, and after sitting so long, he could use a good walk.

But first a stop in the men's room. Entering a stall, he looped his duffel bag strap over the corner of the door, but before he'd even turned around, a hand snuck over the top and yanked the bag up and over.

"Hey, you!" Healy burst from the stall, too late to nab the thief. A guy with spiked hair and a gold stud in his lip shot Healy a smirk before disappearing through the restroom door. By the time Healy made it to the corridor, the creep was long gone.

Angry and out of breath, Healy collapsed against the wall. All his worldly possessions were in that duffel bag—*now what?* The idea of approaching a security guard made his stomach twist, but what choice did he have? Not that he expected he'd ever see his stuff again.

But Tom's Bible. . .he'd do anything to get that back. Spotting a uniformed cop patrolling the terminal, he caught up with him and tapped his arm. "Excuse me, sir. I've just been robbed."

The cop proved nice enough, taking Healy's report without belaboring his ignorance about restroom security. He explained they'd been on the alert for this guy for a couple of weeks now. "You got a phone number where I can reach you?"

"Uh, nope. Just got into town. Can I call you?"

The officer handed him a business card. "Don't get your hopes up, okay? And watch yourself. This is a big city."

As Healy thanked the man, a growl from the depths of his belly reminded him he still needed food. Except most of his cash had just disappeared along with the contents of his duffel bag. *Lord, I'm trusting in Your infinite provision.*

He felt in his pocket to make sure the rest of his money was safe and then found his way to the exit and out onto the street.

A few minutes later, the cashier at a hole-in-the-wall hamburger joint handed him his order in a greasy white bag. He took a seat at a sticky table and unwrapped his ninety-nine-cent burger. As he bit into the flattened sandwich, he felt like yelling, "Where's the beef?" They served better burgers where he came from, but no way did he wish to be there. Never again.

He popped the last french fry into his mouth and washed it down with a swig of watery cola. On the way to the restroom he stopped in the narrow hallway beside a payphone. A gigantic telephone book with soiled, ripped pages hung from a chain beneath the narrow shelf. He stared at the phone for long seconds. "Can't hurt to try, long as I'm here."

Balancing the book on his forearm, he paged through the residential section under *B*. He found a long list of Bishops, including several Toms, Thomases, and just plain *T*'s, but none of the street addresses matched what he remembered. He pictured the countless envelopes he'd addressed to 2418 Ashton Brook Lane, St. Louis, Missouri. Tom could have moved, and if Healy's letters weren't getting forwarded, maybe Tom came to believe Healy had broken off the friendship.

He frowned. He'd finish off his remaining coins long before he tried all those phone numbers. But Tom was worth the risk, whatever the cost.

Okay, better get started. He inserted some change and punched in a number. Two rings, three, four.

"Hi, y'all," chirped a recorded greeting—a woman's voice but heavy on the Southern drawl. "This is Tom and Amy's voice mail. Leave a message at the—"

Healy hung up. Unless Tom had remarried, his wife and college sweetheart was from Massachusetts and her name wasn't Amy. Besides, when Tom wrote several years ago, telling Healy all about his new bride, he sounded forever-after, head-over-heels in love.

He tried the next number. A teenager rudely told Healy he'd never heard of a Thomas Charles Bishop formerly of Gloucester, Massachusetts, and where in the—Healy winced at the curse—was Gloucester anyway?

He had enough change to make one more call. Maybe the restaurant Tom owned? He remembered it was Italian but couldn't recall the exact name. Too much time has passed since Tom's last letter. Too much Healy didn't want to remember. In shutting out the bad memories, he'd blurred a few important things as well.

"Lord, help me here. If I'm not supposed to find Tom, why'd You let me get on the bus to St. Louis in the first place?"

"Hey, buddy, you gonna make a call or not?"

He turned to face a short, tough-looking guy with a red-eyed rattlesnake tattoo glaring from his bicep. Healy edged away from the phone, his hands lifted in surrender. "Sorry. It's all yours."

He trudged out of the restaurant, met once again by intense heat rising off the shimmering sidewalk. With no goal in mind, he walked the sizzling streets until he found himself at the Mississippi River. Sweat ran in rivulets down his torso. He never realized Missouri could get this hot and humid.

And all this way for nothing. If only he could recall more details. Tom's wife had family in the area, Healy knew that much, but he couldn't remember any names, much less what city they lived in.

And Tom's letters were long gone, stolen by another tattooed tough guy, a newbie at the rooming house who didn't share Healy's taste in Christian music. Healy could only watch helplessly as the last ties to his only friend on earth took a nosedive into a flaming trash can.

And now he didn't even have the Bible, the one Tom gave him the last time he visited.

"I'm off to that little college in Boston I told you about," Tom had told him. "Might not get back to Michigan any time soon, so I wanted you to have this Bible to remember me by. Hang on to it, Gus." Tom always called him by the nickname—short for Ferguson—he'd bestowed when they first met on the high school football team. "This book holds the words of life."

Words of life that had sustained Healy through a torturous decade and a half. Now he wanted to find and personally thank the man who'd shared faith and hope with him, who had, at least a long time ago, believed in Healy Ferguson when others turned their backs.

The late afternoon sun reflecting off the murky Mississippi told him he'd soon need to make plans for the night. Maybe he could curl up in one of the bus station seats until morning, then decide how to pay for a ticket back to. . .

No, there'd be no going back. How did the worn-out cliché go? *Today is the first day of the rest of your life.* He'd dreamed of a new start. Tom or no Tom, with God's help maybe St. Louis could be just that.

He made it back to the transportation center shortly before sunset, but his long, aimless walk had left him sweaty, parched, and hungry again. He could wash up in the restroom, then break out his remaining cash and buy himself a little supper. Possibly his last meal if he didn't figure out something quick.

❧

A crash and a shout of pain shattered the afternoon stillness. The fountain pen flew from Valerie Bishop's hand, sending a spray of ink across the journal page. She fought to drag her thoughts away from the bittersweet memories she'd been reliving. *The security system—had someone—*

"Mrs. Bishop, are you up there? I need help."

Her head cleared instantly. "Mr. Garcia!"

She hurried downstairs, gasping for breath by the time she reached the living room. The gray-haired handyman lay in a heap next to his toppled ladder on the paint-spattered drop cloth.

Valerie rushed over to kneel beside him. "What happened? Are you hurt?"

He clutched his thigh, grimacing. "My leg. I think it's broken."

"Don't move. I'll call 911." She raced to the kitchen phone and placed the call, then returned and retrieved a pillow from beneath the plastic tarp covering the sofa. Gently she placed it under Mr. Garcia's head. "An ambulance is on the way. Does it hurt much?"

"Only when I breathe." He offered a weak smile. "My own fault, trying to paint twelve-foot walls with a six-foot ladder. Too stubborn to go out to the truck for the longer one." He shifted his weight and let out a groan.

"Careful, you could be hurt worse than you think." Valerie patted his arm as her glance took in the high walls, where a wide strip of mottled green near the ceiling contrasted with the fresh coat of eggshell white.

"Doc ain't gonna be happy about this," Mr. Garcia said. "I promised him I'd wrap things up by the end of the month."

"You let me worry about my brother," Valerie stated with an encouraging smile. Connor Paige and his wife, Ellen, had spent the last few years renovating the historic two-story Victorian. They'd hoped to have at least the lower floor completed in time for Connor's Fourth of July staff party, less than two weeks away.

"Aunt Val?" came a tentative voice from the top of the stairs. "I heard a bad noise."

"Down here, Annie." Valerie straightened, then strode to the hallway, ignoring the pull in her lower back. Honestly, some days she felt more like sixty than thirty. She rested a hand on the banister and looked up at her sleepy-eyed niece, whose flaxen ringlets lay matted against her damp brow. Except for Annie's natural curls, Valerie could have been looking at herself at age four.

As Annie trudged downstairs, dragging a stuffed rabbit by one ear, Valerie heard the squeal of brakes. Red and blue strobe lights sliced through the curtains. Once again, Valerie fought to still her racing heart and focus on the task at hand.

"Are those the doctor people? What happened?" Hugging her rabbit with one arm, the little girl gripped the hem of Valerie's sundress.

"Mr. Garcia fell from his ladder." As Valerie entered the alarm code on the keypad, she tried not to dwell on the fact that one light blinked steadily, indicating an open window in the living room, left ajar for ventilating the paint fumes.

Two paramedics entered. She directed them through the French doors. "Careful, there's wet paint."

Within seconds, three of the neighbors appeared in the entryway. Maggie Jensen, balancing a plump, red-haired toddler on her hip, spoke first. "We saw the ambulance drive up. Is everything okay?"

"Mr. Garcia took a bad fall." Valerie rubbed her arms and glanced toward the living room.

Jean Franklin, wearing tennis togs, pulled a stretch-terry sweatband off her short gray curls. "That's awful. Is he hurt very badly?"

"It's a broken leg, I think."

"And how are *you*?" Maggie placed her free arm around Valerie's shoulder.

She gave a wry grin and reached across to tousle little Steven's flaming locks. "A little shook up, but I'll be fine."

Cliff Reyna, the third neighbor, shrugged. "I'll get out of your way then, but you know where to find me if you need anything." He nodded toward his bungalow across the street.

Valerie smiled her gratitude. "I know, and I appreciate it more than I can say."

After the paramedics transferred Mr. Garcia to the ambulance and drove away, Valerie closed the door against the stifling heat. Thank goodness Connor's first remodeling priority had been installing central air-conditioning. She expelled a tired sigh, then twisted the dead bolt and reset the alarm.

"Mr. Garcia didn't clean up his mess." Annie pointed to the cream-colored sludge oozing from the overturned paint tray.

Paint smells filled Valerie's nostrils. "Guess I'd better find someone who can finish the job."

Two hours later, Valerie hadn't yet lined up another painter. She shoved the phonebook across the kitchen table.

A key in the lock announced Ellen Paige's arrival home from teaching summer English classes at East Central College. After disabling the alarm, she dropped her shoulder bag on the table next to the phonebook. She dropped a quick kiss on Annie's head and collapsed into the nearest chair.

Valerie saw the fatigue in her sister-in-law's eyes. Probably the heat—it had been affecting them all. She walked to the refrigerator. "You look like you could use a cold drink."

"Sounds wonderful. Thanks." Glancing out the window, Ellen nodded toward the painter's truck parked in the driveway. "Mr. Garcia still at it?"

"Afraid not." Valerie returned with two glasses of ice water. She fortified herself with a long swallow, then explained about the accident.

"Poor man." Ellen furrowed her brow. "I hope he'll be okay."

"I'll call later and check on him. Maybe we could send over a meal." She poked at the ice cubes in her water glass. "I never thought to call anyone about picking up his truck and equipment. Maybe Mrs. Garcia can have someone come by."

"Mommy, you should have seed the doctor people," Annie said. "The amb'lance made a lot of noise. Can I have a cookie?"

"Too close to supper, sweetheart." Ellen coiled one of the tot's blond curls around her finger. "Any ideas where we could find someone to finish the painting, Val?"

"Everyone I've tried is already locked into other jobs, most of them for the rest of the summer." She pried open a bobby pin with her teeth and tucked a loose strand of hair into her topknot.

"Well, that fries it." Softening her expression, Ellen continued, "Honestly, Val, none of this work would be getting done if you weren't here to oversee things. Household manager, nanny, best friend—" She leaned across the table and gave Valerie a grateful hug. "You're the best sister-in-law ever."

"The feeling's mutual." She couldn't bring herself to imagine where she'd be without the generosity of her brother and his wife. Probably in a mental hospital somewhere. . .or worse. She refused to impose on her widowed mother, already overburdened with the care of Valerie's aging grandparents.

Ellen drained her glass. "So what are we going to do? Connor sure can't finish the painting himself, not with putting in ten-hour days seeing patients."

The image of her tall, sandy-haired brother holding a paintbrush made Valerie laugh. "Imagine how long it would take that perfectionist to paint one wall, much less an entire room!"

Ellen chortled. "Right. Connor better stick with plastic surgery, where his perfectionism is truly an asset."

The kitchen door whisked open, and Connor Paige breezed in. He kicked the door shut and tossed his car keys on the table. "You two talking about me behind my back again?"

"Honey, you're home early." Ellen self-consciously tugged at her ash brown curls as she greeted her husband with a kiss.

"Mmm, love you, too, babe." He drew her into his arms. "My last surgery of the day was canceled. The lady decided she liked her nose the way it was."

"Her loss, my gain." Ellen's voice became husky, and she melted into his embrace. "I get to rub noses with the handsomest guy in the world."

Valerie caught Annie's enraptured gaze and smiled to herself, drawing her own vicarious pleasure from seeing Connor and Ellen so much in love.

With a downward glance, she clenched her left fist and felt the pressure of her gold wedding band between her fingers.

Oh, Tom, I miss you so.

Chapter 2

"Hey, hey you." A rough hand jostled Healy awake. "This ain't no hotel, ya know."

Pain shot through his neck as he tried to straighten from his slouched position. "Sorry." He rubbed his eyes and attempted to focus on the wiry, balding man standing over him.

"You been here all night," the man said, leaning on a broom handle. "I know, because I'm the janitor, and so have I." He dragged a sweat-stained handkerchief across his forehead and sank onto the seat beside Healy. "I'd'a had security kick you outta here a long time ago, except you look to be an honest guy who's temporarily down on his luck."

"Yeah, you could say that. Everything I own was stolen in the men's room yesterday."

"Bummer. Security's usually pretty tight here, but I heard they'd had a few problems lately. Wish I could help, but workin' in bus stations for nigh on thirty years, I learned real quick not to keep much cash on me."

"Thanks anyway. It's my own fault for being careless." Healy ran stiff fingers through his tangled hair. His mouth tasted like damp cardboard.

The janitor reached for a discarded section of newspaper and smoothed out the wrinkles. "This yours?"

"Naw, picked it up off the floor yesterday." He reached for the paper, folded open to a half-page advertisement for area churches. Last night, as he'd weighed his sadly limited options, he'd decided the best thing to do would be to seek assistance from a church, and one ad had snagged his attention. A white-haired, bespectacled pastor smiled warmly from an inch-tall grainy photo, bringing to mind Healy's boyhood Sunday school teacher. And the name of the suburb—Aileen—had a familiar ring. He wondered if Tom had mentioned it before in his letters.

"You know that place?" Healy pointed to the ad. "The preacher looks like a nice guy."

The janitor took a closer look. "Aileen's down the road a fair piece. Quiet, country-like. Lots of fancy old homes, good place to raise kids."

Healy looked away, an ache tightening his throat. Aileen didn't sound much like a town where he'd fit in. And kids? Those came with a wife, a job, and stability.

Fat chance.

Still. . . *Aileen*. The name rolled around in his mind like a soothing melody. He glanced sideways at the janitor. "How far you say it is?"

"Maybe forty miles." He pointed over his shoulder. "Take I-44 past Gray Summit, then over toward Villa Ridge."

The highway and town names meant nothing to Healy, but he thanked the janitor and stood wearily. The food court had begun gearing up for breakfast, and the smells of sizzling bacon and brewing coffee pushed Healy's gnawing hunger into overdrive. A wave of dizziness made him stagger.

"Steady, there." The janitor grasped his arm. "When'd you eat last?"

"Yesterday, sometime." He'd spent the last of his money on a package of cheese crackers from a snack machine.

The janitor pulled his wallet from a pocket inside his coveralls. "My shift ends in twenty minutes anyway, so I'll give you what little I have. Buy yourself some breakfast."

Healy tried to shove the money away. "How will I pay you back?"

"Just do a good turn for somebody else you meet along the way." The janitor touched a finger to his forehead and returned to his cleaning cart.

Healy spent about five seconds offering up a prayer of heartfelt thanks to his heavenly Provider, then stepped up to the counter and ordered coffee and pancakes. When he finished eating, he returned to the clerk and asked if he could purchase a tall cup of ice.

"And can you tell me how to get from here to Interstate 44?"

❧

In the relative coolness of the June morning—the temperature just creeping into the eighties—Valerie sat in a wicker porch rocker and watched Annie play on her multicolored swing set. Two tall oaks and an ancient elm shaded the backyard; purple and fuchsia petunias cascaded from planters on the porch rail. The six-foot cedar fence and padlocked gates offered a semblance of security.

A sultry breeze toyed with a strand of Valerie's hair as she lifted the cordless phone from her lap. Reading from Mr. Garcia's business card, she dialed his home number. His wife put him on the line.

"Mrs. Bishop, so kind of you to call."

"I tried to phone last night, but you were probably still at the hospital. How are you?"

"Leg's gonna be fine, but I'll be staying off ladders for a while." Mr. Garcia chuckled, then his tone grew serious. "I'm real sorry to leave Doc Paige in a bind."

"It's okay, really. And Connor said to let you know if his hospital connections can be of any help."

"Thanks, I appreciate that."

The porch boards creaked under the rungs of Valerie's chair. "Any chance you know of someone who might fill in for you?"

"I can give you a couple names. . .but summer's a busy time."

"So I've discovered. I've already tried everyone in the Yellow Pages."

Mr. Garcia apologized again.

"Please, it's not your fault. We'll figure something out." She smirked. "At worst, we'll start a new Fourth of July tradition. We'll pass out T-shirts and coveralls, and Connor can make his get-together a painting party."

"Now there's a plan," Mr. Garcia said with a laugh. He told Valerie his wife and a friend would come by later for his truck and equipment.

She said good-bye and laid the phone on a glass-topped wicker side table.

"Come swing me, Aunt Val," Annie called. "Make me go high."

"Be right there." Valerie slipped her bare feet into the sandals she'd pushed aside.

The sun's glare reminded her of the latest weather report: heat and drought with no immediate end in sight. Valerie didn't miss the long winters and deep snows of Massachusetts, but this summer threatened to do her in. Thank goodness they weren't on mandatory water rationing, because the sprinkler system was the only thing keeping the lawn and garden plants alive.

She reached down to refasten a yellow barrette holding Annie's riot of curls off her damp face, then gave the swing a gentle push.

Annie giggled. "Higher, higher!"

Valerie tickled Annie's ribs on the next pass. "Any higher and you'll fly right over the roof."

The back door slammed, and Valerie looked up to see Ellen striding toward them.

"Hey, squirrel." Ellen waited for the swing to slow and then lifted Annie out. "How about a good-bye kiss before Mommy heads off to work?" As she planted her lips on the girl's head, she wrinkled her nose in disgust. "Sweaty, sweaty, sweaty. Phee-ewww!"

Annie squirmed away. "Oh, silly mommy!"

With a pat on the bottom, Ellen sent Annie off to play, then draped an arm around Valerie's shoulder. "After we get the little stinker into bed tonight, Connor and I have something important to talk to you about."

Concern prickled the back of Valerie's neck. Leave it to Ellen to drop a bomb like that and then make her wait all day for the rest of the story. She could certainly guess what the "something important" might be. A married couple deserved privacy, and Valerie lived in dread of the day Connor and Ellen would tell her she needed to pull herself together once and for all, move out, and live her own life.

And she simply wasn't ready.

❧

If not for the problem of finding another painter, Valerie might have spent the entire day brooding over Ellen's cryptic words.

Father, she prayed, taking the cordless phone from its cradle in the kitchen nook, *I know it's long past time for me to be living independently again—but the very thought terrifies me. Have I taken Connor and Ellen too much for granted?*

Exhaling through tight lips, she pressed the numbers for the pastor's office at Zion Community Church. "Good morning, Pastor. It's Valerie Bishop."

"Hello, my dear, how are you on this sweltering summer day?"

The image of the jolly, white-haired man smiling into the telephone cheered her immediately. With his scholarly mannerisms and cultured accent, he reminded her of an eccentric old Anglican vicar. She often wondered how he'd ended up shepherding their small-town congregation in Aileen, but the folks at Zion adored him.

Valerie peeked into the den to check on Annie, then carried the phone back to the kitchen. "I'm in a bit of a quandary, and I'm hoping you can help. You've probably heard about Phil Garcia's accident." She lowered herself gently into a chair.

Pastor Henke laughed. The painter's wife also happened to be the church librarian. "Harriet has made sure everybody in the office knows, and the ladder gets higher and the leg cast bigger every time she tells the story."

"I feel horrible for him." She sighed. "The problem is, we haven't found anyone else to finish the renovations, and I thought you might know of someone. Perhaps an Eagle Scout looking for a project, or maybe a bored retired person who'd like a little extra income."

"Let me put my thinking cap on. Can I get back to you?"

"Of course." She closed her eyes. "You know where to find me."

"Valerie," Pastor Henke began.

She winced at his cajoling tone. "Please, Pastor, don't start on me again."

"All right, but this has gone on quite long enough, my dear, and I absolutely refuse to give up on you."

As she said good-bye, Valerie couldn't help but smile. The pastor had been offering his tender counsel ever since she moved to Aileen four years ago to live with her brother. The panic attacks had started even before Valerie was released from the hospital after the accident. The doctors called it *post-traumatic stress disorder*. Valerie only knew that on the night Tom died, she lost not only all semblance of security but all her hopes for the family she'd dreamed of creating with the love of her life.

Thank You again, Father, for Connor and Ellen. Their invitation to share their home had been the best thing she could have hoped for at the lowest point in her life.

With a grateful sigh, she retrieved the glass of iced tea she'd left by the phone cradle and pressed its coolness to her cheek.

❧

Hot. Healy couldn't remember when he'd ever been so hot. When he began his trek shortly before eight that morning, a bank thermometer had read eighty-six degrees. Eighty-six that early in the day? What had he gotten himself into? Summer in Michigan would have seemed downright balmy in comparison.

But Michigan held nothing for him now. It felt like a whole other lifetime, one he'd just as soon forget.

Long after he'd finished off his melted ice and refilled his cup several times from gas-station water hoses, a robust trucker pulled over and offered Healy a ride.

"How far you headed, son?" The man shot him a toothy smile.

"Aileen." Healy basked in the cool of the air conditioner wafting through the open cab door. He pulled the rolled section of newspaper from his back pocket and pointed to the listing for Zion Community Church. "I'm going there."

"Aileen, huh? I can get you as far as Gray Summit. That's where I dump my load. Aileen's maybe six or seven miles off the highway from there."

"Close enough." Healy grinned his thanks and climbed into the cab.

The half-hour ride gave him a chance to rest his weary legs and quench his thirst with the frosty lemon-lime soda the trucker offered him from his cooler. The trucker wheeled the big rig into the loading area behind a warehouse. "End of the line for me, son. Hope you can find another ride for the rest of the way."

"God bless you for your kindness."

The driver pointed him in the direction of Aileen, and Healy resumed his sweltering trek.

Following the signs, he trudged along a winding two-lane road. He passed country estates, farms, and rolling meadows where horses, sheep, and small herds of cattle grazed. The withered grass and shrinking ponds gave evidence of the early summer heat wave.

Around the next bend, he caught sight of the Aileen city limit sign. POPULATION 2,376. He groaned. How many job opportunities could there be in a town this small?

But he couldn't shake the sense that God had led him here, led him to Aileen and the kind-faced pastor of Zion Community Church.

When he reached the town square, he spotted the church directly across the green. Stained-glass windows framed the double doors of the white clapboard building. A tall bell tower with a gold cross on top cut a bright slash across the cloudless sky. A sign indicated the pastor's office could be found at the rear of the building. Healy followed a narrow sidewalk between neatly manicured flowerbeds and came upon a small outbuilding behind the church. He knocked and entered uncertainly.

"Come in and close the door," came a cheery voice, "before you let all the cool air out."

Seeing the round-faced man behind the cluttered desk, Healy recognized him as the pastor in the newspaper photo. "Excuse me, sir, I—"

The pastor's mouth dropped open. His eyes widened. Healy could only imagine what he must look like, barging in off the street in a sweat-soaked T-shirt and filthy jeans. Not to mention he needed a shave, and his last haircut wasn't exactly *GQ* material.

Face it. You look like what you are, an ex-con. You were wrong to come here. Aileen is definitely not your kind of town.

"I, uh. . .sorry to bother you." He lowered his head and started out the door.

"Don't go." The pastor scurried around the desk. "Here, have a seat." He took Healy by the arm and guided him toward an ancient sofa upholstered in green corduroy. "Please forgive my rudeness. I was expecting someone else, that's all."

He closed the door and stood before Healy. "Now, young man, you look as if you're in need of some help. Please tell me what I can do."

Healy gulped. Since he'd arrived in St. Louis yesterday, three perfect strangers had befriended him. He didn't know what to do with such undeserved kindness. He braced his arms on his thighs and sighed.

The short, plump pastor plopped down beside him. "My, that's some scar." He pointed to the six-inch strip of dimpled white flesh on Healy's left forearm. "May I ask how it happened?"

Healy pressed his lips together, his answer barely audible. "Knife fight."

The pastor sat back and folded his hands. "Sounds like you have quite a story to tell."

Chapter 3

Valerie sat in Connor's paneled study overlooking the sunny front lawn. One hand resting on a computer mouse, she scrolled down a web page and selected two boxes of shredded wheat to add to her online grocery order.

"What else, Miss Annie?" she asked the squirming girl in her lap.

"Cookies."

"You and your cookies." Valerie tickled Annie's tummy until the little girl doubled over in giggles. She selected another item from a dropdown menu. "Okay, what kind? Oatmeal? Chocolate chip?"

Annie pointed to a picture of peanut butter sandwich cookies. "Those kinds."

Valerie moved the cursor and clicked. "Your wish is my command. Hop down now, and let me finish. Then we'll have time for one more game before Mommy and Daddy get home."

"Yay! I'll go pick one." Spiraled pigtails jiggling, Annie dashed out of the study.

Valerie released an envious groan at the little girl's bubbling energy. Turning to the computer screen, she selected the SUBMIT ORDER button. While she waited for the confirmation message, she wondered again what Ellen and Connor planned to tell her tonight.

After dinner, she had to suppress her anxiety awhile longer as she washed up the dishes and Ellen got Annie into the tub for a bubble bath. Two bedtime stories later, followed by Annie's nightly prayer in which she blessed everyone including the postman, the church custodian, and the Jensens' three-legged dog, Connor and Ellen finally settled their little girl into bed. Valerie followed their kisses and hugs with several of her own, and the three adults tiptoed downstairs to the quiet kitchen.

"Con, honey, a tall glass of cold milk would sure taste good right now." Ellen set out some glasses. "Some for you, Val?"

"Sure. I'll break out the graham crackers."

"Three tall white ones, coming up." Connor hefted the milk jug from the refrigerator.

"All right, you two, what's going on?" Valerie's voice rang with forced brightness as she joined her brother and sister-in-law at the table. Dread tightened its grip on her heart, and she hoped they didn't notice her trembling hand as she passed around the box of grahams.

Connor and Ellen exchanged looks.

"You should tell her, Con," Ellen said.

"I'm surprised you didn't let it slip already." Dodging Ellen's playful slap, Connor glanced at Valerie. "Okay, here's the deal, sis. I, uh, we're. . ." His jaw clenched.

Dry graham cracker crumbs lodged in Valerie's throat. She sipped her milk and swallowed hard. "Just say it, Connor. You're scaring me."

He laughed nervously. "It's just that we're hoping you'll be as happy about this as we are. Ellen and I—we're going to have another baby."

"Oh. Oh, my goodness. That's wonderful!" The knot of anxiety swelled into a teary explosion of joy. She almost tipped over her milk glass in the rush to embrace her brother and his wife. "How long have you known?"

Ellen handed her a napkin to dry her eyes. "I was starting to get suspicious, so we did a pregnancy test last night. According to my calculations, the baby's due in early February—right around Annie's birthday." She held Valerie at arm's length, her brows furrowed. "Are you okay with this? I mean, *really*?"

"Why wouldn't I be?" Valerie hugged her sister-in-law again. "I know how much you've been wanting another child. And Annie will be thrilled to have a new baby brother or sister."

Connor wrapped his arm around her waist. "You've been so great with Annie, and then taking charge of the renovations and all." He glanced up at her with concern. "The thing is, we don't want the baby to be an additional burden."

Valerie stepped back, her fears crashing in again. "Connor, don't you realize that being a nanny to your children is the best thing that could ever happen to me?" *Or second-best.* She clamped down on the fresh surge of regret.

Connor grinned. "We were hoping you'd still feel that way."

Relief flooded her—they weren't sending her on her way after all!

But as she returned to her seat, Valerie's heart constricted with a new concern. "Ellen, the paint fumes. You shouldn't even be in this house."

"Connor and I run the air purifier in our bedroom, and we use those high-efficiency filters in the AC." She cast Valerie a look of loving accusation. "The fumes aren't good for you, either. When we find another painter, I wish you and Annie would. . .could go out. . ." She let her words trail off with a helpless shrug.

"Annie and I are fine. We spend most mornings playing in the backyard. When it gets too hot, we stay in the den with the door closed. And Mr. Garcia was always good about cracking a window for ventilation." Although she never wasted any time closing and locking the windows after he finished for the day.

"You know what Ellen's trying to say, Val," Connor said in a low voice, "and it's not about paint fumes."

She couldn't meet his eyes. "I know."

Later, alone in her bedroom, she permitted her full range of emotions to surface. In spite of the joy flooding her at the thought of a precious new niece or nephew, her heart threatened to break in two. "Oh, dear Lord, when will You take away the pain? When will You fill up this horrible, aching emptiness? Will I ever feel whole again?"

She stared at the ink-stained journal entry she'd been writing in yesterday when Mr. Garcia fell. Words leaped out at her. *My precious one. . .never forget you. . .in my heart to stay.*

She moved the book aside and pulled a crisp sheet of stationery from the drawer. When she reached for her Bible, it fell open easily to one of her favorite psalms, number 139, and she copied the verses with flowing script:

> *For you created my inmost being;*
> *you knit me together in my mother's womb. . . .*
> *My frame was not hidden from you*
> *when I was made in the secret place. . . .*
> *All the days ordained for me were written in your book*
> *before one of them came to be.*

When the ink dried, she carefully folded the paper in thirds and slid it into an envelope. Across the front, she wrote:

> *Dearest Connor and Ellen,*
> *May the Lord continue to bless your very special family.*
> *Thank you for letting me be a part of it.*
> *Valerie*

She tiptoed into the darkened master bedroom and turned on the bedside lamp. Laying the envelope atop Ellen's Bible on the nightstand, she smiled. But when she glimpsed her reflection in the cheval mirror, a wan face looked back at her with haunted eyes.

You have every right to be hurt and angry, an inner voice taunted. *Every right to be jealous of your brother's happiness. Every right to blame God for what happened to you.*

"No. I will never blame God for the wickedness of sinful human beings." She wanted to sink to her knees and beg God's forgiveness for even acknowledging such cold, ugly thoughts.

❧

Healy felt like he'd died and gone to heaven. Heaven couldn't be any sweeter than this, could it? Blueberry waffles dripping with melted butter, hot maple syrup sliding across a shiny china plate. Fresh-brewed coffee with a hint of cinnamon, and was that real cream in the little blue cow-shaped pitcher?

"Sorry the waffles are the frozen kind." Pastor Henke removed two more from the toaster oven and plopped them on Healy's plate. "Being a widower, I've chosen convenience over haute cuisine. More coffee? Orange juice?"

"Pastor, you've done too much already." Healy wasn't real sure what *haute cuisine* was, but these toaster waffles tasted mighty fine. He shoveled in another mouthful and groaned in delicious agony.

The white-haired gentleman filled a mug of coffee for himself and settled his bulk into a chair. "So, my dear boy, are you awake enough to finish that extraordinary tale you began in my office yesterday before the budget committee arrived?"

"Where'd I leave off?" Yesterday already seemed like a blur. Healy spread a pale yellow chunk of butter across the steamy waffles, then added more syrup.

"I believe you'd come to the part about seeing Zion's ad in the newspaper." Pastor Henke stirred cream into his coffee. "I'm still amazed you'd trek all the way to Aileen. Whatever possessed you, especially in this merciless heat?"

Fork poised above his plate, Healy stared thoughtfully. "Couldn't shake the feeling this is where God was sending me."

"You mentioned something about an old friend you were hoping to find?"

"I'm afraid that's a lost cause." Healy exhaled long and loud. "Thought maybe that's why Aileen sounded familiar to me—maybe from a letter or something. Prison sorta messed with my memory. Some stuff I remember real well. Other stuff. . .it's just gone."

The phone jangled, and Pastor Henke jumped up to answer it. He stood with his back to Healy and spoke in muted tones. The best Healy could make out was the occasional "I see" and "Well, well, well."

Finally Pastor Henke said good-bye and turned to face Healy. His mouth formed a thin line. "That was the warden."

The waffles turned to cement at the bottom of Healy's stomach. He knew Pastor Henke had placed some calls to verify his story. Couldn't blame the man, considering the way Healy had walked in off the street, looking awful and smelling worse. Now the big question was, what exactly would the warden have said about him?

"Oh, my boy, my boy." Pastor Henke clucked his tongue and returned to his chair.

Healy pressed back from the table. "It's okay, Pastor. I'll be out of here in—"

"Young man." Pastor Henke seized Healy by the wrist. "You are not going anywhere. At least not until we find you suitable employment and a place to live."

"But—"

"No buts about it. Warden Smithers confirmed everything you've told me. He's faxing detailed reports and letters of recommendation—his own, plus several from the prison chaplain, psychiatrist, job counselor, your parole officer, and others." The pastor released Healy's wrist, then sat back and smiled. "Seems you made quite an impression during your stay as a guest of the Michigan correctional system, and they are more than delighted to help facilitate your new start in life."

All the air rushed out of Healy's lungs. He lifted his gaze to the ceiling. "Thank You, Jesus!"

"Now, where were we?" Pastor Henke folded his hands around his coffee mug. "Ah yes, you were about to tell me about this friend you're looking for."

"Best friend a guy could ever have. We went to high school together, played on the football team. He's the one who led me to Christ."

"And there's a chance he might live in Aileen?"

Healy chewed another mouthful of waffle. "Could be, or maybe he has family here. All I remember for sure is that I used to write to Tom at a St. Louis address, and he owned an Italian restaurant."

"Your friend's name is Tom? He owned an Italian restaurant?"

Healy looked up at the sudden quaver in the pastor's voice. "Tom Bishop, yes, sir."

"Oh dear." Pastor Henke slowly shook his head. "Oh, my dear, dear boy, it's possible I may have some terribly sad news for you."

Chapter 4

As Valerie poured grape juice into a plastic Little Mermaid cup for Annie's afternoon snack, the warble of the kitchen phone startled her. Annoyed with herself, she took a couple of steadying breaths before answering.

"It's me again," came Pastor Henke's cheery voice. "I'm calling with the answer to your prayers."

Valerie laughed as she helped Annie scoot up to the table. "Which prayer would that be? The one for rain, or the one for naturally curly hair, or the one for—"

Pastor Henke guffawed. "I didn't know you had such a long list. No, the one I had in mind is locating another handyman to finish the painting job. . .along with anything else Connor may have in mind."

A relieved sigh burst from Valerie's lungs. "Pastor, that's wonderful!"

"May I bring him right over?"

"Now?" Anxiety tightened her stomach.

"If this isn't a good time. . ."

"It's not that." She pressed a hand to her temple. She knew Phil Garcia from church, and the various other workmen had been referred by trusted family friends. It hadn't occurred to her until this moment that finding a new painter on such short notice might also mean bringing a complete stranger into the house. "Pastor, is. . .is this person someone you know?"

"Actually, he's just arrived in town," the pastor said slowly. "I assure you, he has solid references. However, I'm afraid his pecuniary situation is a bit fragile—"

"His *what*?" Valerie couldn't help but laugh. Pastor Henke had an amusing if sometimes annoying habit of tossing around his extensive vocabulary.

"Sorry, my dear." He gave an embarrassed laugh. "He's in a financial bind, and I know Connor has the apartment above the garage. I thought perhaps your brother might consider making living arrangements a part of the man's compensation."

She hesitated. "Pastor, it's not that I don't trust your judgment, but—"

"I assure you, this young man is a fine Christian with experience in carpentry and painting, not to mention all kinds of other skills." Pastor Henke sighed. "Valerie, my dear, this man's arrival in Aileen seems ordained by God to meet both your needs and his. Have no fears about him. I have thoroughly investigated his background and I trust him completely."

With great effort, Valerie pushed her concerns aside. She'd learned long ago that Pastor Henke's instincts about people were usually right on target. "All right," she said, expelling a sharp breath. "Bring him over and we'll see what we can work out."

Ending the call, she gazed out the window toward the garage, a carriage house in the old days. The long, narrow rooms above had been converted into a modern apartment by the previous owner and now held most of Valerie's belongings from the Ashton Brook Lane house, items she'd never found the strength to sort through, let alone part with. If someone were to move into the apartment, she'd have no choice but to face the daunting task.

Maybe the time had come. *Lord, give me the strength and courage I lack.*

Annie's tap on her wrist brought her back to the present. "Can we play a game now?"

"Sure, sweetie." By the time Valerie caught up with her niece in the den, Annie had all the parts to her Cooties game spread across the coffee table. Valerie eased down to sit cross-legged on the soft, shaggy carpet. "Oh boy, my favorite."

They were halfway through the game, with Annie's Cootie several body parts ahead of Valerie's, when she heard the distinctive rumble of Pastor Henke's red Mustang convertible. Moments afterward, the doorbell rang.

"Who's here?" Annie asked.

"Pastor Henke's bringing over a new painter." Valerie rose stiffly and aimed her index finger at Annie with mock severity. "Don't mess with my Cootie."

A quick peek through the curtains raised second thoughts about Pastor Henke's judgment. Damp, dishwater-blond hair curled over the collar of the stranger's ill-fitting plaid shirt. A razor nick showed dark red on his sunburned face. An ugly scar blazed up his left arm.

A memory clamped down on her heart, sending it racing. She tore herself away from the window.

The bell rang again. "Valerie dear, it's Pastor Henke."

This is ridiculous. She forced her breathing to slow, yet her hands still shook as she deactivated the alarm system. She flung open the door and marshaled all the cheerfulness she could manage. "Hello, Pastor. Please come in."

❧

Healy's first glimpse of the slender woman took his breath away. Her gray eyes sparkled with a brightness to rival the summer sunshine. She wore her pale blond hair pulled back from her face in a fancy clip. Long strands shimmered across the shoulders of her blue-flowered dress.

"Valerie dear, thank you for seeing us on such short notice." Pastor Henke and his companion stepped into the foyer. "This is Healy, the young man I told you about." He paused, cleared his throat. "Healy. . .Ferguson."

Healy held his breath, awaiting Valerie Bishop's reaction. If the pastor's story was true, Healy now stood before Tom's wife.

Correction, Tom's widow.

"Hello." Her tone held the merest suggestion of hesitation, but she gave no sign she'd recognized his name. According to Pastor Henke, Valerie had a few gaps in her memory as well.

When the pastor first came up with the idea of recommending Healy for the handyman's job, Healy wasn't so sure. Pastor Henke had glossed over the details of Tom's death, but he gave the impression Valerie still struggled with the aftermath. What if the sudden appearance of Tom's old buddy the ex-con were too much for her?

But Pastor Henke had already put in a call to Valerie's brother, and both had come to the conclusion that Healy's arrival was God's doing, that somehow, some way, Healy might turn out to be the catalyst for healing that Valerie's family and friends had been praying for.

She slowly extended her hand to Healy. "Pastor Henke tells me you're a jack-of-all-trades, which is what we desperately need around here." She nodded through open French doors toward a room with paint-spattered tarps covering the floor and furniture.

Healy glanced into the living room. "Yes, ma'am, I know a good bit about painting and carpentry. Problem is, I'm in sort of a transition period and don't have my own tools or supplies." He ran a finger around the collar of his shirt. At least two sizes too small, it was the best the elderly preacher could come up with. Pastor Henke had found the shirt, a pair of khakis, and clean socks in a barrel of clothing the church had collected for a homeless ministry.

"We'll arrange for whatever supplies you need," Valerie said. "I understand you also need a place to stay. We have an apartment over the garage, and I'm sure my brother would be willing to negotiate living arrangements as part of your compensation."

She folded her arms and looked away for a brief second. Her voice faded as she added, "I'm afraid it'll take some doing to make the apartment livable, though."

Her kind, honey-soft voice belied the uncertainty Healy read in her posture and expression. Even with a fresh change of clothes, Healy knew he still must look like a down-and-out drifter. He swallowed and met her gaze. "I don't need much, ma'am, and I know how to work hard. If you give me a chance, I promise I won't let you down."

She swept him with an appraising glance, and her gray eyes softened. "Pastor Henke seems to think you're just the man for the job, Mr. Ferguson, and he's never given me reason to question his judgment."

"I really appreciate this, Mrs. . . ."

"Bishop. But Valerie is just fine. I'm sure you'd like to see the apartment." She started down the hall.

Healy's heart flip-flopped. It was all coming back to him now. Tom had written about marrying a beautiful blond wisp of a girl named Valerie. Only with Tom's penchant for bestowing nicknames, he usually referred to her as

"Lady V." And they'd chosen to live in St. Louis because his wife had family nearby. . .family in a little town called Aileen.

A tremor of grief rolled through him. He thrust out a hand and reached for the nearest wall.

Pastor Henke grabbed Healy's elbow. "Easy there, my boy."

Valerie turned and came toward him. "Are you all right? Can I get you some water?"

A towheaded child appeared at the other end of the hallway. "I'm coloring now, Aunt Val. I already put my Cootie together without you." She started toward Healy and pointed at him with a fist full of crayons. "Are you gonna paint Daddy's wall?"

The little girl's questions helped Healy corral his thoughts. He knelt and smiled at her, offering his hand to shake. "Hi, there. My name's Healy. What's yours?"

Her smooth, tiny hand slipped into his calloused one. "My name is Annie Maureen Paige. I'm four and I live here. Where do you live?"

"Uh, well, I'm between addresses right now." He rose awkwardly, glancing at Valerie.

The little girl tugged at his pants leg. "Wanna help me color my picture?"

"Not now, Annie," Valerie said with a quiet laugh. "We're on our way to show Mr. Ferguson the garage apartment. I'll color with you when we finish."

"Don't forget!" Annie skipped through a doorway near the back of the house.

With a tentative smile, Valerie continued down the hall, stopping in the kitchen to select a set of keys from a drawer. Healy and the pastor followed her outside onto a shaded porch, where she halted suddenly, and Healy had to catch himself before he stumbled into her. His face hovered inches from the back of her beautiful blond head. The scent of honeysuckle, intensified by the heat, filled his nostrils.

"The apartment's up there." Her voice had risen a couple of notches, growing stretched and thin. "If you don't mind, Pastor, I'll let you show Mr. Ferguson around."

"I understand," the pastor said softly, taking the keys she offered. "This way, my boy."

Healy tried to keep pace as the older man marched across the lawn and up a flight of weathered stairs. He shuffled his feet while Pastor Henke unlocked the apartment. "Pastor, I'm still not sure this is a good idea. Working here, keeping quiet about my prison record, and knowing Tom—any of it."

The door creaked open, and Pastor Henke pocketed the keys. "In this particular instance, I am relying on the wisdom of Ecclesiastes—'a time to be silent and a time to speak.' And for now, dear boy, this is the time to be silent. When the time is right to tell Valerie who you really are and where you came from, you'll know it."

Pastor Henke flipped a light switch and illuminated the narrow kitchenette to the right of the door. Dust-covered boxes lined the floor and countertops. Healy moistened his lips. "You never finished telling me. What. . .happened to Tom? How exactly did he die?"

"Ah, Healy, it's a heartbreaking story, so hard to talk about." The pastor strode to a streaked window overlooking the driveway and forced it open. "There, perhaps we can air this place out a bit."

Sweat trickled down Healy's ribcage. He could feel wetness spreading under his armpits. "I need to know, Pastor. He was my best friend."

"I know, dear boy, I know. As I said, it was not quite five years ago—October, as I recall. Tom and Valerie had just closed their restaurant for the evening." Pastor Henke shoved a crate out of the way and opened a door at the far end of the living room. "Here's the bedroom. Not large, but a nice view, don't you think? And it has a good-sized closet."

"More than enough room for my stuff. . .if it ever shows up again. Go on, Pastor."

Pastor Henke opened another window, then dabbed his reddened face with a folded handkerchief. "It was a vicious, senseless, tragic accident. Tom was. . .he was killed by a speeding car."

Stricken, Healy pretended to examine the tiny bathroom. He turned on the sink faucet, and brown water gushed out.

"Oh dear, rusty pipes," Pastor Henke said, peering over Healy's shoulder. "Valerie was also injured in the accident, and after she left the hospital, her brother and his wife brought her to live with them."

Healy met the pastor's gaze in the bathroom mirror. "She was there when it happened?"

"Sad indeed. But Valerie has truly been a blessing to the Paige family, and to everyone at Zion Community Church who has gotten to know her. She still has much to overcome, but I've never met a more generous, more loving, more forgiving person."

Staring at his own reflection, Healy glimpsed the deep lines etched around his eyes. So much sorrow, so much pain to absorb in one short day.

❧

Valerie pressed a glass to the refrigerator spigot and watched clear, cold water pour out. Would this heat never break? Connor would have to hold his Fourth of July barbecue indoors, or his guests would collapse from heatstroke.

She curled her fingers around the frosty water glass and glanced out the window. Pastor Henke and the handyman must be sweltering in the airless apartment. Even if they thought to turn on the air conditioners, it would take hours to cool the place down. And if the new handyman planned to move in anytime soon, she—or someone—faced a huge, hot cleanup job. At least he could use Valerie's furniture and dishes and such. Someone might as well, since she began to doubt she'd ever be the one residing in the apartment. She suspected the man owned little more than the clothes on his back and could only wonder about the circumstances that had brought him to Pastor Henke.

When the time was right, maybe he'd tell her more about himself. In the meantime, she'd try to be as kind and compassionate as she knew how.

Sympathy welled for Healy Ferguson—and yet it was more than mere pity she felt for him. A kindred spirit, perhaps? Someone as bound by a difficult past as she?

True, when she first saw him, icy fingers of panic had tightened around her throat. Not that he reminded her so much of *him*, the face that still haunted her nights more frequently than she wanted to admit. But *he* had a scar, too.

"Of course, the scar." She mentally chided herself. "Lord, forgive me for judging a man because he has a scar."

He could have gotten it anywhere. Probably in his carpentry work, with a sharp tool of some kind. A scar didn't make a man a criminal.

Annie danced into the kitchen. "I finished coloring. I made the tree blue and the apples purple. Isn't that silly?" She cocked her head and laughed. "Where's Pastor and that man?"

"Still looking at the apartment." Valerie knelt to give Annie a hug. The gesture reminded her that Healy had also knelt when introducing himself to Annie. She pictured the gentleness—the *guilelessness*—in his eyes, and the trusting way Annie had taken to him immediately.

How could Valerie not like a man who understood so instinctively how to relate to a child?

Chapter 5

"Well?" Valerie poured glasses of iced tea and placed them before Pastor Henke and Healy Ferguson. "Is it utterly hopeless up there, or can we make the apartment livable?"

"It's a fine place." Healy stared at his hands, wrapped around the glass. "A lot more space than what I'm used to."

"I'm sure it will clean up nicely," Pastor Henke said.

"That'll be the fun part." Valerie's teasing tone masked the choking dread that threatened to close her throat. She turned to the refrigerator and exhaled slowly. "How about some milk for you, Annie?"

"Yes, please." Annie scooted her chair closer to Healy's. "Are you gonna live in our 'partment?"

He took a long drink of tea. "I sure would like to, but the decision's up to your aunt and your parents."

Valerie set a plate of oatmeal raisin cookies on the table and settled into a chair. "Sorry, these aren't homemade. I was a business major, never much good in the kitchen." She twisted her wedding band and smiled over the bittersweet memories.

"Valerie, my dear," Pastor Henke began, "I did a bit of snooping upstairs. I came across some boxes of men's clothing that might fit Healy. I wondered—"

Healy looked suddenly flustered. "No, Pastor, I couldn't. I can get by for now."

"It's. . .it's all right." Valerie had kept Tom's things boxed away long enough. Besides, if Tom were alive, he'd give the shirt off his back to help someone in need. To honor her husband's memory, she could do no less.

"Please," she said, squaring her shoulders, "it would make me very happy to see my husband's things put to good use by someone who needs them. Take whatever you need."

Healy murmured a hoarse "Thank you."

Valerie nibbled on a cookie, feeling as if at least a tiny portion of her immense burden had lifted. It was a small step, finally letting go of some of the tangible reminders of the past, but an important one.

In the ensuing silence, she returned her attention to Healy. He reached for a cookie with a hesitant tremor, like a child who feared a slap on the hand for taking something he shouldn't. She had the feeling the tall, lean man had received few breaks in his life.

Lord, he looks as if he could use some friends. Let me be one.

She glanced at the clock. "It'll be at least another hour before Ellen and Connor get home. In the meantime, Mr. Ferguson—"

He held up a hand and gave an awkward laugh. "'Mister' doesn't quite fit, if you know what I mean. Ferguson, or Healy, or just plain 'hey, you' is more what I'm used to."

Valerie looked at him appraisingly. What this man needed more than anything was a heaping dose of self-respect. "Then I'll use your first name, Healy, because that's what a friend would call you. And with that in mind, you can drop the 'ma'am' with me. It's Valerie, okay?"

His voice dropped to barely a whisper. "That'll be just fine, ma'am—I mean, Valerie."

"Good." She nodded firmly and rose to refill his iced tea glass. "What I started to say was, why don't you take another look around the apartment? Help yourself to whatever clothes you can wear. And if you end up staying, feel free to use the dishes, furniture, linens, whatever."

"Yes, go take another look around, Healy," Pastor Henke said. "I have some church business I need to talk with Valerie about."

"Um, okay, if you're sure."

"Here, take some tea and cookies with you." Valerie wrapped three cookies in a napkin. "And turn the air conditioner on, first thing."

When the back door clicked shut, Valerie turned to Pastor Henke. "He seems enormously shy, but. . .there's something special about him, something that makes me trust him." Taking her chair, she ran a fingernail along the edge of the table. "I hope Connor will feel the same way."

The pastor cast her a knowing smile. "I'm sure he will."

"I like him," Annie said. "He looks kinda like the prince in my storybook."

Valerie recalled her first glimpse of Healy Ferguson outside the front door. Although she might call him attractive in a rugged sort of way, *prince* would not have been her first choice of words. The man obviously carried deeper scars than the one visible across his arm.

"I can tell he's had a difficult life, Pastor," she said. "Do you know how he got that ugly scar?"

The white-haired man cleared his throat. "I believe he said it happened with a knife."

She couldn't suppress a sardonic laugh. "I hope it doesn't mean he's another accident-prone handyman."

"Oh no, it wasn't his fault," the pastor said quickly. He coughed again. "Er, do you mind if we change the subject briefly? I was hoping to convince you to take over as the congregation's prayer-chain coordinator."

Valerie touched a hand to her cheek in surprise. "Is Catherine Higgins resigning?"

"Not exactly. The church council is going to kindly suggest that she take a much deserved rest. The truth is, Catherine is getting a bit too hard of hearing for the job." He chuckled. "Never did get it straight that we needed to pray for healing for Howard Nelson's gout—not his *goat*."

Valerie burst out in giggles. "I could barely keep from laughing out loud when she called saying Howard's goat was ailing. I didn't even know the Nelsons had a goat."

"They don't." Pastor Henke's sides shook with laughter. He patted his folded handkerchief to his forehead and exhaled loudly. "So, are you up for the position?"

She thought a moment, remembering the many friends at Zion who had visited and prayed with her over the past few years. It would be a way to give back to them some of the love she had received. Even better, if not exactly the reason Pastor Henke and her family would like to hear, she could handle the responsibilities without ever leaving the house.

"Sounds like it's right up my alley," she said. "When do I start?"

❧

Healy stood amid the boxes of Tom's things and let grief wash over him. He lifted a maroon polo shirt and imagined how Tom's broad shoulders must have filled it out. His fists knotted around the coarse cotton fabric. *Lord, why? Why'd You bring me all this way, only to let me find out my best friend is dead?*

Pastor Henke appeared at the door, carrying a plastic tote containing cleaning supplies. "Valerie thought you might want to start getting the place habitable."

Healy shook off his grief. "Thanks. Good idea."

While they cleaned and sorted, the pastor told Healy a little more about the Paige family and their association with Zion. "Connor's an elder, and Ellen was leading a ladies' Bible study until she passed the baton to Bonnie Trapp last spring."

"And Valerie?" Healy's question was muffled by the stack of musty-smelling beige towels he carried to the bathroom.

"As a matter of fact, she just agreed to be our new prayer-chain coordinator." Pastor Henke clucked his tongue. "A worthy vocation, but such a waste when she could be doing so much more."

Healy's heart clenched with concern for his friend's widow. The moment he first laid eyes on her, he'd felt strong protective impulses rising from deep within his bones. He'd do anything, dare anything, if he could ease her sorrow and erase the fear that lurked behind those shimmering gray eyes.

Within the hour, a blue sedan drove up, and the floor beneath Healy's feet vibrated as the automatic garage door rumbled open.

"That's Ellen," Pastor Henke announced. "I'll just run down and say hello. Be back shortly."

A few minutes later, Healy saw a silver minivan park in the driveway. A tall man dressed in an expensive-looking gray suit got out, unlocked the side gate, and entered the backyard. The man took three steps toward the house only to snap his fingers, spin on one heel, and trot back to the gate to lock it securely.

Healy could only shake his head at such paranoia—bolted doors, locked gates, alarm systems. Poor Tom. Poor Valerie. He shunted his gnawing grief aside with more vigorous cleaning efforts. It seemed forever before the pastor returned.

"The Paiges are home," Pastor Henke called from the landing. "Time to meet your future employer."

The slender, sandy-haired man who'd arrived in the minivan met them at the back door of the house.

"Hi. Connor Paige. Come on in." Though he'd removed his suit coat, his pastel blue dress shirt and loosened tie easily fit Healy's image of a successful surgeon—and made Healy feel more out of place than ever.

With a sweaty palm he shook the doctor's hand. "Healy Ferguson. How do you do, sir?"

"Mr. Ferguson. Nice to meet you." Connor introduced his wife, Ellen, an attractive woman with a cap of short brown curls. She towered over the petite Valerie Bishop, who waited nearby wearing an encouraging smile. The little girl, Annie, knelt on a kitchen chair, printing her name over and over on a sheet of lined paper.

"Have a seat." Connor motioned Healy toward the table, and they sat down. "Pastor Henke explained about your need for work and a place to live. So you have a good bit of handyman experience?"

"Yes, sir." *In a manner of speaking.* Prison vocational training and work assignments, then a year on parole working for a building contractor, ought to count for something. Healy took the chair next to Annie. Though he knew Pastor Henke had already spoken at length with the doctor, the man still seemed uncomfortably formal and reserved. Healy mentally prepared himself in case Dr. Paige decided to send him on his way.

And then his nostrils picked up an enticing aroma coming from the stove. His stomach gave an ominous grumble, and he clamped an arm across his waist.

Ellen's chuckle eased his embarrassment. "Hmm, sounds like somebody's hungry. Don't worry, Mr. Ferguson, you're invited to supper. You, too, Pastor. We have plenty." She went to the stove to stir the contents of a large stockpot.

Pastor Henke released a disappointed moan. "How kind of you to ask, but I'm afraid I can't stay." He glanced at his watch. "In fact, I'm late already for another appointment. I'll leave Healy in your care."

"But, Pastor—" Healy started from his chair. Lowering his voice, he said, "What if this doesn't work out after all? What if—"

The pastor winked. "Where's your faith, my boy?" To the Paige family he said, "I'll see myself out. Have a good evening, all."

Healy could hardly swallow as he sank into his chair. "I, uh. . .I guess I'm stuck here for a while."

"I should certainly hope so," Ellen said, "since you're our replacement handyman." She measured out a fistful of dry spaghetti and dropped it into another stockpot. Steam swirled around her, mirroring the haze of disbelief filling Healy's mind.

Connor pushed his chair back. "Healy, would you join me in my study? It might be easier to discuss the details of this arrangement in private."

All right, Ferguson, get ready for the ax to fall.

He followed the doctor down the hallway into a paneled office lined with bookshelves. Through partially open wooden blinds, the evening sun sketched a ladder-like pattern across the massive desk. The men took seats across the desk from each other, and Healy caught the look of uncertainty in Connor Paige's eyes.

The doctor spoke slowly. "As I'm sure you know, when Pastor Henke phoned me earlier, he told me all about your time in prison."

"Yes, sir." Healy pressed his hands together. "I made a serious mistake, one I'll regret the rest of my life. But I'm not the same person I was sixteen years ago. I'm just praying now to put the past behind me and make a new start."

"I admire you for that." Connor rested his forearms on the desk. "But I'll admit, when Pastor Henke told me his idea, I had my doubts. The faxes from the prison officials, your parole officer, and former employer helped a lot, but what clinched it for me was learning you're Tom's friend Gus. He used to talk about you often, and I know he'd want me to help you any way I can."

"Thank you, sir. Tom was the only real friend I ever had. I can't believe he's dead."

"I'm sorry. We've had over four years to grieve. You've only just found out."

Healy nodded, unable to speak.

After a moment of silence, Connor went on. "I agree with Pastor Henke—your arrival in town may well be the answer to our prayers, in more ways than one. But since Valerie obviously doesn't remember you, I'd rather not tell her anything just yet about your connection to Tom, and especially not about your prison record. My goal is to get her back into therapy soon, and I don't want to do anything to rock the boat until I'm certain she's getting better." Connor rubbed his chin. "It goes against my nature to keep things from my wife, but at this point, I'm not planning to tell Ellen, either. She and Val talk about everything, and I'm afraid Ellen might unintentionally let something slip."

Healy nodded. "I understand. I'll abide by whatever you say."

Connor's eyes narrowed. "But let me make something perfectly clear. If you give me even the smallest reason to doubt your sincerity or your integrity, I'll personally buy your bus ticket back to where you came from." He reached for a yellow legal pad. "Now, let's discuss the working arrangements."

As Connor finished outlining the next few projects he had in mind, his little daughter came to summon them to dinner. Joining the family at the table, Healy smiled his thanks as Ellen Paige set a plate of spaghetti in front of him, next to a bowl of green salad. The marinara sauce and Italian spices smelled incredible.

Connor folded his hands. "Healy, it's our custom to offer thanks before each meal."

"If I may be so forward, sir, I've got a lot to be thankful for today and I wonder if you'd let me ask the blessing."

Connor looked at him with mild surprise. "By all means."

Stealing a glance at the slender, flaxen-haired woman across the table, Healy began, "Precious Lord, how do I thank You for such bounteous care? I came to this town on faith and a prayer, and look how You have rewarded me. What an awesome God You are. Bless this family, bless Pastor Henke, and bless this food to the nourishment of our bodies. In Jesus' name, amen."

A soft chorus of "amens" sounded around the table.

"How's the apartment coming?" Valerie twirled strands of spaghetti around her fork. "Did it ever cool off up there?"

"Took awhile, but it's comfortable now." He paused to savor the rich flavors dancing across his tongue. "I cannot remember when I've tasted anything so good."

Ellen sprinkled freshly grated Parmesan over her spaghetti and passed the container to Healy. "The recipe came from Valerie's late husband's family."

Healy nodded. "From Italy, I—" *I remember,* he'd almost said. He sensed Connor's warning glance. "I mean, this is such great Italian food, his family had to have been Italian."

Valerie smiled, sadness crinkling the corners of her eyes. "Tom's maternal grandmother was Italian. Grandma Carmela taught him everything she knew about cooking, even helped get our restaurant started—while I stayed out of the way and kept the books. Thank goodness Ellen has the talent and patience to re-create the family recipes. My attempts always flop."

Healy poked at his salad, stabbing a mushroom and tomato onto the end of his fork. She seemed to talk easily enough about Tom. And yet he'd been warned she still couldn't venture past the backyard without the effort triggering an anxiety attack.

Father, help me not to do anything to upset Valerie. That's the last thing I'd ever want to do. And I know Tom must be there in heaven with You, so make sure he knows it, too.

Someday, when the time was right, Healy prayed God would allow him to tell her himself about his friendship with Tom, before a chance discovery or someone's slip of the tongue revealed the truth by accident.

Yet the thought of her knowing terrified him, because telling Valerie the truth would also mean revealing the fact that he'd spent fifteen years in prison for manslaughter.

Chapter 6

Valerie watched from the living room doorway as Healy lined up the last strip of an elegant rose-print wallpaper border. The first time she'd seen him wearing one of Tom's old T-shirts, her heart had twisted, but day by day it had grown easier, especially knowing Tom's things were being put to good use.

She stepped into the room. "A little higher on that end—perfect."

With expert strokes Healy smoothed the border above the fruitwood-stained chair rail, trimmed the edge, and rolled the seams. He stepped back to appraise his work and expelled a long breath. "That should do it. The living room's done."

Valerie clapped her hands in delight. "This calls for a celebration. How about an ice-cold lemonade?"

"Let me clean up in here first. Join you in the kitchen in a few minutes?"

"I'll have it ready and waiting." She cast a smile over her shoulder and sauntered down the hall.

Pastor Henke had not overstated Healy's abilities in the handyman department. He'd already finished painting and papering the living room, fixed a leaky faucet in the powder room, stopped an annoying stair step from creaking, and replaced a cracked tile on the kitchen counter.

And all this on top of cleaning and organizing the garage apartment. She regretted being unable to help him sort through all the crates and extra furniture stored up there—most of it was hers, after all—but no amount of good intentions or willpower had been able to propel her across the backyard and up those stairs.

She recalled the verse from 1 John she had clung to so often: "Perfect love drives out fear." Yet despite daily prayer and several failed attempts at therapy, she couldn't seem to make it true for herself.

How much longer, Father? Why is my faith so weak that I can't overcome this?

She had just filled two glasses with lemonade when Healy came through the kitchen, carrying his wallpapering supplies. Tucking a leftover roll of paper under his chin, he reached for the knob to let himself out the back door. As he pulled it open, the warning beep of the security system caught Valerie's attention.

"Oh no, hold on." She rushed over to enter the code before the alarm sounded.

Healy let out a frustrated groan. "Sorry, I keep forgetting."

"It's my fault." Her face warmed. "I just feel safer when the alarm is set."

She locked the door behind him but resisted her compulsion to reset the alarm. "He's coming right back, silly," she told herself, but it didn't keep the apprehension from rising in her throat. She watched for Healy to return from the garage. When she saw him climb the porch steps, she silently unlocked the door and strode back to the table.

"Cold lemonade, as promised." She closed her eyes in gratitude when he remembered to lock the door and set the alarm. "You must think I'm so paranoid." Her forced laugh sounded hollow. "It's a long story."

Healy took the chair across from her and downed a long gulp of lemonade. The awkward silence between them grew.

"The munchkin still napping?" Healy finally asked.

"Mm-hmm." Valerie sipped her drink.

He chuckled. "Figured. Otherwise she'd be in here asking for cookies."

"You've got that right." She felt herself relaxing. "You're so good with Annie. You must really like kids."

"My, uh, buddies where I came from—some of them had kids. I was always a bit envious."

Did his hand shake just now as he lifted his glass?

"You don't talk much about where you came from."

"Not much to tell."

She noticed his sunburned cheeks and nose had started to peel. "I don't mean to pry. I just wondered. . ."

"I'm from up north." His gaze met hers, and he exhaled slowly. "How about you?"

"I grew up in Boston." She swirled the ice in her glass. "My mother still lives there. I'll bet she's having a much cooler summer than we are."

"This heat's the worst I've ever known. What's the deal, anyway?"

Valerie gave him a conspiratorial wink. "I think the weather forecasters made some kind of deal with the air conditioner manufacturers."

"Ah, I see." Healy laughed, and she joined him, relieved to see the troubled look leave his eyes.

She liked this man more every day, shyness and all. Healy was clearly a man of integrity and great patience, someone whose character had been carved out of trials and pain, not unlike her own. She wasn't entirely sure when the pity she had first felt for him had shifted to friendly concern, and then from concern to genuine interest.

Truth be told, she wasn't exactly sure how to interpret her feelings for the Paiges' inscrutable new handyman. She only knew she wanted to get to know him better. . .much, much better.

❧

The rumble of a car caused Healy to look up from his supper of macaroni and cheese. From the apartment window he saw the elderly Pastor Henke emerge from his flashy red Mustang. He couldn't help but chuckle at the incongruity.

Moments later, heavy footsteps shook the outside stairs, and Pastor Henke's round face appeared through the glass in the door.

"Hey, Pastor, come on in."

"Oh dear, I'm interrupting your dinner. I just came by with this." Pastor Henke held out Healy's scruffy, stained duffel bag.

"My stuff." Healy grinned in surprise. He'd braved a call to the police department a few days ago and learned the thief was caught when he tried to rob another traveler. A search of his apartment turned up a whole stash of luggage, including Healy's duffel bag and all its contents—short the twenty-dollar bill, unfortunately. Pastor Henke had a friend in the department who kindly intervened to speed up the release of Healy's property from the evidence room.

"Sorry I couldn't fetch this for you sooner, but things at church became rather hectic this week." A distracted look crossed the pastor's face.

"Thanks, I really appreciate it." Healy set the bag on a cushioned armchair in the sitting area. Returning to the table, he cast an awkward glance at his meager meal. "I don't have much to offer, but you're welcome to join me."

"A glass of ice water would be most welcome." Pastor Henke took a chair at the end of the small gray Formica table. "Please, go ahead and eat before it gets cold."

Healy placed a frosty tumbler before the pastor and self-consciously resumed eating. "Valerie and the Paiges have been real nice about inviting me to take meals with them, but I feel like I'm imposing."

"I'm sure they don't think so. Tell me, how is everything going?"

"Real well." Healy swallowed his last bite and pushed the plate away. "It's good work for good people. I can't thank you enough for making this possible."

"Connor told me at church Sunday that you're doing an excellent job." The pastor gave a half smile and leaned forward. "Of course, Phil Garcia fears you'll steal away all his clients while he's incapacitated with his broken leg."

Healy shot the pastor a worried glance. "Please, I wouldn't—"

"My boy, I'm only teasing. No, no, there's plenty of work in the area to keep Phil and you and any number of handymen amply employed for years to come."

Feeling stupid, Healy sat back and shook his head. "Whoa, I'm almost as paranoid as Valerie."

Pastor Henke grew quiet. "Yes, it's a shame, isn't it?"

Healy gave a huff. "I don't know how many times I've accidentally set off the burglar alarm. Once the cops even came out. I thought I'd have a heart attack right then and there."

Pastor Henke tapped his index finger lightly on the tabletop. "Valerie is still unaware of your past?"

"Connor warned me not to tell her yet. She seems frightened of enough stuff as it is." He pushed back from the table and braced his forearms on his thighs. "Pastor, seeing her so scared all the time. . .it grates on my soul."

The pastor stared at his brown wingtips. "As it does with all of us."

Healy tried to reconcile his impression of Valerie as usually competent and self-controlled with the image the pastor and Connor had painted of a woman reduced to a mass of raw nerves after the death of her husband. "If she's that bad off, how does she manage so well taking care of the house and watching over Annie? I mean. . ."

Pastor Henke narrowed his eyes. "You mean, how can Connor and Ellen entrust their child to someone so unstable?"

Healy's throat closed. He nodded without meeting the pastor's gaze.

"They didn't right away, of course." The pastor sipped his iced tea. "Annie was born a few months after Tom died. Ellen had already planned to take a couple of years off from teaching, so she also used the time to assist in Valerie's recovery. We all soon realized that Valerie needed to feel *needed*. She has a great fondness for children, and Annie became the center of her world. More and more frequently, Ellen left the child in Valerie's care for short trips to run errands and such, and Valerie's confidence blossomed."

"But suppose something happened. I mean, if she can't even leave the house. . ."

"Connor and Ellen introduced Valerie to several trusted neighbors who are usually home during the day. In addition, she's always had a list of friends from church she can call." Pastor Henke folded his hands on the table. "And she is not incompetent, my boy, simply haunted by a terrible trauma."

Healy still fought to grasp the reality of Tom's death. No one seemed willing to talk about the details, but he had to know. "Please, Pastor, tell me more about the accident."

"If you insist." The pastor sadly shook his head. "That night three men had just robbed a convenience store, and the police were chasing them. For some reason Valerie has never remembered, instead of Tom's going straight to their car in the lot next to the restaurant, he was crossing the street."

Cold dread snaked through Healy's gut. He bowed his head. "Oh, blessed Jesus."

The pastor raked a hand through his thinning hair. His gaze held a faraway look. "Tom was hit by the robbers' getaway car. It spun out of control and smashed into a light pole, and the three men tried to escape on foot. Valerie was grabbed and shoved by one of them and had to be hospitalized with severe injuries. As for the rest of the details, her mind is a blank. Police arrived within moments and captured the men."

"Where are they now?" Healy asked through tight lips.

"In prison, for a long, long time."

"Good."

❧

Valerie massaged her back as she settled into her desk chair. She hadn't written in her journal for almost a week now, and her conscience stung. How could she be so neglectful?

Turning to a fresh page, she uncapped her fountain pen and stared into the darkness outside her window. A smile curled her lips as an image of Tom's face formed in her mind's eye.

Then the clean-cut dark hair of her memories paled to a shaggy dishwater blond, the blue eyes turned hazel, and it became Healy's face she pictured, not Tom's. A stab of shame shot through her, but in that moment she could almost hear Tom's voice: *"It's okay, Lady V, I don't blame you. It's all right to move on."*

If only she could. The events of one dreadful night had altered her life forever. With each passing year her hopes of feeling safe and whole again slid further and further away.

She turned to the open journal and lifted her pen.

My dearest,

I still miss you so much—all the joy we might have had—and this is the only place I can come to when I want to be with you. When I see Connor and Ellen's happiness, I only miss you more. I wish I could hold you in my arms just once and tell you how much I love you.

You would like Healy. Annie adores him, and early in the mornings, before it gets too terribly hot, he pushes her in the swing or plays hide-and-seek with her in the backyard. They have such wonderful fun together.

Oh, my love, I wish you could have stayed. I cling to God's promise that someday we will be together in heaven.

She heard a light tapping on the door and quietly closed the journal. "Come in."

"Hi, Val." Ellen stepped into the room. "Am I interrupting?"

"Not at all." She rose to greet her sister-in-law with a hug. "How have you been feeling?"

Ellen sank onto an ice-blue velveteen loveseat. "Tired, mostly. And the morning sickness is kicking in."

"I heard you in the bathroom this morning. Is it really bad?"

"When is throwing up ever fun?" Ellen looked toward the ceiling. "Connor's such an angel, wanting to hover and mop my brow, but when I'm hanging over the commode, in the words of Greta Garbo, 'I vant to be alone.'" She picked up a throw pillow and pressed it to her stomach. "Ugh! It's so. . .humiliating. Mind if we change the subject?"

Valerie chuckled and sat down beside her. "Be my guest."

"Healy's amazing, isn't he? I can't believe all he's done already."

"I know. All I have to do is mention something needs doing, and before I know it, he's finished."

"So, now that the downstairs is in good shape, what should we have Healy work on next?" Ellen's appraising gaze swept from floor to ceiling. "We've done hardly anything in here since you moved in, except slap on a coat of paint and hang curtains."

Valerie shifted sideways and faced Ellen. "Wouldn't you rather fix up the extra bedroom for the new baby's nursery?"

"We have time." She chewed her lip. "You really need some bookshelves. There's room for built-ins between those two windows."

Valerie traced a leaf in the pattern of her capris. "Ellen, what do you think of Healy—I mean, other than as an excellent handyman?"

"He's hard to get to know, but I've liked him from the start. I'm still vague about how Pastor Henke found him."

A twinge of longing gripped Valerie's heart. "Healy sure doesn't talk much, does he?"

Ellen leaned toward her with a probing stare. "What is that look I see in your eyes, Valerie Bishop? Are you getting interested in our tall, handsome stranger?"

"Whatever gave you such an idea?" Rising abruptly, Valerie strode across the room. Why did she feel so jumpy all of a sudden?

"Well, you two do spend a lot of time together."

"He's working, and I'm supervising. I think you could say we're becoming friends, but I don't know him nearly well enough to even consider being *interested* in him."

Ellen rose and paced the room, nodding and casting sidelong glances at Valerie. "Yes, I think we need to have Healy start on this room next. Bookshelves for sure—or if he can do it, maybe some glass-front curio cabinets. And I'll pick up some wallpaper books and paint swatches after classes tomorrow." She winked. "That should keep both of you busy for the next few weeks."

Valerie looked heavenward and laughed. "Ellen, you are impossible."

When her sister-in-law excused herself for bed, Valerie collapsed onto the loveseat. She sighed as Healy's face filled her mind once more. "Lord, I have to admit, there is something about the man."

Fair-skinned and lean, he certainly had little in common with Tom, the muscular, raven-haired ex-football jock she'd fallen in love with in college. Tom had been loud, vivacious, even a prankster at times.

Healy, on the other hand, seemed unusually quiet and reserved. She'd caught only glimpses of his playful side when he spent time with Annie, but even those rare moments warmed something inside her.

"Who am I kidding?" Such thoughts could lead nowhere, not as long as she remained trapped inside a house with an activated security system, hidden behind a high privacy fence with a padlocked gate. Not as long as she feared her own shadow.

She pressed her fingertips to her brimming eyes. "Please, Father, let me live like a normal person. Take away the pain of *that night* and let me heal."

Chapter 7

Valerie closed the oven door on a tray of brown-and-serve wheat rolls—the only cooking task her brother and sister-in-law would entrust to her—and hurried to make a space on the kitchen table for the steaming meat platter Connor had just brought in from the grill. The pungent aroma of mesquite-smoked beef brisket, chicken, and sausage set her taste buds aquiver. She pinched off a bite of brisket and popped it into her mouth.

"Hey, no nibbling." Conner slapped her hand.

"But the temptation is simply irresistible." She snuck another bite and danced away. Savoring the morsel, she narrowed her eyes. "Why, brother dear, is that a trace of barbecue sauce on *your* upper lip?"

Ellen entered from the hall, followed by sounds of laughter and conversation. "Everyone loves what we've done with the house. Mmm, yummy." She snagged a chicken wing.

"Enough, you two." Connor dragged a napkin across his mouth. "Save some for our guests."

Ellen cast him an innocent smile. "But, honey, I'm eating for two."

The oven timer beeped. Donning quilted mitts, Valerie brought out the rolls and slid them into the cloth-lined basket Ellen offered. "Looks like everything's ready."

"Great. I'll announce dinner." Ellen headed toward the dining room with the basket of rolls.

Connor lifted the meat platter. "Isn't Healy coming? I haven't seen him all evening."

"I told him several times he was invited." Valerie parted the window curtains. Behind the garage apartment, the evening sky blazed purple and orange—probably the only fireworks she'd see tonight. She turned away abruptly. "Maybe Healy's uncomfortable about being with so many people he doesn't know."

"Wouldn't surprise me. Well, I'm starved. We're eating now, with or without Healy." He marched out of the kitchen.

Biting her lip, Valerie pulled open the back door and stepped onto the porch. She'd managed four quick steps across the lawn when the inevitable rush of panic swept through her. What if the gates were unlocked? What if someone had crept into the backyard and lay in wait behind a bush or tree?

Her heart raced. She couldn't breathe. Every sound seemed amplified a hundred times. She dare not turn around and run back inside—someone might grab her from behind. Yet she couldn't move forward, couldn't seem to move at all.

God, help me.

"There you are," came Connor's voice from the porch. Instantly he appeared beside her, his protective arms encircling her. "You okay, sis?"

She relaxed against him. "I wanted to try again to convince Healy to come to dinner. But I couldn't get there."

Connor gently turned her toward the house. "You tried, that's what counts."

Her jaw clenched. "It's not enough."

"I know I promised not to push, but I wish you'd try counseling again."

"If it didn't work before, what makes you think things would be different now?"

"We could try other doctors, a different approach. I've read about some new medications—"

Reaching the porch, Valerie stopped and faced her brother with pleading eyes. "Listen to me, Con, I simply can't bear the idea of reliving everything, being prodded to fill in the missing pieces. And I don't want to go through life depending on drugs. I did that for too long after I got out of the hospital, and it almost turned my brain to mush. Please, let me handle this my own way." She reached for the doorknob. "And pray for me."

❧

All afternoon Healy had been inhaling the mouth-watering aromas drifting upward from the Paiges' backyard. He'd never smelled anything as tantalizing as beef sizzling over glowing mesquite embers. From his kitchen window he'd watched a sweat-soaked Connor brave the midsummer heat and the even higher temperatures of the smoky grill.

But he'd seen little of Valerie today and assumed she must be busy in the house, helping Ellen prepare for the party.

And he missed her. More than he dared acknowledge.

Hardly a day had passed in the last two weeks when he hadn't spent at least several hours in her presence. Their conversations were pretty much limited to painting and wallpapering and carpentry, but just being in the same room with her made him feel. . .

Admit it. She makes you feel like a man.

For sixteen years he'd felt lower than the lowest animal. In prison he'd run the gamut of emotions, starting with intense remorse over the incident that had put him there. Self-loathing finally gave way to fleeting glimmers of hope that, with God's help, he just might survive the prison experience, maybe even come through it a better, stronger person.

Best of all, he eventually found himself able to accept the forgiveness in Christ that for so long Tom had tried to convince him could be his for the asking. And in that moment everything changed forever.

But he also had to accept that sin has its consequences. Prison did something to a man. The daily indignities—lack of privacy, the guards' insults, the brutal cruelty of fellow inmates—no matter how secure he felt in God's love, a part of him still hearkened to the murmurs of inferiority and unworthiness.

He settled into the armchair and reached for his Bible. The aging leather felt rough and dry, even in his calloused hands. Smudged fingerprints marred the once white pages, and penciled notes filled the margins. He'd written to Tom awhile ago, telling him how glad he was that his friend couldn't see how dirty and worn the Bible had grown.

"Just means you're using it," Tom had written back, *"and that's a good thing, Gus. Keep it up. I'm praying for you."*

"Aw, Tom." Healy's throat closed with grief as the Bible fell open to the flyleaf. "I can't believe you're dead. Going on five years, and I never knew."

For the millionth time his gaze fell upon Tom's inscription:

To Gus, my best friend and the best placekicker I ever blocked for. When things get tough and you can't see the end, read Joel 2:23–26. God is the great Restorer. No matter what happens, trust in Him.

Tom

The passage from the book of Joel had come to hold great meaning for Healy as the years of his sentence dragged by. He loved the images of God sending the autumn rains, the threshing floors filled with grain, the vats overflowing with new wine and oil.

Most of all, he clung to God's promise: "I will repay you for the years the locusts have eaten. . . . You will have plenty to eat, until you are full, and you will praise the name of the Lord your God, who has worked wonders for you; never again will my people be shamed."

Above the drone of the air conditioner he heard the *pop-pop-pop* of firecrackers. He went to the front window and looked out. Beyond the treetops, the darkened horizon lit up momentarily with a dazzle of green and gold.

Fireworks. He hadn't seen a real Fourth of July fireworks display since he was a teenager. He grinned like a kid as another sparkling spectacle of light mushroomed above the tree line.

Voices from below caught his attention. Down by the street he saw Connor, Ellen, and Annie along with several party guests setting up lawn chairs. His heart quickened as he searched the faces for Valerie's. With regret, he realized he couldn't expect to find her among them. He'd never seen her venture farther out the door than Annie's backyard swing set.

He looked toward the Paiges' house and glimpsed Valerie's profile at her sitting room window. Across the driveway stood an enormous cottonwood tree, which he felt sure blocked her view of the brilliant display.

"She's missing so much, all on account of fear." He lowered his head. "Valerie needs some restoring, too, Father. Show me how I can help her."

Gathering his courage, he started for the door. Then, remembering the spicy canned chili he'd heated up for supper, he made a detour to the bathroom for a quick tooth brushing and swirl of minty mouthwash. Tongue tingling, he strode downstairs and rapped loudly on the Paiges' kitchen door.

❧

Hearing the knock, Valerie turned from the window. She couldn't see much anyway, thanks to that tree. It completely blocked her view toward the Aileen Community Park several blocks away, where the annual fireworks show was staged. It surprised her that town officials would even hold a fireworks show this year, dry as everything was. No doubt the fire department was on high alert.

The knock sounded again. She bristled with irritation. "Doesn't Connor have his key?" As she made her way downstairs, she murmured, "Forgive me, Lord. It's myself I'm upset with, not Connor."

The sight of Healy standing on the porch, hands stuffed in his jeans pockets, sent her heart fluttering. She smoothed her hair into place before opening the door. "Hello," she said, more breathlessly than she liked. "I—we missed you at dinner. There's plenty of food left. Can I warm up a plate for you?"

He entered hesitantly. "Uh, no thanks. I came down because I saw you were missing the fireworks."

She tried to laugh, but it sounded hollow. "Who can get excited about flashes of gunpowder? It's so noisy, and the show's over almost before it starts."

"Yeah, but you gotta admit, it's pretty impressive while it's happening."

"Really, I'm not interested." She strode to the sink, where a greasy serving platter soaked in soapy water. She drained the sink and began refilling it with fresh hot water and a generous squirt of dishwashing liquid.

A hand reached past her and shut off the faucet. She looked up into reproachful eyes. "Valerie Bishop, how long has it been since you've seen a Fourth of July fireworks show?"

"I. . .I can't remember." He stood so close that she could smell his mint-scented breath. She fought the nervous churning of her stomach.

"Then I know for a fact it's been too long." Healy took both her hands and tugged her toward the door.

"I can't go out there. Healy, please." Panic edged her voice. Healy would think she'd gone completely crazy.

"I understand you're scared, but it's okay. Trust me." Releasing one of her hands, he reached behind his back and opened the door.

Unspeakable terrors lurked beyond the reach of the porch light. Her breath quickened. She planted her feet on the doorsill.

Healy stopped and squeezed her hand. "Look at me."

At the force of his words, she settled her anxious, darting gaze on his face.

"Concentrate on my voice. Keep your eyes on me and don't think about anything else." He took a step back and pulled her one shaky step forward.

"Good," he said. "I'm here, and you're safe."

Another step. And another.

Dry grass whispered beneath her sandals. Reassuring eyes beckoned her forward. Soothing words coaxed her up the wooden stairs beside the garage, through a door beneath a yellow porch light swarming with June bugs. When Healy released his hypnotic hold, she found herself standing in the darkened living area of his apartment.

"Come look." He motioned her toward the window. "I got the best view right here."

As she neared, an exploding ball of red, white, and blue lit up the night sky. "Oh my goodness." Breathless, she pressed her palm against the glass. "It's beautiful. I'd forgotten. . ."

Acutely aware of Healy's presence beside her, she watched in awe as one striking display after another sparkled above the treetops. It seemed an eternity and yet only moments until the sky erupted in a grand finale of color and light—pinwheels, mushrooms, chrysanthemums, and rockets. She could only murmur in wonder and delight.

The fireworks faded, leaving a thick cloud of smoke drifting across the starlit night. Below, Connor and his guests folded up their lawn chairs and returned to the house. With a sigh, she smiled up at Healy. "Thank you."

He brushed her cheek, wiping away a tear she hadn't realized had fallen. "We all have our own prisons," he said. "But sometimes the door's standing wide open and we don't even know it. And only a fool would fail to walk out that door if given the chance."

She searched his face. "What if what's outside the door is scarier than what's inside?"

"You'll never know until you step through, now, will you?" He grinned.

She couldn't help but smile back. "I suppose I just took one major step through the door tonight, thanks to you."

"You wanted to, or I'd never have been able to talk you through it." He switched on a table lamp, then ambled to the refrigerator and peered inside. "Want a soda?"

Feeling giddy, Valerie nodded. "A soda would be great."

She did want to change things, to break out of her "prison." Something about Healy made her believe for the first time that maybe she could.

Chapter 8

Valerie slipped off her sandals and tucked her feet under her skirt on the mauve tweed sofa that had once graced the living room of the Ashton Brook Lane house. Looking around the apartment, she noticed Healy had done a pretty good job of settling in. The sitting area was comfortably arranged, with the sofa facing the front windows and accented by a maple coffee table and a side table with an ivory-shaded reading lamp.

Tom's old leather recliner, a huge thing that had always swallowed Valerie, sat catty-corner to the lamp table. Sitting there now, Healy looked as relaxed as she had ever seen him. Their eyes met briefly before he lowered his gaze and grinned, obviously pleased with himself over the triumph of coaxing her upstairs to see the fireworks. And he certainly had a right to be a little smug. Healy Ferguson had achieved what no one else had managed in four years of trying.

She sipped her soft drink and smiled at him over the rim of her glass. "You're pretty proud of yourself, aren't you?"

"I'm more proud of you."

"I think I'm still in shock." She tucked a strand of hair behind her ear. "Healy Ferguson, man of many talents. I wish you'd tell me more about yourself."

"Like I said before, not much to tell." He rose stiffly and paced to the window like a nervous cat.

What secrets lay hidden behind those hooded hazel eyes? Valerie tried for a lighter tone. "Why so secretive? Are you in the witness protection program or something?"

Healy sighed and set his soda can on the windowsill. "I suppose I am keeping some things private." Staring out the window, he shoved his hands into his pockets. "I got into some trouble a number of years ago, bad trouble. I had a temper like you wouldn't believe. I—"

He paused, swallowed. "I hurt somebody. And I paid for it. And thanks to a good friend who never gave up on me, I also found forgiveness in the Lord." His voice shook. "By God's grace, I've been given a second chance."

Valerie's heart ached for him. She knew all too well the torture of reliving her own past. "I'm so sorry, Healy. About your past, and for pressuring you to talk about it. But I'm glad you had such a loyal friend."

"Wouldn't be here at all if not for him." Healy retrieved his soda can, took a long drink, and returned to the recliner.

"Do you and your friend still keep in touch?"

He looked tired. . .or was it sadness that shadowed his gaze? "He, uh. . .he died awhile back."

"Oh, Healy." Valerie scooted to the edge of the sofa and tentatively reached for his hand.

He sat forward, and his warm, calloused fingers slowly relaxed into her palm. "The really sad thing is that I never had the chance to properly thank him for all he did for me. It's the whole reason why I—" He cast Valerie a sidelong glance and abruptly withdrew his hand. "Hey, it's getting late. I should be getting you back to the house before your big brother misses you."

Valerie laughed. "Connor? Don't let him intimidate you. Besides, after what you did for me tonight, he and Ellen will be singing your praises right along with me."

"I hope you're right." He rose and helped her from the sofa. "Think you can make it on your own, or do you want me to walk with you?"

For the first time Valerie gave thought to the necessity of another trek through the darkened backyard. She pressed a hand to her roiling stomach. "Can you cast another of your spells on me?"

"I bet if you set your mind to it, you could make it just fine, but if you want, I'll stay with you all the way."

She gazed up at him with trembling lips. "I want." *Oh, Healy, I want a whole lot more than just a walk across the lawn with you!*

"All righty then." He steadied her as she took a shaky step onto the landing, then guided her slowly down the stairs.

When they arrived on the back porch, she released a grateful sigh. She gripped both his hands and squeezed them with all her might. "I made it," she said in amazement. *"I made it!"*

"Wasn't so bad after all, huh?" Healy's mouth curled into a half smile. Still clutching her hands, he leaned toward her. His lips brushed her cheek.

Her hand flew to her face. The spot where he'd kissed her seemed aflame.

Healy jerked back. He clawed stiff fingers through his hair. "I—I shouldn't have done that. For–forgive me. Guess I got caught up in the moment."

"Oh no, it's all right." She smiled shyly up at him. "It was a nice moment."

The door swung open. Ellen and Connor stood just inside the kitchen, their mouths agape.

"Thought we heard voices out here," Connor said, his brow furrowing.

Ellen grinned. "Why, Val, I thought you'd already gone upstairs to bed."

"I, uh. . ." She clasped trembling hands behind her back.

Healy cleared his throat. "I didn't want her to miss the fireworks, and I've got the best view up there." He nodded toward the apartment.

"Yes," Connor said with an appraising look, "you certainly do."

Valerie slithered past her brother. "Well, good night, Healy. Thanks again." She darted up to her room, leaving Connor and Ellen to ponder the questions she'd read in their eyes.

As she prepared for bed, she studied her reflection in the bathroom mirror. Her cheeks glowed a little pinker than usual, her eyes brighter.

"You look like a silly schoolgirl," she chided her image in the mirror. No man had made her feel this way since she first met Tom, and after his death she'd never expected to experience these feelings again.

She closed her eyes. "Lord, where are You leading me?"

Healy. . .healing. Could they be one and the same for her?

❧

Had he really kissed her? Just a little peck on the cheek, nothing serious. . .right?

Like a zombie Healy began emptying the dish drainer, methodically placing plates and glasses in the cupboard. A knock sounded on the apartment door, and he almost dropped a coffee mug. His heart hammered. *Valerie?*

"Healy?" Connor's voice, and there was a definite edge to it.

"Uh, be right there." Had Connor seen the kiss? He gulped and pulled open the door.

The tall, blond man stepped inside, his knife-sharp stare pinning Healy to the spot. "I don't know what you did or said, but it's a downright miracle." Connor laughed aloud. "A miracle!"

Healy wrinkled his brow. He'd expected a lecture on propriety, if not a swift kick out of town. "I don't. . .understand."

"Do you know how long it took us to get Valerie to venture outside even twenty feet from the back door? And only in broad daylight. Never once since she's lived with us has she ever made it as far as the garage, much less upstairs to this apartment." Connor pressed a palm to his forehead. "Healy, how did you do it?"

He gave an embarrassed shrug. "I just talked to her, that's all. I made her focus on me, not her fears."

Connor's eyes narrowed. "That's all? After everything we've tried, you make it sound way too easy."

"Guess I've had some practice." Healy stared at the floor. "When I was in prison, it seemed like new inmates—especially the young, scared ones—gravitated toward me. I never could forget how scared I was when they first locked me up, and I didn't want to see another kid with a lousy start in life go through that kind of terror without someone in his corner."

"Healy Ferguson, you never cease to amaze me." Connor ambled across the kitchenette and leaned his forearms on the back of the recliner. He stood there for a full minute without speaking. Then, turning slowly, he said, "Even knowing you're Tom's old friend, I had reservations about hiring an ex-con with a manslaughter conviction and letting him take up residence right upstairs from my very fragile sister." He chuckled softly. "I think of her as fragile, but she's really not. Just. . .wounded. Valerie has an inner strength the rest of us can only envy."

"She's got a deep, abiding faith in the Lord," Healy said softly. "That's where her strength comes from."

"Of course, you're right. And maybe I've been too protective of her." He sighed. "Anyway, when I realized what you'd done tonight, I had to come up and thank you."

Healy's face warmed. He shoved nervous hands into his pockets. "Just glad I could help."

❧

"No, I'm telling you, you'll have to come out to the garage to see." Healy stood in Valerie's sitting room. They'd been having this discussion—make that *argument*—for the past twenty minutes. But after Connor's continued encouragement to keep working on Valerie's fears, Healy wasn't about to give in.

"This is ridiculous. Why can't you bring the boards up here for me to look at?" She stomped her foot like a stubborn child, and he couldn't suppress a chuckle.

"Because," he said, rolling his eyes, "there are too many of them and it's too hot. And it's getting hotter by the minute."

"It'll be hot in the garage, too. No sense both of us getting all sweaty." She crossed her arms. "If you need my opinion so badly, bring the boards up here."

He spread his hands. "Hey, it's okay with me if you don't care how the wood grain matches up. I can build your bookshelves any old way if that's what you want."

"Ooooh, you are so stubborn."

"Me? I'm not the one standing here throwing a tantrum."

"Tantrum? Tantrum!" Valerie shook her finger in his face. "I'll give you a tantrum."

Healy burst out laughing and decided he'd never seen anyone so beautiful in his life. Her lips pushed out in a childish pout. A wisp of pale yellow hair had worked itself loose from her hair clip and hung haphazardly across one of her smoldering gray eyes.

"Healy Ferguson, stop laughing at me right this minute." With an angry huff, she swept her hair off her face. It fell right back.

"I know what you're doing." She twisted out of his reach. "I've seen you and Connor whispering, plotting. You're trying to get me away from the house again. Maybe it worked the other night, but"—she shivered—"don't push it, okay? I'm not ready to try again."

"So when will you be ready?" Healy came up behind her. It took all his resolve not to draw her into his arms.

Her voice quavered. "Maybe never."

"It's one thing to be afraid," he said, "and something else entirely to be a coward."

He waited in silence, watching her fine-boned hands clench and unclench. Her shoulders rose and fell with several deep breaths. "I know you're right, Healy, but I—"

"No buts about it. 'I can do all this through him who gives me strength.' You know that verse, don't you?"

"Philippians 4:13. I know it by heart." The fight seemed to go out of her. She turned to him and held out a shaky hand. "Okay, let's go look at some boards."

❧

Day by day, with Healy's patience, prayers, and gentle persuasion, Valerie ventured farther and farther beyond the safety of the house and the enclosed backyard. Her heart hammered with every first step, and her breathing became so shallow that she felt sure she would die. Yet with God's help she reined in her panic and followed Healy's lead.

They began with trips outside the back gate to look at the bookshelves he was building in the garage. They counted off each painted board of the wide porch running along the front of the house, even braved the heat to sit on the white wicker rockers with glasses of iced tea and watch the cars driving by. Sometimes Maggie Jensen and red-haired little Steven from next door joined them, or Jean Franklin stopped to chat on her way to the tennis courts. The whole neighborhood, witnessing Valerie's progress, showered her with encouragement.

Finally, the first week of August, with Healy holding one hand and Annie the other, Valerie made it all the way down the front walk to the mailbox.

"Yay, Aunt Val, you did it!" Annie plucked a scarlet zinnia from the flower bed and handed it to Valerie with a flourish.

"Thank you, sweetie." Though it was too early for the postman, she tugged open the mailbox and peered inside anyway, then happily raised and lowered the red flag several times.

"Way to go, Valerie!" She glanced across the street, where Cliff Reyna looked up from his weed pulling and gave her a thumbs-up.

She waved, then looked toward the house and shook her head. "With all the painting and landscaping Connor and Ellen have done since I've been living here, this is the first time I've seen it from this perspective." Her gaze took in the beveled Victorian porch rail, the gray siding and maroon shutters, the cupola, the brass weathervane. "Connor and Ellen have poured so much love into this home. It truly is beautiful."

"There's a whole beautiful world out here just waiting for you," Healy said. "It's been deprived of your presence far too long."

A car roared past. Valerie cried out and fell into Healy's open arms, burying her face against his rock-solid chest. He held her until the terror subsided, then guided her toward the porch while Annie protectively clutched her other hand. She clambered toward the door, but Healy stopped her.

"No," he said, leading her to one of the wicker chairs, "you're going to stay out here and beat this fear. You're going to see that everything's all right."

"Healy, I can't. Please—" Memories of another car on a dark, rain-slicked street seized her heart, sending it racing all over again.

Healy pressed her backward until she had no choice but to sit down.

"Breathe," he commanded her. "Take it in. . .let it out."

She closed her eyes and obeyed.

"It was just a silly old car," Annie said, stroking Valerie's arm. "There now, no reason to be all a-scared."

"Out of the mouths of babes." Valerie glanced at her niece with a grateful smile.

The pounding in her chest subsided. The terrifying shadows at the edge of her mind withdrew.

"Thanks, sweetie. I think I'm going to be okay." She looked up into Healy's tender gaze, and she actually believed it.

❧

Pastor Henke sat across from her in the living room the following Sunday afternoon. "Valerie, I'm so proud of you. At this rate, I expect to see you in church any Sunday now."

"Nothing would mean more to me." She fingered the crocheted edging of a throw pillow. "But the mere thought of getting in the car and actually driving somewhere still sends shivers up my spine."

Pastor Henke nibbled on a slice of banana bread Ellen had baked yesterday. "From the very start, I had such an extraordinary sense that Healy was sent here by God. And just as I thought, he was meant to do far more than painting and carpentry."

Valerie absently twisted her wedding band. She could hear Connor and Ellen's muted laughter as they watched an animated video with Annie in the den. "Pastor, Tom's been gone almost five years now. Am I being foolish? I mean, do you think it's possible. . ."

A shadow crossed his face. "Are you becoming interested in Healy as more than a handyman and friend?"

"Yes, I think I am." She bit her lip. "It feels right somehow, and yet when I think of Tom and all we shared. . .and all we lost. . ."

The pastor rubbed his hands along the arms of the beige brocade chair. "Healy has lost a great deal, too," he said slowly. "He's a good man, and worthy of your affection, but tread carefully, my dear."

She studied his expression. "Why do I get the feeling you're keeping something from me? And Connor, too. You both know more about Healy's past than you're letting on." Her insides clenched. She pressed a hand to her forehead. "I get so tired of people walking on eggshells around me."

"If it seems that way, my dear, it is only because we all care about you so much."

"But I'm getting stronger, and I think I'm entitled to know the truth." She sent up a prayer before blurting out the question plaguing her heart. "Pastor, Healy has already told me about his temper getting him into trouble. Is there any reason to think he might be. . .dangerous?"

"Oh no," the pastor answered quickly. "Healy is a changed man. He would never physically hurt you or anyone else—of that I'm entirely confident."

She sat forward, her confusion deepening. "Then why do I get the impression you're warning me not to let myself become involved with him?"

Pastor Henke released a gentle laugh. "I'm a crusty old widower. I would never presume to give anyone advice about matters of the heart."

She couldn't suppress a laugh of her own. "Since when have you ever been short on advice about any topic? Please, Pastor." She grew serious again. "If there's something I should know, then tell me."

"Trust your heart, my dear. It will tell you all you need to know for now."

She looked away and trembled. "I don't know if I dare trust my own heart in this situation."

"But you can trust the Holy Spirit. Don't be afraid of where God leads you." Pastor Henke touched her arm. "In the meantime, my only advice is to take plenty of time to get to know Healy. . .and to let him get to know you."

His cryptic words only added fuel to her mounting frustration. "Won't you give me even a small clue about his past, something that might help me understand him better?"

"Better he tells you himself, when the time is right. . .for both of you."

Valerie rose and crossed to the window. Heat shimmered off the pavement as the August sun beat mercilessly down. "But if everything you've hinted at so far is true, then Healy and I have both wasted too much time already."

"We all have our own prisons," he had told her after the fireworks ended that night.

She spun around and locked her gaze upon the pastor. "Healy's been in prison, hasn't he?"

Chapter 9

"You're awful quiet today." Healy chewed the inside of his cheek as he positioned a glass-front door on Valerie's new built-in curio cabinet. "Matter of fact, you've been quiet all week."

Valerie handed him a pencil, and he marked the screw holes for the hinges. "I've been doing a lot of thinking."

His stomach did a flip-flop. Second thoughts about him, he imagined. Fearing Connor's wrath, he'd never let himself come even close to kissing her again, not even a chaste peck on the cheek, since the Fourth of July.

But, oh, how he'd wanted to. Had she sensed it? More than once he'd prayed about his growing feelings for his best friend's widow. But how could she—how could anyone—love a man who'd served time for killing someone?

So what if he'd accepted Christ, repented, paid his debt to society? He had no education beyond his prison vocational classes and a GED. When he walked out the prison gate a year ago, he'd started his new life with nothing but Tom's Bible, a couple changes of clothes, and the little money he'd saved. No woman in her right mind would even consider a relationship with a loser like him.

True, Valerie didn't know about the prison part yet, but from the moment he showed up at her front door in castoff clothing from Zion Community Church's donation barrel, the rest had to be obvious. She was way too good for him, and she must have finally started to realize it. Nothing else could explain her recent coolness.

He reached for the electric drill to make his pilot holes. Valerie supported the door as he secured the satin-finish hinges with matching brass screws. They repeated the process for the opposite door.

"It looks beautiful," Valerie said, stepping back. "Healy, you're a fine carpenter."

He murmured his thanks and raked a hand through his sweat-dampened hair. "One more set of doors and it'll be finished."

She sighed. "And on to Connor and Ellen's next project. Probably the new baby's nursery."

Did he only imagine a wistful tone in her voice?

She pressed a hand to her back and crossed to the delicate-looking antique desk. He'd noticed her writing in a book there a few times while he worked but sensed she preferred to keep the contents private.

Kind of like him and prison.

"Looks like a good time to break for a cold drink." He started for the hallway.

"Healy, wait." She turned toward him.

His heart thudded. "Yeah?"

"A few days ago Pastor Henke admitted to me what he and Connor have known about you from the beginning." He saw pity in her eyes, a look he'd never wanted to receive from a woman he cared so much about. "Healy. . .I know you've been in prison."

Thank the Lord little Annie had already gone down for her nap. He rubbed his jaw. Okay, so Valerie knew the truth now, at least that part of it. "I sure didn't mean to deceive you. It's just that the pastor and your brother thought—"

"I understand." She reached out, almost touched him, but drew back at the last moment. "I know they were. . ." She bit her lip. "They were concerned about my reaction because of what happened to my husband."

"Tom." He hung his head.

"Yes. His death and everything surrounding it has haunted me all these years." She stared at the floor. "You've helped me so much with my panic attacks when no one else seemed able to. But when I found out you had. . .you were. . ."

"Sent to jail for manslaughter," he supplied throatily.

She lifted her gaze to meet his. "It came as a shock, just when I felt we were getting to know each other. I knew you must have been through some rough times, but I had no idea. I wasn't prepared for the truth."

He tried to laugh. "Hard to ever be prepared to learn that kind of truth about somebody." He thought of Tom and the look of shock and utter despair in his eyes when he came to see Healy in jail the day after his arrest.

"What I'm trying to say," Valerie continued, "is that I should have come to you right away. You're a good man, Healy. A godly man. How could I doubt for an instant that you are a different person from who you were so many years ago?"

She reached out again, and this time her touch shot tingling currents of electricity through him. "Healy, will you tell me. . .in your own words. . .what happened?"

❧

She pulled him over to the loveseat and sat next to him without releasing his hand. His palm felt cold and damp. She longed to wrap her arms around him and take away the fear, just as he had helped her confront her own private terrors.

"I was seventeen," he began, his voice low and tremulous. "My sister had been dating this older guy. I'd seen bruises and suspected he slapped her around, but she always denied it. She seemed so hungry to be loved."

Valerie squeezed his hand. "I can't imagine any woman needing love so much that she'd willingly put up with such treatment."

Healy made a harsh noise in his throat. "Guess she didn't know any better. When we were little, our dad got killed in a construction accident, and Mama had to work long hours to provide for us. Years later, she got sick and died.

Bethy, my sister, was fifteen, and I'd just turned twelve. We went to live with an aunt."

He clasped his hands between his knees. "Bethy dropped out of school and started hanging with a rough crowd, doing all sorts of things our mama had tried to teach us not to do. She did her best to raise us right, got us to Sunday school and all, but it was hard to believe in a God who'd let such horrible things happen to a good woman."

Valerie nodded. "I went through a time when I asked similar questions, myself."

"I'm not saying all this to excuse myself, but maybe it helps you see where I got off track. I lived on anger back then, but I made it to my senior year without much more trouble than occasional suspension for giving somebody a black eye or broken nose." He gave a cheerless laugh. "My temper actually gave me an edge on the football field."

"You played football?" Valerie gave him a half smile. "My Tom played in high school, too. He used to say it helped him burn off his raging teenage hormones."

Healy cast her an unreadable look before glancing away. "Teenage hormones can't be blamed for what I did. When I saw that guy hitting my sister one night, I knew real anger, real hatred, for the very first time." His whole body trembled. "I heard his car pull into the driveway near midnight. He was drunk and yelling for Bethy. He accused her of being with another guy and carried on about how he'd beat the tar out of them both."

"Oh, Healy."

He went on as if she weren't even there. "I tried to stop her, but she told me it would be okay. She thought she could talk some sense into him before he woke the whole neighborhood. Then he grabbed her arm and slapped her over and over again. Her mouth was bleeding, and she kept whimpering, begging him to stop, and suddenly I couldn't take it anymore. I ran out and started punching him. He fell backwards and hit his head on the concrete." He let out a shuddering breath. "He never got up."

A hush descended around them in the sun-brightened sitting room. Slowly, with immense tenderness, Valerie drew him into her arms and held him. She stroked his dark blond hair and breathed in the masculine smells of wood stain, sawdust, and sweat as he emptied himself of tears against her shoulder.

"It's all right, Healy," she whispered. "It's all in the past now. It's over." *And I love you.*

❧

Valerie, I'm falling in love with you. He wanted so badly to say the words aloud to the woman who had finally pierced the armor around his heart.

He pulled away with a sniff. "Sorry, didn't mean to lose it like that." He grabbed some tissues and blew his nose. "Just when I think I've gotten past it, the disgusting truth jars me back to reality. No two ways about it, I'm a murderer."

"But you were defending your sister. Didn't the courts take that into consideration?"

Methodically he folded the damp tissues. Their baby powder smell lingered in his nostrils, playing sweet counterpoint to the bitter memories. "Oh sure, until they heard testimony from my high school principal, counselor, and a couple of football coaches whose players I sent to the hospital after some post-game brawls."

"But surely that wasn't enough—"

"It gets worse." He hauled in a long, shaky breath. "The coroner testified I hit the guy so many times that he was probably already unconscious when he fell."

She rose and crossed the room, then spun around to face him, an explosive fire brightening her eyes. "I don't care what they said about you in court. Healy, you've paid the penalty for your crime. And just like the Bible says, you're now a new creation in Christ. When I look at you today, I see a good, honest, decent man. I see a man of immense talent and skill."

She ran a finger along the cabinet door, and her voice grew hoarse with emotion. "The past is behind you. You have a wonderful future ahead. Oh, Healy, I just know it."

"If you're going to give me the God-isn't-finished-with-you-yet speech, you don't have to. If I didn't already believe He has a better plan for my life, I wouldn't have made it this far."

He should tell her about Tom now. She should know the part her husband had played in Healy's redemption. "Valerie, there's something else—"

"Hey, Aunt Val." Annie sauntered into the room, dragging an oversized stuffed rabbit. "I waked up from my nap and I want my snack now."

"Hi, sweetie. Did you sleep good?" Valerie gave Healy a regretful look that told him they'd have to put their conversation on hold for a little while. "Come on downstairs, and we'll see what kind of cookies we can find."

"Healy, you come, too." Annie reached for his hand.

As he grasped her pudgy pink fist and allowed himself to be dragged downstairs, he indulged in a few pleasurable moments of fantasizing—Valerie, himself, a kid or two of their own. With steady carpentry work maybe he could someday afford a nice little house for his family. Jesus had been a carpenter, after all. It was honest, respectable work, and Healy knew he was good at it.

Maybe it was a gift from God that he'd been stopped from telling Valerie about his connection to Tom. At least this way, whatever she felt for Healy, he could be sure it wasn't clouded by any sense of obligation or pity toward her deceased husband's old buddy from prison.

So he'd wait—wait to tell her that part until he got the okay from Connor or Pastor Henke. . .or from the Lord.

And, Lord, if I'm not supposed to be falling in love with her, You'd better stop me quick, because I'm falling hard and fast.

Chapter 10

Valerie peered around the corner of the open garage door and stood watching Healy. Sweat gleamed on his tanned, muscular arms as he measured and marked a piece of lumber for the new sink cabinet for the upstairs guest bathroom.

Smiling, she crept up from behind and snaked her arm around him until the booklet she held was right in front of his face.

"What in the world—" He grabbed it out of her hands with feigned annoyance. "Can't a guy get any work done around here without some pretty lady pestering him?"

"Pretty lady, is it?" Her heart thrilled. "When the guy is as handsome and talented as you are, what do you expect?"

Color rose in Healy's face. He hid it behind the booklet he'd wrenched from her grasp. "All right, let's see what you found so important that you had to come all the way out here and interrupt my work."

Fizzy as a shaken-up pop bottle, she blurted out the answer. "It's a course catalogue from East Central College. I asked Ellen to bring one home with her yesterday."

"College?" Healy held the catalogue away from him as if it were on fire.

"There's still time to register for the fall, and they offer business and vocational courses, and I thought—"

She cut herself off at the terrified look in Healy's eyes. "I—I thought going back to school might be another positive step toward your new start in life."

He edged away and slowly turned the pages. His Adam's apple quivered. "I used to dream about going to college. . . ."

"Well, here's your chance." Urgency filled her. She fixed him with a determined stare. "Healy, you can do it. You can do anything you set your mind to."

He rubbed the back of his neck with a dirty hand. "You're forgetting I don't have a car, or even a driver's license. How would I get there?"

"If you can plan your class schedule to match Ellen's, you can ride with her. If not, something else will work out."

He looked askance at her. "You seem awful sure of yourself."

"Hey, aren't you the guy who's been quoting Philippians 4:13 all summer?"

"Okay, but you're forgetting one major detail. Even with what Connor pays me, I haven't saved near enough for college."

Valerie set her hands on her hips. "Healy Ferguson, for a man of faith, sometimes you sure don't show much. You happen to be looking at the church prayer-chain coordinator, remember? The calls have already been made. People are praying as we speak."

His mouth spread into a broad grin, and his hazel eyes lit up. "You are truly the most amazing woman I have ever known." Then he let loose a whoop of victory. He swept Valerie into his arms and whirled her around the hot, stuffy garage. "Hey, world, I'm gonna be a college man!"

"Healy, oh, Healy!" Laughing, she wrapped her arms around his neck. Her head still spun when he finally set her down. She pressed a hand to her lower back but smiled in spite of the nagging ache.

Worry filled Healy's eyes. "Did I hurt you? Are you okay?"

"I'm fine. I'm just so happy to see you this excited."

He held her at arm's length. "Valerie, I. . ." His throat worked, and he seemed to want to tell her something but couldn't get the words out.

Say it, Healy. Say you love me.

Lowering his eyes, he murmured, "I can't believe how lucky—no, how *blessed* I am to have found you. Nobody has believed in me like you have since—"

"Oh, hush." She silenced him with a finger to his lips. She looked up at him coyly, surprising herself with the sudden yearning she felt. "If you really think I'm so amazing, then why don't you kiss me?"

❧

Kiss her?

He didn't need to be asked twice. He drew her to him, so close that he could smell the delicate honeysuckle scent of her shampoo. His lips hovered over hers for the briefest of moments before he gently, tenderly kissed her. The warmth of her mouth made his head swim. He relished an ecstasy he never imagined possible. No wonder Tom had fallen helplessly, head-over-heels in love with this woman.

He drew back, and for a moment her lips seemed to follow his. He sensed in her the same keen urgency welling up in himself.

"Valerie, oh, Valerie!" He gave a ragged sigh. "Tell me I'm crazy, tell me it's hopeless, but I'm in love with you. I think I have been since the first minute I laid eyes on you."

"You're not crazy," she said, her voice like liquid silver. "I'm falling in love with you, too."

Resisting every urge churning inside him, he pushed her away. His pulse throbbed in his ears. "You'd better go inside. It's safer. . .for both of us."

Her honeyed laugh floated in the sultry air. "Sorry, Healy, but as hard as you fought to get me through that locked door, you're going to find it a lot harder to banish me to the house again."

He couldn't help but grin despite the doubts coiling around his heart. She was so incredibly beautiful. And stubborn as they came. "I just meant that we should both slow down here. You haven't known me very long, and with what you do know, you ought to be at least a little cautious, don't you think?"

A shivery sigh escaped her lips. "I'm not afraid of your past or of who you used to be. But you're right, we should take things slowly." She ran a slender finger along the jagged white scar on his left forearm. "We're both scarred from old wounds, and we need to make sure we're fully healed."

Sadness crept into her eyes. Every time Healy thought about how Tom died, it made his stomach wrench. The pain must be a million times worse for Valerie. She saw it happen. She watched her husband's blood drain away in a senseless, pointless act of carnage.

"Hey, seriously, it's the hottest part of the afternoon." He covered the catch in his voice with a cough. "You should go inside. We can talk more about. . .us. . .later."

"Will you join us for supper?"

He chewed his lip. "Okay, as long as you and Ellen and Connor don't gang up on me about this college stuff."

"But you will think about it, won't you?"

"Count on it." He brought the catalogue to his forehead in a mock salute before stuffing it into his back pocket. "Now get out of here so I can finish up."

❧

As Valerie sauntered toward the house, she could still taste the delightful warmth of Healy's lips and feel his rock-hard arms around her.

O Lord, I know my feelings for Healy are real, but I'm scared.

Not like the paralyzing fear of her panic attacks, but the fear of falling deeply, hopelessly in love with this man and then losing him. Losing him the way she lost Tom. Maybe not to a violent act of crime, but what about a car accident, or a hair dryer falling into the bathtub with him? Or alone in the garage he could injure himself with one of those noisy power tools and bleed to death before anyone found him.

"Perfect love casts out fear. Cast all your worries on Me."

"I know, Father." She glanced toward the cloudless blue sky. "I'm trying. Help me, as only You can."

As she bent down to pick up one of Annie's toys, another searing pain shot through her back. She gasped and doubled over, bracing her hands on her knees, and silently acknowledged one more reason she could lose Healy.

She'd have to tell him. Soon.

The back door opened. "Val, are you okay?" Ellen hurried down the porch steps and helped Valerie inside.

"I'll be all right in a minute. Just let me sit down and rest." She eased into the nearest kitchen chair.

"Turn around. I'll rub it for you." Ellen pressed firm hands against the painful spot on Valerie's back, kneading the soreness away.

"Thanks. That feels great." She rested her head on the table and relaxed into her sister-in-law's massage.

"How's Healy coming with the bathroom cabinet?"

Valerie gave a soft chuckle in spite of her discomfort. "We didn't talk much about the cabinet."

"Hmmm. Okay, what did you talk about? You were out there long enough." Ellen gave Valerie's back a final brisk rub and plopped down in the chair across from her.

Sitting up, Valerie smoothed her hair away from her face. "I showed him the college catalogue."

"And?"

"It might take some doing, but I think he can be convinced."

Ellen sipped the cranberry juice she'd left sitting on the table. "I'll be happy to help him register and show him around campus. He'll have to go through some testing, but maybe I can pull a few strings to smooth the process for him." She winked. "But I have a feeling you and your prayer chain will soon have the entire situation under control."

"I really appreciate how accepting of him you and Connor have been." Valerie reached across the table to squeeze Ellen's hand.

"I admit, I was stunned when Connor finally told me about Healy's time in prison. I can't believe he and Pastor Henke kept it between themselves for so long." She grimaced. "Well, yes, I can."

Valerie shot her sister-in-law a wry grin. "Right. What is it Connor always says? 'Telephone, telegraph, tell Ellen.'"

"Ugh, don't rub it in." Ellen went to the stove to stir a pot of marinara sauce. The garlic-and-tomato aroma filled the kitchen.

"Anyway," Valerie continued, "you can see what a good man Healy is. That part of his life was so long ago, and he paid for his mistake."

Ellen smiled over her shoulder. "You're falling fast, aren't you?"

"Am I so obvious?"

"Like a neon sign." Ellen laid aside the wooden spoon. "Valerie Bishop is"—she flashed the quotation marks symbol with the first two fingers of each hand—"*in love*."

Valerie cast her a pleading look. "What am I going to do? One minute I'm sure it's so right, and the next, I'm quaking in my sandals."

Tenderness softened Ellen's voice. "Honey, you've been in love before, and you know how it works. You take it one day at a time. And if Healy is the man God wants you to be with, He'll take care of the details."

"I'm not being a traitor to Tom's memory, am I?"

"Of course not. And I think you already knew the answer to that question. Come on, what's really bothering you?" She dropped several handfuls of bowtie pasta into a pot of boiling water. "Are you more hung up on Healy's past than you can admit to yourself?"

Valerie rose and stretched, then went to the cupboard and took out a stack of dinner plates. "It threw me for a loop at first, but all I have to do is spend ten minutes with him and I know what a wonderful man he is."

"Then what's the problem?"

The back door swung open and Connor breezed in. "Mmm, Italian. My favorite." He planted a noisy kiss on Ellen's cheek.

"Come back here," she demanded when he turned away. "You can do better than that." Grabbing a chunk of his blond hair, she pulled his face to hers and kissed him passionately.

The color rose in his face as Ellen released him. "It's the marinara sauce," he said, winking at Valerie. "Always does that to her. You know, Italian, the food of romance?"

"Oh, and I thought it was the bloom of pregnancy." Valerie raised an eyebrow as she busied herself arranging flatware.

"Well, romance is in the air," Ellen said brightly.

Valerie looked up at a light tapping on the back door. Connor strode over to answer it. "Hey, Healy, come on in."

He looked scrubbed and fresh from the shower, his wet hair slicked back and dark blond curls brushing the collar of a pale blue polo shirt. "Am I too early? Valerie invited me for supper."

Connor clamped a hand on Healy's shoulder. In a loud stage whisper he said, "We're having Italian. Enter at your own risk."

At Healy's questioning look, Valerie could only shrug. *Lord, if You're going to let Connor and Ellen play matchmaker, I'll need an extra dose of Your courage.*

Chapter 11

Healy settled into the passenger seat of Ellen's blue Mazda, then looked up at Valerie. "I wish you'd come with me."

She wanted to, more than she could ever tell him, but her heart still raced at the mere thought of venturing far from the familiarity of home. She shook her head and gently closed his door, forcing her thoughts toward the surprise she planned for Healy when he returned. Bending toward his open window, she said, "I'll stay here and pray for you the whole time you're gone."

Ellen laughed and climbed in behind the steering wheel. "We're only going to get him registered for school, Val. You make it sound like he's headed to death row." She threw her hand over her mouth. "Oh, Healy, I'm so sorry. I wasn't thinking."

"If I'm not used to prison jokes by now, I never will be." He blew a limp strand of hair off his damp forehead and grinned at Ellen. "What do you say we get this show on the road before I chicken out or we both melt from the heat, whichever comes first?"

Ellen started the car and turned the air conditioner on full blast. She leaned over the steering wheel and gave Valerie a thumbs-up. "If all goes well, we should be back by six."

Valerie tilted her head to give Healy a quick kiss. "I'm so glad you're doing this." She waved as they backed out of the driveway.

❧

Ellen flipped on her signal and turned at the next corner. "You don't have to look so scared, you know."

"Can't help it. This college thing is almost as scary as prison ever was. I don't know if I can cut it." He could feel himself breaking into a cold sweat despite the frigid air blowing in his face.

Ellen tossed a smile in his direction. "Val has every confidence in you. I know you'll make her proud."

"I'd like to do more than make her proud." He rubbed his brow. "I'd like to. . ."

"I know you're falling for her." Ellen spoke slowly as she stared at the road ahead. "Be careful, Healy. She's a strong, determined woman, but she still has some healing to do."

"Believe me, I'm not rushing into anything. Besides, what do I have to offer someone like her?" The old feelings of worthlessness welled inside him. "She deserves so much more, someone who can give her a real home, someone who can provide for her the way she deserves." *Someone without a past.*

"Love doesn't usually take those details into consideration," Ellen replied. "It just happens."

"Still, I can't even let myself dream about a future with Valerie unless I know I could give her a decent life. She's already been married to the best and most upright guy who ever walked the face of the earth." He stared forlornly at the passing countryside. "Why she even gives me the time of day, I'll never understand."

Ellen cast him a quizzical glance. "You almost talk as if you knew Tom."

His stomach knotted. "I did."

By the time Ellen parked her car in the faculty lot, Healy had told her everything about his connection with Tom and how the search for his friend had brought him to St. Louis and finally Aileen.

She cut off the engine and drummed her fingers on the steering wheel. "I am going to have a serious talk with my husband later. Is there anything *else* he and Pastor Henke have neglected to tell me about you?"

Healy ducked his head. "That about covers it. After Valerie guessed I'd been in prison, I thought maybe Connor would go ahead and tell her about me and Tom. I even asked him about it a couple times, but he said we had to take it one step at a time, said he still has hopes of getting her back into counseling before we lay too much more on her."

"I suppose that makes sense. But still. . .I can't believe Valerie hasn't put the pieces together for herself. Why, even I remember Tom mentioning his correspondence with a friend in prison."

Healy rubbed perspiring hands on his thighs. "When I think about how Tom died, all she went through herself—it's no wonder she can't remember some things."

Ellen gave her brown curls a rapid toss as she reached into the backseat for her purse. "And you, Healy, losing your best friend. . . I'm so sorry."

"Tom was too good a man to suffer that way." With a ragged sigh, Healy shoved his door open and stepped into the August heat.

Coming around the car, Ellen touched his arm. "It seems to me you have two people to make proud with this decision to go to college. Tom holds as much a stake in your future as Valerie does."

Healy stared across the sloping lawns toward the rambling brick buildings. "And I owe him. I owe him big-time."

❧

Valerie hummed along with a Christian radio station while she put the finishing touches on a banner she'd been creating on the computer:

FOR WISDOM WILL ENTER YOUR HEART, AND KNOWLEDGE WILL BE PLEASANT TO YOUR SOUL.

AUTUMN RAINS

—Proverbs 2:10
Congratulations on Your Exciting New Beginning!

While bright yellow paper slowly fed through the color printer, she went to check on a sheet of cookies in the oven. The tempting aroma of melting chocolate chips swirled around her. Unable to wait a second longer, she dipped a spoon into the tub of pre-mixed cookie dough and scooped out a gooey, delicious mouthful.

She was still savoring the chocolaty sweetness when the phone rang a few moments later.

"Good afternoon, Valerie. How's my favorite prayer-chain coordinator?"

"Hi, Pastor! Couldn't be better. You sound as if you have an assignment for me." She took one last lick from the spoon.

"In fact, I do." Pastor Henke sighed softly. "You're familiar with the Sanderson family."

Valerie had met the Sandersons once when she and Tom visited Zion, and she'd read about the family often in the church newsletter since coming to live with her brother. Harold Sanderson owned a prominent investment company and held the reputation of being one of Zion's biggest financial contributors. However, both Connor and Ellen had hinted on more than one occasion that Harold had a tendency to throw his weight around until he got things done his way.

But Harold's money had not been able to ensure a trouble-free family life. Seemed as if one or another of his four spoiled children was always getting into mischief—drinking binges, speeding tickets, vandalizing the high school, truancy. The older ones had somehow managed to grow up, shape up, and move out on their own. That left only the Sandersons' teenage daughter. Valerie chewed her lip. "Oh no, what's Marsha done this time?"

"She and a friend were in a car accident last night. Marsha wasn't seriously injured, praise God, but her friend Tina Maxwell has a broken rib and a mild concussion."

"Oh dear. Is there no end to trouble for that family?"

"I'm afraid it gets worse. Marsha's accident occurred after she and Tina were caught shoplifting." Pastor Henke paused, cleared his throat. "Seems they were trying to make a quick getaway."

She pressed a hand to her stomach and mentally pushed away a disturbing memory. "Have charges been filed?"

"For Tina, yes. Marsha was taken into custody but, as always, Harold's attorney pulled some strings and got her charges dropped." His crisp tone left no doubt concerning his opinion of such tactics.

The oven timer chimed. Valerie removed the sheet of cookies while balancing the phone against her shoulder. "Somebody needs to talk to the Sandersons about tough love."

"I assure you, I have tried." Pastor Henke huffed. "At any rate, would you please activate the prayer chain for Tina? Her family doesn't attend Zion. In fact, I'm not sure they're Christians at all, but all the more reason why she needs prayer. And, of course, add the Sandersons to the list. . .for obvious reasons."

"I certainly will." Valerie jotted a note on the tablet by the phone.

"Moving on to a more pleasant topic," Pastor Henke began, "did you get our budding new student off to matriculate?"

Valerie's heart lightened. "Ellen should be walking him through the registration process as we speak." She tacked the prayer reminder on the bulletin board next to her list of emergency phone numbers. "I'm so excited for him. He deserves this chance for a better life."

"I'm still planning to be there for his celebratory dinner. Six thirty, right?"

"Bring your appetite. Connor's going to throw some salmon steaks on the grill, and, of course, Ellen has lots of fixings already prepared. I'm in charge of dessert."

Silence met her ears. Then she heard a tentative, "You. . .made dessert?"

"Oh, please. You sound as if you don't think I'm capable."

"Er, well, I do recall the pumpkin pie you attempted a couple of Thanksgivings ago."

She pursed her lips. "I can't help it if I never made pie from a real pumpkin before. How was I supposed to know to remove the seeds first?" She laughed. "Anyway, you don't have to worry. Everything is store-bought, from the premixed cookie dough to the old-fashioned vanilla ice cream."

"Whew, I am utterly relieved."

"I'd better go, Pastor." Valerie dropped her spoon into soapy dishwater. "I'd like to get those prayer-chain calls made before Annie wakes up from her nap. She's going to help me decorate Healy's apartment while he's out."

They said their good-byes, and Valerie reached in the drawer for her prayer-chain phone list. The calls went quickly—no one seemed to require much explanation about another Sanderson sibling in trouble.

As she hung up from the last conversation, Annie skipped into the kitchen. The curly-haired child sniffed the air and broke into a grin. "I smell cookies, Aunt Val."

"You sure do, sweetie." Valerie swiftly moved the tray of cooling cookies out of Annie's reach. "But we have to save these for later."

"Healy's party. Yay!"

Valerie whisked the container of dough into the refrigerator. "Come on, Annie-girl, let's go decorate. Afterward, I'll let you have one cookie with a glass of milk."

Already perspiring as she unlocked Healy's door, she mentally thanked him for leaving the air conditioner running. She set her armload of decorating supplies on the kitchen table and surveyed the room. Her mouth curled into an approving smile. "My goodness, this place is neat as a pin. You'd never guess a bachelor lived here." Ever since he'd been working on Connor's house, Valerie had observed Healy's meticulous care of everything, from the professional power tools Connor had rented to the tiniest paintbrush. She admired and respected Healy more every day.

"Put the banner right there." Annie pointed to the wide archway between the dining area and living room.

"Good idea." Valerie positioned a chair and climbed up carefully, ever conscious of the twinge in her lower back.

With the banner hung to her satisfaction, she carried a package of balloons to the sofa and sat down to start inflating them. After blowing up the first three, she felt a twinge of lightheadedness and leaned back to catch her breath. She could hardly restrain her laughter as Annie took up the project, puffing and spitting but making little headway with the stiff, stubborn balloon.

Suddenly the balloon shot out of Annie's mouth and landed on an end table. She scurried over to retrieve it. "Hey, Aunt Val, Healy has a big Bible like Daddy's. I wonder if his has pictures, too." She tossed the balloon aside and began paging through the black leather-bound book.

"Oh, Annie, be careful." Valerie reached to rescue Healy's Bible. "You don't want to tear the pages. Healy wouldn't like—"

The Bible fell open in her lap, revealing the flyleaf. As she glanced down, the sight of familiar handwriting wrenched her heart.

To Gus, my best friend. . .

Shock and disbelief sent chills up her arms. *"Tom?"*

Memories long submerged flooded her consciousness. Gus, Tom's high-school football buddy from his hometown in Michigan, the kid who had accidentally killed someone in a fight and ended up going to prison. How many times had Tom talked about visiting his friend at the state penitentiary, giving him a Bible, helping him find forgiveness in Christ? Though Tom never got back to Michigan, he faithfully wrote to his friend, sometimes as often as once a week.

Including the day he died.

"I'll be ready to leave in a minute, Lady V."

The chasm of the past four years was bridged in a moment, and she could hear Tom's tired but cheery voice as clearly as she did that night.

"I know it's late, but I just want to finish this letter to Gus. We can drop it in the corner mailbox on the way home."

She remembered leaning in the office doorway, feeling so sleepy that she could scarcely keep her eyes open. The aromas of olive oil, Italian sausage, and pungent spices still lingered in the air. Commingled with the sharp odor of disinfectant cleaner, the smells conspired to nauseate her.

"Good night, Pablo. See you tomorrow, Manny," she called to the busboys, yawning as she followed them to the back door to lock it behind them. With each step, the boys' rubber-soled shoes squeaked on the tile floor, still wet from the last mopping of the day.

Returning to the office, she watched Tom seal the envelope and peel a stamp from the roll in his desk drawer. He gave her an apologetic smile as he rose and slipped his arms into his jacket. "Is my little Italian mama about to fall asleep standing up?"

"I'm Irish, not Italian, and yes." She leaned into the comfort of his embrace.

Tom held the front door open for her, and the October evening met them with a cold, misting rain. Across the street, the U.S. mailbox shimmered under a haloed streetlight.

"Wait here. I'll be right back." Tom sprinted across the slick pavement, letter in hand.

She stood in the shelter of the green awning over the door, hands stuffed into the fleece-lined pockets of her coat. A few blocks away, a police siren wailed. It seemed to be moving closer. Tom waved and started back across the street.

Suddenly tires screeched. Headlights blinded her. A sickening thud and a woman's scream—her own. A car spun out of control. Metal slammed against metal. Glass shattered.

A stranger's face filled her vision. A rough hand clamped around her arm; another covered her mouth. She tasted sweat and fear. A dangerous, hate-filled voice shouted in her ear, "Lady, you're coming with me, or I'll kill you right here!"

Dear God, help me. Tom, get up, get up—please!

The police sirens were upon them now, splintering the night air. Blue and red strobes sliced through the mist and reflected in her captor's wide, panicked eyes. Blood oozed from a gash on his temple, crisscrossing an angry scar across his left cheek.

"Let the lady go," someone shouted. "Don't make things worse than they already are."

He made an ugly noise in his throat—half terror, half rage—before thrusting her hard against something metal, something sharp. Pain shot through her back, and she screamed. With one hand she groped for something to brace against; with the other she cradled her abdomen. She raised her head as her assailant and the two men with him plunged into the night, police in pursuit.

And then blessed blackness.

Chapter 12

"Aunt Val? Aunt Val, why are you crying?" Annie's shrill, frightened pleas slowly penetrated the fog of Valerie's mind.

"I'll be all right, honey. Just. . .give me a minute." Dazed, emptied, she barely recognized the sound of her own voice, taut and thin as an overstretched rubber band.

As long suppressed memories converged with reality, the unspeakable truth jolted her with brutal force. If Tom had not crossed the street, if he hadn't chosen that moment to mail the letter to Gus. . .to *H. P. Ferguson, Prisoner #6397104*. . .he would still be alive.

It seemed impossible, and yet the evidence lay before her in Tom's own handwriting in the front of Healy's Bible, the one Healy told her his best friend had given him fifteen years ago.

How could she not have known? Hadn't she carried Tom's letters to the mailbox on many occasions? Tom had always called his friend Gus, but why hadn't she at least recognized the last name? If nothing else, she might have pieced things together listening to Healy describe the fight that sent him to prison. *Defending his sister. . .got carried away.* . .weren't those the words Tom had used when he first told her about his friend in prison?

You didn't remember because you didn't want to. You couldn't bear the pain of remembering.

The truth pressed on her heart like a crushing weight. How could she ever look at Healy the same way again?

O God, why? I loved him so!

With trembling hands she returned the Bible to the end table. "Let's go, Annie."

"But the balloons. And the streamers." Annie tugged on Valerie's wrist. "Aren't we gonna decorate?"

"We have to go now, Annie." She staggered out into the oppressive heat.

Reaching the house, she closed the kitchen door and mechanically punched in the code to arm the security system, which, with strange detachment, she realized she had not felt the compulsion to do in weeks.

❧

"Here you go, Mr. Ferguson." The gray-haired woman behind the counter slid a stack of computer printouts across to Healy. "Your class schedule and receipts. The bookstore is open if you'd like to purchase your textbooks."

Ellen touched Healy's arm. "Valerie's probably bitten her nails to the quick by now. We can get your books another day."

Healy chuckled. "After handing over so much money for tuition and fees, I could use a few days to recover from the shock before laying out another small fortune on textbooks."

"Getting an education is not cheap," Ellen said as they headed toward the parking lot. "But the grant information Mrs. Kelsey gave you should help, at least for next semester."

He shook his head. "I still can't get over the idea of total strangers from your church offering to cover my expenses to get me started. I don't know how I'll ever repay them—or you and Connor for all you've done."

Ellen aimed the key-chain remote at her shiny blue car and punched a button. "Get it through your head once and for all, Healy Ferguson. This is not about payback. It's about accepting help when you need it."

"But still, I don't know what to say."

She tugged on his shirt collar and winked. "It's easy. Just say *thank you.*"

He swallowed over a lump in his throat. "Thank you."

On the way back to Aileen, Healy reviewed his class schedule with Ellen, and they discussed how best to work out his transportation. As they had hoped, he could ride to campus with her for most of his classes, but a couple of his labs would require returning in the evening.

"You could apply for a driver's license, you know," Ellen suggested.

Healy smirked. "And drive what?"

Ellen looked at him with feigned astonishment. "Don't tell me you've already forgotten the proficiency of our esteemed prayer-chain coordinator. After all she's managed so far, I'm sure coming up with a vehicle would be small potatoes for her."

Warmth spread through Healy's chest as he pictured the fair-haired woman he fell more in love with every day. "She is something, that's for sure."

Ellen parked in the driveway, and they stepped through the side gate. "Thanks again for all your help," Healy said. "And remember, you promised to let me be the one to tell Valerie about Tom when the time is right."

Ellen made a zipping motion across her lips. "It'll be hard, but I'll try." She waved as Healy started up the stairs to his apartment.

Turning his key in the deadbolt, Healy realized with confusion that the door was already unlocked. He distinctly remembered locking the apartment before leaving with Ellen. Cautiously he pushed open the door and stepped inside. At the sight of the bright yellow banner taped across the archway, he broke into a grin.

"Oh, Val, you are really something."

He ducked under the banner and dropped his stack of college papers on the end table. On the other side of the coffee table, three inflated red balloons rolled aimlessly across the floor, propelled by the gentle breeze from the air conditioner. A cellophane bag containing more balloons lay on the sofa, along with a roll of masking tape and two unopened packages of crepe paper streamers.

An uneasy feeling tugged at Healy's insides. Had Valerie had another panic attack? She'd come so far, and the last thing she needed was a setback. He spun on his heel and hurried downstairs, thumping loudly on the Paiges' back door.

"Healy, come in." Ellen's worried look confirmed his fears. "Something's happened with Valerie. I found her shut in her room with Annie and Jean Franklin from next door, and she hasn't told any of us what's wrong. Maybe she'll talk to you."

Healy strode across the kitchen. "Did Annie say anything?"

"Just that they were decorating your apartment, and then Aunt Val started crying and said they had to leave. At least Val had the presence of mind to ask Jean to come over." Ellen hugged herself and stared toward the hallway. "I don't like this, Healy. She was doing so much better."

"Let me see what I can find out." He took a steadying breath before marching upstairs.

He paused outside Valerie's sitting room door. "Valerie? It's Healy. Can I come in?"

"Go away," came the muffled reply. "Please. Just go away."

"Valerie, I—"

The door opened slowly, and Jean slipped out with Annie clutching her hand. The latch clicked shut behind them. Annie looked up at Healy with a solemn frown. "You can't 'sturb Aunt Val right now. She's very sad."

Healy cast the silver-haired woman a searching look, and she shrugged. "All I know is, something upset Valerie enough that she didn't trust herself to take care of Annie. She phoned and asked if I could come over—first time she's ever needed to call on me, so I knew it must be serious. I asked her several times to let me phone Connor, but she didn't want me bothering him at the office."

Healy pulled a hand across his face. He knelt and caught Annie's small pink hands in his, squeezing them gently. "Sweetheart, do you know why Aunt Val is sad? Can you tell me what happened in my apartment?"

Her bottom lip trembled. "I think she got mad at me 'cause I was looking at your Bible. I'm real sorry, Healy. I didn't tear it, I promise. I just wanted to see if it had pictures like Daddy's."

Healy lowered his head. "Did Aunt Val look at my Bible, too?"

"Uh-huh." Annie's voice quavered, and he glanced up into worried blue eyes. "Are you mad at Aunt Val for looking at your Bible? Because she was real careful, and she put it right back on the table where it was."

He drew the child into his arms and stroked her pale yellow curls. "No, darlin', I'm not mad at you, and I'm not mad at Aunt Val."

Tiny arms wound around his neck. "Then can you make her happy again? We were gonna have a party for you 'cause you went to college with my mommy." She drew back and searched his face. "Did you see the big yellow sign? Did you like it?"

"I loved it." He swooped her up as he rose. "Tell you what. Let's go back downstairs and talk to Mommy."

"Shall I stay with Valerie?" Jean asked.

"I'd really appreciate it if you'd keep an eye on her for a while. Until we sort through this mess, I don't think she should be alone."

"I understand." Jean quietly re-entered the sitting room as Healy started downstairs.

He found Ellen pacing the kitchen, paring knife in one hand, a glossy green bell pepper in the other. She looked up anxiously. "Well?"

Healy set Annie on a kitchen chair and gave Ellen a meaningful look. "I think she knows."

"About you and Tom? But how?"

With a sidelong glance at Annie, he moved a few steps away and lowered his voice to tell Ellen about the inscription in his Bible and what Annie had said.

"But why would she be so upset?" Ellen plopped the pepper onto a cutting board. She stabbed the knife into it and sawed viciously around the stem. "This makes no sense, none at all. I mean, sure, she might be surprised, maybe even miffed at you for not telling her sooner. But even I remember Tom talking about an old friend he kept in touch with who was serving time. I should think Valerie would be happy to finally know who you are."

Healy slicked back his shaggy hair. "Maybe it's *because* I'm Tom's friend. Maybe it brings me too close." *Why, Lord? I wanted to be the one to tell her. Now what do I do?*

"Did you know my uncle Tom?" Annie asked. "I didn't. I wasn't even born yet when he went to live in heaven."

"Annie, why don't you go see what's on TV?" Ellen sent a forced smile her daughter's way. "Or pop in one of your Veggie Tales videos."

The little girl skipped out of the kitchen, and Healy sank onto the chair she had vacated. Ellen tossed her paring knife onto the cutting board at the same moment the doorbell rang. "It's probably the pastor," she said, starting toward the front door. "Maybe he can help."

Moments later Healy heard the jolly man's voice echoing in the hallway. "Ellen, my dear, hope I'm not too early. Is our college man all enrolled?"

Ellen's response was subdued. "Pastor, I'm afraid Valerie's had a setback."

Healy rose as Ellen escorted Pastor Henke into the kitchen. The white-haired man took Healy's hand and shook it. "Well, well. I thought I was coming for a celebratory dinner in your honor. But I gather we have something much more serious to contend with."

They all sat around the table, and Healy and Ellen took turns explaining to Pastor Henke what sketchy details they had pieced together.

When they finished, the pastor rubbed his chin and sighed. "Clearly Connor was wise to be so cautious about revealing Healy's friendship with Tom. But that knowledge alone shouldn't have produced a reaction this severe. No, there must be something more to it."

"But what?" Ellen spread her hands in a helpless gesture.

"I suspect," the pastor began thoughtfully, "that seeing Tom's inscription in Healy's Bible triggered a memory her subconscious mind has intentionally suppressed all this time."

"You may be right." Ellen moistened her lips and turned to Healy. "Valerie was seriously injured herself the night Tom died. Days went by before she could talk coherently to the police. By then, she couldn't remember—or else she didn't want to remember—exactly what happened. All we've ever known is based on the evidence the police found at the scene."

Healy rose, then stalked across the kitchen, hands jammed into his back pockets. "She *has* to talk to somebody. She can't go on like this."

"Don't you think we know that?" Ellen slapped the table. "From the day she got out of the hospital and came to live with us, we have all tried to convince her to continue therapy."

"I'm sorry." Healy tucked in his chin. "I know you have."

"Has anyone called Connor?" Pastor Henke asked.

Healy shook his head. "Jean said Valerie wouldn't let her."

"Then we must do so right away." When Ellen started to rise, the pastor placed a hand on her arm. "You're exhausted, my dear. Let me."

As Pastor Henke phoned Connor's office, Ellen cast an apologetic glance at Healy. "I didn't mean to snap at you. I know how much Valerie means to you."

"It's all right. I understand." He noticed the glass of fruit juice she had left on the counter and carried it to her. She smiled her thanks.

"Connor is finishing up with a patient and will be right home," Pastor Henke reported. "In the meantime, perhaps I should see if Valerie will speak to me."

"Yes, she trusts you." Ellen looked at him hopefully. "Please try."

The pastor disappeared up the stairs, and moments later Jean Franklin peeked into the kitchen. "I wish I could have done more. I feel so helpless."

Ellen gave her neighbor a quick hug. "I'm just grateful you were there when she called."

"Me, too. Please let me know how she's doing."

"I will." She thanked Jean again, and the woman slipped out.

Healy returned to his chair and pressed his palms into his eye sockets. "This is my fault. If I'd told Valerie everything from the start, this would never have happened."

"You can't know that for sure," Ellen said. "If discovering your identity did trigger Valerie's memory of the night Tom was killed, *when* she found out wouldn't have made a difference. The memories themselves are the problem here, not you."

Again Healy leaped to his feet. The chair scraped backward across the floor. "How do you know?" he shouted. "How do you know I'm not the whole problem? Tom died a violent death at the hands of criminals. I'm a criminal. I killed somebody, too."

Breathing hard, he stormed out the door. Beating a man to death was the biggest mistake of his life. Coming to Aileen was the second. He knew what he had to do.

Chapter 13

Darkness settled over the Paige house. Silent tears streaming down her cheeks, Valerie capped her fountain pen and laid it on the blank page. Words had failed her tonight; not even the comforting ritual of pouring her heart into her journal could soothe her troubled spirit. Wearily she rose and leaned her head against the bookcase Healy had built.

Oh, Healy. . .Healy, why you?

"Healy is not to blame," a gentle voice reminded her.

"I know, Lord, but still. . ."

No one could understand. Not Pastor Henke with his godly wisdom and prayers, nor Connor and his relentless attempts to break down her resistance to counseling. Especially not Ellen, whose life as wife, mother, and teacher continued full and happy.

"We all have our own prisons." Healy's words.

"I did not choose this prison." Her fists knotted. "Lord, I don't want to live any longer in fear and isolation. I don't want to live without love."

"Then forgive."

For the life of her, she thought she had—years ago. When the trial began several months after Tom's death, the judge excused her from court appearances because of her persistent back pain and the debilitating anxiety attacks. Instead, both the defense and prosecuting attorneys deposed her on videotape. She said what she had to say and then tried to put the trial out of her mind. It seemed the only way she could function without losing her mind completely.

Many weeks later, the assistant district attorney paid her another visit. She listened stoically as he informed her the three men had been convicted and sentenced to lengthy prison terms, including a life sentence for her assailant, the man who was also driving the getaway car. Valerie had expected some sense of finality, but she'd felt only emptiness.

As the attorney got up to leave, Valerie remembered something she had read in an inspirational book her mother had sent her. She reached for the man's arm. "Do you. . .have photographs of the men?"

He looked askance at her. "Why?"

"I need to see their faces. It will help me try to forgive them."

Searching his briefcase, he pulled out photocopies of the men's police mug shots. "If you say so," he said, handing them to her. "But if you can forgive these guys after all they took from you, you're a better person than I'll ever be."

"If I don't forgive them, in the Lord's eyes I'm no better than they are."

Every day for months afterward, she purposefully studied the photos, memorizing their faces and praying over each one. "Jesus, grant me the strength to forgive. Take away my anger and fear, and help me to desire Your love and goodness for each of these men. Lead them to repentance. Show them the blessed life they could have in knowing You."

She'd struggled at first, her voice tear-choked and her heart full of bitterness and doubt. She remembered the day she finally knew in her soul the forgiveness for which she prayed. It was mid-October, almost a year to the day after Tom's death. Still suffering from recurring back pain, she had been propped up in bed, reading her Bible. A verse from Isaiah 49 leaped out at her:

"Can a mother forget the baby at her breast and have no compassion on the child she has borne? Though she may forget, I will not forget you! See, I have engraved you on the palms of my hands; your walls are ever before me. Your sons hasten back, and those who laid you waste depart from you."

God's reassurance of His everlasting justice and mercy rang out through the words. He had not forgotten her in her sorrow and never would. God alone would deal with those who had hurt her. And in precious memories He would restore to her what she had lost.

Laying the Bible aside, she had eased out of bed and limped to the closet. She tugged some things aside until she found the flat box containing the cream-colored leather-bound journal Tom had given her less than a month before he died.

"This is a special time, my sweet Lady V," he'd told her with a kiss. "I thought you might want to keep a diary of your thoughts and feelings. Someday," he said, gently patting her rounded belly, "those words may mean a lot to the little one growing in there."

Continually busy at the restaurant, she had never gotten around to writing in the journal, and after the night she lost everything important to her, she had seen no reason to. But on the day she had finally sensed God's love and forgiveness settling around her heart, she knew the time for remembering had come. From then on, writing in the journal became a sacrament of remembrance. In the sanctuary of those lined white pages, she found expression for both the agony of her double loss and the joy of eternal hope.

Now she must learn to forgive all over again. "O Father," she said, moving from the bookcase to the window, "I love Healy with all my heart. I don't want his connection with Tom's death to come between us. Help me."

The apartment windows were dark. Perhaps Healy was still downstairs with Ellen and Connor. They must all be so worried. She had to talk to them, to apologize to Healy, to explain.

Muted voices led her to the den. Pausing at the door, she glimpsed Ellen curled on the sofa, resting in Connor's arms.

"If she won't talk to anyone, what else can we do?" Ellen flicked away a tear.

"Just pray, I guess. Maybe in the morning—" Connor glanced up. "Val."

She entered shyly. "I'm sorry I worried everyone."

Connor rose and enveloped her in his arms. "Sis, whatever happened, you need to talk to us. You can't keep holding it inside."

"I know." She drew comfort from the softness of his cotton shirt. "I just needed time to sort through it all."

Ellen laid a hand on her shoulder. "Val honey, did you remember something?"

Valerie pressed a hand to her mouth, a sob choking her. "I need to talk to Healy. Do you know where he is?"

Connor and Ellen exchanged glances. "He's. . .he's gone," Connor said.

"Gone?" Valerie shook her head. "What are you saying?"

"Connor tried to stop him—we both did—but he packed his things and left with Pastor Henke a couple of hours ago." Ellen's eyes brimmed. "He kept saying it was his fault, and he didn't want to hurt you anymore."

"But it *isn't* his fault." Valerie sank into a chair, despair overwhelming her.

Connor sat on the edge of the sofa and reached for her hand. "Valerie, it's time you told us exactly what's going on here. Is it. . .do you know about Healy and Tom?"

She nodded, unable to speak.

Connor cast Ellen a knowing glance. "Healy realized you must have figured it out when you looked in his Bible."

"What happened?" Ellen pleaded. "Did it trigger your memories from the night of the accident?"

Again she nodded. Tears coursed down her cheeks.

"Oh, honey." Ellen knelt in front of her. "What did you remember that could be worse than what we already know?"

She took a steadying breath. "Tom crossed the street that night to mail a letter to Gus—to Healy. If he hadn't, we'd have gone straight to our car. Tom would still be alive."

She pressed a hand to her abdomen, her voice choked with emotion. "And so would our baby."

❧

Healy awoke from a fitful sleep, forgetting for a moment that he was no longer at the apartment. He set his bare feet on the plush carpeting of Pastor Henke's guest bedroom and exhaled tiredly. Life without Valerie seemed unthinkable, but he would not cause her more pain, and if that meant leaving Aileen, so be it.

Now, if only he could figure out what God wanted him to do next. Unfortunately, the Lord had been strangely silent since last night.

Maybe a hot shower would help. He took his shaving kit and a change of clothes from his duffel bag and trudged to the bathroom. When he emerged twenty minutes later, the aroma of brewing coffee lured him to the kitchen.

"Good morning, my boy." Pastor Henke cracked an egg into a bowl. "Oh my, you had a bad night, didn't you?"

Healy helped himself to a cup of coffee and took a seat in the sunny breakfast nook. "I feel like my whole life has been ripped out from under me. . .again."

"I'm sure you do." The white-haired pastor fumbled through a drawer and pulled out a wire whisk as butter sizzled in a skillet. After beating the eggs, he poured them into the skillet. "These won't take long. Would you start some toast, please?"

Healy dropped two slices of wheat bread into the toaster. "I promise I won't trouble you for long. As soon as I find another place, I'll be on my way."

"And where exactly do you plan on going?"

"People from your church have invested in my education, and I don't intend to let them down. But I can't stay in Aileen, not if it means upsetting Valerie. I thought I'd look for a place over near the college. Maybe find some work there, too."

Pastor Henke waved a spatula. "Healy Ferguson, I gave you more credit. Have you no faith that God can work out whatever difficulties lie between you and Valerie?"

Healy sighed and stared out the window. "It isn't that I don't trust God, Pastor. I just don't trust my own judgment anymore. At least not where Valerie's concerned."

"Humph. All the more reason you should not be jumping to conclusions and going off half-cocked." Pastor Henke divided the scrambled eggs onto two plates and carried them to the table. When the toast popped, Healy handed a slice to the pastor and methodically spread butter and jam across the second one for himself. They ate in thoughtful silence.

Finally Pastor Henke spoke. "Healy, do you recall what you told me the day we first met?"

Healy sipped his coffee. "I said a lot of things."

"Yes, but what stands out in my mind is how certain you were of God's hand being with you every mile of your journey, from getting on the bus to St. Louis, to seeing the advertisement for Zion Community Church, to finding your way to my office here in Aileen."

"It all seemed right. . .then." Healy pushed his empty plate away. "But that was before I knew Valerie was Tom's wife. Before I started falling in love with her. Before something—God knows what—made her shut me out."

The phone rang. Pastor Henke angled a concerned glance toward Healy as he spoke to the caller. "Yes, he's right here. Hold on." He handed the receiver to Healy. "It's Connor."

Healy's throat tightened as he took the phone. "Hello?"

"Hi, Healy. How are you?" The tension edging Connor's voice belied his polite greeting.

"Okay." As far as Healy was concerned, Connor could cut the small talk and say what he had to say. It couldn't be good. "How are things there?" he asked, meaning Valerie.

"Better, I think. Valerie finally talked to us last night." Connor released a pent-up breath. "Healy, she wants you to know why she reacted the way she did."

"Like I don't already know? I'm a loser, and she finally figured it out."

"No, it's not that at all. Here, let me put her on—"

"Don't. I can't talk to her."

"All right, then, you'll have to hear it from me."

Healy forced himself to listen. His remorse only intensified as Connor related Valerie's recaptured memories of the night Tom died. And he recalled—suddenly in vivid detail—the last letter he'd ever received from his faithful friend. Tom had rambled on and on about soon becoming a father. *"Never thought it would happen to me,"* he wrote. *"Can't wait to see what kind of amazing creation God's going to bring from a crusty, black-haired part-Italian and a sweet little blond Irish girl."*

Healy covered his eyes. "Oh, dear Lord, forgive me." Would he never stop paying for a sixteen-year-old mistake? How could he live with himself knowing Valerie had lost her husband, lost her baby, all on account of Tom's devotion to a man who in no way deserved it?

Connor spoke firmly. "Valerie doesn't blame you, Healy. None of us do. She feels terrible about yesterday. She wants you to come back."

Muffled voices sounded in the background. "Here, Valerie wants to tell you herself. I'm giving her the phone."

"No—"

"Healy."

He dissolved at the sound of her voice.

"Healy, please—I'm sorry. I never wanted to hurt you." She released a small sob. "This is too hard over the phone. Come back so I can explain."

Healy took a shuddering breath, almost choking on his next words. "I'm not good for you. You deserve better. Please. Don't call me again."

"Healy, wait—"

"Good-bye, Valerie." He hung up the telephone before he could change his mind.

❧

Stunned, Valerie handed Connor's desk phone back to him. Tears filled her eyes. "He hung up on me."

Connor circled the desk and hugged her. "Give him some time. Finding out the truth has been a shock for both of you."

Valerie eased out of her brother's embrace and turned to the window. Along the eaves of the front porch, thirsty petunias drooped from their hanging baskets. The grass near the curb looked brown and dry. It was not yet nine o'clock, and already waves of heat shimmered off the pavement. The whole landscape looked as parched and desolate as the wilderness of her heart.

"It's been almost five years, Connor. I've wasted so much time hiding from the truth. I couldn't face knowing Tom's faithfulness to someone I'd never even met cost me everything I held dear."

"Tom's friendship with Healy isn't what killed him or your baby. Three criminals fleeing from the law killed them."

"I know. Deep inside, I know." She moved her head slowly from side to side, her hands curling into tight fists. "Oh, Connor, I wish you'd never told him about the letter. The pain in his voice—I can't even bear to think about how much he's suffering now."

"He's with the pastor. He couldn't be in better hands." Connor gently smoothed Valerie's knotted fists. "God's going to see both of you through this, I'm certain."

"I know, but. . ." How did that old cliché go—one step forward, two steps back? That's how her life felt lately. It was an old game, and she was tired of it. Things had to change.

Lord, help me. Help me take the next step forward.

She tilted her head to look up into her brother's shimmering blue eyes. With effort, she sent him a weak smile. "I honestly wasn't ready before," she said, finally understanding why, "but now I think I am. It's time I got serious about some counseling."

Chapter 14

Under the glow of the brass chandelier, Healy sat at the pastor's kitchen table and studied his math book. High-school algebra stumped him as a teenager. He found it no easier in his thirties to comprehend how *x*'s and *y*'s could stand for actual numbers, much less how he was supposed to figure out what those numbers were.

Pastor Henke laid a hand on his shoulder. "Looks as if you're experiencing a slight case of dyscalculia."

Healy rolled his eyes. Where did the pastor come up with these words? "If that means I can't do algebra, you're right. Maybe I should just stick to carpentry." He tossed his pencil onto a sheet of notebook paper worn thin by frequent erasures.

"Of course you are never required to use algebra when constructing something with hammer and nails, correct?" The pastor settled into a chair and looked expectantly at Healy.

Healy stared back at the pastor. "Well, Jesus was a carpenter, and I don't recall one single reference in the Bible about Him studying algebra."

Pastor Henke drew his eyebrows together. "You don't think math was involved in multiplying five loaves and two fishes to feed the five thousand? Or what about our Lord's instruction about how many times you should forgive your brother when he sins against you?"

"Seventy times seven. Okay, I get the message." Healy sat back and rubbed his eyes. "But I still don't get this *x*-equals-*y* stuff."

"You've been back in school less than a month, after how many years? Don't be so hard on yourself. It'll come."

Maybe, Healy thought as the pastor left him to his studies, but even if he did manage to earn any kind of college degree, would it matter? At this point, he felt as if he were merely going through the motions, and only because he refused to disappoint those who had so caringly expressed confidence in him—not the least of whom was Pastor Henke.

Healy had insisted several times that he should find his own place, but the pastor would not even acknowledge such discussions. "My dear wife has been with the Lord nearly ten years now," the man had reasoned, "and our children live out of state. It gets rather lonely around here, and besides, you need some time to get your feet on the ground and develop a sound financial strategy for your future."

Strategy? The only "financial strategy" he ever had was to make sure he always had at least two bills to rub together in his wallet. And sometimes even that was hard to manage.

In the end, he had finally agreed to live rent-free in the pastor's guestroom in exchange for doing various odd jobs around the house. Ellen also insisted on driving him to school as planned until he got a license and could afford his own car. Pastor Henke or another church member provided transportation to his evening classes. Though his new friends from Zion patiently explained time and again that they expected nothing in return, he made them promise to call on him for any home maintenance chores he could help with.

Still, all enthusiasm had vanished the day he walked out of Valerie's life. Not even Pastor Henke's steadfast support and Ellen's continued friendship could fill the void.

As he stared unseeing at the math book, he realized if he made it through college—if he made anything at all of this second chance he'd been given—he would have to do it for himself and for God.

With a determined sigh, he picked up his pencil and tackled the algebra problem once more. Amazingly, it suddenly made sense. His brain cranked out the solution in a matter of minutes, and he mouthed a silent "*Hallelujah!*"

"Well, well." Pastor Henke, returning to the kitchen, paused to adjust his tie. "Is that a smile of victory I see?"

"I may survive this class after all." Healy yawned and stretched. "You're all dressed up. Headed out this late?"

The pastor's expression turned grim. "Yes, I'm afraid so. Young Tina Maxwell goes to court in a few days, and I'm going to visit her at the detention center and try to offer some encouragement."

Healy recalled his conversations with the pastor about a teenager who'd been picked up for shoplifting with the daughter of one of Zion's families. "I'm sure she's very scared," he said. How could he forget his own terror upon entering the courtroom to face judge and jury, knowing they held the rest of his life in their hands?

"Indeed she is." Pastor Henke picked up his car keys and Bible from the kitchen counter. "But just when I think I'm breaking through her shell, she closes herself off again."

Healy shut his math book and placed his assignment in the pocket of a green folder. "At least she hasn't told you to stop visiting. That's a positive sign."

"It should be, I know, but I'm so far removed from her, both in age and experience." The pastor narrowed his eyes at Healy. "But you, on the other hand. . . Healy my boy, can I persuade you to accompany me tonight?"

"Aw, Pastor, I don't know." Healy extended one leg and stared at his dirt-stained sneaker. "You're trained in this kind of thing. I'm not. Besides, what would I say to a teenage girl?"

"You only need some common ground and a compassionate heart." The pastor pulled out a chair and sat down, resting an elbow on the table. He leaned close and looked Healy in the eye. "And have you already forgotten your extraordinary success helping Valerie conquer her anxieties? I've watched you with little Annie, too. The child adores you."

The mention of Valerie and Annie tore at the empty place in his soul. "I don't have any special knack. It was only because I know what fear feels like. I cared, and I wanted to help."

"That's exactly what I'm talking about." Fixing Healy with a thoughtful gaze, the pastor rubbed his chin. "I don't know why this never occurred to me before. You have incredible people skills, Healy. Others instinctively trust you—your openness, your honesty, your genuine concern. This is a God-given gift, and you would be remiss not to use it in His service."

Healy rubbed perspiring hands on his jeans. Part of him wanted to deny everything the pastor had said, but when he examined his heart, he realized helping others had been his constant goal ever since he came to know Christ in prison.

As if reading his thoughts, Pastor Henke said, "Remember when you first came to Aileen and I phoned the penitentiary to confirm your story? The chaplain's letter told about all the inmates you had brought to Christ, all the lives you helped to turn around."

He laid a hand on Healy's arm. "And my conversation with the warden was no different. He held you up as a model prisoner, going the second mile with every task, taking advantage of vocational training, helping new inmates avoid trouble, even risking injury yourself to break up the inevitable fights."

Instinctively Healy's right hand covered the long, ugly scar streaking across his left forearm. As if it were yesterday, he remembered forcing himself between a huge, angry convict and a cowering new arrival who'd made the mistake of crossing the big man's path. Without warning, the big man whipped out a shiv—a piece of jagged glass taped to the handle of a spoon stolen from the cafeteria. Before Healy could dodge the makeshift weapon, he felt it slash through his arm and watched his own blood pour out on the asphalt of the exercise yard. The wound had required twenty-nine stitches to close. He'd felt and counted every one.

"So what do you say, Healy?" the pastor asked. "Will you go with me to talk to Tina?"

Maybe helping someone else was exactly what he needed. Maybe in some small way it could make him feel useful again. "All right, Pastor, if you really think I can help."

❧

After joining Connor and Ellen to hear Annie's bedtime prayers, Valerie slipped out to the back porch and settled into a wicker rocker. Crickets and cicadas serenaded the muggy twilight; heat lightning flickered on the horizon. She wished the signs portended rain, but the weatherman on the six o'clock news had offered no hope for a break from the intense drought under which the entire Midwest baked.

At least she could be outdoors in the dark again and not feel afraid. The counselor Connor had found, a soft-spoken Christian woman, truly seemed to be helping. For the first several visits, Dr. Miller came to the house, but as Valerie gradually recovered the ground Healy had helped her gain over the summer, the doctor encouraged her to attempt the trip to her office. Today Connor had driven Valerie to her first appointment there, and in spite of a shaky start and arriving forty-five minutes late, she had somehow managed to hold herself together.

Thank You, Lord, thank You, she prayed in rhythm with the creak of the chair.

She glanced up at the sound of the back door and smiled to see her sister-in-law.

Ellen drew a chair closer. "Is this a private party, or can anyone join in?"

"You're welcome to stay if you can stand the heat."

"If I were any more pregnant, I probably couldn't." Ellen settled into the cushioned chair with a contented sigh. "Connor said you did great today. We're very proud of you."

"Dr. Miller is wonderful. She seems to sense exactly how much I can handle."

Ellen reached across the space between them and gave Valerie's hand a squeeze. "Connor and I have been praying for this ever since you came to live with us."

They rocked in silence for several minutes, until Valerie could no longer hold back the question she had wanted to ask for weeks. "Ellen, how is Healy?"

Ellen cleared her throat. "His classes seem to be going okay, except for math. He has his nose buried in his book on the way to and from campus almost every day." Crossing her legs, she continued, "Now his carpentry class is another story. Word around campus is that he can out-carpenter the instructor. I wouldn't be surprised—"

"I mean, how *is* he?" Valerie fixed Ellen with a look. "Please, how's he doing. . .in here?" She pressed a hand to her heart.

"I don't know how to answer that question." Ellen angled her a sideways glance. "He obviously misses you terribly, though he won't talk about it, at least to me."

Valerie rose and leaned on the porch rail, staring across the shadowy backyard. A mockingbird's strident call sounded from near the top of one of the oak trees.

She spun around. "I don't understand why he won't at least talk to me."

Ellen leaned over the arm of her chair to pinch a brown leaf off a wilting ivy plant. "What does Dr. Miller say?"

"She says we both need some space to heal." Valerie's tone became flippant. "That's such a cliché. 'I need my space.' Well, I tried hiding inside my own little 'space' and still never healed completely. Opening my heart to Healy became my first real glimmer of hope."

She lifted her hands. "And now everyone's telling me *Healy* needs space.

Why did he have to pull away from me just when I find myself coming fully alive again?"

Ellen didn't answer, and Valerie knew how selfish and unfair she sounded. But when she glanced toward the dark windows of the garage apartment, she missed Healy more than ever. She sank onto a step and buried her face in her hands.

Dear heavenly Father, please watch over Healy. You know his needs. You know the desires of his heart. I only want what's best for him, so I ask You to help me accept whatever decisions he makes about his life. . .even if those decisions don't include me.

❧

Several days later Healy rose from his seat near the back of Zion Community Church as Pastor Henke announced the closing hymn. He'd attended a few times with Connor and Ellen over the summer, but not consistently. More often he had preferred to join Valerie in her sitting room on Sunday mornings to read and discuss Bible passages with her. He found her love for the Lord inspiring, and he could listen for hours as she read from scripture in her quietly firm, expressive voice.

Since moving in with the pastor, he'd become a regular at Zion. Although he remained shy about meeting people, he encountered many warm and friendly individuals. He couldn't help silently speculating about which members had anonymously made it possible for him to enroll in college.

After Pastor Henke pronounced the benediction, Healy placed his hymnal in the rack and turned to step into the aisle. A small, dark-haired man in a tan polo shirt blocked his way.

"Mr. Ferguson?"

Healy nodded. The man looked familiar, but for a moment Healy couldn't place him. "If I should know you, I'm sorry. I've met so many new people lately."

"Ed Maxwell, Tina's father." He extended his hand. "I want to thank you for all you've done for her."

"Of course. We met at Tina's hearing." Warmth spread through Healy's chest as he took Mr. Maxwell's hand. "How's she doing, sir? I heard about her sentencing." The girl had received one month in juvenile detention and one year's probation with community service.

"It could have been a lot worse if not for you." Mr. Maxwell crushed Healy's knuckles in his tenacious grip. "Your coming to court and putting in a good word for her—I know that's what made the difference with the judge."

Healy waved away the man's praise. "I'm sure the judge saw what we already knew. Tina hasn't been in serious trouble before. She's young, and she made a stupid mistake. She learned her lesson and has every intention of staying out of trouble from now on."

"Yes, but it took both you and Pastor Henke to get through to her in the first place." The man blinked brimming eyes. "I still can't get over the fact that perfect strangers would take an interest in my daughter. I mean, Pastor Henke came to see Tina while she was still in the hospital after the car accident. And then you both visited her regularly at the detention center."

"The pastor's a good man. I'd hate to think where I'd be today if not for him."

"Well, he's the reason I'm in church today." Mr. Maxwell glanced toward Pastor Henke as the elderly man worked his way down the aisle, greeting people along the way. "Actually, both of you are. After Tina's mother divorced me, I pretty much gave up on God. That's when Tina first started acting out—just little signs of rebellion then, but if I'd had any idea what it would lead to. . . Anyway, you and the pastor have reminded me what Christ's love is all about."

Mr. Maxwell lowered his voice. "Truth is, I almost turned around and walked out this morning when I saw the Sandersons sitting there with Marsha like nothing had happened, while my Tina's locked up. But then I thought, God loves them, too. And we're all sinners, right? That's what church is for."

"You're right. People like the Sandersons may have a different way of handling their problems, but at least they're here, and God will keep working on their hearts."

"Yeah, I hope so. Well, I just wanted to say thanks. Nice talking to you." Mr. Maxwell gave Healy's now bloodless hand a final squeeze before departing.

As Healy jiggled his fingers to restore feeling, Connor and Ellen walked over, Annie between them. He couldn't help noticing the slight bulge of Ellen's pregnancy beneath her loose-fitting black-and-beige print dress.

"Don't worry, I won't shake your hand," Connor said with a chuckle. "Who was that man, anyway?"

When Healy explained it was Tina Maxwell's father, both Connor and Ellen gave him a knowing look.

"Pastor Henke told us how great you were with Tina," Ellen remarked.

"It felt good to be able to help."

A tiny hand tugged on his pants leg. "Healy, when are you coming back to my house? I miss you."

He caught Ellen's apologetic glance as he knelt to give Annie a hug. "I see you in church every Sunday now, sweetie." He gave her corkscrew curls a gentle tug. "Afraid that's the best I can do for now."

"Is it 'cause you're going to college? My mommy goes to the college, and she lives at my house. Why can't you live there anymore?"

"I'm sorry," Connor said. "We've tried to explain, but what can I say? My daughter is smitten with you."

"And she's not the only one," Ellen muttered.

Connor jabbed her with his elbow, and she shot him an exasperated glare.

Healy pretended not to notice as he stood upright again. Relief swept over him when he saw Pastor Henke approaching.

"I saw Mr. Maxwell talking to you." The pastor loosened the knotted rope at the waist of his white cassock. "So good to see the man in church today."

"Did you get a chance to speak with him?"

"Yes, for a few moments, but he was in a hurry to visit Tina." He turned to Connor. "Any Sunday now, I expect to see our dear Valerie accompany you to church."

"Us, too. At the rate things are progressing, I think she'll be ready very soon."

Pastor Henke beamed. "I'm so glad. I hear the counseling sessions are going extremely well."

Ellen put her arm around Connor's waist and looked straight at Healy. "Better than we ever dared hope. She's so looking forward to living a full life again."

A suffocating heaviness pressed down upon Healy. He edged toward the door. "Sorry, would you excuse me, please? I, uh, I really need some air."

At the far end of the rapidly emptying parking lot, he leaned against Pastor Henke's red Mustang. The noonday sun raised beads of perspiration on his forehead as he looked toward the gold cross atop Zion's white steeple.

Dear Jesus, please help them understand. Especially Valerie. And please help me get it right this time.

For several days now, he'd been preoccupied with a scripture he'd come across in the book of James: "Let perseverance finish its work so that you may be mature and complete, not lacking anything." Until he became a whole person himself, he could not give himself fully to Valerie or any other woman.

He had only recently come to understand how incomplete he remained. Even knowing he had full forgiveness in Christ, he struggled for years with the need to atone for taking the life of another human being. He once thought he'd feel whole again after serving out his prison sentence. Last year, when the prison gates closed behind him for the last time, he decided his life would not be complete until he could finally leave Michigan, find Tom, and thank him for literally saving his life. When he amazingly discovered himself falling in love with Valerie and realized she loved him, too, he hoped he'd at last find wholeness in this extraordinary new relationship.

Finally, God showed him that completeness had to begin on the inside. His security, his salvation, his very worth as a human being must have only one source: the Lord.

Chapter 15

Valerie pressed perspiring hands against her thighs. Her wide-eyed gaze darted side to side through the windows of Ellen's Mazda. "There are so many people. We shouldn't have picked a Saturday. I don't think I can do this."

"Then you'll have to sit out here and fry, because this is the only day I had off this week and I'm not leaving the engine running for you." Yanking her keys from the ignition, Ellen shoved open the car door and stepped out into the Walmart parking lot.

A blast of heat rushed in, and Valerie sucked in her breath. "Ellen Paige, you are the meanest woman alive."

Peering through the open door, Ellen shot Valerie a challenging look. "Dr. Miller said you were ready for this. Are you going to flunk your homework assignment? Because I'm not signing your excuse this time."

Valerie made a growling sound in her throat. "Okay, okay. I'll. . .try."

As the next step in getting Valerie out of the house, Dr. Miller had given her a choice: a brief shopping trip, or accompany her family to church. Stupidly, she imagined shopping would be easier, without the added embarrassment of facing people she knew in case she suddenly found herself in the grip of a panic attack.

She flung open her door, instantly regretting her carelessness when it scraped against a shiny black Ford Explorer in the adjacent space. A warning *beep* sounded from the hulking vehicle. Valerie clambered out and examined the Explorer for damage.

Ellen stalked around to Valerie's side of the car. "Do I need to get out my insurance card?"

Valerie rubbed her hand along the car door. "I think it's okay. Don't see any—"

"You are standing too close to the vehicle. Move away at once."

At the computerized warning, Valerie sprang back in astonishment. "Did you hear that?"

Ellen grabbed her arm. "Let's just do our shopping, okay?"

"But that car talked to me." Valerie glared over her shoulder as her sister-in-law tugged her toward the Walmart entrance.

"It can talk all it wants as long as it doesn't mention any names when its owner comes back. Hurry up, it's hot out here."

A welcome gust of cool air greeted them inside. Before Valerie could react to the bright fluorescent lighting and the hordes of Saturday shoppers, Ellen thrust a shopping cart in front of her. "Here, push. It'll give you something to do." She rested a hand on Valerie's shoulder and added in a gentler tone, "And don't forget to breathe."

Breathe. Memories of Healy's encouraging smile and soothingly persuasive voice flooded her thoughts. She fought the lump in her throat and tried to concentrate on steering the cart.

"You're doing great," Ellen assured her. "Turn up this aisle."

Valerie clutched the cool blue cart handle. "What are we shopping for? I already forgot."

"Clothes for Annie, golf balls for Connor." Ellen paused and consulted her list. "And I need some blush, conditioner, and raspberry tea."

Valerie nodded, mentally repeating the list and trying to match the items with the store's information signs. *Keep your mind busy. You can do this.*

"What do you think of this?" Ellen held up a bright yellow children's shorts outfit with a watermelon appliqué. "It's on sale. Summer closeout, fifty percent off."

Valerie looked toward the ceiling. "I don't believe you. With Connor's and your combined income, why do you even care about bargain hunting?"

"Because it's *fun.*" Ellen grabbed another outfit off the rack. "This is adorable. Annie will love the little poodle on the front. And see, since they're on sale, I can buy twice as many for the same price."

Twenty minutes and four outfits for Annie later, Ellen scurried over to a display of ladies' swimsuits. She snatched up a slinky tropical-print tank suit. "Valerie, this is absolutely *you.*"

Intent on watching Ellen's shopping exploits, Valerie had relaxed considerably. She leaned on the shopping cart and narrowed her eyes. "And, oh, look," she said dryly, "it's marked down seventy-five percent. Seriously, where would I wear something like that?"

"Connor and I have been talking about putting in a pool." She fanned herself dramatically. "Especially after this summer. The fitting room is right here. Try it on, okay?"

Valerie couldn't remember the last time she'd shopped for herself except from a catalogue or online. Even more, she'd missed the girlish fun of a shopping expedition with another woman. She took another quick inventory of her emotional state. No shortness of breath, only the slightest flutter in her chest—but that could just be excitement. Yes, she was managing pretty well. And what could happen in a fitting room?

She bit her lip and took the bathing suit from Ellen. "Okay, I'll try it on, but I draw the line at coming out here to model for you."

Ellen grinned. "Fair enough. I'll wait for you right outside the door."

An attendant pointed Valerie to a vacant stall. She let out a long sigh as she closed the door, the tiny cubicle restoring her sense of security. Hanging the bathing suit on a hook, she took a moment to reorient herself before slipping out of her sundress.

As she donned the skimpy swimsuit, her excitement returned. Though she hadn't been able to be as physically active since the accident, the ten or fifteen minutes she attempted on Connor's treadmill several times a week had obviously kept her in pretty good shape. She looked at her figure from every possible angle and realized she liked what she saw. "I wonder if—"

She groaned. No matter how hard she tried, she could not get Healy Ferguson out of her mind. *Dear Lord, please, if it's Your will, bring him back to me. Soon.*

Wearing her sundress again, she sank onto the narrow bench and fumbled with a confusing array of slides and clips to reattach the swimsuit to the hanger. She became vaguely aware of a muted conversation going on in the cubicle next to hers.

"Just stick them in your purse. They're small enough," a young voice said.

"I don't know. . . . What if we get caught?"

"We won't. I've done this a hundred times. Do you want the bikini or not?"

"But the attendant counted how many items we brought in. She'll know if we don't bring them all back."

"It's Saturday. There's a million people here. She's too busy to notice anything." An exasperated sigh. "Come on. Just do it."

The fine hairs rose on the back of Valerie's neck. She gathered up her purse and the swimsuit and slipped into the passageway. Taking a steadying breath, she approached the attendant. "Excuse me, but you should probably call security. I think you have a problem in cubicle number 11."

The plump woman tossed a handful of empty hangers into a box below her counter and turned with a distracted sigh. "What kind of problem, ma'am?"

"I heard two girls—"

Ellen caught her arm. "Valerie, is everything all right?"

Laughter rang out in the passageway behind her. She turned to see two teenagers sauntering their way, each carrying several different articles of clothing.

The tall, auburn-haired girl plopped her stack on the counter. "None of these fit," she stated. "Come on, Jackie, let's go to the mall."

Acting on pure instinct, Valerie blocked their way. "My, you sure seem to be in a hurry." She couldn't miss the deer-in-the-headlights look in the eyes of the girl called Jackie. Glancing toward the attendant, she said, "I suggest you count the items they're returning and make sure they're all there."

"Lady, you should mind your own business," the first girl said, glaring at Valerie.

Ellen stepped closer now. "Well, hello, Marsha. Do your parents know you're out shopping today?"

"Marsha Sanderson?" Valerie suddenly recognized the girl from the church pictorial directory. She shook her head in dismay. "Oh, honey."

"Jackie, keep walking. They can't do anything." Marsha gripped her friend by the elbow. As the attendant picked up the phone, the girls dashed out of the dressing room.

"Come on, Val, you're a witness." Ellen parked her shopping cart next to the attendant's desk and told the woman she'd be back for it, then grabbed Valerie's hand.

Adrenalin pounded in Valerie's ears by the time they reached the exit. A burly uniformed man jogged over just as Marsha and Jackie plowed between the security gates, setting off a strident alarm. With Valerie and Ellen falling in behind him, the guard chased the girls outside. He caught up with them at Marsha's car, illegally parked in a handicapped spot.

Jackie started crying hysterically. "I didn't mean to go through with it, honestly." She dumped the contents of her large shoulder bag on the hood of the car and tossed a crumpled wad of green and yellow bikini parts at the security guard. "Please don't call my parents. They'll kill me. I'll never do it again, I swear."

"I don't have a choice, young lady." The security guard turned to Marsha and asked to see the contents of her handbag.

"I don't have to show you anything," she said smugly. "I know my rights."

"Fine. You can do it here, or you can do it down at the police station." He keyed the TALK button on his two-way radio and requested a patrol car be sent over. "It's pretty hot out here. Let's all take a walk inside to my nice, air-conditioned security office, shall we?"

After giving statements to the police and finally completing their shopping, Ellen and Valerie emerged from the Walmart. They crossed the scorching parking lot and found Ellen's Mazda, now steamy from sitting under the sun.

"Dear Lord," Ellen muttered as she turned on the air conditioner full blast, "You can put an end to this heat any time now. Have You noticed it's October?"

Valerie felt as if she'd been run over by an army tank. She let her head drop against the headrest. "I think I should get triple credit for this assignment."

"I think Dr. Miller would agree." Ellen backed out of the parking space. "But just think, kiddo." She tapped Valerie's arm with the back of her hand. "You came out of this ordeal with a really cute swimsuit."

"Which I will never get to wear since I am planning to immediately go back into permanent hibernation."

"Come on, you did great." Ellen turned onto the highway heading toward Aileen. "I mean, how many recovering PTSD sufferers can say they faced down a talking car, cleaned out Walmart's sale racks, and single-handedly captured two shoplifters all in the same day?"

Valerie puckered her lips. "I can't believe Marsha Sanderson almost got off scot-free again."

"The girl is clever, I'll give her that. At least now we know her modus operandi."

"Yeah, get your friend to steal the merchandise so you're never caught with it."

"But this time you can testify to what you overheard in the dressing room. With an actual witness, it won't be so easy for her daddy's expensive lawyers to get her off the hook."

A new fear clutched at Valerie's throat. She shot her sister-in-law a terrified look. "They'll summon me to court, won't they?"

"Let's deal with this one step at a time. God will help you do whatever you need to do when the time comes."

Valerie nodded, knowing her sister-in-law was right. She closed her eyes and made an effort to relax. When Ellen nudged her a short while later, she awoke in amazement to discover they were sitting in the driveway at home. She'd actually calmed herself enough to fall asleep in the car. *Praise God!*

❧

"Healy, the brakes, the brakes—*now*!"

"All right already." Healy stomped on the brake pedal of Pastor Henke's Mustang convertible. The tires squealed, and the car lurched to a halt behind a grimy dump truck. "Two feet to spare. No sweat."

Pastor Henke whipped out his handkerchief and mopped his forehead. "No sweat indeed. You may say 'no sweat' when you're driving your own vehicle and choose to tailgate a gargantuan mass of unforgiving steel." He caressed the dashboard. "It's all right, my dear little car. Healy is sorry he frightened the living daylights out of us."

The traffic light turned green, and the dump truck lumbered forward. Healy eased his foot onto the gas pedal and inched ahead. "Better?"

"Oh yes, much."

"You gotta remember, Pastor," Healy said, gliding onto the freeway on-ramp, "I haven't been behind the wheel of a car in over sixteen years. And as a teenager I didn't exactly drive like a grandma."

"Defensive driving is a virtue, my boy." The pastor cast Healy a scathing look. "And it's the *only* way you'll ever be allowed to drive my car again."

"Sorry, Pastor. I really do appreciate your helping me practice for my test." Healy flipped the turn signal, then checked both mirrors and glanced over his shoulder before changing lanes. "How was that?"

"Excellent. And a respectable distance between you and the car ahead. Let's keep it that way."

Over the next several miles Healy relaxed into his driving, finally giving up the urge to floor the gas pedal and see what the sweet little red sports car could do. He couldn't understand Pastor Henke's complaints, however. On more than one occasion he'd witnessed the pastor peel out of the driveway or church parking lot. He'd even been in the passenger seat numerous times when the old guy sat at a traffic light and gunned the engine in a taunting challenge to the driver in the other lane. Guess the pastor still cherished his fantasies of youth and speed.

Sounding more at ease, Pastor Henke said, "Have I told you the latest in the Marsha Sanderson saga? Take the next exit, by the way."

"I heard something about her and a friend being picked up at the Walmart last weekend." Healy eased onto the exit ramp and turned right at the stoplight, passing an electronics store and some restaurants.

The pastor clicked his tongue. "Honestly, that child's mendacious nature is going to be the ruin of her."

"Pastor, how many times do I have to tell you? Your twenty-dollar words are wasted on my two-bit ears. Speak English, okay?"

"Sorry, my boy." He sighed. "I mean, as long as the Sandersons let Marsha get away with her lies, she will never straighten out. Once again, she has gotten another of her gullible friends in trouble."

"Seems to be a habit with her." They drove in silence past apartments, churches, and several housing subdivisions. Healy slowed as he approached a four-way stop. "Straight ahead?"

"Yes, then left at the next intersection. You're doing very well, Healy. My toes have finally uncurled."

Healy gave a low whistle and patted the steering wheel. "This little baby purrs like a kitten."

"She may purr for you all she likes. But remember, she only growls for me."

On the interstate again, heading toward Aileen, the pastor continued his story about Marsha Sanderson's latest run-in with the law. "Naturally, our dear Marsha is out on bail while her friend Jackie sits in juvenile hall. However, there is a small break in the case," he added slowly, "someone who actually overheard the girls plotting the crime and witnessed their attempted escape."

"Oh yeah?"

"Yes." A pause. "Valerie."

The car swerved. Angry horns sounded to their right.

"Healy!"

"I got it, I got it." Healy's fingers bit into the steering wheel.

"My fault," the pastor murmured. They both sucked in sharp breaths. "I knew it would take you by surprise."

When they turned onto the quiet country road to Aileen, the calming scenery of shady oaks, farmland, and livestock grazing in the stubbly fields helped restore Healy's equilibrium. "How. . .how is Valerie involved?"

As the pastor talked, all Healy could think about was that Valerie had actually made it outside her home, successfully negotiating a trip to a busy department store. He almost burst with joy at the news of her accomplishment. *O Lord, thank You.*

Healy parked in the pastor's driveway and handed him the keys. "Thanks again for the driving practice. Next time I could use some pointers on parallel parking."

A pained look crossed Pastor Henke's face. He gulped. "I. . .suppose so."

Entering the kitchen, Pastor Henke said, "I'm afraid I don't have much time for preparing a meal this evening. I have an appointment to meet with Jackie and her parents tonight." He turned to Healy. "You're welcome to come along, if you haven't too much homework."

Healy smiled. "I'd like that." He still basked in the glow of his success with Tina Maxwell. If God could somehow use him to help young people stay on the right path and avoid life-altering mistakes like his, he wouldn't pass up an opportunity.

Chapter 16

A pale pink dawn filtered through the lacy curtains as Valerie reached for the creamy white journal. She'd filled several pages since beginning her therapy with Dr. Miller, and rereading her latest entries, she gave thanks to God. What a joy to discover that the underlying tones of sorrow and grief gradually faded before an ever-increasing sense of hope.

Now she must make one final entry. Uncapping her fountain pen, she turned to a fresh page.

My little one,

When I first started writing to you in these pages, my body and spirit were so broken that I was afraid I'd never find peace again. I still miss you and your daddy more than I can say. Your daddy would have loved and cherished you as I do your memory, and I thank God for the blessed assurance that you and Daddy are together in heaven now.

Child of my heart, it has been a long journey, but you would be so proud of your mommy. The old terrors are finally letting go. It all started when Healy Ferguson came into my life, and even though it was hard to face the truth about Healy's past, I am humbled daily by how dearly your daddy loved him as a friend.

I love him, too, deeply and inexpressibly. When we met, we both had so much growing and healing to do, but I believe this is also part of God's plan. Maybe we needed to find each other for the healing to begin.

So, my precious one, it's time for me to say a last good-bye to you—although you will always be a part of me. My love for you is forever sealed within these pages, but now I must look toward the future, which I pray will include Healy.

My greatest regret is knowing I may never be able to give Healy the family he deserves. I pray the doctors were wrong and that someday you may yet have a little brother or sister—not to take your place but to continue the legacy of love I so wanted to share with you.

I miss you, my darling, my sweet little baby. May God and His holy angels watch over your spirit and keep you ever in His presence.

Love always,
Mommy

Tears streamed down Valerie's cheeks as she closed the book. Tenderly she wrapped it in the pastel green monogrammed baby blanket she had saved all these years. As she bent to tuck the precious bundle away in the bottom drawer of her dresser, a shaft of sunlight touched her left hand and set her engagement diamond ablaze. She sank onto the edge of the bed, her eyes brimming with fresh tears.

"Oh, Tom, I need to say good-bye to you, too, my love." She slipped her rings from her finger and held them to the light, gazing at them deeply, longingly, one last time. "Oh, my darling, I will always love you, but I know you would want me to be happy again. Please give me your blessing."

She removed another white box from the dresser drawer, this one containing her wedding album and mementos from that special day. Folded neatly atop the album lay the lace-trimmed white handkerchief her mother had given her to carry with her bouquet. She placed her rings within the folds and pressed the handkerchief to her lips for a parting kiss before closing it away with the other treasures.

Filled with new peace, she dried her eyes before going downstairs. She found Connor and Annie at breakfast. She poured herself a glass of orange juice and carried it to the table. "Where's Ellen?"

"Mommy's throwing up again." Annie seized her milk glass with both hands and took a big gulp. She swiped at a drip on her chin before scooping up a spoonful of multicolored O-shaped cereal.

The sound of running water in the downstairs bathroom preceded Ellen's ashen-faced appearance in the kitchen. "I thought this morning sickness thing would have ended weeks ago. Must be another girl."

"That's an old wives' tale." Connor laid his paper aside and sipped his coffee. "Have you talked to your OB/GYN about why you're still throwing up so often?"

"I have an appointment this afternoon—" Slapping a hand over her mouth, Ellen raced toward the bathroom.

Connor stared after his wife, his brows drawn together. "She wasn't sick this long with Annie."

Valerie paused before filling a bowl with shredded wheat. "She seems to be feeling good otherwise. I remember even at five months I still felt nauseated sometimes. . . ." Her voice trailed off and she sighed. "Would you like me to go check on her?"

"Give her a minute. She prefers not to have an audience."

"I understand." Toying with her spoon, she stared into her bowl.

Connor touched her arm. "Are you sure *you're* okay? You look a little sad this morning."

"Not in a bad way. Just came to another crossroads, that's all." Two, actually, but she would savor those tender moments awhile longer before explaining to her brother.

Ellen returned, a wet washcloth pressed to her neck.

"Did you throw up again, Mommy?" Annie asked.

"Darling daughter,"—Ellen gulped and jammed a hand to her stomach—"you and your father will not use those words in my presence again." She heated water in the microwave and dunked a raspberry teabag in the steaming mug, then retrieved the box of saltines from the pantry. "So what's on everybody's agenda for today?"

"The usual office appointments, then a rhinoplasty later this afternoon." Connor adjusted his tie. "Should be routine."

Valerie finished a soggy mouthful of shredded wheat. "Annie and I are going to work on her reading skills after breakfast, and then Pastor Henke is taking me to my counseling appointment."

"And I'm going to look at storybooks in the waiting room." Annie lifted her cereal bowl and drained the last dribble of milk.

Ellen planted a kiss on Annie's head. "Great, you can read me one of your stories when I come home." She glanced at the clock. "I need to get a move on, or I'll be late picking up Healy for class."

Connor went to the cupboard and got his wife a travel mug for her tea. Walking her to the door, he enveloped her in a hug. "Hope you feel better, honey. Be sure to talk to your doctor about this morning sickness thing—"

"Please, not another word." Ellen planted three quick kisses on her husband's lips and grabbed her purse. "Have a good day, everyone." The back door banged shut behind her.

After Connor left, Valerie helped Annie sound out words in a picture book and then finished getting ready for her appointment with Dr. Miller. On the drive over, Pastor Henke brought Valerie up-to-date concerning the latest prayer needs at church.

"And, of course, keep the Sanderson family on the list. I still pray for a miracle with Marsha."

"So do I." Valerie smoothed her khaki slacks, then stared at her folded hands. "Ellen told me Healy has been going with you to visit Tina and Jackie."

The pastor fairly beamed. "He is quite amazing with those troubled young ladies. They both seemed to trust him readily."

"I'm not surprised." She gazed out the window, only half listening while the pastor chatted on about Tina's and Jackie's spiritual and moral progress. A stab of remorse pierced her heart, and she silently apologized to the Lord for her indifference toward the delinquent teens. The person she really wanted news about was Healy.

Following her appointment, Pastor Henke took her and Annie to lunch at a small, colorfully decorated Mexican restaurant on Aileen's town square.

The waiter seated them at a corner table under a pink piñata in the shape of a pig. "I can't remember the last time I ate out," Valerie said before opening her menu. At least the restaurant wasn't busy yet. "Warn me if I get something stuck between my teeth, okay?"

Pastor Henke chuckled as he studied the menu. "The enchiladas *al carbon* are excellent here. Annie, what interests you, my dear?"

The curly-haired child seized a handful of tortilla chips. "Corny dog and french fries."

"A truly authentic Mexican dish. Good choice." Pastor Henke winked at Valerie.

The waiter took their order and returned shortly with their meal. Dabbing taco juice off her chin, Valerie noticed two men in business suits enter the restaurant. Recalling the church directory photo, she identified the taller man as Harold Sanderson, Marsha's father. She tapped Pastor Henke's ankle with the toe of her shoe.

He caught her eye and casually glanced over his shoulder. "Oh dear."

Mr. Sanderson sauntered over and offered his hand. "Pastor, good to see you. And Mrs. Bishop, isn't it? I understand you're still suffering from your, er, emotional distress. How are you doing these days?"

An icy shiver went up her spine. "Very well, thank you."

"Mind if I sit down?" Without waiting for a reply, the tall, beefy man pulled out the empty chair across from Annie. He inclined his head toward his athletically trim and equally well-dressed companion, now seated with his back to them at a table near the window. "That's our family attorney, Jason Albright. He's in the process of preparing a defense for Marsha and, of course, would be very interested to interview your psychiatrist, Mrs. Bishop."

Valerie cringed. "My doctor is a licensed Christian therapist, not a psychiatrist. And I'm sure she would be happy to answer any of your attorney's questions. Although I can't imagine how she could help Marsha's case."

The swarthy man cast Valerie an oily smile. "I've read that post-traumatic stress disorder can make people delusional, hear voices, confuse fantasy with reality."

Pastor Henke removed his glasses and glared at Mr. Sanderson. "Harold, your remarks are highly indecorous and patently uncalled for. Perhaps you should excuse yourself and stop insulting my friend and *your* fellow parishioner."

"Yes, well, we all know Mrs. Bishop hasn't been attending church services since she moved to Aileen." Sanderson returned the pastor's direct gaze. "And perhaps you should remember where a high percentage of Zion's financial support comes from. In addition, you might consider rethinking your associations, Pastor. First a mental patient—now I hear you've taken a convicted murderer into your home."

Valerie's mind burned with fiery retorts, but she couldn't find her voice.

"You should spend less time protecting your own reputation and more time reading your Bible," Pastor Henke countered. "Our Lord Jesus Himself welcomed all kinds of 'sinners' into His company."

Even as her own agitation heightened, Valerie sensed Annie's growing distress. The little girl drew her knees under her and leaned across the plate containing her half-eaten corny dog and ketchup-smeared fries. "You're a mean man and I want you to go away *right now*." She punctuated the last words with a pointed finger and accidentally tipped Pastor Henke's glass of iced tea into Mr. Sanderson's lap.

"Why you—"The startled man bolted to his feet, expletives exploding from his mouth.

Sputtering, Pastor Henke grabbed for the overturned glass. An observant busboy rushed over with a dishpan and cloths. He swept the scattered ice cubes into the pan and mopped up the table and floor in front of the fuming Mr. Sanderson, then made a rapid departure.

Valerie wanted to shove her hands over Annie's tender ears, but the child continued her own tirade against the "mean, mean man."

"Annie," Valerie pleaded, "please sit down and be quiet, okay?" With trembling hands, she grabbed a napkin to dab at the ketchup now staining the pink-and-green appliquéd watermelon on the front of Annie's new shorts set.

"This is an outrage," Jason Albright shouted, joining the mêlée. "Believe me, Mrs. Bishop, I'll remember this when we go to court. You are certainly an unfit caregiver if you can't even prevent a small child from such an impudent display."

"Unfit—how dare—" Valerie's hammering heart threatened to explode right out of her chest. She thought she would surely expire right here in Don Reynaldo's Mexican Restaurant, facedown in her Acapulco Special.

"Enough!" Pastor Henke bellowed. "Gentlemen—and I use that term loosely—you will please leave this establishment at once, or I guarantee you will both be hearing from *my* attorney."

With departing glowers, Sanderson and Albright stormed out of the restaurant.

Valerie fought to keep from collapsing into a quivering mass of raw nerves. Pastor Henke came to her side and wrapped a protective arm around her. "It's all right now, it's all right. They're gone."

"Oh, wow, I handled that well." Gasping, she took a shaky sip of water. At least Annie had settled down and now calmly polished off her corny dog.

"I'd say you handled the situation very well indeed, all things considered." The pastor pulled up the chair Harold Sanderson had so brusquely vacated and sat down close to Valerie. "Take a moment to pull yourself together, and I'll drive you home as soon as you're ready."

At the sound of someone clearing his throat, Valerie glanced up in dread. A thin, dark-complexioned man with a moustache stood next to Pastor Henke's chair. "Pastor, please accept my apologies. I was tied up on a phone call when the wait staff informed me two men were harassing you. Can I assist you in some way? Should I call the police?"

"That won't be necessary, Ray. This is a problem we'll have to entrust to the Lord."

"If the need should arise, both the waiter and busboy witnessed everything. They agree the other men started the altercation."

"Thank them for me. I'll call if their help is needed."The pastor turned to Valerie. "Are you ready to go home, my dear?"

She nodded and attempted to stand on quivering legs. Her breathing had yet to return to normal, and tears threatened.

Pastor Henke reached for his wallet, but the man stopped him. "Today your meal is compliments of Don Reynaldo's. I only hope you will return another day, when perhaps you can enjoy a more pleasurable dining experience."

❧

Hours later, in the seclusion of her darkened sitting room, Valerie finally calmed down enough to relate to Connor and Ellen what had transpired at the restaurant.

Ellen's fists knotted. "I always knew there was something I didn't like about Harold Sanderson. What a creep."

Connor sat on the floor, his back resting against Ellen's knees. "Three cheers for our Annie-girl, though. Wish I could have seen Harold's face when that iced tea landed in his lap."

Valerie curled her legs under her and hugged a throw pillow. "Mr. Sanderson really scared me, and I don't just mean the panic attack. I seriously believe he intends to use my emotional illness to discredit me as a witness against Marsha."

Ellen shook her head. "The man will go to any lengths to keep his daughter out of trouble so *his* reputation won't be soiled. What is wrong with people like that? And how did he ever become a member of Zion Community Church?"

"His wife, Donna, is a good Christian woman," Connor stated. "However, I don't think she has the intestinal fortitude to stand up to him."

"How do you know so much about her?" Ellen asked.

"I, uh. . .I have to plead doctor-patient confidentiality."

"Aha, so Donna Sanderson is a patient of yours." Ellen narrowed her eyes. "Interesting. Tummy tuck? Nose job?"

Valerie mentally tuned out the conversation as she laid her head on the arm of the loveseat. *Father, I know You are fully capable of protecting me and bringing good out of this for all of us. Grant me a huge dose of Your courage, because I have a feeling I'm going to need it. . .and very soon.*

❧

Healy headed to the campus cafeteria to grab something for supper and do a little studying before his evening carpentry class. It had not been one of his better days. He got an important date wrong on his history quiz, and math problems he had solved easily last week now baffled him. When he tried to wade through a chapter of his business textbook, his eyes blurred. An uneasy feeling plagued him, but he couldn't identify the source.

A church friend picked him up later and drove him home to an empty house. He found a note on the kitchen counter from Pastor Henke saying he would be late because of a committee meeting. Tired as he was, Healy propped himself up in bed to make a last-ditch attempt at his reading assignment. His eyelids grew heavy, and his mind soon went numb from trying to absorb endless facts and figures.

Around ten forty-five, the pastor returned, tapping lightly on Healy's door.

"Still up, are you?" the white-haired man asked with a yawn.

"Not for long. Can't seem to concentrate."

"I've had one of those days, too." Pastor Henke sighed, a faraway look in his eyes. "I'll tell you about it in the morning. For now, let's both try to get some sleep. Good night, my boy."

" 'Night, Pastor." Finally giving up on his studies, Healy turned off the lamp and settled into bed.

Sleep eluded him. For hours he tossed and turned, kicked covers off, punched his pillow, got up for a glass of water, adjusted the speed of the ceiling fan. Nothing seemed to help.

"Lord, You must be keeping me awake for a reason. What is it?"

"Valerie. Pray for Valerie."

His throat tightened as an image of her delicate face formed in his mind. He fought the urge to wake the pastor, but by now it was almost two o'clock a.m., and he could hear the elderly man snoring loudly even through two closed doors.

"Okay, God, You know what's wrong, and You know what Valerie needs. Be with her and protect her from whatever danger she faces. Calm her with Your holy peace."

As he murmured his "amen," a measure of God's peace settled over him as well, and his restlessness finally ebbed.

Chapter 17

"Val?" Ellen's voice sounded muffled through the closed bedroom door. "It's almost nine. Honey, are you getting up?"

Valerie rolled away and pulled the thin cotton blanket up around her chin. Since her encounter with Harold Sanderson at the restaurant, every day had been a struggle. One moment she felt strong and confident. In the next the phone would ring or a car horn would sound, and she'd be trembling from head to toe.

A persistent knock sounded from the hallway. This time she heard Connor's voice. "Valerie, you promised you'd go to church with us. Don't chicken out on me, sis. You can do this."

Yes, she'd promised. . .in a weak moment. Connor had the bright idea that if Valerie showed up in church, it would undermine Harold Sanderson's ability to cast doubt upon her reliability as a witness.

And Marsha's hearing was set for Tuesday morning.

Valerie's stomach lurched. She lunged to the bathroom and hung over the commode seat, succumbing to dry heaves.

The outer door opened and Ellen slipped in. She dampened a washcloth and pressed it into Valerie's shaking hand. "Looks like you're doing worse than I am this morning. Today's the first day I *haven't* thrown up."

Valerie laid the cool cloth against her cheeks and glimpsed her pallid face in the mirror. "Maybe Harold Sanderson is right. I'm such a bundle of nerves, why would anyone believe anything I had to say?"

"You don't believe that for a minute." Ellen angled a stern gaze at Valerie's reflection. "You have the power to finally make the Sandersons face the truth about Marsha. If you back out, who knows what kind of trouble that kid will get herself into by the time she's twenty?"

"Oh, Ellen, why does it have to be me?" Then she thought of Healy. Suppose an adult had taken a firm stand with him and his sister, rebuking Healy for his temper, insisting Bethy abandon dangerous relationships? Would a man's life have been saved, sparing Healy sixteen years of regret and inner torment?

"Okay. I know you're right." She leaned against the bathroom sink and drew in a shuddering breath. "I need to shower and wash my hair. Do I have time?"

Ellen drew her into a hug. "We'll make time."

The congregation had just risen for the opening hymn when Valerie and the Paige family entered. Connor found seats on the back pew, placing Valerie on the end in case she felt the need for a quick departure. For a dizzying moment, her thoughts flashed back to the last time she'd worshipped at Zion—when she and Tom visited Connor and Ellen the Easter before Tom's death. She closed her eyes and let the memories wash over her. Blessed relief filled her when she felt more gratitude than sorrow in remembering. Tom had once been her whole life, her very reason for living. But he was gone, and nothing would ever bring him back. She must look toward the future now, whatever God had in store for her.

She opened her hymnal as the organ strains of the familiar tune evoked timorous sounds from her vocal cords. *O God, it's been too long. Thank You for bringing me back.* She focused on the words and music of "What a Friend We Have in Jesus," and soon found herself singing with joyous enthusiasm.

❧

As Healy attempted the tenor line of his favorite hymn, he glanced around hoping for a glimpse of the Paige family. Valerie had been heavily on his mind and in his prayers for days now, even more so after Pastor Henke told him about her unnerving experience at Don Reynaldo's. Another family occupied the Paiges' usual pew today, he discovered with chagrin. He prayed it didn't mean Valerie's condition had worsened to the point that they didn't want to leave her home alone.

From a few rows behind him, a strangely familiar voice caught his ear, a voice he couldn't recall hearing at Zion before, and yet. . .

He casually turned his head, scanning the faces at the rear of the church. His gaze settled on the petite, fair-haired woman standing near the aisle in the very last pew.

Valerie.

The words of the hymn froze in his throat. His heart leaped. It was all he could do to resist the urge to shove aside the people next to him, charge down the aisle, and sweep her into his arms.

Her gray eyes met his. She wiggled her fingers in a shy greeting as a bittersweet smile curled her lips. He smiled back, then ducked his head and swiveled to face front again.

When the service ended an hour later, he had not the remotest guess as to what scripture lessons had been read, the subject of Pastor Henke's sermon, or even who had been mentioned in the congregational prayers. He thought he would explode before the others in his pew finished their after-worship hellos and chats and finally made room for him to exit.

❧

"Carol and Dave O'Grady, I'd like you to meet my sister, Valerie," Connor said, introducing her for what seemed to Valerie like the hundredth time.

"How do you do? Nice to finally meet you in person." She recognized many names. A few people she remembered meeting when she and Tom had visited. She'd read about some of the other families in the church newsletter or heard Connor, Ellen, or Pastor Henke speak of them. Several people she knew from her prayer-chain phone calls, or personally from evening Bible studies hosted at the Paige home. Others were part of the congregational care team that visited her on occasion. All expressed delight to see her out and about at last.

When space cleared around her, she tried not to be too obvious as she stood on tiptoe to look for Healy. *Oh, please, Lord, don't let him have left without speaking to me.*

Just when she thought she glimpsed him beyond some bobbing heads, another face filled her vision.

"Mrs. Bishop."

Her blood ran cold, but she bravely lifted her chin. "Good morning, Mr. Sanderson." She felt Connor's arm slip around her waist, giving her the courage to cast the towering man a confident smile. "Sir, you look surprised to see me."

"I—" He cleared his throat. "I'm so glad to see you're well enough to worship with us this morning. But I wouldn't want you to become so overwrought from these little outings that you are unable to appear in court this Tuesday."

She hoped he couldn't hear her throbbing pulse. "How kind of you to be concerned. However, I wouldn't dream of missing the opportunity to do my civic—and Christian—duty."

A plump, mousy woman appeared at his side, with a bored-looking Marsha lingering a few steps behind. "Harold, dear," said the woman, "we should be going."

Something prodded Valerie to reach for the woman's hand. "Mrs. Sanderson, I'm so glad to meet you." She ignored Harold's icy glare. "I've been praying for Marsha. I know you only want the best for her, but sometimes what's best for our children is that we *don't* protect them from the consequences of their mistakes."

"Yes, I. . .I know." The woman glanced toward her husband. "It's been hard—"

"Donna," Sanderson snapped, seizing her wrist, "let's go."

The woman cast Valerie an apologetic grimace as her hulking husband dragged her toward the exit. Marching behind her parents in a self-righteous huff, Marsha suddenly whirled around and narrowed her gaze at Valerie. "People like you, you just don't get it with your holier-than-thou attitudes. Stop sticking your nose where it doesn't belong."

The teen's words stirred an angry passion in Valerie. She followed them outside into the glaring noonday sun.

"Mr. and Mrs. Sanderson." She caught them at the edge of the sizzling parking lot.

The man spun around. "Careful, ma'am, or you really will work yourself into a state."

"You tell her, Dad."

"Harold, please—"

Valerie took a long, steadying breath and spoke in measured tones. "Sir, there is absolutely nothing you can do to hurt me more than I have already been hurt. My wounds go deeper than you can possibly imagine. And why you would waste your time attempting to rattle me enough that I would appear incompetent before a judge is beyond me."

She paused, searching his face, searching for the right words. Her gaze drifted briefly to Marsha. "You have a lovely daughter who is going to grow up not knowing right from wrong. You're teaching Marsha that no matter how badly she messes up, Daddy's going to fix it. But she'll be an adult soon, and Daddy won't always be able to cover for her mistakes. Then what?"

"Dad, are you going to let her talk—"

"Marsha, be quiet." Donna Sanderson tugged on her husband's arm, looking up at him with a tear-streaked face. "Mrs. Bishop is right, Harold. It's long past time someone held Marsha accountable."

Marsha screwed up her face. "Mom—"

"First your brothers and sister, now you—this has gone on too long, and it has to stop."

Valerie became aware of Pastor Henke beside her.

"Harold," he said, "are you listening? How much trouble does Marsha have to get herself into before you finally tell her enough is enough?"

The man faltered. "She's just a kid, Pastor. Kids make mistakes. That's part of growing up."

"It doesn't have to be." The low, insistent voice at Valerie's left commanded everyone's attention. Healy stepped forward. "You want to hear about mistakes, Mr. Sanderson? How about if somewhere down the line Marsha finally does something bad enough to get her sent to prison? How will you feel then? Let me tell you, it's no walk in the park."

Sanderson lifted his chin. "How dare you—"

"How dare I what?" Healy leaned into his tirade. "How dare I tell you about real life, about what could happen when a kid takes a wrong turn and gets away with it? About how one 'free ride' gives you the guts to take the next chance, and the next?"

He moved to stand directly in front of Marsha, his determined gaze penetrating her defiant one. "Young lady, if you had any clue what real jail time is like, you wouldn't be looking so cocky right now. You'd be on your knees before the judge on Tuesday, begging for mercy."

Relentlessly he bombarded her with the gruesome details of his life in prison: the embarrassing lack of privacy, fights—or worse—with other prisoners, daily harangues from arrogant guards, not to mention the sometimes grueling, often disgusting manual labor.

The girl's lower lip trembled. She took a small step backward and lowered her eyes. "I. . .I didn't do anything. It was them. Tina and Jackie."

Valerie found her voice once more. "No, Marsha. It was you. And it's time you admitted it."

❧

Healy watched tiredly as the Sandersons got into their silver Lexus and drove away. He could only hope he'd gotten through.

And Valerie—she was amazing. She and the Paiges stood in the shade of a cherry tree a few feet away. Valerie hugged herself and sucked in huge gulps of air. Her brother and sister-in-law patted her back and spoke encouragement while their towheaded daughter scooped up a handful of dried grass clippings and tried to entice a skittery blackbird. At least Ellen had kept little Annie out of the fray.

"Here, looks like you need this." Pastor Henke handed him a folded white handkerchief.

Healy took it gratefully and drew it across his damp forehead, then wiped his perspiring palms. The heat seemed even more oppressive today, or was it merely his nervous tension?

He shook his head. "When I saw Valerie in the back pew, I was flying higher than a kite. And then. . ." He lifted his hands in a helpless gesture.

"And then the Sandersons happened." Pastor Henke released a tired groan. "It certainly appeared Harold and Donna—even Marsha—were moved by what you and Valerie said. Let's pray for a miracle, shall we?"

Healy nodded toward the family under the cherry tree. "My miracle is standing right over there."

"Then don't you think it's about time you told her so?"

Maybe it was. The past few weeks had brought Healy a long way toward the maturity and sense of personal completeness he'd been striving for. Returning to school had brought a measure of confidence, and a contact he had made through the vocational department promised steady part-time work with a reputable building contractor.

And maybe. . .someday. . .he'd have the experience and resources to start up his own construction business.

Hope and a future, the years of the locust restored. *Lord, thank You.*

An even fuller sense of satisfaction swelled because of the time he spent with Pastor Henke at the juvenile detention center. Last week the pastor had introduced him to a chaplain heading up a new troubled teens ministry, and the man had encouraged Healy to join him.

Yes, if God could finally bring some good out of those wretched prison years, Healy would cooperate 100 percent.

The pastor nudged him and gestured toward the Paiges. "Er, Healy my boy, you're about to miss your opportunity."

Healy looked up to see Connor unlocking the Paige family minivan. Panic spurred him into action. No way was the woman of his dreams getting away from him today. He sprinted toward the parking lot. "Valerie, wait."

Chapter 18

At the sound of her name, Valerie's heart climbed into her throat. Healy jogged toward her, his eyes filled with single-minded purpose. How many times had she prayed for this moment? One foot on the running board, her fist wrapped around the handgrip, she stared at the approaching figure and dared to hope.

She recalled her first glimpse of Healy in church this morning, sensing something different about him even then. His dishwater-blond hair, though still brushing his collar in the shaggy style she found so endearing, had been neatly trimmed. He no longer wore homeless-barrel hand-me-downs or Tom's slightly too large shirts and jeans. Today he looked casually handsome in pressed khakis and a trim-fitting blue plaid polo shirt.

But he also carried an air about him that went much deeper than surface appearances. She'd never seen him looking so relaxed and self-assured. No one meeting him for the first time today would ever suspect he had been a troubled youth, much less believe he'd served time in prison. When he spoke his mind to the Sandersons, his natural eloquence filled her with awe.

In truth, the only thing about him that seemed unchanged was the telltale scar disfiguring his left forearm. Yet even the scar spoke of his godly character, especially after Pastor Henke had told her the story behind it one day as he drove her to an appointment with Dr. Miller.

Panting, Healy staggered to a halt within arm's reach of her, and she realized her own breath had quickened. He opened his mouth, but no words came out. He jammed his hands into his pockets and backed off a few steps. That purposeful air of only minutes before had vanished, replaced by a cloud of uncertainty.

"Healy, hi!" Not yet buckled in, Annie jumped up from the seat and poked her head between Valerie and the door frame.

"Hey, munchkin." A hesitant smile briefly eased the tension lines in Healy's face.

The little girl grinned flirtatiously. "Did you come over to kiss Aunt Val?"

"Annie Maureen Paige!" Ellen twisted around and gaped at her daughter, but the twinkle in her eye betrayed her delight.

Valerie's cheeks flamed. She lowered her gaze as Ellen reached around to guide the little girl back inside the van. With Connor's help, Ellen buckled Annie into her safety seat.

Then, lowering her window, Ellen spoke to Healy. "Actually, we're all dying to know. *Did* you run all the way over here to kiss Valerie?"

Valerie gasped. She noted with chagrin that Healy's embarrassment matched her own. And yet he displayed a grin a mile wide.

"Truth be told, ma'am, I sure would like to." He cast Valerie a sidelong glance. "That is, if the lady consents."

She inhaled a deep, shaky breath. Of course she wanted to kiss him, desperately! She fingered a loose strand of hair falling across her shoulder. "Um. . .maybe we should go somewhere and talk first."

Pastor Henke appeared beside Healy. "I, er, didn't mean to eavesdrop, but. . ." He jangled a set of keys. "Healy, my boy, the Mustang is yours if you'd like to borrow it for the afternoon. I'm sure Connor and Ellen will be happy to drop me off at home."

Valerie eyed Healy with a puzzled smile. "You're driving now?"

"Passed my test a couple of days ago." Turning, he caught the keys as the pastor tossed them over. "Thanks, Pastor."

"Treat her with respect, my boy," Pastor Henke cautioned. "The car, that is. I know you'll do right by Valerie."

"Yes, sir." Healy gave a mock salute.

Pastor Henke winked at Valerie, then gently bumped her aside and climbed in beside Annie.

Slack-mouthed, Valerie found herself standing on the hot pavement alone with Healy. She kicked at a loose pebble with the toe of her beige leather pump. "Looks like I'm stranded. Care to give a girl a lift?"

"My chariot awaits." Healy escorted her to the pastor's shiny red convertible.

Once both their seat belts were fastened, he turned to her and grinned, one eyebrow lifted provocatively. He revved the engine a few times before steering the car out of the parking space in a slick maneuver rivaling James Bond.

Valerie smiled in mute admiration and gripped the armrest. She finally released her pent-up breath when he slowed three blocks later and turned in at the Sonic Drive-In. Pulling into a space next to one of the menu boards, he lowered the windows and shut off the engine. A warm, zesty breeze swept through the car, ruffling their hair.

"It's not fancy," he said with an apologetic half smile, "but it's within my budget. Hope it'll pass for Sunday dinner for you this once."

After all Valerie had been through this morning, sitting in the privacy of the car at a drive-in sounded just fine—in spite of the fact that even in October it remained ninety degrees in the shade, and the humidity must be close to 100 percent today. "Works for me. What do you recommend?" She undid her butterfly clip and wound all her hair off her damp neck before replacing it.

Healy ordered burgers, tater tots, and cherry limeades, then added into the speaker, "Make that order to go, please." Glancing at Valerie, he said, "Thought we could have a picnic. There's a small lake nearby, with a neat spot the pastor showed me. It's shady and breezy. . .a nice, quiet place where we could talk."

Valerie nodded. The delay would give her that much more time to calm her roiling emotions and regain some perspective about this incredible new man sitting beside her.

❧

Healy hoped he appeared calmer than he felt. Under his new plaid shirt from JCPenney's—bought with money he'd earned replacing kitchen faucets for one of Zion's parishioners—his heart roared louder than the Mustang's supercharged V8 engine.

Maybe he was rushing things. Valerie had an awful lot to cope with, what with her scheduled court appearance Tuesday and all the hassle the Sandersons had been giving her. But to look at Valerie now, so poised and serene, not a worry line in sight to mar that beautiful brow. . . *Oh, dear Jesus, thank You for the miracle of healing You are performing in her life. And let me be worthy, if it's Your will, to share my life with her.*

The server brought their order. Healy passed the bags over to Valerie, and she balanced them on the floorboard next to her feet. Leaving the Sonic, Healy suggested they put the top down on the convertible and forego air-conditioning in favor of the brisk breeze. Conversation proved impossible over the wind noise, but Healy didn't mind. He could use the time to settle his nerves and frame his words. There was so much he needed to say to her, and he had no idea where to begin.

He parked near a secluded picnic area overlooking the sun-dappled lake. A sharp gust of wind whipped around the car as he helped Valerie out. "Hold on to your skirt. The breeze is really picking up."

As they settled opposite each other on benches at a sheltered picnic table, a sudden gust toppled the bag containing their burgers. Valerie snagged a loose napkin. "Maybe we'll get lucky and a cool front will come through."

"That would suit me just fine." Healy peeled back the foil wrapper on his burger. "Even better if it brought some rain. The lake looks even lower than the last time I was here."

When at last Healy had deposited all but their limeade cups in a nearby trash receptacle, he climbed onto the bench next to Valerie so that both of them looked out toward the wind-stirred whitecaps dancing across the lake.

"Thank you for coming with me." He reached tentatively for her hand, sighing inwardly when she intertwined her fingers with his.

She glanced wryly at him and took a sip of her drink. "Face it, neither of us stood a chance with Ellen, Annie, and Pastor Henke all playing matchmaker."

A fuzzy sensation tickled his insides. "Matchmakers, huh? How do you feel about that?"

"Well, I. . .I sort of liked it." Her voice softened to nearly a whisper. "How about you?"

Healy almost couldn't make out her words over a deep rumbling in the distance. Probably a truck on the highway. Or maybe a jet, he reflected as a shadow passed over the lake.

When the sound subsided, he answered, "I liked it, too." He stared at their entwined hands. "I don't want to put any pressure on you, I mean, with all you're facing right now, but. . ."

"But what?"

He looked up, and their gazes locked.

But I'm deeply, crazily in love with you, Valerie Bishop, and I can't spend another day without you. His chest pounded so violently that he couldn't catch a full enough breath to speak the words.

Her shimmering eyes became pleading. "Say what's on your heart, Healy. Don't be afraid. I'm not. Not anymore."

His gaze drifted to the gently curving bow of her lips. White heat shot through him. "Maybe if I"—he leaned closer—"could just kiss you. . ."

Those sensuous lips arched into an inviting smile. "I thought you'd never get around to it," she said huskily, and laced her arms around his neck.

Healy thought he would drown in the ocean of love filling those gorgeous gray eyes. He drew her close, pressing his lips against hers, tasting their warm sweetness until tears coursed down his cheeks.

"I love you, I love you," he murmured against her hair, holding her ever more tightly. "These last few weeks—I missed you so much. I can't even imagine my life without you in it. Somehow. . .some way. . .I want to prove myself worthy of your love in return."

"You don't have to prove anything to me, Healy Ferguson." Her words fell against his ear in warm, breathy wisps. "You are worthy. I've known it—and I have loved you—almost from the day we first met."

He pulled back, searching her face. "You have?"

She nodded.

A sudden thunderous *crack* startled them both, and Valerie buried herself in his arms. Her heart beat like a fluttering bird against his chest.

Only then did he notice how dark the day had grown. A mass of thick, ominous clouds swept in from the northwest. On the metal roof above them came another sound, almost unrecognized after the long, dry summer—heavy, clattering raindrops. He looked out at the dry ground and watched huge drops splatter in the dust. Ever-expanding rings formed as rain pelted the surface of the lake.

Autumn rains.

It felt like a sign from heaven confirming the promises of the scripture Healy had clung to for so long. *Thank You, Lord.*

The next gust of wind carried a chill, and the fat, spattering drops abruptly became a downpour. Valerie lifted her head and burst out laughing. "Rain! Healy, it's finally raining!"

Chapter 19

Healy's momentary elation erupted in a panicked cry. "Oh no, the car!" He raced to the car, leaped over the door, and scrambled into the already drenched driver's seat. He stabbed the keys into the ignition, then pressed the switch to raise the top. "Come on, *come on*!" He thought it would never reach the up position and finally lock into place.

He looked up to see Valerie dancing around puddles and shielding her head with both hands. She fell into the passenger seat and slammed the door. Her rain-soaked hair hung limply around her shoulders. Mud speckled her dainty beige pumps.

He grinned at her. "You look like a drowned rat."

She pushed a wet curl off his forehead, sending a shiver down his spine. "You look. . .incredible."

He took her hand and simply held it, gazing at her while the rain thundered against the roof. In a matter of seconds, their warm bodies and breath had the windows completely fogged. His conscience urged him to turn the car around and get them home at once, before the love in Valerie's eyes and the seclusion of their damp but cozy cocoon destroyed what little resistance he had left.

❧

Valerie gazed through the rain-spattered side window and sent up a prayer of thanks that Healy's willpower proved stronger than hers. Having experienced the full breadth and depth of married love, she longed to share such closeness again. . .as Healy's wife. She believed with all her being that God had brought them together.

But she also knew that they must wait. Their love was still so young, and they had much to talk about, so many issues yet to deal with.

Including Marsha Sanderson's appearance in juvenile court on Tuesday.

The rain had let up by the time they reached the Paige house. Valerie ran inside long enough to grab several towels, then helped Healy dry the car interior as much as possible.

"Do you think anything's ruined?" she asked as Healy wiped water drops off the dashboard.

"Sure hope not." He frowned. "But I doubt Pastor Henke will ever let me near his car again."

"We were both taken by surprise. You got the top up as quickly as you could." She drew the towel around the stick shift and center console.

Healy knelt on the driver's seat and tugged at a strand of her wet hair that had come loose from the butterfly clip. "That storm isn't the only thing to take me by surprise today."

Her pulse quickened. "Me neither."

Healy helped her carry the damp towels to the laundry room and start the washing machine. Standing on the back porch, he sighed and shoved his hands into his pockets before bending to kiss her lightly on the lips.

Recognizing the wisdom of his posture, she locked her arms behind her back. "Call me?"

"Count on it."

When she turned from closing the door, she found herself staring into Connor and Ellen's eager faces. Suppressing a smile, she brushed past them and headed toward the stairs. "I'm desperate for a long, hot bath," she announced without pausing. "I am soaked to the skin."

Let them wonder.

❧

Healy checked the thermometer outside Pastor Henke's kitchen window—a pleasant fifty-eight degrees. Fall had finally arrived! He slipped a crisp khaki windbreaker over his white dress shirt and navy print tie. He wanted to look his best when he met Valerie at the courthouse for Marsha's hearing.

"Ready, Healy?" Pastor Henke reached for his car keys on the kitchen counter. "I shall drive, naturally." He'd been none too happy to learn that his precious automobile had suffered even a few moments under Sunday's unexpected torrent.

Half an hour later, they gathered with Valerie and the Paiges in the corridor outside the courtroom of the Honorable Judith K. Houser. Healy had been in this same courtroom for Tina Maxwell's hearing, and he knew the judge to be fair-minded and frank.

Good, just the kind of judge to deal with Marsha Sanderson.

And, he hoped, the kind of judge who would make sure the Sandersons' attorney didn't emotionally abuse Valerie.

He edged close to the woman he loved and took her hand. "How are you doing?"

"Nervous."

He detected a slight tremor in her hand and gripped it more firmly.

"Val, they're calling everyone inside." Connor nodded toward the bailiff standing in the open courtroom doors. He planted a quick kiss on her cheek. "We'll be waiting for you right here, and praying like crazy."

Valerie inhaled deeply. "I'll need all the prayers I can get."

With Healy holding her hand, they followed the Sanderson entourage into the small, wood-paneled courtroom. Jason Albright shot them a scathing glance. Healy fired back his own threatening glare as he drew a protective arm around Valerie's shoulder.

At least the Sandersons themselves no longer displayed the same animosity toward Valerie. Healy hoped Marsha's red-rimmed eyes signified true remorse, not a dramatic performance intended to impress the judge. If only she would show even a hint of the willingness to turn her life around that both Tina and Jackie had demonstrated.

Lost in prayer, he paid little attention to the court proceedings until the juvenile prosecuting attorney called Valerie to the stand. His senses sharpened, and his gaze riveted on the slender blond woman as she strode to the witness chair. Healy could tell by the set of her mouth and the way she repeatedly smoothed the fabric of her dark green dress that every moment was a battle for control.

The prosecutor's questions were simple and straightforward, allowing Valerie to relate the Walmart incident in her own words. After a few minutes, the tight lines around her mouth relaxed, and she spoke as if she and the attorney were the only ones in the room. At least Jason Albright had the decency to keep his mouth shut. After all, how could he object to the truth?

"Thank you, Mrs. Bishop. No further questions at this time." The prosecutor returned to his chair.

Judge Houser finished jotting some notes on a legal pad and looked toward the defense table. "Mr. Albright?"

"Yes, Your Honor, thank you." The slick lawyer rose and buttoned his suit coat. He ambled toward the witness stand and presented his arrogant profile to those seated in the courtroom. "Mrs. Bishop, how are you today?"

Healy read phoniness in every aspect of the man's demeanor. He stiffened.

"I'm fine, thank you, Mr. Albright." Valerie folded her hands and smiled serenely back.

"No hallucinations today, no voices, no panic attacks—"

"Objection," snapped the prosecutor. Healy wrestled back the urge to leap across the railing and nail Albright on the chin.

Judge Houser removed her glasses and glared at the Sandersons' attorney. "Objection sustained. Mr. Albright, you will please confine your questions to the matter at hand."

"Your Honor, my question cuts to the heart of this witness's credibility. The defense intends to prove that Mrs. Bishop's mental health issues—"

"Must I remind you, Mr. Albright, that Mrs. Bishop is not on trial here today. The court is fully aware of Mrs. Bishop's 'mental health issues,' as you choose to call them, and you are surely aware of Dr. Karen Miller's deposition in which she describes the causes, treatment, and, I reiterate, *excellent* prognosis for Mrs. Bishop's recovery from post-traumatic stress disorder."

The judge flipped through a file on her desk. "So unless you have some new evidence that would convince the court otherwise, I find no reason to excuse Mrs. Bishop's testimony on the grounds you are claiming."

For once, Jason Albright look flustered. "Er, in that case, Your Honor, the defense requests a brief recess."

"Very well. Ten minutes."

"But, Your Honor—"

With a tired sigh, Judge Houser folded her arms atop the desk. "Mr. Albright, all the time in the world isn't going to change the facts. Either you are ready to proceed with your client's defense, or you are not."

"I object, Your Honor."

The judge pinched the bridge of her nose. "To what, Mr. Albright?"

Jason Albright lifted his chin. "To the fact that Your Honor has obviously already decided this case before hearing the defense arguments."

"*If* that is true, then you are the only one to blame. You seem to have forgotten your job, sir, which is to present *credible* evidence on your client's behalf. Now, do you want that ten-minute recess or not?"

Albright swallowed. "Yes, Your Honor."

Healy winked at Valerie and caught the almost imperceptible relaxation in her shoulders.

The judge turned to Valerie with a look of mutual understanding. "Mrs. Bishop, you're excused for the time being. Thank you for your patience."

❧

In the corridor, Valerie tucked her arms under Healy's jacket and sagged against his warm chest. "Is it over?" she asked tiredly. "I mean, my part?"

Connor patted her shoulder. "From what little we overheard, it sounded like the judge did a good job of putting Albright in his place. I can't imagine he'd dare try anything else."

Ellen smoothed Valerie's hair. "You did great, honey. How are you feeling?"

Valerie and Healy shared a knowing look. "I should get an Academy Award."

"You've got my vote." Healy touched her cheek. "How are you doing, babe, I mean really?"

She liked the sound of that, *babe*. "Actually, I'm doing great. I feel. . .*empowered*. I feel triumphant. Like I've just survived the Boston Marathon. More than survived—*conquered*."

All the while she was on the stand, she had mentally repeated a scripture verse from Isaiah: *"You will keep in perfect peace those whose minds are steadfast, because they trust in you."*

Perfect peace. Was it possible, after so many years, that she had found it at last?

The bailiff's strident announcement brought an abrupt end to the ten-minute recess. Judge Houser swept in, her black robes billowing, and Healy and Valerie took their seats.

The judge peered at Jason Albright. "Shall we continue?"

Albright rose and cleared his throat "Your Honor, Marsha Sanderson has asked to speak on her own behalf."

Valerie grasped Healy's arm. Perhaps what they'd all been praying for would finally happen.

"Very well." The judge gestured Marsha to the witness stand. "Young lady, what is it you would like to say?"

Marsha lowered her eyes, her hands clasping and unclasping. "I–I'm really sorry for what I did."

"Before you say anything further, dear. . ." Judge Houser fixed Jason Albright with her steely gaze. "Mr. Albright, have you discussed with your client the possible implications of what I believe she is trying to tell this court?"

"Yes, Your Honor, I have." Albright's jaw muscles flexed. "Marsha Sanderson and her parents have made this decision against my advice. Miss Sanderson wishes now to throw herself upon the mercy of the court and accept whatever disciplinary actions your honor deems appropriate."

"I see." The judge cast her patient gaze upon Marsha. "All right, dear, in that case I'd like you to explain exactly what it is you are sorry for."

More hand wringing and a desperate sidelong glance toward her parents. "I'm sorry for. . .for talking my friends into shoplifting and then lying about it so I wouldn't get blamed."

Thank You, Father! Valerie gave Healy's arm another squeeze, and he patted her hand, nodding almost imperceptibly. If not for the solemnity of Judge Houser's courtroom, both of them would surely have leaped and shouted for joy.

Chapter 20

It had taken a full week for Valerie to come down off her post-trial high. She savored the heady feeling of wholeness and inner peace, hers at last by God's grace. And yet, despite the long years of grief and fear, she knew in her heart that God had never abandoned her, never stopped being in control of her healing.

The greatest blessing of all was God's wonderful gift of Healy. They grew closer and more in love every day, spending as much time together as his class schedule and part-time work would allow—and no longer within the confines of the Paige house. Yet those few short hours they shared together each day didn't seem nearly enough, and Valerie could barely control her urgency for things to change.

In the meantime, she'd been contemplating how to solve another problem. Though they'd taken Pastor Henke's car to the detail shop for a thorough cleaning and waxing, it appeared he had only grudgingly forgiven them for leaving his precious red Mustang unprotected during the downpour.

In a last-ditch attempt to win him over, Valerie invited him for tea and fresh-baked brownies—from his favorite bakery in town, not homemade, she quickly informed him. The next afternoon, while Annie watched a favorite movie on the den TV, they nibbled brownies and chatted in the Paige kitchen.

"My dear Valerie, homemade or not, these are delicious." The pastor dabbed crumbs off his chin with a paper napkin. "Not on my diet, of course, but a delightful treat."

She topped off his cup of Earl Gray. "I've been meaning to ask you about Marsha. What's the latest news?"

"She's none too happy about serving time in detention," the pastor replied, "but I think it has finally put the fear of God into her, and I hope I mean that literally. As you know, Healy's troubled teen ministry is now involved with her case, and it appears her shell is beginning to crack."

He blew across the surface of his tea and took a sip. "And the Sandersons are now attending my biblical parenting class. Donna had to coerce Harold with untold threats to get him to their first session, but he has made an astounding turnaround in a very short time, praise God."

"That's wonderful, a real miracle." Valerie smiled coyly and rested her chin on her interwoven fingers. "Certainly such encouraging news should more than make up for any remaining hard feelings over the completely unintentional blunder of your two very favorite parishioners."

The white-haired man eyed her suspiciously. "First you ply me with brownies, then you play upon my good humor. Since I am already quite willing to forgive you and Healy for your negligence, I am afraid to ask where all this munificence is leading."

She traced a finger around the rim of her teacup. "I need to retake my driver's test, too, before I can get a new license. Your little red car is so cool, and I was hoping. . ."

"Oh no. No, no, *no*!" He lifted his hands. "I was fool enough to entrust my precious automobile to Healy, and look how he repaid me. And on top of everything else, the ungrateful lout is planning to move out and leave me to fend for myself once again."

Valerie's heart lifted at the reminder of Healy's return to the garage apartment next Saturday. Connor had already discussed additional remodeling projects with him, a top priority being the new baby's nursery. And transportation to school and work was no longer a problem since Healy had arranged to purchase a reliable used car from a church member. In every aspect, he grew more independent and self-possessed with each passing day.

The pastor laid a hand on Valerie's arm. "You know my petulance is all a sham. I could not be happier for any two people in the world than I am for you and Healy."

She leaned over to kiss his round, ruddy cheek. "After all, you're the one who introduced us."

He wiggled his bushy white eyebrows. "So. . .should I anticipate a wedding in the near future?"

"As much as I want that, it's way too soon. We still have issues to work through." Her throat tightened. "Pastor, I haven't told him everything yet about the night Tom died."

His brows drew together. "Oh, my dear, do you think it will matter to him, honestly?"

"But he loves Annie so. And look how great he is with the kids at the detention center. He'd make a wonderful father. He deserves children of his own."

The pastor grasped both her hands and held them firmly. "But he is in love with *you*."

"I know." A tear slipped down her cheek. *But I wanted to give him so much more.*

Later, when Healy stopped by between his after-school construction job and a teen ministry board meeting, she grabbed a sweater and took him out to the wicker rockers on the back porch. Cheery clusters of yellow and orange chrysanthemums filled the porch-rail planter boxes, and the whole earth smelled moist and alive again.

"You look like you have something on your mind." Healy pulled his chair closer, his forehead wrinkled in concern.

In the gathering darkness she absently massaged the empty spot on her ring finger and struggled for words. "Healy, the night Tom died. . . I never told you the whole story."

She could feel him tense. His mouth grew tight. "It's okay. You don't have to."

"Yes, it's important that I do." She set her chair to rocking, hoping the rhythmic motion would soothe her, but it only served as a poignant symbol of a joy she might never know, the joy of rocking her own child.

"When it happened," she began, her throat constricting, "I was five months pregnant. My baby died that night, too."

Healy exhaled sharply. "I know, babe. I'm so sorry."

"You know about my recurring back pain." She forced herself to continue before courage failed her. "One of the men pushed me backward, and I fell across one of those metal picket fences they put around trees in the sidewalk. That's what caused me to lose the baby. And the internal injuries I suffered. . ." She swallowed a sob. "Healy, there's a good chance I may never be able to have more children."

He knelt at her feet and enveloped her in his strong arms while she gave in to her grief all over again. When her tears subsided, he pressed her hands between his own. "My precious Valerie," he said, his eyes filled with tenderness, "if you thought telling me this would change my feelings for you. . ."

She sucked in her breath, both anxious and terrified to hear his next words.

Healy's voice grew husky. "At this moment my feelings for you are deeper and stronger than they've ever been. You are the bravest, most loving woman I have ever known or ever hope to know."

"Oh, Healy, I'm sorry, I'm so sorry." She pressed her face against the collar of his soft flannel shirt and twined her fingers through his hair.

"You have nothing to be sorry for." He drew her once again into his sheltering embrace. Then his body stiffened, and his tone became tentative as he added, "Unless this is your way of saying you want me out of your life."

She pushed him to arm's length but kept her hands locked around his neck. "That's the last thing I'd ever say to you, Healy Ferguson." Her chest ached, her heart pulsed. "Healy, if you'll have me, I want to spend the rest of my life showing you how much I love you. I want to be your wife."

Healy recoiled as if she had punched him in the belly. He sputtered, fumbled for words, raked a trembling hand through his hair. "Hey, I know I missed out on a lot while I was in the slammer, but I thought the guy still did the proposing. Anyway," he added with a chuckle and a downward glance, "I'm the one on my knees here."

Valerie looked at him with puzzled amusement. "In case you haven't noticed, this is the twenty-first century. Not that I'd exactly call myself a women's libber, but I have learned how to ask for what I want." She tapped her toe with mock impatience. "Now, is that a yes, or a no?"

With a crooked smile he lifted her left hand and caressed her fingers. Abruptly he stopped and held her hand toward the amber glow of the porch light. His brows knitted. "You're not wearing Tom's rings. I hadn't noticed before. When did you take them off?"

With a tender sigh, she thought back to the day she'd said her final good-byes to Tom and the baby she would never hold in her arms. "A few weeks ago, when I realized how desperately I wanted to spend the rest of my life with you."

"But are you absolutely sure? You and Tom, you had so much—"

"Tom was my first love. Yes, what we had was amazing and wonderful, and it can never be replaced." A tear slipped down her cheek. "But the love I feel for you, though different, is equally strong. And I think I can love you better for having loved Tom. . .and for knowing how much Tom loved us both."

Speechless, his own depth of passion shining in his eyes, Healy drew her ring finger to his lips and kissed it. She caressed his face with the palm of her hand before brushing away a streak of dampness from his cheek. She cast him an expectant glance. "You still haven't said yes to my proposal."

"Yes," he said in an explosion of laughter and tears. "Yes, yes, *yes*!"

Epilogue

"All rise."

Valerie reached for Healy's hand as they stood with their attorney to await the entrance of the Honorable Judith K. Houser. How appropriate they should find themselves in Judge Houser's courtroom again after all these years, and for such a significant occasion. The statuesque judge, who now presided over family court, settled into the leather chair behind the bench.

"My, my," the judge began when the rustle of shuffling feet and chairs had ceased, "this is quite a family I see before me, Mr. and Mrs. Ferguson." Slipping on her reading glasses, she perused the contents of a thick file folder. "Four happy children, all thriving, I see."

A lump rose in Valerie's throat as she glanced over her shoulder. On the long bench behind them, sandwiched between Connor and Ellen on one end and fourteen-year-old Annie and her ten-year-old brother, Thomas, on the other, sat four fidgeting children, each as different from the others as night and day.

Jenny, age seven, wore her chin-length black hair in a smooth bob. Five-year-old Kim rubbed sleep out of her dark, almond-shaped eyes, while her coffee-complected younger brother, Andrew, age four, bounced the toes of his polished shoes off the railing in front of him.

Tucked under Annie's protective arm sat three-year-old Bethany, her blond curls rivaling Annie's. Soft green eyes danced in her round, flat face. She grinned at Valerie. "Mommy, I love you."

"I know, sweetie. Mommy loves you, too."

"Let's be quiet now." Annie gave Bethany a quick kiss on the top of her head.

Judge Houser lowered her reading glasses. "Mr. and Mrs. Ferguson, your petition to adopt little Michael appears to be in good order."

Sighing inwardly, Valerie gazed with tenderness at the seven-month-old baby sleeping in the infant seat on the table in front of her. Healy reached his arm around her. He looked handsomer than ever in his cocoa brown suit and paisley tie, especially with the distinguished flecks of gray at his temples.

Continuing, the judge folded her hands. "Before I grant this adoption, however, I have a few things to say. Mr. Ferguson." She fixed intense brown eyes on Healy. "The court is, of course, fully cognizant of your background and the challenges you have had to overcome to reach this place in life."

Healy bit his lip and nodded. Under the table, Valerie patted his knee.

"I must say," the judge continued, "your diligent efforts to establish yourself as a model citizen are well documented. I well recall your frequent appearances in my juvenile courtroom on behalf of teens in trouble. I have also read with great pleasure the innumerable letters of commendation written by everyone from your pastor, to the warden and chaplain where you served your sentence, to your former college instructors and employers."

Judge Houser slipped on her glasses to consult her notes before continuing. "This latest home-study report describes you as an exceptional father and a conscientious provider for your family. I see that you are the successful owner of your own construction business, the cornerstone of a vibrant ministry for troubled youth, an elder of your church. . ." She paused and caught her breath. "Sir, I applaud you for a life well lived."

Healy cleared his throat. "Thank you, Your Honor."

"I would also like to commend both you and your wife for opening your home and hearts to special-needs children, those dear ones who are so often overlooked by today's society. I see that your church has assisted you in adopting orphans from China and South America"—she nodded toward Kim and Jenny—"and also that you are parents to a biracial son and a daughter with Down's syndrome. Admirable indeed."

Little Michael squirmed and whimpered. Valerie reached for his pacifier and patted his tummy until he quieted.

"And now," Judge Houser continued, "you are petitioning to adopt a little boy suffering from fetal alcohol syndrome. With any other couple I would seriously question your preparedness for such an undertaking. But I have only to look into the faces of your other four children to know that you have not only the necessary patience and tenacity but an endless supply of love."

The judge lifted her gavel. The firm *crack* echoed throughout the courtroom. "Petition granted. Congratulations, Michael Connor Ferguson. In my considered opinion, you are one of the luckiest little boys in the world."

A cry of joy erupted from Valerie's throat. She and Healy fell into each other's arms. Moments later their other children, along with Connor and his family, Pastor Henke, and Valerie and Connor's mother, pushed through the gate and encircled them with more hugs and tears.

"I think this calls for a prayer of thanksgiving," Healy said in a choked voice. One arm around Valerie, the other hovering protectively over baby Michael's infant seat, he bowed his head. "Gracious heavenly Father, again You have shown the power of Your promise. What a quiver full of children You have given me. Thank You for my precious wife, Valerie, and for the wonderful blessings these dear little ones have brought into our lives. Help us always to be the best parents we can be and to model Christ's love for them. In Jesus' holy name, amen."

"Amen indeed," Pastor Henke interjected. "'Be glad, O people of Zion'!"

ROMANCE BY THE BOOK

Dedication

For Julie Lessman, my favorite real-life Missouri author, and for Candy, the hairstylist who always makes me look my best!

Chapter 1

"Is it in yet?" Sailor Kern stretched her thin frame across the library checkout counter. Her elbows dug into the yellow Formica. "*Please*, Kathy, tell me you have it."

The dark-haired woman behind the counter arched one eyebrow as she scanned the bar codes on a stack of returned books. "Have what?"

Sailor huffed. "Come *on*, Kathy. You're supposed to be my best friend. Don't keep me in suspense."

With infuriating slowness Kathy Richmond scanned another book and placed it on the rack behind her. "Are you referring to the new Chandler Michaels novel?"

"What else?" Sailor stood erect, one sneaker-clad foot tapping out her impatience. "You promised I was next on the waiting list."

An impish grin skewed Kathy's lips. She turned away and dug deep into the back of a filing-cabinet drawer, spun around with a flourish, and plopped a book on the counter. "Ta-da!"

Sailor snatched up the book and hugged it to her chest. "Do you have any idea how long I've been waiting to read this?"

"Seeing as how you've checked out every one of Chandler's fourteen previous books at least twice and have been bugging me about his latest release every day for the past month, I would say. . .yes." Kathy groaned and glanced toward the ceiling. "You could have picked up your own copy over at Dale & Dean's Book Corner the day it came in."

"Buy it? At hardcover price? Do I need to remind you what they pay me at the Y?" Sailor held the novel at arm's length and slid admiring fingertips across the slick, shiny book jacket. It pictured a raven-haired, Victorian-era songstress in the arms of her dashing hero. "*Love's Sweet Song*. This one has got to be his most tender romance yet—proof you don't need graphic love scenes to tell a great story."

"On that much, I can agree." Kathy motioned Sailor aside while she assisted an elderly library patron. She tucked the gentleman's receipt into the top book and pushed the stack toward him. Speaking slowly and distinctly, she said, "These are due back on the sixteenth, Mr. Crenshaw."

"Thanks"—Mr. Crenshaw squinted toward Kathy's chest—"Kandy. It's a date, sweetheart." With a wink he gathered up his books and headed toward the exit.

"What a flirt." Sailor planted one hip against the counter. "And did he just call you Kandy?"

"His eyesight's almost as bad as his hearing. You did notice everything he checked out was the large-print edition?"

"I also noticed his gaze lingered a bit longer than necessary on your, uh, name tag."

"He's a harmless old coot." Grinning, Kathy resumed her book scanning. "Besides, we thirty-something single girls have to take romance anywhere we can find it."

"Don't remind me." An old, familiar ache settled under Sailor's breastbone. Between her incurable shyness and ordinary looks, the only romance she could expect came from the pages of books like the one she held. She eyed the alluring songstress again and heaved an envious sigh before handing Kathy the book along with her library card.

"Oh, Sailor, I was kidding." Kathy checked out the book for her and then motioned one of the other librarians over to help the next patron. She stepped around the counter and gave Sailor's shoulder a squeeze. "I only get a half-hour lunch break today. Can you join me in the snack bar just this once? There's something I've been dying to talk to you about."

Kathy hummed softly, avoiding Sailor's probing gaze as they entered the glass-walled elevator that would whisk them to the lower level. Sailor's stomach twisted—and it had nothing to do with her noontime hunger pangs or the disgustingly fattening aromas of hot dogs and fries wafting their way. Nope, when Kathy Richmond got that look in her eye, it usually meant she was about to push Sailor way out of her comfort zone.

And it didn't take much.

❧

"Ow! That hurts, Doc!" Parker Travis cringed and ducked from beneath Andy Mendoza's probing fingers.

"Hold still, will you? How else do you expect me to diagnose your back pain?"

"X-rays. MRI. CT scan." Parker reached around to rub the sore spot behind his right shoulder.

"Man, what a hypochondriac." The doctor dug his thumbs deep into the center of Parker's aching back muscle, eliciting another yelp. "An X-ray or MRI isn't going to tell me anything I don't already know. This is clearly an overuse injury, probably from spending too many hours a day wielding a hair dryer."

"So you don't think it's anything serious?" Health issues always made Parker slightly nervous, especially since so many men on *both* sides of his family tree had died before age fifty. He wanted to be around to make sure his widowed mom and grandmother were well cared for as long as they lived.

"Nope, you're as healthy as a horse." Andy jotted notes in Parker's file. "Although maybe you should've chosen a different career. Not to mention how you have to twist your upper body to hold a flute."

Parker groaned at the reminder. On Sundays he and Andy played in their church's praise team band—Parker on flute and Andy on drums. But lately the sets had left Parker almost as crippled from pain as his salon work. "I love what I do. You expect me to give up the things I enjoy most?"

Andy took hold of Parker's arm, moving the shoulder through its range of motion. "Actually, being on your feet for hours at a time, I'm surprised you aren't complaining about your knees."

"Ouch! Will you stop that?" Parker almost wished he'd never made this appointment. Suffering in silence had to be easier than dealing with his old high school–band buddy's razzing. No way he'd admit to his chronic knee pain now, especially if the esteemed Dr. Andrew Mendoza had nothing more helpful to offer.

"Sorry, Park. Seriously, the best thing for you is a course of NSAIDs for the inflammation and some therapeutic exercise." He jotted something on a prescription pad.

"But I already work out. I run several days a week, do free weights in between."

"A regimen that only exacerbates your issues. The muscles have tightened up and need to be stretched." Andy perused the rack of health-related brochures mounted on the exam room door. He selected one and offered it to Parker. "Have you ever considered water aerobics?"

Only a know-it-all show-off like Andy would use words like *regimen* and *exacerbates*. Parker glimpsed the red and black symbol for the YMCA but kept his hands firmly planted beside his thighs. His grandmother and her friends at the assisted-living center did water aerobics. He loved those gals, but. . . "Can't you refer me to a physical therapist, or maybe a personal trainer?"

Andy smirked. "A bit image conscious, are we? Water aerobics is a great way to exercise without stressing the joints. Especially good for sore knees," he added with a wink. He tapped Parker's arm with the sharp edge of the brochure. "Sign up. Doctor's orders."

Parker slithered into his black polo shirt with the Par Excellence Salon and Day Spa logo embroidered on the breast pocket. He'd worked hard to get to this place in life, overcome a lot of kidding and even more innuendos. Male hairstylists, even guys like him who owned and managed their own salons, weren't exactly seen as the strong, macho type. Neither were closet hypochondriacs or men who played the flute. It didn't matter that he played on his church's men's softball team and could easily slug one over the fence. Didn't matter that his Birkenstock High 100-yard-dash record remained unbroken. If folks around town found out he'd joined his grandmother's water aerobics class, the teasing would never end.

Later, pulling into a vacant space in front of the Willow Tree Assisted-Living Center, he'd about decided to call Andy again and insist on a referral to a specialist. If Birkenstock didn't have one, Springfield was just up the highway.

Then he reached into the backseat for his styling kit, and the stabbing pain in his back made him grab the door frame and suck in his breath.

Two hours and six little old ladies' gray heads later, he was ready to dress in tights and a pink tulle skirt if it would make the pain go away.

❧

Sailor sat in her cramped cubicle behind the YMCA reception area and paged through a stack of registration forms. Her introductory water aerobics class starting tomorrow looked to be an interesting group. A pair of sixty-something twins who were more than a tad overweight. A new mom hoping to return to her prepregnancy fitness level. A stressed-out paralegal. Three high school teachers who signed up together for fun. All women, of course. Never any cute guys. They all hung out in the weight room or the lap-swimming lanes.

The reminder sent Sailor's thoughts careening back to her lunchtime discussion—make that *arm-twisting*—with Kathy. She made a correction in her computer file, stabbed the ENTER key, and flipped the third teacher's registration form facedown on the completed pile. "I cannot believe that girl."

Kathy, of course. Not the teacher. What had possessed her friend to think Sailor could possibly be coerced into joining the Bards of Birkenstock committee? She glared at the computer monitor. "I don't *do* committees—as if the whole universe doesn't know that already."

And yet. . .Kathy had let that one tempting morsel slip out. Chandler Michaels had been selected to receive the Birkenstock Arts and Letters Association's annual award for outstanding literary achievement. Every year they honored prominent Missouri authors at the Bards of Birkenstock Festival, an event that brought in Missouri's brightest literary luminaries for readings, book signings, a parade, and a $100-a-plate fund-raising dinner that culminated in the gala awards ceremony.

Chandler Michaels—right here in Birkenstock! And if Sailor joined the committee, she'd be guaranteed actual face time with the author who had set her heart aflutter with his heart-tugging love stories too many times to count.

An insistent buzzing nagged at her from somewhere beneath a pile of papers. She shuffled them aside until she exhumed her desk phone then jabbed the intercom button. "Hi, Gloria. What's up?"

"Phone call on line 3," the front-desk receptionist chirped. "It's your friend Kathy."

Expecting an answer, no doubt. "Thanks, Glo." She pressed another phone button and grabbed up the receiver. "I told you I needed some time to think about it."

"What's to think about? You're dying to meet Chandler Michaels. Admit it."

Sailor stretched her legs under the desk. "He's been away from Missouri so long, it would be just my luck he won't even come to town for the ceremony. You've seen the Oscars. The biggest stars are so busy with their next movie that they pre-tape their acceptance speeches and don't bother attending."

"Birkenstock's hometown hero? He'll come back if for no other reason than to gloat."

Sailor sat up straight, her breath quickening. "Chandler Michaels is from Birkenstock?"

"You didn't know? Since you love his books so much, I figured you'd know everything about the guy."

"I am *not* some crazed fan." Sailor winced. "Anyway, he's a very private person. His website bio just says he grew up in a small town in the Missouri Ozarks."

"Well, I just found out from our committee chairperson that Chandler was born and raised right here in little ol' Birky. His real name is Chuck Michalicek. 'Chandler Michaels' is his pen name." Kathy chuckled. "Can't say I blame him. Chuck Michalicek is quite a mouthful."

"Michalicek? The name's vaguely familiar. . . ." Sailor twisted the phone cord.

"I did a Web search myself. You're right—nothing linking Chandler Michaels to Birkenstock. But I dug up a mention of Chuck Michalicek on the Birky High Facebook page. The old guy graduated way before our time then apparently left for college and dropped off the local radar."

"*Old guy?* He can't be *that* old."

Kathy snorted. "I'm staring at his picture in a BHS yearbook as we speak. He looked way different then—mutton-chop sideburns, long-haired hippy 'do. 'Peace, brother' all the way."

Sailor cringed. "But he looks so handsome on his book covers."

"Surely you realize that publicity photo is a masterful work of airbrushing? And the dinner jacket, black tie, backlighting, the whole I'm-as-suave-as-James-Bond thing? Please."

"Well. . .it's a persona. Would you want to read a romance novel by an author who looked like Bill Gates?"

Kathy roared then quickly lowered her voice a notch. "If somebody as rich as Bill Gates wanted to romance me, I wouldn't care what he looked like."

Sailor looked up to see Gloria poking her strawberry blond head around the cubicle wall. The receptionist handed her another registration form and tapped a french-manicured fingernail on the printed name. "He's waiting out front right now—wants to ask some questions about your class."

He? Sailor's eyes widened then narrowed to slits. Probably an elderly retiree who found out the tai chi class was full. "I've got to go, Kathy," she said into the phone. "Can we talk about this later?"

"Just say yes. This is your chance, Sailor." Kathy mimicked a hyper game show host. "You, the one and only Sailor Kern, could be picking up Chandler Michaels from the airport. Driving Chandler Michaels around town. Arranging Chandler Michaels's autograph parties. Presenting Chandler Michaels with the Bards of Birkenstock commemorative plaque, engraved with his name—"

"Stop. Just stop!" Sailor grimaced and thrust out a hand. "Okay, I'll be on your stupid committee. Just promise I can stay in the background. No phone solicitations. No public speaking."

"We'll keep it very low-key, I promise. It'll be fun!"

Low-key, my toenail. Could there be *anything* low-key with Kathy? Sailor hung up the phone and wondered if she'd completely lost her sanity. Then a giggle erupted from deep in her belly and worked its way up through her chest until it exploded from her throat. She squeezed her eyes shut and pumped her fists.

"I'm going to meet Chandler Michaels!"

❧

Parker paced the YMCA lobby, first peering through the steamy windows overlooking the indoor pool then pausing to watch the patrons using the health center. Swimming. Why couldn't Andy have suggested swimming? Wouldn't it stretch his back out as well as some wimpy water aerobics class?

"Hi. You wanted to see me?"

The tiny voice came from behind him, almost too soft to be heard over the clang and groan of the health-center weight machines. He glanced over his shoulder—stupid move, considering the jolt of pain it caused—and then had to drop his gaze nearly a foot to find the source of that voice.

"Hi. Are you the water aerobics instructor?" Couldn't be. . .could she? Five foot two if that, face devoid of makeup, dishwater blond hair pulled into a messy ponytail. She didn't even look old enough to have a driver's license.

"Sailor Kern. And you're Mr. . . ." She scanned his registration form. "Parker?"

"Travis."

"Hi Travis, nice to meet you. What can I tell you about the class?"

"No, it's Parker. Parker Travis."

She crossed her arms and retreated a step. Eyes the color of the indoor pool shimmered under the fluorescent overheads. "Now I'm confused."

Perfect. He felt like he was in elementary school again. Except his teachers were never this youthful. Nor as unpretentiously pretty.

Yikes. *Get a grip, man.* "My name is Parker Travis, not Travis Parker."

Her gaze flitted across the form. "People are always missing that it says last name first and putting their first name first, so I thought. . ." Those aqua eyes gave an embarrassed roll and her tone grew even softer. "Well, anyway, Mr. *Travis*, Gloria said you had some questions."

"Yeah. My doctor recommended your class." Parker glanced around the lobby. A couple of jocks in gym shorts and sweaty T-shirts strolled out of the health center, their jibes and deep-throated laughter bouncing off the walls. Parker waited while the testosterone cloud dissipated. He could bench-press 200 pounds, and Andy wanted him to sign up for *water aerobics*?

"You were saying?"

Parker huffed a resigned sigh. "See, I've got this pain behind my right shoulder and the doc thought your class would help."

The girl shifted. A dubious gleam lit her narrowed eyes. "But you're not convinced."

Parker stared at the toes of his black sneakers. A dusting of gray hair clippings clung to them, reminding him of his conversation with the spunky ninety-year-old in the apartment next to Grams's. While he styled her hair today, he'd let it slip that he might be signing up for this class. She proudly flexed her rounded bicep, giving credit to her three-times-a-week water workouts with the "sweet little instructor" at the Y.

"Little" certainly described the pint-sized mass of lean muscle standing before him. He'd hold off on the "sweet" verdict for now. Striking a pose to mirror Miss Kern's, he said, "Let's just say I'm not sure if the class is right for me."

She shrugged. One eyebrow slowly lifted in what could only be interpreted as a challenge. "Only one way to find out."

Parker chewed his lip. He'd never live it down if he showed up for church Sunday and had to tell Andy he chickened out. "Okay, hit me with your best shot."

❧

Sailor tried to keep the delighted look off her face. Ever since her first glimpse of Parker Travis, she'd been fighting to keep her heartbeat steady. In nearly ten years of teaching at the Y, she'd had *maybe* that many male students, and most of them had been at least twice her age. She hadn't expected a halfway good-looking man in his midthirties *without* a weight problem and *with* a full head of hair. Parker was obviously physically fit, boyishly charming, good-looking in an understated sort of way. . . .

She double-checked the registration form.

Yes, and single!

Still in shock, she led her newest student through the double glass doors into the pool area. Immediately a deep sense of peace washed over her—the clear, ice blue water splish-splashing against the tiles, the moist heaviness in the chlorine-scented air, the broad windows overlooking the Y's forested jogging path. This place meant much more to her than merely a cavernous space housing an Olympic-size swimming pool. It had literally saved her life.

Parker Travis stepped up beside her. "Nice view."

"Isn't it?" Turning toward him, Sailor exhaled a calming breath.

His gaze swept the full length of her body before his mouth turned down in a doubtful grimace. "So do I need any special equipment?"

She shook off the shivery feeling his slow perusal had evoked and drew herself up taller, not that it helped. "I usually e-mail the information to my students before the first class, but since you're here. . ." She strode across the deck, opened the door of a tall cabinet, and pulled out various pieces of gear. "You'll need a flotation belt, webbed gloves, aqua blocks, noodles—"

"Noodles? What are we going to do, make spaghetti?"

Laughter bubbled up from Sailor's abdomen. "A pool noodle is a five-foot length of compressed foam rubber. We use them for resistance or as a flotation aid." She retrieved a lime green noodle from the molded-plastic storage bin next to the cabinet. "The Y keeps all this gear on hand, but if you'd rather purchase your own, Sports and More carries a basic water aerobics kit. Just mention you're in my class, and they'll know what you want."

"Okay." Parker nodded thoughtfully. "Guess I'll see you tomorrow. Four o'clock, right?"

"Four o'clock."

Another crazy, tingly, girly feeling raced up her arms as she watched him leave. She recalled the logo on his shirt. Par Excellence Salon and Day Spa, that ritzy place just off downtown, where Birkenstock's beautiful people hung out to get even more beautiful. A memory clicked into place—wasn't Parker Travis the high school track star-turned hairstylist? Maybe she could garner some tips on how to look her best when Chandler Michaels arrived in town. Her reflection stared back at her from the tinted glass doors—a limp strand of stick-straight hair falling across one eye, knobby knees poking through faded sweatpants, a figure that was more soda straw than hourglass.

If she wanted to impress Chandler Michaels, she'd need all the help she could get.

Chapter 2

Parker adjusted the folded towel behind Donna DuPont's neck and eased her head into the shampoo bowl. "Comfortable?"

"Perfectly. Use that luscious peach-scented stuff. I packed a bottle for our Maui vacation, and Howard went wild over it."

"Glad our illustrious mayor approved." Grinning, Parker turned on the sprayer to rinse out the Platinum Diva #39 he'd applied twenty minutes ago. "How was your trip?"

While the mayor's wife described luaus, dolphin watching, and snorkeling excursions, Parker nodded and set to work. No denying it, shampooing remained one of his favorite aspects of being a hairstylist. After wetting Donna's hair, he applied a generous dollop of Peaches 'n' Crème Ultra-Conditioning Shampoo and massaged it into frothy, fragrant suds. His fingers glided across Donna's lathered scalp in overlapping circles, the sensation as relaxing to him as it was to his sleepy-eyed client. *Let's see that water aerobics instructor top this for the ultimate in stress reduction.*

Great, just when he thought he'd put the dreaded class out of his mind. He checked his watch. *Hoo-boy.* The class started in less than an hour.

"Ouch!" Donna jerked beneath his fingers. "Good grief, Parker, you're not kneading bread dough."

"Sorry." He finished with a gentler massage and reached for the sprayer.

"You seem a tad distracted this afternoon," Donna said later as they returned to his station.

He rotated his shoulders a few times before removing her towel and beginning her comb-out. "Having some back trouble. I'm supposed to start an exercise class today."

"Ugh. Getting older is the pits." Donna turned her head from side to side. "Do you think I should go shorter?"

"Sure, we can do that." Parker squinted into the mirror. Was that a tinge of gray in his sideburns? *You're sure not getting any younger, Travis.* In only four years he'd hit the big 4-0. . .not that he was keeping track.

"Not Jamie Lee Curtis short, mind you. I need a little fullness around my face, don't you think?"

Parker shook off his depressing thoughts. "Now, Donna, have I ever let you walk out of here looking anything but gorgeous?"

"That's why I keep coming back." She giggled like a teenybopper. "You are quite a handsome man, you know."

The scissors slipped. Parker did a quick recovery and evened out the minor mishap before Donna could notice. He shot her an embarrassed smile through the mirror. "What would the mayor think if he knew you were flirting shamelessly with your hairdresser?"

"If I weren't already. . ." She tittered and dropped her volume. Not that it mattered with the constant chatter and the whir of blow-dryers emanating from the other cubicles. "What I mean is, any gal in town would have her socks knocked off to nab you for a husband. When are you going to find yourself a wife and settle down?"

He exhaled sharply and reached for the dryer. "Haven't met the right one, I guess."

"How do you expect to develop a lasting relationship, putting in the hours you do? And then donating your services at the assisted-living center, doing all those old ladies' hair?"

The ache in Parker's shoulder gave way to a bristle of irritation. "I love those sweet old gals."

Donna flicked a stray hair clipping off her nose. "Well, you ought to at least ask if any of them have a cute, available granddaughter—oops, at their age, better make it *great*-granddaughter."

❧

Seated on the poolside bleachers, Sailor looked from the registration forms to the aging "Doublemint Twins" bursting out of skirted fuchsia bathing suits. She'd been stunned to learn they really had starred in one of those Wrigley's gum commercials back in the '70s. "So. . .which one is Lucille and which one is Lorraine?"

"I'm Lucille."

"I'm Lorraine."

Sailor's breath whistled out. "My goodness, you *are* identical, aren't you?"

"It's easy to tell us apart once you get to know us." Lucille—or was it Lorraine?—cocked a plump hip and fluttered her sparse lashes. "I'm the cute one. My sister's the smart one."

Both burst out in gales of laughter. They pranced to the far end of the bleachers and began laying out their water aerobics gear.

Sailor groaned. This class could prove the most challenging mix of students yet. She turned her attention to the next arrivals, the three teacher friends from Birkenstock High. All reasonably fit, thank goodness, probably midfifties at most. Sailor checked them off her roster in time to welcome the new mom and the paralegal. She introduced them to the other ladies then peeked into the lobby. One more student expected, and he was already ten minutes late. Probably a no-show. Like she'd be surprised.

She let the glass door whisk shut then returned to the bleachers. Her students sat hip to hip on the first row, their expressions somewhere between eager and terrified. Maybe she should assure them she hadn't drawn and quartered anyone. . .yet. Offering a shy smile, she slid out of her sweatpants and adjusted the straps of her teal blue tank suit.

"Wel—" She cleared her throat of first-day jitters. "Welcome, everyone." She ought to be used to this by now. She always relaxed once the class got going, but those first moments facing a new group of strangers turned her insides to gelatin.

"Okay, let's get started." She collected her personal exercise equipment from the storage cabinet, along with extras for those who hadn't purchased their own. "Hop in the pool. I'll explain how to use everything once we're in the water."

With practiced ease she strode to the four-foot mark and stepped off, bouncing lightly as her toes hit bottom. The chilly water made her gasp.

The Doublemint Twins—she *must* get their names straight—tested the water with fuchsia-painted toenails.

"Oooh, that's cold!" Lorraine—or was it Lucille?—shivered and hugged herself.

"Once we get moving, it won't be so bad." Sailor motioned to the ladder. "You can ease in more gradually if you'd rather."

While the twins made their way down the ladder, huffing and complaining all the way, the other ladies put their legs over the edge and splashed themselves before sliding into the pool. Sailor began by showing them how to hold their noodles at arm's length, moving them forward and back just below the surface as they marched in place.

The door from the lobby burst open. The guy from yesterday careened around the end of the bleachers. What was his name? Travis Parker, Parker Travis, whatever. "Sorry I'm late."

Sailor pursed her lips and kept marching. Good-looking and single he might be, but she despised having her class interrupted. "It's"—*inhale*—"okay"—*exhale*. "Please get a noodle and join us. We're beginning with warm-ups and stretches."

"Noodle. Yeah, the long foam thingy." He grabbed one and tossed it into the pool then kicked black sneakers off sockless feet, tore a white T-shirt over his head, and splashed into the water next to the paralegal. "Hi. I'm Parker Travis."

"Oh, the Par Excellence stylist! I just moved to Birkenstock, and I've been meaning to make an appointment. Everyone says you're the best in town." The paralegal released one end of her noodle and stuck out her hand. "Miranda Wright."

Sailor choked on a chuckle and covered it with a cough. Seeing the name on a registration form was one thing, but hearing it aloud was even funnier. Did Miranda's parents have any clue she'd end up in a law profession?

Sailor composed herself and raised her voice. "*Quiet* warm-ups and stretching, everyone. Please save your social time for after class."

"Sorry, my bad." The hairdresser. And wearing cutoff jeans, of all things. Goose bumps rose on his pale chest beneath a tanned V that suggested he spent time outdoors in a T-shirt. A runner—of course. His muscled limbs bore the telltale look of someone who worked out but didn't take stretches seriously. No wonder his doctor had recommended Sailor's class.

Sailor slanted him an annoyed frown. "Are you aware the Y has a no-cutoffs policy?"

He apologized again. "My old suit was worn-out. Didn't think you'd appreciate the, uh, view."

With effort Sailor kept her cool through the rest of the class, despite the twins' giggling and the hairdresser's grunts and groans as they attempted various exercises.

Chandler Michaels. Chandler Michaels. Chandler Michaels.

That name would sustain her for the duration of this class. The third weekend in May and the Bards of Birkenstock Festival could not come soon enough.

❧

The water aerobics class could not end soon enough. Parker only thought he'd kept himself fit. He hadn't felt this hammered down, twisted up, and bent out of shape since third grade, when he wrapped his bicycle—and himself—around a sycamore sapling. And Andy said this would be good for his back pain? He'd be lucky if he could pry himself out of bed tomorrow morning, let alone make it through a day at the salon. Hard to believe Grams and her friends actually did this stuff several times a week—and claimed to enjoy it.

The last to trudge up the pool steps, Parker stowed his exercise equipment in the cabinet. He limped up beside Sailor as she answered some questions from those plump, giggly twins with the bad perms.

"It gets easier, right?" one of the twins asked.

"Of course." Sailor handed each woman a sheet of paper. "Here's your practice routine. Try to work in at least two or three sessions before next time, and—"

Parker eased his cramping left thigh. "You mean we're supposed to do this on our own, too?"

Sailor nailed him with her aquamarine stare. "You can't expect to reap the benefits if you only work out once a week."

"I get that, but—" Parker sucked air between his teeth. Man, one hour with this skinny little water aerobics teacher and he felt like a bumbling oaf.

One of the twins released a chirpy laugh. "Honey, if two old biddies like us can do this, you sure can. Let's go shower, Lucille. We can have the early bird special at Audra's Café and still be home in time for *Wheel of Fortune*."

The twins gave him an eyeful of their fuchsia-clad rumps as they waddled toward the ladies' dressing room. He should have given them his card and offered to do something about those horrible perms.

Sailor's shoulders lifted in an exaggerated sigh. She pressed one of the practice sheets into his hand. "You'll get it. Just. . .try not to be late next time. And get some trunks."

"Guess I didn't make a very good first impression on the teacher." He stared at the page, a series of photographs with brief descriptions. Jogging in place. Arm extensions. Side-to-side lunges. Maybe Grams could give him some pointers.

"Don't be so hard on yourself. This was only your first class." With the grace of a ballerina, Sailor glided across the deck and bent from the waist to gather up her gear.

Parker found himself staring at the sleek curve of her profile, the muscle definition in those skinny arms, the wet tangle of her ponytail curling across one shoulder.

Whoa, fella! He gave himself a mental shake. Donna DuPont had done a fine job of reminding him he was *way* over the hill already. This little thing was probably fresh out of high school, if that. There were laws.

She carried her gear to the storage cabinet then looked his way in surprise. "Did you have more questions?"

Parker rubbed his chin. "I, uh. . ."

"I'd be happy to talk more on the way out, but I have another commitment this evening."

"Don't let me hold you up." Parker slid into his shoes and edged toward the door. "Same time next week?"

"Every Tuesday at four o'clock." She gave an exhausted moan. "For seven more weeks."

❧

"Seven more weeks of the Douglas twins?" Kathy draped an arm around Sailor's shoulders. "I've been putting up with their screechy voices in church choir for two years now. Oh, how I pity you!"

"Douglas, Doublemint. Lorraine, Lucille. I never did get their names right." Sailor sank into one of the empty chairs around the massive table in the library conference room. "So are we early or what?"

"The rest of the committee usually drags in by ten after seven." Kathy began distributing notepads and pens around the table. "And Donna DuPont, the chair, just got back from vacationing in Hawaii, so she's probably still on aloha time."

"Hawaii. Sounds wonderful." Sailor slid deeper into the padded seat and folded her hands across her purple sweater. "Someday I'm going to take a vacation. A real one."

"You're already a world traveler. India, Guyana, Kenya. . . The farthest I've been outside Birkenstock is the librarians' convention in San Diego last year."

"Visiting my missionary parents every few years doesn't exactly constitute a vacation." Sailor's gaze settled upon an easel displaying a poster-size print of Chandler Michaels's latest book cover. Her heart faltered. "When I'm Mrs. Chandler Michaels, I'll invite you to my vacation villa on the Riviera. You can stay as long as you like."

Coming around the table, Kathy whacked her on the head with a notepad. "When are you going to pull your nose out of those romance novels and get serious about a real guy? Besides, how do you know Chandler isn't married with ten kids?"

"His bio says he lives in a New York apartment with his Siamese cat. No mention of a wife or kids."

"But if he keeps his private life private. . ."

"I'm reading between the lines." *And hoping.* Maybe it was a silly schoolgirl fantasy, but she couldn't stop herself from dreaming.

Two more committee members drifted in, and Sailor pulled herself erect. A twinge of nerves churned the remains of the tofu stir-fry she'd made for her and Uncle Ed's supper. Poor guy, she'd turn him into a healthy eater if it took the rest of his life.

"Hello, I don't believe we've met." An elderly gentleman with a shock of white hair took the chair next to hers. The mixed aromas of coffee and wintergreen tickled her nose. "Allan Biltmore, at your service."

Oh yes, the retired English teacher. Sailor had missed his class by one year. "Sailor Kern. I'm Kathy's friend." Except right now she wanted to strangle Kathy. How had she ever let her friend talk her into joining the Bards of Birkenstock committee?

Ba-ding. Chandler Michaels, that's how.

A few more committee members arrived, taking seats around the table. They took turns introducing themselves, but Sailor knew she'd never keep them all straight. Her brain felt like a washing machine on spin cycle, and the meeting hadn't even started yet.

As Kathy predicted, Donna DuPont didn't grace them with her presence until nearly seven thirty. The platinum blond mayor's wife breezed to the head of the table, a Hawaiian-print muumuu swirling around her hips. "Sorry, sorry, sorry to keep you all waiting. I see Kathy's been playing hostess. Thanks for getting the room ready, dear."

Kathy nudged Sailor's chair and slipped her a Cheshire cat smile. "My pleasure, Donna. How was Hawaii?"

"Marvelous!" She took her seat then spent the next ten minutes describing the sights, smells, and sounds of Maui, until Allan Biltmore interrupted her with a loud *ahem* and suggested they get on with the meeting.

At least with everyone else present, Sailor could blend into the background. She tuned out the conversation and doodled on her notepad until Donna announced the next item on the agenda: Chandler Michaels's arrival in Birkenstock.

"It's confirmed, ladies and gentlemen, and I am *so* excited." Donna stood, as if to give her next words even more import. "Chandler will be flying in on the Tuesday before the festival, so we'll have him in town for five glorious days!"

Applause and cheers sounded around the table. Goose bumps traveled Sailor's limbs beneath her sweater and jeans.

"Some of you already know that Chandler is actually Birkenstock's own Charles Michalicek." Donna paused for a couple of surprised gasps. "Yes, it's true. And he's so excited for the chance to visit his hometown again. However, his family no longer lives in the area, so Allan has graciously offered to host

Chandler in his home, which will save the committee some hotel expenses."

More applause and nods of approval. "And now I'll turn this portion of the discussion over to Kathy Richmond, who is heading up the Chandler Michaels welcome-committee task force." Donna extended her hand toward Kathy and sat down.

Kathy gave Sailor a quick wink as she scooted closer to the table. "Actually, the task force is just two of us at this point. My friend Sailor here is a huge fan of Chandler's, so she's agreed to help coordinate his schedule while he's in town."

Heat slithered up Sailor's neck. She could feel everyone's gaze shifting in her direction. Arms crossed over her midsection, she eased her chair backward a quarter inch and kept her eyes lowered.

Kathy flipped through a folder of notes. "I'm still waiting for a return phone call from Chandler's assistant, a Mr. Easley, but I assume he'll want as much PR exposure as possible." She itemized preliminary ideas for Chandler's visit—book signings, dinners, tickets to see his favorite Branson entertainer, the festival parade through downtown Birkenstock.

"Wonderful ideas, Kathy. It sounds like you have it all under control. And welcome to our committee, Sailor." Donna checked off another item on her agenda. "That about wraps up our business for tonight. Do I hear a motion to adjourn?"

❧

Sailor slumped into the living room and sagged against the back of Uncle Ed's recliner. While teaching a water aerobics class usually energized her—at least until today's group showed up—meetings of any kind drained the life out of her.

"Late night, eh?" Uncle Ed slid a bookmark into his John Adams biography and laid the book on the end table. "Your parents called."

Disappointment blanketed Sailor's shoulders. She and her parents e-mailed regularly, but with their crazy schedules and the time difference, she hadn't talked to them in over a month. She trudged to the sofa and sank down. "Rats. Sorry I missed them. How are they?"

"Your dad's knee-deep in another Bible translation, and your mom is heading out to the wilds tomorrow to set up a health clinic." He clucked his tongue. "Why they want to burn themselves out trying to save folks in some third-world country is beyond me."

"They're not burning themselves out, Uncle Ed. They're serving God."

"Like I said, burning themselves out." A look of loneliness darkened his eyes. He sighed and reached for his book.

Sailor shook her head. Poor Uncle Ed hadn't been the same since Aunt Trina died of a heart attack eighteen years ago, the day after Christmas the year Sailor turned fifteen. Uncle Ed blamed Aunt Trina's death on the stress of cooking for the 172 needy and homeless folks who signed up for the Mission Hills Bible Church Christmas dinner. He never went to church again, and his mental state began a slow but steady decline. Staying with her uncle might not be the greatest thing for her already limited social life, but Sailor didn't have the heart to leave him to fend for himself.

The mantel clock chimed nine forty-five. Sailor heaved herself off the sofa. "I'm heading to bed. Good night, Uncle Ed." She patted his shoulder, but his only response was a grunt.

Without turning on the light, she sank onto the edge of her bed. Truth be told, she wasn't all that much closer to God than her uncle. She still believed, but God seemed even farther away than her missionary parents in that tiny Kenyan settlement.

When had it started, this sense of aloneness? Probably the year she entered second grade and her parents decided to leave her in the States. Already past forty when Sailor was born, Ogden and Hazel Kern weren't exactly kid people anyway. They'd hoped she'd have a better life with Uncle Ed and Aunt Trina, who desperately wanted children but had none of their own.

Then Aunt Trina died. Sailor's parents arranged a hasty three-month furlough but then returned to the field, leaving Sailor to manage a grieving man's household while surviving high school. Without the guidance of church friends Josh and Deb Fanning—almost like second parents—she might not have made it. As Uncle Ed retreated into his biographies and woodworking, Sailor found solace in romance novels and comfort food. She must have put on seventy pounds between her freshman year and graduation. Her parents, returning home for the big event after nearly three years of seeing their daughter only in photographs, hardly recognized her.

Framed by the light from the hallway, Sailor glimpsed her dim reflection in the dresser mirror—a shadow of her former self, literally. It took a brush with borderline diabetes in college before she got serious about losing weight. Her doctor's threats, combined with encouragement from Josh and Deb, turned her onto healthy eating and exercise. She slimmed down, shaped up, and before she knew it, the Y had promoted her from part-time receptionist to water aerobics and swimming instructor.

But even after dropping sixty-five pounds and getting into the best shape of her life, Sailor still had trouble thinking of herself as pretty. Plain, boring Sailor Kern, the missionaries' kid. Whatever possessed her to imagine she could turn the head of someone like Chandler Michaels?

Chapter 3

The following Tuesday Parker met his grandmother in the assisted-living center's small two-station salon. She beamed up at him from her motorized wheelchair. "Thanks for making a special trip. Yesterday was the only day Dr. Mendoza could work me in for my checkup." She fluffed her white curls and studied her reflection. "Do you think it's time for another perm yet?"

Parker tugged on a soft, silvery lock. "Couple more weeks maybe. You've still got a lot of body."

Grams chuckled. "You're the expert. I do think it's getting a bit long around the ears, though."

"Let's get you shampooed, and I'll have you trimmed up in no time." Parker helped her to the shampoo bowl.

Finishing up, he reached for a dry towel on the shelf above the sink. Pain arced across his shoulder blades. "Yow!"

"Parker, are you all right?" Grams sat forward, her old bones creaking.

"Just a cramp." Parker shook off the twinge before he worried his grandmother any further. Suffering from rheumatoid arthritis, she had enough problems of her own.

"Just a cramp indeed." Grams gripped the arms of the chair and skewered Parker with her steely blue gaze. "You've been moaning about your sore back for weeks. Isn't the water aerobics helping?"

"Hard to tell yet. I've only had one class." Parker helped Grams across the small space to the styling chair then patted her hair with the towel. He tried not to let the pain show in his face, but one glimpse in the mirror and he knew he couldn't fool anyone.

Grams absently massaged the gnarled knuckles of one hand. "I can't even imagine how much worse off I'd be if not for that sweet little instructor. I've been taking her classes for five years now, and she's always so patient and understanding."

Parker stifled a grimace as he combed up sections of his grandmother's wet curls and reshaped her style with precision snips. Sweet little instructor, huh? How about a ninety-five-pound Ivan the Terrible? The petite Miss Kern would not be pleased to know he'd opted to run and do weights rather than practice his pool exercises.

He flicked on the blow-dryer and coaxed strands of Grams's hair around a ceramic styling brush. The slick, soothing feel of each curl beneath his fingers drew his thoughts away from the ever-present ache between his shoulder blades. As he worked, a snippet of Grams's earlier remarks resurfaced. He paused and switched off the dryer. "She's been teaching five years already? What'd she do, start in kindergarten?"

Grams shot him a puzzled glance through the mirror. "Don't be silly. She has a college degree in exercise therapy from Missouri State."

He was now officially impressed. He sectioned off a lock of hair and wrapped it around the brush. "Well, she doesn't look a day over sixteen. That's all I can say."

❧

"Sailor Kern, you disgust me." Kathy drizzled ketchup on the mound of french fries next to her double-deluxe bacon burger. "You never let a gram of saturated fat slip past your lips, you're skinny as a model, and you don't look like you've aged a day since college."

Sailor flaked off a bite of broiled salmon topping her Asian salad, one of her favorites when she met Kathy for lunch at Audra's Café. "You know very well what I looked like my first year at MO State. Some days I'd kill for a greasy burger. But I love being healthy too much to risk it."

"What—eating the burger or getting nailed for murder?"

Laughing, Sailor flicked a spinach leaf across the table. "One of these days I'll convince you to try my class. I've incorporated a nutrition segment into my continuing series."

"No thank you. In the official Kathy Richmond dictionary, *nutrition* is a four-letter word." Kathy dabbed a dribble of hamburger juice off her chin. "Psyched for another class with the Douglas twins?"

Sailor slumped. "Why'd you have to remind me?"

"A slice of Audra's homemade turtle cheesecake would sure help ease the pain." Kathy signaled their server. "Want me to order one for you?"

"I'm almost desperate enough to be tempted, but. . ." Sailor sat back and patted her abdomen. "Two words: *Chandler Michaels*."

"Puleeeze, you are not still harboring romantic notions about the guy?"

When Sailor didn't answer right away, Kathy made a growling noise and hammered the table with her fists. "Sailor, honey, Chandler Michaels is a fantasy. Find yourself a nice, stable, hometown guy. Somebody who's proud enough of his Birkenstock roots not to run off to the big city and change his name."

Sailor's chest tightened. "I'm thirty-two years old, and I have yet to meet one eligible guy who'd even look at me twice."

"Come on, Sailor. . ."

"No, it's true." An image of the raven-haired beauty gracing the cover of Chandler's latest novel filled her mind. She whispered a sigh and stared at a soggy lettuce leaf at the bottom of her salad plate. "Maybe you should get someone else for the committee. I don't think I'm the right person after all."

Kathy poked Sailor's arm with the tines of her fork. "You stop talking like that right now. There's no one I'd rather have working with me."

"I know, but—"

"I know how much you admire Chandler. But it kills me to see you mooning over an aging literary snob, when I'm certain God has someone really, really special in mind for you."

Sailor huffed. "Well, He's sure taking His own sweet time." Her shoulders relaxed, and a shy grin crept across her face. "But I admit, I've let myself get a little too starry-eyed over the idea of meeting Chandler."

"He will be one lucky guy having you squire him around town." Kathy finished off the last of her burger. "And if he turns out to be totally cool and even a tenth as charming as his story heroes, I'll be incredibly jealous."

Audra, the café owner, arrived at their booth to personally deliver Kathy's turtle cheesecake. "I heard Chandler Michaels is coming to town for the book festival." She flipped her auburn pageboy off her shoulder. "Back when he was just plain 'Chuck,' he gave me my first kiss. Any chance you can wrangle me a date with him?"

Kathy shrank back, one hand to her chest. "Why, Audra, aren't you and Hank celebrating an anniversary soon?"

"Number twenty-seven." Audra tipped her head back and laughed. "But I'm dying to see how the years have changed Chuck. I've already scheduled my hair appointment at Par Excellence for that week. Gotta look my best for the gala. I'm catering, you know."

Sailor fingered the end of her ponytail. Par Excellence—the logo on her new student's shirt. "Audra, do you know the guy who works there—Travis something?"

"Parker Travis. He's the *best*." She smoothed the curve of her pageboy. "Wouldn't let anyone else lay a hand on these tresses."

Kathy nudged Sailor's ankle with her toe. "How do you know Parker?"

"He's in my water aerobics class that just started."

"*He's* the weirdo guy you were telling me about—the one who showed up late and then griped for the entire hour?" Kathy guffawed. "Why didn't you tell me?"

"Can I help it I have a problem with names?" Sailor crossed her arms. "So what's the big deal?"

Kathy shared a look with Audra. "Good grief, Sailor. Parker Travis is probably *the* most eligible bachelor in Birkenstock."

Audra scooted onto the seat next to Kathy and clicked her enameled fake nails on the tabletop. "Not to mention he's one marvelous hairstylist."

"Well, he's a lousy student." Sailor looped her arm through the strap of her tan microfiber ergonomic purse and edged out of the booth. "I'll let you two dish the hairdresser. I've got to get back to the Y."

❧

In the Willow Tree parking lot, Parker dropped his styling kit onto the backseat of his Camry then collapsed behind the wheel and gave his shoulder a rub before starting the engine. Just enough time to run home and change into his new swim trunks before heading to the Y.

That was the plan anyway. Now, as he stood before his closet mirror, he took one look at himself in the psychedelic orange fabric and decided to risk Miss Kern's ire one more week with his faded cutoffs. After he explained the local department store was a little late stocking its spring line of bathing suits and was still selling off last year's leftovers, maybe she'd cut him some slack.

The pool area stood empty except for the lifeguard and two guys doing the backstroke in the lap lanes. Sailor Kern was nowhere in sight. He gathered a set of exercise gear from the tall cabinet and chose a bright yellow noodle from the storage bin. In the water he turned toward the windows overlooking the jogging trail and tried a few stretching and warm-up exercises. At least now he could truthfully say he'd practiced.

Between the hushed water sounds and the pleasant view, Parker found his shoulders relaxing into the stretches. His breathing deepened. His heart rate steadied.

"Nice. Very nice."

Parker jerked his head around. The voice may have been gentle, but the effect on his psyche—and his achy shoulders—was anything but. He shifted to face his petite instructor. "Just warming up."

"So I see." Holding an aqua blue noodle, Sailor descended into the pool as softly as a feather on a spring breeze. Arms draped across the noodle, she drew her knees up and frowned. "Didn't I mention the Y's policy about cutoffs?"

Parker wiggled an eyebrow. "If you saw the only trunks Mabry's had in my size, you'd be thanking me for wearing the cutoffs."

The corner of her mouth turned up in the beginnings of a smile, but she quickly looked away. Embarrassed? Shy? Funny how she masterfully took control of a class of complaining adults, yet every other time he saw her, she conveyed a bashful vulnerability. Confident one moment, timid the next. . . He found it hard to believe she wasn't as youthful as she appeared.

Maybe the perennial haze shrouding the pool had something to do with it. The misty air would certainly mask a crow's-foot or two. But when he signed up for the class last week, he'd seen her in the full, harsh glow of the lobby lights. Nope, not a wrinkle or crow's-foot in sight.

He stretched his legs behind him and draped his arms over the noodle. "I heard you've been teaching classes here for several years."

"Close to ten, I guess." That shy smile again.

Parker tried to keep his face expressionless while he did the mental arithmetic. Eighteen when she finished high school, at least twenty-two out of college, then another ten years teaching for the Y. So. . .thirty-something?

No way! An enigma. Sailor Kern was definitely an enigma.

She stretched from side to side with the elegance of a water nymph. He attempted a few nonchalant lunges with the grace of a hippopotamus.

Her barely disguised smirk did nothing for his ego. "How's your back this week? Any improvement?"

He gave a noncommittal grunt.

"It'll come. Here, try this." She showed him how to adjust his stance to increase the stretch.

He felt the release in his tender back muscle and huffed out a long, slow breath. "Wow, that helped. I do the ladies' hair over at Willow Tree Assisted-Living Center. They all rave about you, in case you didn't know it."

Sailor's face brightened. "I really look forward to those classes."

As opposed to this one, judging from the wistful look in her eyes. She checked her watch then shifted a nervous glance toward the door.

He was about to ask how she got started teaching water aerobics when giggles and high-pitched voices announced the arrival of the Douglas twins. Sailor hoisted herself out of the pool to greet them, the phoniest smile he'd ever seen plastered across her face. After last week he felt pretty certain she couldn't be *that* glad to see the noisy duo. Nope, he suspected this was all about avoiding further conversation with him.

Within a few minutes the other students filtered in, and by the time everyone got situated in the water, Sailor had her confident instructor persona firmly in place. She hardly glanced in Parker's direction for the duration of the class.

And he couldn't take his eyes off her.

❧

Sailor stuffed the last neon-colored noodle into the storage bin and slammed the lid shut. Though Parker Travis and the rest of her class had left ten minutes ago, she could still feel the sinewy hairstylist's penetrating stare. Time for a long, hard lap swim.

After eight laps of churning up the water with her freestyle, she switched to breaststroke, stretching her limbs and enjoying the easy glide. When she reached the wall at the deep end, she looked up to see her friend Josh Fanning, the silver-haired swim-team coach, grinning down at her.

"Too bad you're not in high school anymore. We could sure use you on the team."

"In high school you wouldn't have wanted me on the team." In one smooth move Sailor pushed out of the water and onto the deck. She scraped both palms along her slicked-back hair and wrung out her ponytail, water droplets cascading across her shoulders. "Remember when you first gave me swimming lessons? I could barely make it half a length without choking."

"Ah yes. Fishing you out of the pool, drying your tears—"

"Throwing me back in, making me swim another lap." Sailor smirked. "If you hadn't stayed on my case about exercise, plus Deb's insistence on healthy eating, I hate to think where I'd be today."

"How many times do I have to tell you? Deb and I love you like one of our own kids." Josh knelt to dip his goggles in the pool then tugged them on and pressed them into his eye sockets. He stepped off the edge and plunged deep before bobbing to the surface and treading water. "Almost forgot. Deb told me to invite you over for dinner one night this week. When's good for you?"

"Any night but tonight. I've got a"—Sailor cringed—"a meeting."

"A meeting? You?" Josh moved his goggles up to his forehead and squinted at her. "Can't be anything at the Y, or I'd know about it. What have you gotten yourself into, young lady?"

"Promise you won't laugh?" She dangled her feet in the water while she told him about the Bards of Birkenstock committee and Chandler Michaels's expected arrival. "I had no idea he grew up here. His real name is Chuck. . . Chuck. . .something Eastern European, I think."

"Not Chuck Michalicek?"

"That's it. Did you know him?"

"Oh yeah." Josh hooked one tanned arm over the coping. A funny smile quirked his lips. "So ol' Chuck Michalicek is coming back to Birkenstock. He was a couple years behind me in school. Biggest cutup on the swim team. Late for practice, smoked in the locker room. Loved playing practical jokes, especially on the girls." Josh chuckled. "Had us guys convinced he'd hidden a camera in the girls' dressing room. After two weeks of the girls complaining and the guys begging Chuck to show him the pictures, he finally admitted it was a hoax."

Sailor ignored the prickles climbing up her spine. "I'm sure he's matured since then."

"One can only hope." Josh settled his goggles into place again and pushed off the wall in a powerful butterfly stroke.

Sailor watched in admiration for a few minutes before grabbing her towel and heading to the dressing room. Clad in jeans and a forest green pullover, she returned to her desk and retrieved her purse from the bottom drawer. Beneath it she found the copy of *Love's Sweet Song.* She turned it over and gazed at the photo of Chandler Michaels. If a trace remained of the "bad boy" Josh had described, she couldn't see it. . .unless it shone in that mischievous sparkle behind his enticing baby blues.

Man, he was handsome! Sailor's heart did a deep *ker-thump* that made her catch her breath. So what if he was several years older? What she wouldn't give to have Chandler Michaels turn those dreamy eyes her way!

And the likelihood of that? Slim to none. Sailor flicked the end of her damp ponytail off her shoulder. Looking like a drowned rat sure didn't increase her odds. She sank onto her steno chair, her hopes evaporating once again.

Then her glance fell upon the water aerobics class roster, and the name *Parker Travis* jumped out at her. Everyone claimed he was the best hairstylist in town. Maybe it was time she scheduled an appointment.

Chapter 4

Mmm, smells good." Parker planted a hello kiss on his mother's cheek before lifting the lid off the slow cooker. When Mom phoned yesterday with a last-minute plea for his flute-playing talents then bribed him with an early lunch of his favorite beef Stroganoff, how could he refuse? Fortunately his Saturday-afternoon clients were willing to reschedule or see one of the other stylists.

His mother slapped his hand. "Careful, you're letting the heat out."

"Picky, picky." He let the glass lid drop into place. "Can I do anything?"

"You can see if Grams has any last-minute tips. She's in the den, watching the video of last Saturday's show."

"I can't believe I let you talk me into this." A part-time dental hygienist, Mom also sang backup for Frankie Verona on weekends at the legendary jazz singer's Branson theater. Parker had been invited to jam with Frankie's band a few times when he'd gone down to watch his mom at rehearsals, so when Frankie's regular flutist came down with the stomach flu following last night's show, Mom had volunteered Parker as a convenient substitute for the Saturday matinee and evening performances.

She set a salad bowl on the counter and unscrewed the cap from a bottle of Caesar dressing. "What's this your grandmother tells me about your taking water aerobics?"

"Guess I forgot to mention it." Parker plucked at a strand of his mother's chestnut hair. "Your roots are showing. Want to come in next week for a touch-up?"

"Can't. I traded my day off with Missy. She has another prenatal appointment." His mother carried the salad bowl to the table. "And changing the subject will not get me off your case. Why didn't you tell me about the exercise class?"

Parker sank onto a chair. "I just. . .feel kind of weird about it."

"Because water aerobics is not—*ahem*—macho?" His mother fussed with a plaid placemat. "So you're no Marc Bulger. You don't have to play pro football for the St. Louis Rams to be considered manly."

He looked askance toward the coatrack by the back door. A dry cleaner's bag covered the black leather jeans and silver satin shirt his mother had borrowed from the ailing flutist, who—also conveniently—was close to Parker in size. "Dressing like a magician's assistant doesn't exactly help."

"Parker Travis, when have you ever cared what other people thought?"

He combed his fingers through his hair. When *had* he started caring how others perceived his masculinity? Certainly not in high school as the only male flutist in the marching band. He got teased plenty back then, but it rolled off his back like shampoo suds sliding down the drain. Manliness, in his mind, had more to do with strength of character, integrity, honoring your responsibilities. Secure in his identity as a child of God, he'd scoffed at his detractors and went on to pursue the career he felt called to.

True, there were those in the church who liked to quote Proverbs 31:30 to him, especially the line, "Charm is deceptive, and beauty is fleeting." Or the passage in 1 Peter addressed to women: "Your beauty should not come from outward adornment, such as elaborate hairstyles and the wearing of gold jewelry or fine clothes. Rather, it should be that of your inner self, the unfading beauty of a gentle and quiet spirit, which is of great worth in God's sight."

Personally Parker took great joy in helping a woman's outer beauty reflect the beauty he saw inside, and he'd always had the sense that God approved. The Lord sure didn't skimp on beauty in scripture—beauty for ashes, the beautiful feet of the messenger upon the mountain, the beauty of Queen Esther, Jerusalem's Beautiful Gate. . . .

The soft hum of a motor preceded Grams's entrance. One of the most beautiful women in Parker's life, she coasted her motorized wheelchair to a stop next to his elbow. Gnarled fingers reached up to pat his arm. "What's got my boy looking so glum? Did that sweet little gal from the Y turn you down?"

"Sweet little gal?" Parker's mom plopped a stack of plates on the table and skewered him with her stare. "What else haven't you told me?"

Parker angled his grandmother a warning glance. "Nothing. Really."

Grams shot him a feisty look of her own. "Parker Travis, how do you ever expect to find the right girl if you refuse to ask anyone out?"

Mom turned to Grams. "Who is it? Someone from his exercise class?"

"The instructor." Grams nodded. "The same young lady my Willow Tree friends and I take from."

"Sailor Kern?" His mother's eyes lit up. "Why, Parker—"

"Mom!" He rose and marched to the other side of the table. Anything to put space between him and his meddling, matchmaking matrons.

His grinning mother planted her knuckles on the table and leaned toward him. "What's keeping you from asking her out? She's such a nice girl."

Mom would only scoff if he confessed how inept he felt in the romance department. Donna DuPont was right—between his salon work, volunteering, and making sure he was around whenever Mom or Grams needed anything, he'd kept himself too busy to even think about a relationship.

He crossed his arms. "She's nice, all right, if you go for the drill-sergeant type."

"That little bit of a thing? She's one of Dr. Simpson's patients. I've cleaned her teeth a few times, and she's as sweet as can be. And so pretty, too. I've always admired her eyes, the color of polished turquoise."

Just listening to his mother describe Sailor made his insides go all mushy. He circled the table and grabbed the water glasses Mom had left sitting on the counter. "Let's eat. We don't want to be late for the preshow rehearsal."

❧

"Dibs on the remote."

"No fair! I had it first."

"Hey, it's my turn. I was going to play my new video game."

Laughing at the squabbling Fanning boys, Sailor ducked in time to avoid a badly tossed sofa pillow. Whenever Josh and Deb's five sons were all home at once, the place became a madhouse. Sailor didn't mind, though. This was one crowd scene that didn't make her want to hide under her bed.

"Boys!" Deb stood in the kitchen doorway, carrot-colored curls framing her warning glare. "You break your dad's new HDTV, and you'll be mowing lawns for the next ten years."

The "boys"—a brawny high schooler, three handsome college men, and a newlywed barely back from his honeymoon—turned to their mother with a collective groan. Tom, the newlywed, made an exaggerated display of fluffing the pillow and placing it just so on the sofa. Under his breath he muttered, "Party pooper."

Deb merely rolled her eyes and motioned Sailor out of the line of fire. "Come keep us girls company in the kitchen. I need your opinion on a new quinoa recipe."

"I love that stuff—so versatile." Sailor dodged number two son Ken's feigned bout of stomach upset. The boys didn't share their mother's penchant for health food.

In the kitchen Sailor joined Jeannie, Tom's perky bride, at the breakfast bar, where Deb had set out forks next to a savory sampling of curried quinoa.

Sailor tasted a bite and grinned her appreciation. "Yum. Make sure you give me the recipe."

Jeannie sampled a forkful, but the look on her pixie-shaped face suggested the dish wasn't exactly the most delicious thing she'd ever tasted. "Interesting mix of flavors."

"It's an acquired taste, but really healthy." Sailor helped herself to another bite. "How long are you and Tom in town, Jeannie?"

"Just for the weekend." Jeannie popped the top on a diet soda. "We both have to be back at work in KC on Monday morning."

The low rumble of the garage door sent a vibration through the floor beneath Sailor's feet. Seconds later Josh stepped into the kitchen. "Hello, ladies." He buzzed a kiss across Deb's lips before whipping an envelope from his back pocket. "Guess what I have in my hot little hands."

Deb fingered her chin. "The deed to our own private island in the Caribbean? The title to a new Mercedes?"

Josh snickered as he made a show of lifting the envelope flap. "Nope, what I have here is our evening's entertainment—four tickets to the Frankie Verona show tonight in Branson."

"Be still, my heart!" Deb faked a swoon and landed in Josh's arms.

Jeannie arched an eyebrow. "Who's Frankie Verona?"

"You've never heard of Frankie Verona, jazz singer extraordinaire?" Sailor glanced around the kitchen in search of one of the CD cases Deb usually left lying around. She spotted one on the verdigris baker's rack and handed it to Jeannie. "Frankie's 'Moonlight over Missouri' is Josh and Deb's favorite song."

Deb started humming the tune, and Josh swept her into an impromptu waltz around the kitchen. "I can't believe it," Deb said. "We're seeing Frankie tonight? How'd you manage that?"

"A gift from an anonymous Y patron, that's all I know. I found the envelope on my desk after my swim classes." Josh lowered Deb into a dip. "Eight o'clock show, front-row seats. Now we just have to decide who gets to go with us."

"Go where?" Tom ambled into the kitchen. "And what's with the *Dancing with the Stars* routine?"

Sailor finished off the sample plate of curried quinoa and licked her lips. "Your dad got tickets to the Frankie Verona show. You and Jeannie should go with them." She'd keep it to herself that the tickets had actually been left for her. A courier had delivered them to the Y around eleven that morning but refused to reveal the benefactor. Sailor guessed it had to be one of her students, but knowing how much Josh and Deb loved Frankie, she decided they'd enjoy the tickets even more than she.

Jeannie snuggled under her husband's arm and stole a kiss. "Sounds like fun, but tonight's my friend's baby shower, remember? That's why Tom and I are in town."

"Oh, right." Deb disentangled herself from Josh's embrace. "Then who can we share the other two tickets with?"

Tom swiped a swig of Jeannie's diet soda. "You can still take me. I'm sure not going to any ol' baby shower."

"Great, but that leaves one more." Josh fanned out the tickets and wiggled an eyebrow in Sailor's direction. "Doing anything tonight, Miss Kern?"

❧

Sailor made a quick trip home to change, and an hour later the Fannings picked her up for the drive to Branson. As she followed Josh and Deb down the aisle to their theater seats, she stifled a delighted shiver. She hadn't expected her secret gift would garner an invitation to attend with them. The Fannings had brought her to a Frankie Verona show for her eighteenth birthday, and she and her friend Kathy enjoyed the occasional weekend getaway to see other Branson performers. Andy Williams, the Lennon Sisters, Dolly Parton's Dixie Stampede—sometimes Sailor couldn't believe she lived only a few miles up the highway from so many classic entertainers.

Tonight, however, would be her first time to experience the up-close-and-personal thrill of a front-row seat. Faux starlight twinkled in the arched blue ceiling. A simulated harvest moon shimmered above the maroon velvet stage curtain. The hivelike hum of anticipation grew louder as the theater filled for the eight o'clock show.

A timpani fanfare silenced the auditorium, and an announcer's voice reverberated overhead: "Ladies and gentlemen, welcome to Frankie Verona's Moonlight over Missouri Theater!"

The lights went down, the curtain rose, and a live stage band picked up the strains of Frankie's theme song. Three ladies in sequined ankle-length gowns swayed in unison as they harmonized to the opening lines. Then Frankie Verona himself strode onstage in a gem-encrusted tux, his ink black hair slicked into a pompadour. The audience applauded and cheered, its enthusiasm sweeping Sailor along until she found herself clapping so hard her palms stung.

It didn't matter that sitting this close she could see every line and wrinkle in the aging entertainer's face. Frankie remained the consummate performer, his voice as strong and resonant as on Josh and Deb's CDs. The syncopated rhythm and reflected glow from the stage lights wrapped around Sailor, filling her, lifting her, making her feel as though Frankie sang only to her.

When the opening number came to an end, she finally found a full breath. She sank into her seat cushion and sighed.

"Isn't he incredible?" Deb squeezed her hand.

Sailor squeezed back. "Amazing! Thanks for bringing me."

"Good evening, Missouri lovers!" Frankie stepped to the front of the stage, so close that Sailor could almost look up his nostrils. His tux sparkled under red, blue, and amber spotlights. "So glad you could join me tonight. Let me introduce my wonderful singers and musicians. Singing lead soprano, the lovely Laura Travis."

A statuesque woman took one step forward and bowed slightly from the waist, the spotlight bringing out red highlights in her upswept hair. If not for the fancy dress and stage makeup. . .

Sailor grabbed Deb's arm. "Oh my goodness, that's my dental hygienist!"

"From Dr. Simpson's office—you're right." Deb elbowed Josh. "Did you know she sang?"

Sailor lost Josh's response to a surge of applause. She missed the names of the other two backup singers and strained to catch Frankie's introduction of the musicians, beginning with the drummer, bass guitarist, keyboard player, saxophonist, and finally—Sailor's eyes popped open. She hardly recognized the man in black leather jeans and a silver satin shirt with softly billowing sleeves. Ash brown hair curled over his ears and shirt collar. A boyish grin lit his face when he stepped forward to take his bow.

The gray green gaze met Sailor's, and her stomach plummeted to her toes.

❧

"And last but not least, Parker Travis on flute. My special thanks to Parker for stepping in at the last minute after our regular flutist became ill. And did I mention the lovely Laura is his gorgeous and talented mom?"

Parker tore his gaze from the stunned face of the girl in the front row and hoped his own surprise didn't show. Sailor Kern, here tonight? *Look, Lord, I know I've been avoiding the whole boy-meets-girl thing. You trying to tell me something here?*

Gathering his wits, he acknowledged the applause with a nod and a quick kiss on his mother's cheek. Before returning to his position, he cast a nervous grin toward the wings, where Grams watched from a plush recliner. A flutist in a Branson show band herself before rheumatoid arthritis destroyed her fingers, she never missed her daughter's performances if she could help it.

Parker's gut clenched. If he ever found out Grams had anything to do with Sailor Kern showing up in the audience, they'd have to have a serious talk about boundaries.

Somehow he made it through the next couple of numbers but only with the firm resolve not to lower his glance to the first row, center section. Unfortunately his eyes wouldn't cooperate. Halfway through "Love Me Baby" he glimpsed the sharp-looking guy sitting next to Sailor, and the way they laughed and tilted their heads together gave every indication they were more than casual acquaintances.

Way more.

He had no right to be this bothered that his pretty little water aerobics instructor had a date. All he knew was that Sailor Kern evoked something inside him that he'd never allowed himself to feel before, and he had no clue what to do with it.

Two hours later, when the curtain closed after a couple of encores and their final bows, his breath whooshed out in relief. Playing for friends and family at church services was one thing. Performing onstage with a jazz legend while dealing with an unexpected attraction to a girl who clearly had eyes for someone else. . . *Lord, help!*

His mother grabbed his elbow as he ran the cleaning cloth through a section of his flute. "Do that later. Frankie's waiting for us."

"For what?"

Mom gave him one of her get-your-act-together looks. "You know—time to mingle with the audience and sign autographs."

"I'm only a sub. Nobody's here to see me." Anyway, if he stalled backstage long enough, maybe Sailor and her date would be long gone.

"Oh, just come on. Bask in the glory."

Following his mother out front, he spotted Sailor and her guy with an older couple, all surrounding Frankie while he chatted with them and signed their programs.

Frankie waved a hand, his gold rings flashing. "Laura, Parker, come say hello to these nice folks. They say they know you."

The tall woman with the carrottop extended her hand to Parker's mother. "Hi, Laura! Deb Fanning. You cleaned my teeth once when I couldn't get an appointment with my regular dentist. If I had any idea you sang with Frankie, I'd have been bugging you for tickets."

Parker's mother bumped shoulders with Mrs. Fanning and gave a meaningful smile. "Exactly why I don't make a big deal of it."

"Oops, good point." Mrs. Fanning cast a smile in Parker's direction. "So this handsome flute player is your son. Our friend Sailor tells me he's also in her water aerobics class."

"Sailor, how *wonderful* to see you here!" Parker's mom seized Sailor's hand as if greeting a long-lost relative. "My, my, it's one coincidence after another."

Parker hooked his thumbs in his back pockets. "No kidding."

"Just like old home week, eh?" Frankie Verona handed back their programs and excused himself to mingle with the other audience members.

The silver-haired Mr. Fanning took a half step back. "Well, we shouldn't keep you. . . ."

"Oh no, it's perfectly okay." Parker's mother linked her arm through Sailor's. "I'm dying to hear how Parker's doing in your class."

Sailor glanced at her date, who edged sideways as if to avoid the pushy woman in sequins. "He's, um—"

"Mom, we should go check on Grams, huh?" Parker aimed one foot toward the stage.

"She's fine, having her usual cup of chamomile with the makeup lady. Now, Sailor," she went on, drawing the wide-eyed girl to one side. "By the way, did I ever tell you what a beautiful name you have? I'm thrilled Parker's taking your class. He works way too hard, you know."

They moved out of earshot, leaving Parker shuffling his feet next to the Fanning couple and the wimp who wouldn't lift a hand to rescue his girl from the clutches of Parker's meddling mother. He searched for something to say. "So you're all friends of Sailor's?"

Mrs. Fanning nodded. "We've known her since she was a teenager. She used to babysit for our rowdy bunch of sons. Right, Tom?" She elbowed Sailor's date.

"Mo–om." The red-faced guy grimaced and rolled his eyes.

Parker palmed a sudden pinch under his ribcage. "Sailor babysat *you*?"

"Guilty as charged." Tom—Tom Fanning, apparently—flashed a pearly grin, and for the first time Parker could tell he was much younger than he first thought, probably midtwenties at most. "But don't believe anything she says about me. And for heaven's sake don't repeat it to my wife. She still thinks I'm Mr. Totally Cool."

"You're married." Parker felt a silly smile creep across his face. "So you and Sailor aren't. . ."

"Are you kidding? No way!" Tom's eyes crinkled. "Sailor only came with us because some stranger gave my folks four tickets and my wife had to go to a baby shower."

"Some stranger?" Parker glanced toward the wings, imagining Grams smugly sipping her chamomile. No. Not possible. How could she possibly have known the Fannings would bring Sailor to the show?

Paranoia, thy name is Parker.

Chapter 5

Sailor heaved a reluctant sigh and dropped *Love's Sweet Song* into the book return. "Alas, farewell, my love. 'Twas such sweet agony sharing these past few days with you."

"Spare me!" Kathy pressed the back of one hand to her forehead. She might be teasing, but her tone sounded noticeably edgier than normal.

Had she been listening to the rumors about Chandler's "bad boy" past?

Kathy retrieved the book and scanned it in. "Two weeks to the day. How many times did you read it?"

"Only three." Sailor lowered her eyes. "Four, if you count skimming for all the best romantic scenes."

"Wow, a new all-time low. Didn't you read his last one six times before returning it? And three days late, if memory serves."

"I've had a busy couple of weeks." Sailor propped an elbow on the counter. "See, this so-called *friend* coerced me into being on her committee."

"Hmm, would that be the same friend who made you Chandler Michaels's official Bards of Birkenstock social director?" Kathy set a stack of returned books on the counter and began scanning them. "And since we've only had two meetings since you joined the committee, you must have some other reason for staying so busy."

"My classes *have* been a little more draining than usual. And I spent Saturday with the Fannings. They took me to a Frankie Verona show."

"In Branson? Cool!"

A funny ripple rolled up her spine. "Guess who was in the band, subbing for the regular flute player."

Kathy shrugged and scanned in another book.

"My new student. Parker Travis."

"Seriously? How cool!" Kathy's eyes narrowed. "Why, Sailor Kern, what's that look I see on your face? Please tell me you're about to give up this Chandler Michaels infatuation and set your cap for Birkenstock's premier hairstylist instead."

"No!" Sailor hugged herself against a sudden shiver. No, she most definitely was *not* interested in Parker Travis. "I'm trying to get up the nerve to make an appointment. You know, so I look my best for the festival."

As Kathy's gaze drifted toward the entrance, her brows shot up. "Here's your chance."

"Huh?" Sailor swiveled to see the hairstylist in question ambling across the lobby. Her mouth dropped open. He hesitated long enough for her to clamp her teeth together and force a smile.

"Hi again." Parker edged toward the counter and stuffed his hands into his pockets. "Hope you enjoyed the show the other night. Sorry if my mom monopolized you."

Sailor recalled Mrs. Travis's probing questions and lifted one shoulder. "She was just being a mom." *As if I would know.* If not for Deb Fanning, she wouldn't have much of a clue about how real mothers acted.

But come to think of it, Deb had acted pretty motherly the other night, too. Like she and Mrs. Travis were trying to match up their "kids."

Her stomach lurched. She crossed her arms. "Anyway, you were great. I mean, Frankie was great. The *show* was great. It was all. . .great."

"I think he got the 'great' part." Kathy angled a smile toward Parker. "Hi, I'm Kathy, Sailor's very best friend."

Parker did a double take. "Kathy Richmond? Weren't we in band together? Flute, right?"

"I was a lowly freshman, and you were already first chair as a sophomore. I was so intimidated."

"Yeah, right," Parker smirked. "Didn't you drop out of band?"

"Halfway through the first semester. Passed out on the field during marching practice and never went back." Kathy straightened a stack of complimentary bookmarks. "I don't think I've seen you in the library before."

Parker's glance shifted between Kathy and Sailor. "It's my day off, and I just thought I'd. . .come in and look around. . . ."

Sailor's eyes narrowed to slits. People did not simply drop in at the library to "look around." Especially classy flute-playing hairstylists who most likely had a billion other, more interesting things to do. Like maybe style some famous person's hair or rehearse for another Branson show.

Sailor decided it was none of her business. Anyway, she didn't want to hang around and risk reinserting foot in mouth. More like foot, ankle, calf, and knee. "I should probably go. I need to find another book."

"But isn't there something you wanted to ask Parker?" Kathy wiggled her eyebrows meaningfully.

"Oh." Sailor gulped. She slid the toe of her sneaker across a beige floor tile, following the swirl in the design. "I. . .I was thinking about doing something different with my hair."

"Really?" Parker's voice softened in a way that sent tingles across Sailor's shoulders. "I'd be glad to help. Just call the salon and make an appointment."

Something lightened deep within her, like cola fizz finding its way to the surface of a shaken two-liter bottle. "Okay, I will."

❧

Parker became aware of one corner of his mouth curling upward as he watched Sailor scurry toward the shelves. She disappeared between A–F and G–M of the romance section at the same moment he heard the sound of a tornado blowing through—his own explosive sigh. He cringed.

"Packs quite a punch for as quiet as she is, huh?"

Parker jerked his head toward Kathy. "What?"

"Sailor. Most people never look beyond her shyness." She shot him a grin that punched a hole in his gut. "But I can tell you already have."

He stepped up to the counter. "Have you known Sailor long?"

"I was the resident assistant in our Missouri State dorm in Springfield when she was an incoming freshman." Kathy leaned forward, forearms resting on the counter. "So what are your intentions toward Sailor Kern?"

"Intentions?" Parker sucked in a quick breath then blew it out slowly. "All I know is, she throws me way off balance."

Kathy studied Parker as if she were sizing him up for a straitjacket. She slid a furtive glance toward the rows of bookshelves. "If you really are interested in Sailor, you should know something. She's got a megacrush on her favorite romance novelist, and she isn't going to get over him without a fight."

Kathy's concerned frown told him she was anything but happy about this so-called crush. "Who is this guy? Are they seeing each other?"

"They haven't met—yet." Another visual sweep of the bookshelves. "But he's coming to town for the Bards of Birkenstock Festival, and idiot that I am, I invited Sailor to be on the committee."

"Does this have anything to do with her sudden interest in getting a makeover?"

"You guessed it."

Parker scratched an imaginary itch along his jaw and stared off in the direction Sailor had disappeared to. "But she's gorgeous just the way she is." His mouth went dry. Did he *really* just say that out loud?

"I completely agree. I ask God every day to help her believe it for herself." Kathy paused to help another library patron check out a stack of books. Finishing, she returned her attention to Parker. "You never said. Is there a particular book you're looking for?"

Just what he needed—letting a casual acquaintance see how unnerved his growing attraction to Sailor had made him. He massaged the back of his neck. "The thing is, I'm a little out of practice in this whole. . .relationship thing."

Out of practice? How about completely out of touch? His last real date was probably the night he took second-chair flutist Marie Zipp to their high school band banquet. Just because most of his clients were female didn't give him any advantages in the romance department. And face it, no woman he'd met thus far had even come close to capturing his heart.

Until Sailor.

"So. . .you came to the library in search of a book on relationships." Kathy drummed her fingers on the counter. "May I assume you mean something a little deeper than friendship?"

Parker swallowed. "You may assume."

A grin spread across her wide mouth, a grin that looked more Machiavellian than friendly. "I have exactly the book you need."

Motioning for one of the other librarians to cover the front desk, Kathy reached for something on a lower shelf. She tucked a slim, shiny paperback under her arm, stepped through a swinging gate, and hurried Parker to one of the study carrels behind the reference section.

"Have a seat, Parker, and prepare to be enlightened." She took a chair across the narrow table from him and laid the book between them. "The library got in a shipment of advance review copies a few days ago, and when I came across this one, I squirreled it away before anyone else could grab it. I'm betting it'll give you exactly the ammunition you'll need to woo Sailor away from her fantasy man."

He studied the silhouetted couple on the cover, their lips meeting for a kiss in the center of a stylized red heart. "*Romance by the Book*, eh? So simple even a dork like me can learn?"

"Haven't you heard the rumors?" Kathy gave a low chuckle. "Word on the street is, you're the most eligible bachelor in Birkenstock."

Parker flinched. "Guess I'm hanging out on the wrong street corners."

"Or maybe you haven't been paying attention." Kathy crossed her arms and waited while Parker paged through the book.

The first few chapter headings seemed straightforward enough. "What to Say after You Say Hello." "Make Your First Date First-Rate." "You Can't Go Wrong with Roses." "What to Do When 'Like' Turns to 'Love.'"

Okay, maybe he was still in the "like" phase with Sailor. But the incessant pounding behind his sternum every time he was around her—or even thought about her, truth be told—had him wondering if she was the girl he'd been holding out for his entire life.

He flipped the book over and scanned the back-cover blurb and author's photo. The guy in the white dinner jacket reminded him of an aging Daniel Craig straight from a James Bond movie. "Chandler Michaels. So he knows about this romance stuff, right?"

Kathy gave a doubtful huff. "That's what he claims."

"Wait. You recommended this book."

She did a slow eye roll. "What I said was, it'll give you the ammunition you'll need to beat the man at his own game."

Understanding dawned. Parker whistled through his teeth. "You mean this guy"—he knuckled the photo of Chandler Michaels—"is the author she has a crush on?"

"You got it." Kathy's jaw tensed. She gave her head an annoyed shake. "Ever hear of a BHS alum named Chuck Michalicek?"

The name settled like a block of ice in the center of Parker's chest. "Chuck Michalicek is Chandler Michaels?"

"One and the same." Kathy checked her watch and stood. "I have to get back to the desk. Just take the book and read it. You'll get the picture."

Alone in the carrel, Parker stared at the photo of Chandler Michaels while the urge to hit something writhed beneath his rib cage. He'd been only eight or nine at the time, but he could still remember crouching on the stairs, listening to his mother trying to comfort her younger sister, his aunt Ruthy, after her fiancé ditched her two days before their wedding. They'd gotten engaged right out of high school, but the guy left soon afterward to attend an out-of-state college. Turned out he was cheating on Ruthy the entire time they were apart, and it was a blessing she didn't end up married to the creep.

A creep named Chuck Michalicek.

Chapter 6

Sailor drew a chair up to the conference table and clicked the button on her ballpoint. She stared at the blank yellow legal pad before her. Guilt plagued her—not a single new idea of her own for Chandler's stay in Birkenstock. If she didn't prove she could make a valuable contribution to this committee, they might decide to vote her off.

Her practical side, the part intent on self-preservation at all costs, thought that might not be such a bad thing.

Her romantic side—sorely neglected except for a steady diet of romance novels—screamed ugly threats at her for even considering backing out of this once-in-a-lifetime opportunity.

The conference room door swung open, and Kathy breezed in. "Hey, Sailor, you're early. The meeting doesn't start for another twenty minutes—and that's only if Donna shows up on time."

She swiveled her chair around and pulled the legal pad into her lap, propping it on her knee so Kathy couldn't see the blank page. "Just doing a little brainstorming for Chandler's visit."

"Come up with anything interesting? Like maybe a necktie party?"

"Kathy!"

"Did I say necktie? I meant *black* tie." Kathy began aligning chairs and setting out extra notepads and pens.

Sailor rotated her chair to follow Kathy's movements. She jotted numbers one through ten in the left margin then tapped her pen on the first line. "At the last meeting you mentioned taking him to a Branson show. I bet I can get more tickets to see Frankie Verona."

"Good idea. They're from around the same era. Oldies but goodies and all." Kathy checked the thermostat and made a small adjustment.

Sailor smirked. Nothing subtle about Kathy Richmond. "I'm sure Frankie's got several years on Chandler. Remember, I had a front-row seat the other night. Stage makeup covers a multitude of. . .wrinkles."

Kathy plopped into the chair next to Sailor's, her dark hair puffing out around her shoulders. She sat forward and gripped Sailor's armrests. "What's it going to take for you to realize you deserve someone way better, not to mention *younger*, than Chuck Michalicek?"

Resentment pricked Sailor's spine. "Age is only a number. And what's it going to take for you to realize maybe a guy can change? Isn't it possible Chandler. . .Chuck—whatever you want to call him—has moved beyond the silly pranks he pulled as a teenager?"

Kathy straightened. "I gather I'm not the only one who's been talking to you about Chuck."

"I've heard a few rumors." Sailor hugged the legal pad against her chest. "But that's all they are—rumors. And anyway, doesn't it say in the Bible that we're all new creations in Christ? How do you know Chandler hasn't changed?"

"How do you know he has? Or that he's even a Christian?"

"I'm giving him the benefit of the doubt. Isn't that what good Christians are supposed to do?"

Kathy narrowed one eye. "I'm starting to really worry about you, Sailor. And I don't mean only where Chandler Michaels is concerned."

Sailor stiffened. "Why?"

"I've had this sense lately that you and God are. . .well, not as close as you ought to be."

Sailor sucked her lower lip between her teeth. The truth stung, and she couldn't stop her next words. "I don't think my relationship with the Lord is any of your business."

Kathy's chin lifted. Hurt shimmered in her deep brown eyes. "I'm your friend, Sailor. That should be plenty of reason—"

"Good evening, ladies." The white-haired Allan Biltmore waltzed into the room and pulled out the chair on Sailor's other side. "You two have the privilege of being the first to hear my exciting news."

Sailor smiled a silent apology to Kathy—she knew her friend only spoke out of concern—and folded her hands atop the legal pad as she swiveled toward Allan.

Behind her she heard Kathy's sharp exhalation and the forced smile in her voice. "What's up, Allan?"

"Did I mention I was Chandler Michaels's high school English teacher?" He chuckled softly. "Of course I knew him as Charles back then, and indeed he was a live wire. How well I remember—"

"Your news, Allan?" Kathy scooted her chair closer and propped one elbow on the table.

"Ah yes, I digress. Since Charles—Chandler—will be staying with me, we've been in touch about his travel plans." Allan's grin broadened to reveal a set of pearly false teeth. "You, my dear Sailor, are going to be one busy young lady. It turns out Chandler is so thrilled about returning to Birkenstock for this momentous occasion that he has decided to move up his arrival. He'll be coming to town next week."

"N–next *week*?" Nausea seethed up Sailor's esophagus. Should she be thrilled? Terrified? Catch the next bus out of town?

"Wow, Allan, that's. . .amazing." Kathy's voice held an edge that only increased Sailor's panic. A hand reached over the back of Sailor's chair and squeezed her shoulder.

"Indeed. However, Chandler will have some special requirements that—"

The arrival of three more committee members interrupted Allan's explanation, and he couldn't resist boasting to the others about this little coup.

Soon the entire committee had assembled, and the louder the conversational hum became, the deeper Sailor withdrew inside herself. Donna DuPont called the meeting to order, and though Sailor tried to look interested and take notes as the chairwoman worked through the agenda, her mind wouldn't cooperate. Soon she'd be asked to give a report on her ideas for keeping Chandler Michaels entertained, and Allan Biltmore's announcement had thrown a megasized monkey wrench into the mix. Nearly four extra weeks to fill? Not to mention Chandler's "special requirements"! Allan explained that Chandler had asked him to keep the details confidential for now, but that everything was under control. Still. . .what exactly would Chandler expect of her?

God, are You there?

No answer.

I know Kathy's right. You and I haven't really talked in ages. But I'm in trouble here. The chance to meet Chandler Michaels is the most wonderful, exciting thing that's ever happened to me. How will I ever be ready by next week?. . . God?

Still nothing.

And Donna DuPont was looking her way.

❧

"Thanks for working me in, Parker." Donna DuPont fluffed the black protective cape over her knees as Parker secured the Velcro closure around her neck. "Howard and I are hosting a dinner party tonight for the city council members, and I want to look my best."

"Have no fear, your favorite stylist is here." Parker cupped his hands around Donna's hair and pushed it one way and then another. "I'm thinking a little upsweep on the left side to play up those classy pearl earrings Howard bought you in Maui."

"You remembered." She winked at him through the mirror. "And I thought all my babbling went in one ear and out the other."

Sometimes he wished it did. There were days he'd like to remind his clients he was their hairstylist, not a gossip columnist. Or worse, their shrink. . . although he firmly believed what he did for his clients gave their self-esteem a bigger boost than any psychiatrist could ever hope for.

Could he do the same for Sailor Kern?

He wished she'd call. It was Thursday already, not that he was keeping track. Tuesday at the water aerobics class, things had seemed awkward between them, at least from his perspective. She remained all business, unflappable beneath her instructor persona, never even mentioning their encounter at the library.

And of course he wasn't about to mention his reason for being at the library in the first place. Or the fact that her interest in the infamous Chuck Michalicek aka Chandler Michaels had him spitting nails—and not the acrylic kind.

"Parker? Yoo-hoo, Parker Travis!" Donna's singsong voice interrupted his thoughts.

"Sorry, let's get you over to the shampoo bowl."

"What has you so preoccupied lately?"

Parker guided her head into the bowl and tested the water. "Just a little concerned about a friend." *Friend?* His stomach clenched at the realization of how badly he wanted it to be more. Somewhere along the way, he'd ceased resigning himself to bachelorhood and started tripping over his own feet in the presence of one excruciatingly naive and unbearably beautiful woman.

Donna wriggled her bottom deeper into the chair and closed her eyes. "As often as I've confided my secrets to you, you can certainly unburden yourself to me if you feel like it. I'm all ears, honey."

"Thanks, but this isn't something I can talk about." He squirted her favorite peach-scented shampoo into his palm and massaged it into mounds of foam.

He'd just rinsed out the shampoo and applied conditioner when Carla, the receptionist, pranced over, a loose-fitting leopard-print tunic swishing around her thighs. "Can you take a call, Parker? I've got a gal on the line who will only speak with you."

Great, probably another client who'd insist on being worked in before the weekend. His schedule was already jam-packed. At this rate, whatever pain relief the water aerobics class provided would soon be undone. Even with only sporadic attempts to practice on his own, neither his shoulders nor his knees had felt this good in a long time.

He chewed the inside of his cheek. "Let me get Donna to my station, and I'll pick up there."

Donna sat up and adjusted the towel he had wrapped around her head. "Don't take long, honey. I've got to get home to let the caterers in."

"This will only take a second." As Donna settled into the chair, he grabbed the cordless extension from the wall base. "Parker here. How can I help you?"

"Um, hi. I hope this isn't a bad time. . . ."

His heart did a crazy spin and thud. He'd know that quiet voice anywhere. "No, not at all." He eyed Donna through the mirror then stepped around the corner and lowered his voice. "I've got all the time in the world." *For you.*

Silence stretched between them, and he started to wonder if he'd lost the connection. When she finally spoke, frantic desperation filled her tone. "Parker, you've *got* to help me. Everyone says you're the best stylist in town, and Chandler Michaels is coming *next week*, and I haven't done anything with my hair in years, and I look like. . .like. . ." She made a gurgling sound, like a sob catching in her throat. Then a huge, ragged sigh rasped out.

He wanted to tell her she looked like an angel. He wanted to tell her to stay far, far, far away from Chuck Michalicek. He wanted to tell her she deserved somebody with a lot more class. Somebody who would cherish her and love her just the way she was.

Somebody like him.

Donna tapped him on the shoulder. "My hair's drying all funny. Hurry up!"

He pasted on an obliging smile and motioned her back to the chair. Speaking into the phone, he said, "Can you come in Saturday at four? My last appointment is at three thirty. After that we can spend all the time you need."

"I'll be there." Relief thick as honey poured through the phone line. "Thank you so much!"

"You're more than welcome. 'Bye, Sailor." He set the phone in its base and reached for a comb.

"Sailor?" Donna quirked an eyebrow. "Not Sailor Kern? She's on my Bards of Birkenstock committee. Sweet little thing." She gave a tiny gasp, her mouth forming an O. "She made an appointment with you? All I can say is, it's about time. The poor girl's as plain as a country mouse."

Parker felt a pinch in his gut. "I don't think—"

"It was all I could do to keep from saying anything when Kathy Richmond invited her to help with the arrangements for Chandler Michaels's visit. Why, for goodness' sake, she hardly says a word at our meetings. I can't imagine her holding her own in a social setting, least of all with a literary luminary like—"

Parker flicked the blow-dryer switch to its highest setting. "Sorry, Donna, can't hear you over this noise."

Chuck Michalicek, *literary*? A celebrity, maybe. A legend in his own mind, for sure. Parker had spent the last couple of evenings skimming the contents of *Romance by the Book* and wondering what kind of slimeball would come up with this stuff.

An egotistical, womanizing, male-chauvinist slimeball, obviously. Whether Sailor ever looked twice in Parker's direction or not, he'd keep her away from Chuck Michalicek if he had to kidnap her and tie her up in the salon storeroom until the book festival ended and "Chandler Michaels" had left Birkenstock in the dust.

Chapter 7

Sailor angled her aging green Honda Civic into the only vacant parking space she could find along Willow Avenue, two blocks south of Par Excellence Salon and Day Spa. She tipped her head to check her reflection in the rearview mirror. As usual, several escapees from her perennial ponytail now drooped across one eye. Parker Travis had his work cut out for him.

She only hoped he didn't charge by the hour.

Slinging her back-friendly—but not so fashionable, she suddenly realized—handbag over one shoulder, she locked her car, fed the meter, and headed up the street. Three shops down from the salon she slowed her pace then drew up short next to a big blue mailbox at the curb. She swallowed the butterflies swarming her throat, not that she felt any better having them flutter around inside her stomach.

You can do this, Sailor. Keep your objective firmly in mind.

Dodging a couple of kids on skateboards, she tramped the rest of the way to the salon. With a final steadying breath she pushed through the amber-tinted glass door.

"Hi, can I help you?" A perky receptionist with asymmetrically cut blue black hair looked up from filing her nails. The brass plaque at one end of the counter indicated her name was Carla.

"I made—" Sailor cleared the squeak from her voice. "I made an appointment with Parker Travis. My name is—"

"Sailor Kern. Four o'clock." Carla ran a finger down her computer screen. "Parker's finishing up a lowlight. Can I get you a soda or some coffee while you wait?"

"No thanks." She glanced around the seating area and spied a basket of hairstyle magazines. She scooped up the top three. "I'll just look through these."

"That first one's my favorite. It's chock-full of trendy styles." Carla came around and plopped onto the plush black leather sofa next to Sailor. She snatched the magazine and riffled through the pages; then she flipped it open on Sailor's lap and pointed to a photo. "The minute you walked in the door, I could *see* you in this 'do. I have a knack for these things, you know. Just show it to Parker, and he'll—"

"Thanks, Carla, I'll take it from here."

The sound of Parker's voice, strong and sure, sent nervous prickles up Sailor's arms. She jerked her head up to see him escort a sixty-something woman into the reception area. A stunning mass of bronze and golden waves set off the woman's warm complexion.

"Have a wonderful time at the theater tonight, Mary." He gave the woman a chaste peck on the cheek then signaled Carla over to the counter. "Would you please set Mrs. Blodgett up for another appointment in four weeks?"

Sailor rose, the magazine clutched against her abdomen. Parker seemed so different here than at the water aerobics class, or even when she ran into him at the library the other day. A confident grace marked both his posture and his tone, the complete opposite of his self-conscious bumbling while trying to master the pool exercises.

He turned to her, and she glimpsed the tiniest flicker of uncertainty in his awkward smile. It quickly vanished when he extended his hand. "Hi, Sailor. Come on back."

She followed him through a maze of styling cubicles, past a bay of hood-type hair dryers, and around a center atrium where an out-of-control ficus plant stretched its shedding limbs toward a skylight. A hallway branched to their right, and Sailor glimpsed a series of door signs: MANICURE/PEDICURE. FACIALS AND DEPILATORY. BODY TREATMENTS. MASSAGE.

"Wow, you do everything here." An envious sigh whispered between her lips. It would take all those salon procedures and more to transform this plain-Jane nobody into drop-dead gorgeous. No use drooling over the impossible though. She'd probably have to work overtime for the next century to afford what Parker would charge for a simple cut and style.

Oh well, if it made the impression on Chandler Michaels she was hoping for, it would be worth every penny.

They arrived at a brightly lit cubicle with a window overlooking the street. Vertical blinds admitted soft sunlight upon a black-lacquered shelf covered with ferns, begonias, and English ivy. Forest-print wallpaper echoed the greenery and lent an airy, outdoorsy feel.

Parker motioned her into the chair and angled it toward the mirror. With a gentle touch he tugged the coated elastic band from her ponytail and combed his fingers through the strands until her hair flowed around her shoulders like a silken curtain. The sensation gave her chills. She breathed slowly in and out, a tremor vibrating deep in her throat.

"You have beautiful hair." Parker's voice held a mellow tone that matched the look in his eyes. He smiled at her through the mirror. "When was the last time you did anything to it?"

She bit her lip. "Well, I washed it this afternoon after I finished my lap swim."

"Other than shampooing, I mean." Parker fingered a strand. "I see just the slightest damage from pool chlorine. You must use a good conditioner."

"It's specially made for swimmers." Sailor smirked. "I may not know much about styling, but I do know I don't look good in green hair."

Parker shot her a knowing grin. "Do you trim it regularly? Have you ever used a coloring product? Had a perm?"

"My aunt Trina tried to give me a home perm for Easter Sunday one year, but it didn't take very well. Not to mention the smell."

"Ah yes, the ammonia. Perms have come a long way since those days—not nearly so smelly and much kinder to the hair. Have you always worn your hair long?"

"Mostly. I like being able to pull it into a ponytail and not fuss with it." She grimaced. Nothing like admitting to a beauty professional that she avoided spending time on her appearance.

"Actually, an updo enhances your classic oval face." Parker smoothed her hair away from her temples and swept it up into a pile on the back of her head.

This time she couldn't suppress a visible shiver. The thought occurred to her that she could sit in this chair with Parker running his hands through her hair for the rest of their lives.

❧

Parker wasn't sure whether the sudden quiver up his arms originated in Sailor or himself. He only knew he'd like to spend the rest of his life running his fingers through her soft, silky tresses. He hadn't even needed to ask whether she'd used any kind of chemical process recently. Except for minor pool-related dryness at the ends, this was the cleanest, healthiest, most *un*processed hair he'd handled in a long, long time.

He pulled himself out of his self-indulgent reverie and recalled her real reason for being here: to make herself attractive for Chandler Michaels. His shoulders tightened. He squeezed out a sharp breath. "Okay, let's get started. Did you find a style you like in one of the magazines?"

"The receptionist was just showing me this one." The magazine fell open in Sailor's lap, revealing a photo of a model with purplish red hair cut long at the sides and tapering to a high V in back. Spiky bangs fringed her heavily made-up eyes. Judging from Sailor's sudden flinch as she glanced down, Parker guessed she hadn't looked closely at the photo until now.

He swept the magazine from her hands and tossed it onto the work space behind him. "Carla's taste leans toward the avant-garde. I had something more natural in mind for you."

Sailor released a thankful-sounding chuckle. "Just so it's something I can manage on my own, especially with being in the water every day. I'm not real handy with a blow-dryer, and I wouldn't know what to do with gel or mousse or even a curling iron."

"I'll keep all that in mind." Parker ran a comb through her hair and pondered various styles, his sense of calling more powerful than ever. He'd felt the first inklings years ago, helping Grams brush out her tangles as rheumatoid arthritis slowly stole away her grip. "Thank you, Parker. You make me feel so pretty," she would say.

Now he had the chance to share this gift with the one person who most needed it, a woman who had not the slightest concept of how beautiful she really was. Yet if he helped her, he might send her straight into the arms of the one man who least deserved her affection.

His gut cramped. What choice did he have? She'd come to him expecting a makeover miracle, and he had the skill to give it to her.

He also had Chandler Michaels's treatise on romance tucked away in the bottom drawer. Obviously Kathy Richmond hadn't read it all the way through. If Sailor could be swayed by such corny macho tactics, maybe she was already too far gone.

"Think outside the box, Parker."

He tensed. Where had that thought come from?

"Think outside the book. *Trust Me."*

Sailor caught his eye in the mirror. "So do you have any ideas, or am I totally hopeless?"

"Hopeless? Not a chance." He laid the comb aside and rested his hands on her shoulders. "Do you trust me?"

She gulped. "I. . .I think so."

He gripped the sides of the chair and spun Sailor 180 degrees. Gasping, she clutched the chair arms and shot him a terrified look.

He grinned. "You said you trusted me, right?" At her wide-eyed nod, he continued. "Hold on to that thought then, because when you look in that mirror after we're finished today, you'll see Sailor Kern the way I see her. . . ."

He clamped his teeth together before he could add, *Beautiful beyond imagining.*

❧

Sailor sucked in her breath as Parker swept around her, swirling a shimmery black cape like a matador. Beneath the slick fabric her fingers clawed the armrests. A thousand fire ants nibbled at her nerves. What was she thinking, putting herself at the mercy of a mad hairstylist? He must be mad if he thought he could change Sailor from an ugly duckling into Cinderella.

Or was she mixing up her fairy tales?

No matter. Nothing short of a fairy godmother could make her glamorous enough to attract the likes of Chandler Michaels. Besides, even if Parker succeeded in improving her outward appearance, sooner or later she would have to actually *talk* to Chandler. And when she opened her mouth and nothing came out but her typical shy little squeaks, her dream come true would turn into her worst nightmare.

Parker stood to one side, mixing something white and frothy in a square plastic container. The sharp smell bit at her sinuses. She put a finger beneath her nose. "Wh–what's that for?"

He laughed, a throaty, reassuring laugh—or at least she hoped he meant to be reassuring. "Don't panic. You promised you'd trust me."

Trust him? Oh man, that's what got her into this mess in the first place. When he pulled a stack of foil squares out of a drawer and moved toward her with something resembling a rattail paintbrush, she decided the wisest course of action would be to close her eyes and hope for the best.

She felt each stroke as he sectioned off her hair then tucked the foil close to her scalp. The scratchy brushing and crinkling sounds suggested he was painting on the white stuff then wrapping each strand in a neat little foil package. Part, tuck, brush, wrap. . .part, tuck, brush, wrap. . . . The rhythm lulled her into a languid calm.

"Sailor? You awake?" Parker jiggled her arm.

She popped her eyes open. "Sorry, I think I dozed off."

"Time for the next step. Come with me." With one hand on her shoulder, Parker guided her around the shedding ficus plant and down the hallway they'd passed earlier. The door to the manicure/pedicure room stood open, and Parker showed Sailor inside. He introduced her to a regal-looking woman seated behind a table.

"Nice to meet you, Sailor. I'm Pamela. Have a seat." A cap of reddish brown curls framed the woman's wide, exotic-looking eyes. She reached for Sailor's hand and studied the short nails.

Sailor's gaze skimmed the array of manicurist paraphernalia and bottles of polish in every shade imaginable. Painfully aware of her ragged cuticles and too-short nails, she wanted to jerk her hand back. "I've never had a professional manicure. But I guess that's pretty obvious." Not to mention she must look like a space alien or possibly a human TV antenna, with all that foil poking out around her head.

"First time for everything." The warmth in Pamela's coffee-brown gaze matched her tone. She slanted a grin in Parker's direction. "Go put your feet up for a while. I'll take good care of her."

The door clicked shut, and Sailor released a nervous chuckle. "I thought I was just here for a haircut. I hope the salon takes credit cards."

"Don't even think about money. This is your time to relax and enjoy." Pamela eased Sailor's fingers into a bowl of warm water. "Parker's been planning your appointment ever since you called. He's got all kinds of fun stuff lined up for you."

She gulped, a crazy mix of elation, anticipation, and stark terror rippling through her. Would she even recognize herself when Parker completed his work?

She couldn't wait to find out.

Chapter 8

Parker stretched one leg along the reception-area sofa and checked his watch—almost six. Sailor should be close to finishing her session with the makeup artist. He hoped Sandra followed his instructions to keep Sailor's look understated and natural.

He couldn't suppress a chuckle as he wondered how Sailor was handling all this special attention. She'd seemed more than slightly dumbstruck when he dropped her off for her mani/pedi. After she finished there, he brought her to the shampoo station to rinse out the highlighting solution and apply a deep conditioner. Then he'd sent her for a facial and eyebrow shaping. He'd debated scheduling a brown sugar scrub, full-body massage, and wardrobe consultation, but on such short notice and so late in the day, there wouldn't be time. Besides, he didn't want to completely overwhelm her. Maybe his selective introduction to pampering would encourage her to come back for more.

All that remained today was Parker's signature cut and style, and he knew exactly what he wanted to do. Subtle layering, a wisp of bangs, and the strategically placed highlights he'd applied earlier would set off Sailor's features beautifully.

He'd been trying all afternoon not to think about why he was doing this—or rather, for whom—but the image of Chandler Michaels gazing seductively from the back cover of his book wouldn't leave Parker alone. After the salon emptied out, and with Sailor ensconced with his skilled associates down the hall, he'd fished out the dreaded *Romance by the Book*. Might as well brush up on the competition.

The chapter that lay open before him made him want to gag: "Dressing Her for Success." Though the author cloaked his meaning in high-sounding prose and euphemisms, after two paragraphs Chandler Michaels's definition of *success* became crystal clear. The intervening years hadn't changed bad-boy Chuck in the slightest. Parker had the sick feeling that giving Sailor a makeover might only be playing into Chuck's hands—although he doubted a guy like Chuck could ever truly appreciate the unadorned beauty and artless charm of a woman like Sailor.

He closed his eyes and gave his head a helpless shake. *Lord, protect her.*

Footsteps clicking on the marble floor drew his attention. He slammed the book closed and tucked it beneath a sofa cushion as Sandra entered the reception area. She swept long blond waves off one shoulder. "All done. I sent her back to your station."

Parker stood. "How'd it go?"

"I did exactly what you asked. Mineral makeup in natural shades, and the lightest touch possible. I think you'll be suitably impressed." Sandra offered a sly smile. "She sure seemed to be."

Sandra's words buoyed Parker's steps as he headed through the salon. He found Sailor admiring her own reflection. Seeing him in the mirror, she brightened.

He grinned. As usual, Sandra's expertise proved flawless. "So far, so good?"

"I never realized what a difference a little makeup could make. And Sandra made it easy enough that I think I can actually learn to do it myself. She even gave me a product list and some samples."

Was she sitting a little straighter, her smile a tad more self-assured? He tugged the towel loose from around her hair and swiveled her away from the mirror once more.

She grabbed his wrist. "Hey, I trusted you through all this other stuff. Can't I watch while you do my hair?"

He shook off her hand and reached for a spray bottle to dampen her towel-blotted tresses. "Nope. I want you to be surprised."

"Today has already been full of surprises." Her tone became pleading. "Come on, Parker, let me watch."

He couldn't help but laugh. "When did my Simon Legree water aerobics instructor become such a whiner?"

If a little makeup and nail polish could produce this much spunk, he couldn't wait to see how she'd react when she saw the finished product.

❧

When Parker laid the dryer and brush aside and reached for a can of hair spray, Sailor clamped her eyes shut. A fruity scent lingered in the air as the light mist tickled her nose. When Parker whisked away the protective cape and rotated the chair toward the mirror, she shivered, afraid to open her eyes.

"You might as well look and get it over with." His voice rang with self-satisfaction. The guy was good, and he obviously knew it.

So why was she so afraid? It had nothing to do with Parker Travis's hair-styling skills.

It had everything to do with her doubts that she could live up to a new-and-improved version of herself. Who would she be when she walked out the front door? Who did she *want* to be?

She drew in a deep breath, exhaled slowly, and willed her eyes to open. "Oh. My. Goodness."

Parker gave her a hand mirror and turned the chair so she could see the style from all angles. "Just enough layering to give some lift but still long enough for your ponytail. I added the highlights to enhance the golden undertones and brighten your face."

"Everything looks so. . .natural. Totally me, only better." Using her toe, she turned the chair toward the mirror again. She wanted to drink up the image before her.

Then reality hit. Her shoulders caved, and she groped for her purse. "I should have asked sooner. How much is all this going to cost?"

Parker stepped between her and the hook where her purse hung. "This was entirely my pleasure. Everything's on the house."

"I can't let you do that." She dodged around him and swept her purse into her lap. "Seriously. How much do I owe you?"

"Don't argue, Sailor. I guarantee I'll win." He plopped into a forest green leather side chair, a smug smile twisting his lips. "The look on your face when you saw yourself just now is all the payment I need."

Her heart lifted in a series of staccato beats. Something in the way Parker was staring at her made her insides go all fizzy. She'd caught a similar look in his eyes during their last water aerobics class. Today, though, the intensity rocked her.

She gave herself a mental shake. Probably nothing but an overreaction to her very first spa day and the fact that for the first time in her life, a man was actually paying attention to her. A heady sensation, to be sure. But she'd better keep her eye on the real prize and hope the new Sailor Kern would attract equal attention from Chandler Michaels.

Giving an exaggerated eye roll, she unzipped her purse and retrieved her wallet. "Please let me pay you something, Parker. Otherwise I'll feel indebted to you for the rest of my life."

He chuckled and raised his hands in surrender. "Okay, okay. Here's my final offer. Since you only asked for a cut and style, that's all I'll charge you for—but of course you get my special discount for friends." He quoted an amount that still seemed on the high side.

She reminded herself he was the best, after all. "But what about Pamela and Sandra? Not to mention the products they used."

Parker rubbed his jaw and studied the ceiling. "You into bartering?"

"What exactly did you have in mind?"

"A few private water aerobics sessions ought to cover your spa services." His eyebrows drew up in the center, giving him a hopeful, little-boy look. "I mean it, there's a lot more to the workouts than I expected. I could really use some one-on-one coaching."

There went her heart again. What was wrong with her? She tapped her charge card against her chin. Her gaze slid to the mirror, and a fresh wave of confidence swept through her. "It would have to be in the evenings. Daytime hours are pretty much taken up with my classes and office work."

"Suits me. When shall we start?"

❧

Who'd have thought finagling more face time with Sailor could be so easy? Parker mentally patted himself on the back as he shut off the salon lights and locked the front door behind him. It was after eight, the sidewalks of Birkenstock bathed in the pink gold glow of sunset. He found himself whistling on his way across the street to the public lot where he parked his Camry.

Halfway to the car he felt his cell phone vibrate and retrieved it from his pants pocket. The screen displayed the name Katherine Richmond. Oh yeah, Kathy the librarian. "Hi, Kathy. What's up?"

"Sailor just left my house. She couldn't wait to show me her new look. I had to call and tell you how. . .how. . ." Something between a groan and a squeal sliced through his eardrum. "Wow!"

He grinned and pumped one fist, unable to resist a moment of prideful gloating. "I take it you approve?"

"More than approve. I am totally amazed, astonished, and astounded. What you've done for that girl's self-esteem today is immeasurable."

"Then I've done my job. Except. . ." His stomach twisted. "The thought of her with Chuck Michalicek—"

"I know. Have you read the book?"

"Some." Parker tugged the small paperback from the pocket of his Windbreaker and held it to the light. "He is one egomaniacal skunk. And this stuff is supposed to *help* me keep Sailor away from him?"

Kathy was silent for a moment, a thoughtful sigh hissing through the phone. "I didn't have time to explain very well the other day. Could you meet me for coffee in twenty minutes?"

❧

Sailor breezed through the front door. "Hi, Uncle Ed. Sorry I'm so late. Did you find the dinner plate I left for you in the fridge?"

"You take real good care of me, sweetie." With a contented smile, her uncle glanced up from his book. "Did you get some supper?"

Reveling in her new look, she'd hardly even thought about being hungry, until her stomach chose that moment to utter a rolling growl. "Maybe I'll open a can of tuna and make myself a salad."

"Hold on, young lady." Uncle Ed reached for her hand and guided her around to the front of his chair. Removing his glasses, he scanned her up and down. "Something's different about you."

She shrugged and forced a smile. On her way home from Kathy's she'd started worrying about her uncle's reaction. Since she came to live with Uncle Ed and Aunt Trina, they'd tried to raise her as her ultraconservative parents expected. The Ogden and Hazel Kern Child-Rearing Manifesto consisted of six cardinal rules: church every Sunday, no rock music, only squeaky-clean TV programs, no makeup, no miniskirts, and no dating until age eighteen.

Rock music had never appealed to her, and she'd always found books much more entertaining than TV (although she doubted her parents would be happy to know her reading tastes now centered on schmaltzy romances). Church every Sunday? Old habits were hard to break, even if God seemed distant these days. And with her tipping the scales at nearly 170 pounds by her eighteenth birthday, miniskirts were out of the question and dating was a nonissue. Makeup? Wouldn't have mattered anyway.

She flinched beneath her uncle's probing gaze. "Please, Uncle Ed, you're staring."

"Just trying to figure out what's changed." Finally one corner of his mouth curled upward. "You're wearing your hair down. Looks nice, real nice." He sat back with a satisfied sigh and returned his attention to his book.

The tension drained from Sailor's shoulders, replaced by a sense of elation. She recalled the approving look in Parker's eyes earlier. Now a similar reaction from her typically unobservant uncle? Never in her adult life had she felt so acutely aware of her womanhood.

Now the six-million-dollar question: Would Chandler Michaels notice?

Chapter 9

Parker arrived at Logan's Bistro a few minutes before Kathy. He claimed a table beneath a beaded lampshade that cast rippled blue shadows across the floor. When Kathy arrived, he waved her over and then placed their coffee orders with the barista. Returning to his chair, he slapped *Romance by the Book* on the table between them and snorted in disgust.

Kathy rolled her eyes. "My sentiments exactly."

"Has Sailor seen this book?"

"I told you, it's a review copy. Not in the bookstores yet, and Chandler hasn't even announced it on his website. Which is weird, if you ask me." She paused while the barista set their coffees on the table, then she took a cautious sip of her mocha latte. "Frankly, I hope Sailor *never* finds out about this book. It would break her heart."

Parker shot her a puzzled frown. "Wouldn't you want her to know the kind of guy she's harboring this misguided crush on?"

A sad sigh escaped Kathy's lips. "If you knew Sailor like I do, you'd understand. She's led an extremely sheltered life." Briefly she told him about Sailor's missionary parents and how for most of her childhood they had left her in the care of relatives. "After her aunt died, her world revolved around school and taking care of her uncle. Even at college I could hardly drag her away from the books. Social life? Forget it! She went home every weekend to check on her uncle. If not for the Fannings, she'd hardly know what having a real family is like."

Parker popped the spill-proof lid off his decaf cappuccino and swirled a wooden stir stick through the froth, releasing the brisk coffee aroma. "The Fannings. They brought her to the Branson show last weekend. Nice people."

"Very. But enough about Sailor's past. You and I need to concentrate on her future, and Chandler Michaels will be here next week."

"Yeah, Sailor said something about that when she made her appointment."

"It came as a surprise to everyone." Kathy leaned closer. "Remember Mr. Biltmore?"

"Senior English, third period. Hard to forget the teacher who gave me the one and only D of my high school career."

"You got a D in English? Really?"

"Let's keep this about Sailor, okay?" Parker crumpled his napkin. "What's Mr. Biltmore got to do with any of this?"

Kathy described Allan Biltmore's boastful announcement at the last committee meeting. "I guess ol' Chuck couldn't pass up the chance to extend his stay and bask in the glory—although what his 'special requirements' are is anybody's guess."

Parker grimaced. "After seeing this book, I don't even want to imagine."

"Why do I get the feeling your animosity stems from a lot more than reading a few chapters in his tacky how-to romance book?"

"Chuck and my family go way back. Let's leave it at that."

Kathy used the tip of one finger to push the book in a slow half circle. She stared at the cover and massaged her temples. "I don't get it. I've read several of Chandler Michaels's romance novels. They're all about virtuous heroines and gallant heroes finding true love. That he'd even write garbage like this just blows my mind."

Parker couldn't get the image of his brokenhearted aunt Ruthy out of his thoughts. "People will do all kinds of things for money."

"But his books top the bestseller lists regularly. He can't be that hard up for cash."

Frustration simmered in Parker's belly. He pushed his half-empty cup to one side and folded his hands on the table. "We can sit here and ruminate over Chuck's finances, or we can figure out how to keep Sailor from falling for his fake charm. When you suggested this meeting, I thought you were going to explain exactly how this book is supposed to help. Short of showing it to her so she can see Chuck Michalicek for the dog he is, I don't see any value in it whatsoever."

"Don't you understand? Sailor idolizes Chandler Michaels—or rather the romantic heartthrob she imagines him to be. I won't be the one to crush her dreams. I don't think you want that either." Kathy fisted one hand atop the book. "So use your head, Parker. Think outside the box."

The words knocked him backward like a punch to the sternum. *All right, Lord, You've got my attention.* He heaved a weary breath. "So what am I missing here? Obviously you have a plan in mind."

"Oh, you are dense, aren't you?" Kathy groaned. "No wonder you're pushing forty and still available."

"Hey, forty's a few years off yet. Get to the point, will you?"

"My point," Kathy said with a smirk, "is that if Chandler Michaels tries these tactics on Sailor, she'll see for herself what kind of guy he is."

"But won't that be even more devastating than just handing her the book?" Parker's gut clenched. "Not to mention more dangerous. Letting her actually spend time with him would be like sending her to the wolves—make that *wolf.*"

"That's where you come in. While she's mooning over Chandler and escorting him to various writerly functions, you will be romancing her in true heroic fashion—doing the exact *opposite* of everything he describes in this book."

Parker couldn't stifle a pained laugh. "Now you're the one who's acting dense. In case you haven't figured it out, I don't have a romantic bone in my body."

Kathy drained the last of her latte and stood, hands braced on the table and her nose in Parker's face. "Then I suggest you go dig one up somewhere before Sailor rides off into the sunset on Chandler's not-so-lily-white steed."

❧

As the first glimmer of morning light filtered through her mini-blinds, Sailor's eyes popped open. Had she only dreamed the whole salon and spa experience? Hesitantly she touched her hair. Wispy bangs tickled her forehead. Soft layers brushed her cheeks. She sat up with a start and found her reflection in the dresser mirror. Even mussed from sleep, her hair fell across her shoulders in flattering lines.

"Wow," she told the image in the mirror, "you're looking pretty good there, girlfriend." She tilted her fingertips toward a sunbeam and admired the shiny, perfectly shaped nails.

Afraid she'd never be able to reproduce Parker's styling results without several practice sessions, she clipped her hair atop her head and tried not to get it damp during her morning shower. Afterward she made several attempts to match Sandra's light touch with the makeup brushes. Finally satisfied, she stood in front of her closet, pondering what to wear to church.

Her shoulders drooped at the meager choices. She'd definitely need a wardrobe update before she spent much time in Chandler's company. Opting for a khaki skirt and navy twinset, she finished dressing and hurried to the kitchen for a quick breakfast.

Uncle Ed turned toward her with the oversize brown coffee mug he'd just filled. Again he cocked his head as if trying to figure out what was different about her. She hoped she'd kept the makeup subtle enough that he wouldn't come unglued and report to her parents that their daughter was turning into a shameless hussy.

"'Morning, Uncle Ed. Sleep well?" She busied herself preparing a bowl of organic wheat flakes.

"Fair to middlin'." He harrumphed. "How you can pour watery blue milk on that cardboard and call it breakfast is beyond me."

"I like skim milk." She carried the bowl to the table. "And the cereal is full of bran and nuts and flaxseed. It's good, really."

"And good *for* you, too," he mimicked. "You're mighty dressed up for work today."

His occasional mental lapses stabbed her heart. "It's Sunday, Uncle Ed. I'm dressed for church. You're always welcome to come along."

He muttered something unintelligible and carried his coffee to the living room.

Alone in the kitchen Sailor paused between bites and asked herself why she continued church attendance when her spiritual life seemed almost as dry as Uncle Ed's. Part of it was habit, of course. Part of it was obligation. How could she explain to Josh and Deb Fanning and her other friends at Mission Hills Bible Church that her relationship with God had been faltering for years?

If only she could understand why. Unlike Uncle Ed, she couldn't blame it on

Aunt Trina's untimely death, and there'd been no other tragedies or upheavals to cause her to doubt God's love. No, hers had been a gradual drift, a cooling of the spiritual flame, a sense that though God was indeed out there somewhere He couldn't be bothered with a meek little mouse of a girl like Sailor.

The monstrous old black telephone jangled in the hallway. Startled, she dropped her spoon. On her way to the phone, she wished for the millionth time that her uncle wasn't so old-fashioned and antitechnology. Could it really hurt to subscribe to the caller ID service so she could at least prepare herself before picking up the receiver?

"Hi, Sailor. Didn't wake you, did I?" Deb Fanning sounded her usual cheery self.

Sailor smiled into the phone. "Are you kidding? I've been up since the crack of dawn."

"Should have known. Josh and I have to swing by the bakery to pick up doughnuts for our Sunday school class. We could pick you up on the way."

"Thanks, that's—" Sailor bit her lip. "Um, Deb, I just had this crazy idea." Crazy—and completely out of the blue. "I've been feeling a little. . .stale. . .in my attitude toward worship lately, and I was thinking it might help to visit some different churches, maybe get a fresh perspective."

Deb's soft breath whispered through the phone. "I've sensed for a while that you were struggling. I don't blame you a bit. Do you have someplace in mind?"

"Kathy's always told me I'd be welcome to attend with her." Then she remembered Kathy saying Lucille and Lorraine Douglas sang in the choir there. Nope, once a week with the Doublemint Twins was all Sailor could handle. "But I'm open to suggestions if you have any."

Deb remained quiet for a moment. "I've seen ads for a big church across town that looks interesting. Rejoice Fellowship, I think it's called. Josh told me the pastor is on the YMCA board of directors, and he likes him a lot."

The Fannings' recommendation was enough for Sailor. After saying goodbye to Deb, she looked up Rejoice Fellowship in the phone directory and called to ask the service times. Checking her watch, she found she could just make it for the ten-thirty worship.

The massive stucco sanctuary looked new. Narrow, beveled-glass windows framed the entrance and paraded around the hexagonal-shaped exterior. Sailor parked in a spot reserved for visitors, checked her reflection in the rearview mirror, and did a double take. Would she ever get used to seeing the new and improved version of herself?

As she exited the car, a young couple passed her on their way to the sanctuary. The woman, several months pregnant, paused and smiled over her shoulder. "Visiting? Glad to have you."

"Thanks." Sailor returned a quivery smile and fell in step with them on their way up the sidewalk.

"My name's Missy Underwood, and this is my husband, Zach. Are you new to Birkenstock?"

"Um, no." It occurred to Sailor that she actually enjoyed being noticed. Feeling braver she introduced herself and confessed her need for a fresh perspective on worship.

"You'll definitely find that here," Zach said. "Rejoice Fellowship is a real Spirit-filled congregation."

Sailor's steps faltered briefly. Did she even know what it meant to be Spirit filled? An image of her parents slaving away on a new Bible translation flitted through her thoughts. Yes, they were dedicated workers for the Gospel. Yes, they always prayed openly and studied the scriptures. But Sailor wasn't sure even her very pious parents could be described as Spirit filled.

She was missing something—something vital. If what Zach said was true, maybe she would find it here.

She glanced up to see Zach holding open one of the broad double doors. As she and Missy stepped through to the marble and glass foyer, Missy cocked her head and gave Sailor a hard stare. "Wait a minute. I know you. Aren't you a patient of Dr. Ivan Simpson's?"

Sailor drew in her chin. "Dr. Simpson is my dentist."

"I'm a part-time hygienist there, but I just started my maternity leave." Missy's crystal laugh echoed in the cavernous foyer. "I'm not so good with names, but I'm usually better with faces. You look different with your hair down. I love it, by the way."

"Th–thank you." Sailor smoothed a flyaway strand and stood a little straighter.

"So you probably know Laura Travis, the other hygienist. She attends here, too." Missy started toward the sanctuary doors, where sounds from a praise band grew louder. "You'll sit with us, won't you?"

Sailor's feet felt superglued to the marble tile. If Laura Travis worshipped here, in all likelihood so did her son. The possibility of running into Parker sent Sailor's heart plunging to her toes.

Get over it, Sailor. She gave herself a mental shake and forced her legs into motion. Parker was her water aerobics student and now her hairstylist, nothing more. In only a few days she'd be face-to-face with Chandler Michaels, the man she'd been dreaming about since high school—ever since she fell in love with his book jacket photo on the back cover of *Love's Eternal Melody*.

Chapter 10

Parker gave his grandmother a kiss on her crinkly cheek, waved goodbye to the other sweet old gals at Willow Tree, and jogged out to the parking lot. With a grateful lift of his brow, he realized his knees hadn't felt this good in years—or his shoulders either. He checked his watch—just time to grab a root beer and burger at the Sonic drive-through, and then run home to scarf it down and change into his swim trunks before heading to the Y. Probably not the best idea to work out on a full stomach, but the hour between six and seven was all Sailor had available tonight for the extra coaching she'd promised him.

He still couldn't get over her showing up at church yesterday. Was the Lord intentionally bringing them together? *If that's true, Father, then You'll have to keep working on me.* Could he really hope to have it all—a successful business, his volunteer service at church and Willow Tree, looking after Mom and Grams, *and* true love?

Could he live with himself if he passed up the chance to find out?

He gulped down the rest of his burger, gave his teeth a thorough brushing, and swished with mouthwash. If he'd had his head on straight, he'd have asked the Sonic folks to hold the onions. Choosing not to chance Sailor's disapproval by showing up in cutoffs again, he tightened the string at the waist of those hideous orange swim trunks. He pulled an oversize gray T-shirt over his head, slid his feet into flip-flops, grabbed a towel, and headed out the door.

On the way to the Y, he mentally recapped the chapters he'd read last night in *Romance by the Book.* Clearly ol' Chuck was all about flash and dash. He'd devoted whole sections to choosing the perfect babe-magnet car, decorating the ideal bachelor pad, practicing tried-and-true come-on lines, setting the mood for the first kiss.

Parker grimaced. All the other stuff aside, he doubted he'd have to worry about a first kiss anytime soon. . .if ever.

Entering the pool area, he spotted Sailor finishing a mom-and-tot swim class. She climbed the steps behind a toddler in a flowery pink tank suit and bent to share a drippy hug. The sight made Parker's stomach clench. He clamped his lips together, marched across the deck, and wondered why his mouth had gone suddenly dry.

"Hi," he said hoarsely. One of Chandler Michaels's cheesier pickup lines came to mind, something about asking if she knew CPR because she took his breath away. He was almost tempted to use it.

"Perfect timing. Just let me get my gear." Sailor fastened a towel around her waist and started for the storage cabinet. Before she'd taken two steps toward him, she drew to a halt, her eyes the size of volleyballs. "Oh my. No wonder you'd rather wear your cutoffs."

Heat shot up Parker's neck. He dropped his towel open and held it in front of him like a curtain. "I told you, Mabry's was a little low on choices. Believe me, I'll be shopping for another suit first chance I get."

Sailor's suppressed chuckle came out as a grunt. "Excuse me while I go get my sunglasses."

Since when did giving a girl a classy haircut turn her into Miss Snark? Had he created a monster? He tossed his towel, T-shirt, and flip-flops onto the bleachers, collected a set of workout gear from the cabinet, and slid into the water before he blinded too many innocent bystanders.

Dropping into the pool with barely a splash, Sailor offered a repentant grin. "Sorry for teasing you. Ready to get to work?"

The next hour was all business, Sailor's natural confidence in her teaching skills hiding every trace of insecurity. They finished the intense workout with a series of stretches. Parker heaved himself onto the deck and shook out arms that felt like rubber. "I apologize for ever thinking water aerobics was for wimps."

Sailor sat next to him on the edge of the pool. "I did work you a lot harder than I would most of my students." She grinned and aimed a splash at his midsection. "But I knew you could take it."

He splashed her back. "Thanks. I *think*."

She flicked water droplets off her cheek. "I was wondering. . ."

"Yeah?"

"Allan Biltmore is hosting a welcome dinner for Chandler Michaels this Friday, and I—"

Parker didn't realize his snort of disgust was audible until he caught Sailor's surprised glance. He scraped the back of his hand across his face. "Water in the nose. You were saying?"

"I'm worried about being able to get my hair to look as good as you did. I was hoping maybe you could. . .help."

"Do your hair for you? Sure, come by the shop Friday afternoon and I'll work you in. On the house, of course." He cast her a cockeyed grin and rubbed a tender calf muscle. "Consider it part of our trade agreement."

"That's really nice of you." Her shy vulnerability had crept back in, and it tugged at Parker's heart. He found himself staring at the curve of her lips and imagining what that first kiss would be like.

He cleared his throat and tore his gaze away, fixing it on a middle-aged swimmer churning up whitecaps in the lap lane. "If you want, you could also come over after class tomorrow, and I could shampoo your hair and then give you a few pointers with the styling brush and blow-dryer."

"That would be great!" Sailor beamed him a thankful smile. Then her shoulders sagged. "Except the Bards of Birkenstock committee meets every Tuesday. I have to get home and fix supper for my uncle before I head to the library."

"Wednesday then. Or Thursday. I'll make time for you whenever." *Just say the word.*

Her eyes sparkled as if he'd just offered her the Hope Diamond. "I have an extralong lunch break on Wednesdays. Would sometime between twelve and two work for you?"

Parker did a mental recap of his Wednesday schedule. He could probably shift his insurance agent's haircut and mustache trim a half hour earlier. Sandra, the makeup consultant, had asked him to touch up her highlights, but she wouldn't mind waiting another day or two.

Anticipation fizzed beneath his rib cage. "Come at twelve. I'll order takeout for us, and afterward I'll show you some styling tricks. What sounds good for lunch?"

"I can't let you do that."

"My pleasure. We both have to eat, don't we?"

Sailor chewed her lip. "At least let me bring lunch. How does salads from Audra's Café sound?"

"Make mine the Tuscan grilled chicken, extra meat, and you've got a deal."

❧

Sailor noticed Parker's new navy pin-striped trunks the moment he walked in the door for their Tuesday class. When she complimented him, he struck a male model's pose, swim towel slung over one shoulder. His quirky grin and wink turned her insides to gelatin. She spun around and dropped into the pool before the rest of the class could notice the blush warming her face.

After the class ended, another ten laps of full-out freestyle barely made a dent in her nervous energy. What was it about Parker Travis that so distracted her? Chandler Michaels arrived in town tomorrow! She needed to keep her eye on the goal and her mind off the unnervingly endearing hairstylist.

Later, at the Bards of Birkenstock meeting, Sailor presented the list of ideas she'd put together for Chandler's extended visit: speaking at a high school assembly, holding a series of readings at the library, giving talks at local business clubs' weekly meetings, sitting in on book discussion groups, and of course all the requisite book-signing events.

"Wonderful ideas, Sailor." Donna DuPont jotted notes on her legal pad. "I'll let you take care of handling all the arrangements."

Great. She should have known.

Kathy patted her arm. "Don't worry, I'll help you make the calls."

Allan Biltmore leaned toward Sailor with a concerned frown. "Before you confirm too many of those engagements, let me run the list by Charles—excuse me, *Chandler*. We wouldn't want to overwhelm him."

Donna nodded. "Good point. Would you give us an update on Friday's dinner plans, Allan?"

"It's shaping up to be a delightful evening. Chandler wants things relaxed and homey, so the attire is dressy casual. For the menu, he reminded me his favorite meal growing up was something his Polish grandmother made called *bigos*, or hunter's stew. Nelda, my wife, has been scouring the Internet for recipes. I understand it's very meaty, with bacon, sauerkraut, and spices."

Sailor's stomach lurched. Maybe she should fill up on veggies before the dinner and hope no one noticed if she only took a few bites.

"I'd like a really good turnout," Allan continued, "so feel free to bring a family member or friend. Just let me know by noon Thursday so we know how many to prepare for."

On the way to the parking lot after the meeting, Kathy stopped by Sailor's car. "Think you'll invite anyone to go with you to Chandler's dinner?"

"Me? No." Sailor juggled her folder of meeting notes and poked around the side pocket of her purse for her car keys. "You're my best friend, and you'll already be there. And poor Uncle Ed would be completely adrift at a function like that."

Kathy rested a hip against the fender and crossed her ankles. "I wasn't talking about your uncle. I thought maybe. . ." She wiggled her eyebrows. "Parker Travis?"

Sailor's keys slipped from her grasp and clattered to the pavement. When she stooped to retrieve them, her folder splayed open, and a gust of wind sent her notes skittering between the parked cars. "Great, just great."

She chased papers in one direction while Kathy scurried in another. With most of the pages corralled and back in the folder, Sailor unlocked the car and shoved everything across to the passenger seat. Huffing, she straightened to face Kathy. "Thanks for helping. Sorry I snapped at you."

Kathy folded her arms around her zippered portfolio. "I didn't realize mentioning Parker's name would throw you into such a tizzy."

"It didn't. I—" Sailor inhaled a calming breath before her pitch rose any higher. "I can't imagine what made you think I'd even consider asking Parker."

"Well, I know you've been seeing more of each other lately."

"He's in my class, and he did my hair. I wouldn't exactly call that *seeing* each other." Why Sailor felt she had to be so defensive, she had no clue. She dropped into the driver's seat and stabbed her keys into the ignition.

Kathy leaned over the top of Sailor's open door. "Then maybe I'll invite him. I wouldn't mind showing up with a handsome guy on my arm."

Sailor's fingers tightened around the steering wheel. "I didn't know you knew Parker that well."

"We had a nice chat at the library the other day and found out we have some. . .common interests."

"That's great. Then you should invite him." Sailor forced a tight-lipped smile and reached for the door handle. "It's getting late. Uncle Ed will worry."

Kathy waved good-bye as Sailor backed out of her parking space. Something about her friend's self-satisfied smile evoked a twinge of suspicion.

Then it dawned on her that Kathy hadn't once lectured her this evening about her crush on Chandler Michaels. In fact, she'd hardly even alluded to it in almost a week. If Kathy's budding interest in Parker Travis diverted her from bad-mouthing Chandler, it would sure make life easier for Sailor.

Chapter 11

"There you go, Pete. Good for another month." Parker swirled the black cape off his mustachioed insurance agent, strewing salt-and-pepper hair clippings across the floor.

"Fastest trim I ever got." Pete Walden collected his tan blazer from the coat hook. "If I didn't know better, I'd think you were rushing me out of here for a hot date."

Parker reached for the broom and dustpan. His sweeping motions hurried Pete out of the cubicle. "Carla will set up your next appointment. Good seeing you."

"I'm going, I'm going!" Pete looked skyward with a chuckle and strode toward the front. The last words Parker could make out were, "Must be one special lady."

Oh, she is, believe me. Not that he was happy about being so transparent. Everyone in the salon seemed to have picked up on his agitation this morning. Now, as he started rearranging tables in the break room and setting out the lime green picnic ware he'd borrowed from his mother, the rumors started flying big-time. By then there was no sense denying the obvious: He'd invited someone special to lunch.

He turned from adjusting the mini blinds over the back window to see Carla leaning in the doorway. A wide grin lit her face. "She's here. Shall I send her on back?"

Parker's stomach catapulted into his throat. Would he look too anxious if he hurried out front to meet Sailor? He'd have a hard enough time convincing her he regularly set out real plates and flatware for takeout.

He gulped. "Thanks, Carla. And maybe you and the others wouldn't mind eating at your stations today?"

"No prob." She winked an aqua-frosted eyelid. "Enjoy your lunch date."

While he waited, he tried a few nonchalant poses. First he leaned against the counter with his hands in his pockets. Nope, too bored looking. He grabbed a styling magazine off a bookshelf and plopped into a chair. Uh-uh, too disinterested. He tossed the magazine onto the shelf.

His nose twitched as the odor of burned coffee wafted his way. He glanced toward the other end of the counter and leaped to his feet. Someone had emptied the coffeepot without turning off the heating element.

"Terrific." He flicked the OFF switch and jerked the carafe off the burner. Without thinking he turned on the sink faucet and stuck the carafe under the flow. The shock of cold water hitting hot glass shattered the carafe instantly. Parker released the handle with a yelp.

Something hit the floor behind him a split second before Sailor appeared at his side. "What happened? Are you hurt?"

"I don't think so—" Then he saw the blood seeping from his left palm. Pain sliced up his arm.

"Here, hold it under the water." Sailor guided his hand beneath the tap, and he sucked in his breath as the stream washed over the wound. Red swirls circled the white porcelain sink and slid down the drain.

Sailor tore several paper towels from the dispenser. When the flow of blood diminished, she turned off the water and wrapped the towels around his hand. "It looked a lot worse at first, but I don't think it's deep. Come sit down, okay? And keep pressure on it."

Rewind, rewind. Not exactly the way Parker had envisioned their lunch date starting out. How could he have been so stupid? He caught sight of the Audra's Café take-out bag where Sailor had dropped it near the door. "Nothing like a little blood to ruin your appetite, huh?"

She followed his gaze. "Don't worry about it. Here, let me see if your hand has stopped bleeding." With gentle fingers she peeled aside the paper towels.

His palm looked pink and puckered from the cold water, but only the slightest traces of red oozed from the cut. He blew through pursed lips. "Whew. I think I'm gonna live."

"Oh please. It's hardly a scratch." Sailor gave an exaggerated shudder and strode to the sink. "What were you trying to do here anyway?"

"Someone left an empty coffeepot on the burner." Parker dabbed at his cut, now barely visible. Embarrassment aside, he'd been enjoying Sailor's TLC and was almost sorry the bleeding had been stanched so quickly.

"Don't tell me you stuck hot glass under cold water! That's incredibly dangerous." Sailor started opening drawers and cabinets. "Do you have any paper sacks around?"

He stood. "Leave it. I'll take care of it later."

"I don't mind." In the next cupboard she found a stack of paper grocery bags. She spread one open and set it on the floor then began extracting the larger pieces of glass and dropping them into the bag.

"Be careful. I don't want you getting cut." Parker nudged her aside and used the paper towel to finish clearing glass from the sink. He rinsed the smallest shards down the drain and turned to find Sailor carefully folding the top of the bag closed. "Let me take that out to the Dumpster, and you can open up those salads for us. There's bottled water and iced tea in the fridge."

When he returned from the alley, Sailor had dished their salads out of the plastic take-out containers and onto the picnic plates. She unscrewed the cap from a water bottle and poured it over the ice cubes in her glass. Looking up with a shy smile, she said, "I wasn't sure what you wanted to drink."

He grabbed an iced tea and sank into his chair. "Thanks for picking up lunch." With a grimace he added, "And no extra charge for the floor show."

Sailor spread an aqua-and-green-patterned napkin on her lap. "I don't know what I'd do if my new hairstylist were incapacitated. I'm counting on you for Friday night, you know."

He knew. All too well. "Shall I say grace?"

"Please." Sailor folded her hands on the edge of the table.

As he offered up thanks for the meal, Parker had trouble keeping his eyes lowered and his thoughts reverent. After the "amen," he tacked on a silent plea for the Lord's guidance in helping him protect Sailor from the lecherous Chuck Michalicek.

He picked up his knife and fork and tried to slice through the chicken breast without putting undue pressure on his cut. Maybe it was minuscule, but it stung like crazy. "What time is the dinner?"

"We're invited at six for mingling and appetizers, with dinner at seven. They're serving some kind of meat stew Chandler's grandmother always made. It sounds really artery clogging." She made a face and pushed aside a fried wonton. "Audra knows I don't eat these. Guess whoever filled the order didn't get the message."

One of the chapters in Chandler's guidebook dealt with how to get your date to share your interests. Parker decided he'd rather learn Sailor's likes and dislikes and show her he cared about her as a person. *Note to self: Sailor eats healthy.* "Your salad looks good. Is that salmon?"

"It's the Asian salad with grilled salmon and ginger dressing on the side—my absolute favorite."

"I'll have to try it sometime." He popped the cap off the small container of Italian dressing that came with his salad and drizzled it over the greens. "If you come in around four thirty for me to do your hair, will that give you time to change for dinner?"

"Four thirty should be fine." She sagged against the chair. "Except I have no idea what I'm going to wear. Mr. Biltmore said dressy casual. Casual for me is sweats over my bathing suit."

Parker didn't dare say out loud how fabulous she looked in a bathing suit. "We do have a wardrobe consultant here. I'd be happy to—"

"No, Parker, you're doing enough already. I'll see if Kathy can go shopping with me after work tonight." She gave her head a sudden shake. "Scratch that. She has choir practice on Wednesday evenings. Maybe tomorrow. She'll probably want to find something cute to wear, too, since—" She drew her lip between her teeth and angled him a secretive look.

He laid down his fork. "What?"

"You'll find out soon enough."

Whatever it was, the warning pinch in his gut told him he wasn't going to like it.

❧

Back in her swimsuit, Sailor gazed at her reflection in the ladies' locker room mirror. What a shame she had to get in the pool again and ruin the perfect style Parker had helped her achieve. After lunch he'd given her another luxurious shampoo that turned her brain to languid mush beneath his fingers. Then he'd shown her step-by-step how to use a round styling brush to section off her hair and dry it into soft curves around her face. When they finished, he'd selected a few of the products he'd used from a display case in the reception area but once again refused to charge her for anything.

"Goodness, he's a nice guy." She turned from the mirror and checked the wall clock—nearly three. Allan Biltmore should be on his way home from the Springfield-Branson National Airport after picking up Chandler Michaels.

Sailor's stomach flip-flopped. Of all the days to be stuck teaching classes at the Y! The ladies from Willow Tree would be arriving any moment for their water aerobics class. Much as she loved them, she'd much rather be saying her first hellos to Chandler right about now—even though the very idea reduced her to a bundle of raw nerves. With a frustrated groan she pulled on a pair of sweats and hurried to the lobby.

The Willow Tree passenger van had just pulled up in front of the sliding glass doors. Donning her competent instructor facade, Sailor joined the driver at the rear of the van to retrieve a couple of walkers and a folding wheelchair then helped the ladies out the side door.

"Oh Sailor, I love your new haircut!" The white-haired Mrs. Parker plopped into the wheelchair. "You've been to see my grandson, haven't you?"

Sailor sucked in a breath. "Parker Travis is *your* grandson? He mentioned his grandmother took my classes, but I hadn't put two and two together. Why didn't you say something before?"

Mrs. Parker waved a hand in front of her face. "Didn't want to come across as a meddling old granny."

"You, meddling?" Sailor laughed and gripped the wheelchair handles. "The name Parker—I should have realized."

"My husband and I didn't have any sons, so Laura and our son-in-law named their boy Parker to pass along the family name."

"It's a nice name—although confusing at first." Sailor steered the chair through the double doors into the pool area.

"I'm so glad you and my grandson are getting acquainted. His mother and I have been waiting a long, long time for him to meet a nice young lady like you."

Sailor's cheeks tingled. She halted the wheelchair near the pool steps and locked the brakes. "I may have to change my mind about that 'meddling' business."

The elderly woman chuckled and allowed Sailor to help her out of the zip-up terry robe covering her skirted blue swimsuit. "I suppose by now you've figured out who gave you the tickets to the Frankie Verona show."

"That was. . .very nice of you." *And why am I not surprised?* Sailor bit her tongue to keep from saying how she really felt about such manipulative tactics while she aided Mrs. Parker's cautious descent into the pool.

A few of the more mobile ladies were already splashing around doing their warm-up exercises. Buoyed by the water, the arthritic Mrs. Parker moved with a freedom she could never enjoy on dry land—a sight that warmed Sailor's heart even as she mentally chided the woman for her misguided attempts at matchmaking.

❧

On Thursday evening Parker followed Grams's wheelchair down the long corridor to her apartment and held the door as she rolled inside. "Thanks for inviting me for supper," he said. "The Willow Tree buffet sure beats the frozen Szechuan chicken I was planning to heat up in the microwave."

"You're welcome to join me anytime." Grams allowed Parker to help her into her favorite chair and then reached for the pull chain on the nearby table lamp. "Want to start some decaf? My friend Margaret brought me a loaf of zucchini bread yesterday."

"Sounds good." Parker flipped the light switch in the kitchenette and found a package of french vanilla decaf in the freezer. "One cup or two?"

"Just one for me. Tell me more about this dinner party you're going to. The Biltmores are hosting, you said? That old goat's been around almost as long as I have."

He should have known once he mentioned the Chandler Michaels dinner engagement that he'd never hear the end of it from Grams. "Mr. Biltmore may be getting up in years, but apparently he's very active with the Birkenstock Arts and Letters Association."

Grams gave a cynical laugh. "Unless my memory's getting as unreliable as my joints, literature was never your best subject. How'd you end up on your former English teacher's guest list?"

"A friend on the committee invited me. Kathy Richmond, the librarian." Kathy's call last night had thrown him for a loop, but he couldn't refuse a chance to size up Chuck Michalicek in person. *And* keep an eye on Sailor. He filled the water reservoir and turned on the coffeemaker. "Want your zucchini bread warmed up?"

"With a dollop of butter, please. I heard our sweet little Sailor Kern is on the Bards of Birkenstock committee. She'll be there, I'm sure."

"Probably so." He found the zucchini bread wrapped in foil in the refrigerator. Finding a cutting board, he sliced off two good-sized slabs, spread them with butter, and set the plate in the microwave. The coffeemaker beeped the ready signal a few minutes later, and he served their dessert and coffee in Grams's cozy sitting room.

Parker slid a forkful of zucchini bread between his teeth and let the moist, buttery sweetness dissolve on his tongue. "Mmm, good stuff."

Grams blew across her coffee and took a careful sip. "*Probably* so?"

He shot his grandmother a confused look. "Probably so, what?"

"You said Sailor would *probably* be at the Biltmores'. Come now, Parker. You're not fooling anyone." She set down her mug and dabbed her lips with a pink paper napkin. "There's only one reason you'd ever be caught dead at a fancy dinner party, much less a *literary* dinner party, and that's because *she's* going to be there. You're smitten, and there's no use denying it."

Parker slid his dessert plate onto the low table in front of him. He scraped his palms up and down his temples. "Maybe I am. But *she's* smitten with Chandler Michaels."

"Does she know he's really Charles Michalicek? Does she know how that man hurt your aunt Ruthy, not to mention countless other young women blinded by his charms?"

"Yes to the first question, no to the second. And that's what scares me to death."

❧

Uncle Ed flaked off a bite of the pecan-crusted tilapia Sailor had prepared for their supper. "Sissy food, that's what this is. Your aunt Trina knew how to fry up a tasty batch of catfish."

Sailor stabbed a forkful of green beans. "I'd be happy to *grill* you some catfish sometime."

"Not the same. Not the same at all."

It wouldn't do any good to remind him how pleased his doctor was when his latest cholesterol reading dropped fifteen points from last time. Uncle Ed seemed happiest when he had something to complain about, and Sailor's cooking was as safe a target as any.

Finishing her meal, she carried her dishes to the sink. "Kathy's picking me up in a few minutes to go shopping. Anything you need?"

"Can't think of a thing. Can't think what you need to go spending your hard-earned money on either."

Sailor capped the salad dressing and set it in the refrigerator. "I told you, I need something nice to wear to the dinner at Allan Biltmore's tomorrow night."

"Oh right, for that loony tunes romance writer." Uncle Ed poked at a cherry tomato on his salad plate and flinched when the juice squirted him in the eye. "Do your parents know how you're spending your evenings?"

Guilt niggled Sailor's nape. No doubt her parents would have a few things to say about her infatuation with Chandler Michaels—exactly why she purposely kept her e-mails vague when describing her involvement with the Bards of Birkenstock committee.

The sound of a car horn saved her from coming up with a reply to her uncle's question. "There's vanilla pudding in the fridge for your dessert. I'll be home before ten."

Scooping up her purse, she fled out the front door and plopped into the passenger seat of Kathy's car. "Let's shop till we drop!"

Kathy threw the gearshift into REVERSE. "This has got to be a first—Sailor Kern excited about a shopping excursion."

"I've never had a reason to care before. But tomorrow night—"

"I know, I know. Tomorrow night you get to meet the romance writer of your dreams." Kathy turned at the next corner and aimed her car toward downtown.

"I can hardly believe he's here already." Sailor's feet did a happy dance on the floorboard. She felt sixteen again—or at least how sixteen *should* have felt. "We probably shouldn't drive by the Biltmores' to see if we could catch a glimpse of him."

Kathy angled her a look. "Probably not."

Birkenstock's shopping district wasn't huge, so it didn't take long for Sailor and Kathy to investigate the ladies' apparel offerings. If Kathy hadn't been along, Sailor might have settled for the first long-sleeved, calf-length basic black dress she laid eyes on in Mabry's Department Store.

"Give me a break, Sailor. You're going to a party, not a funeral." Kathy steered her to a rack of tops and slacks in bright spring colors. "This peasant blouse is *you.* And the swirls of aqua will bring out your eyes."

Sailor squinted and held a hand to her brow. "I've never worn anything that colorful in my life."

"And it's about time. Go try it on with these white cropped pants."

"For a dinner party?" Sailor frowned and tried to shove the garments back on the rack. Despite her intentions to choose something stylish and tastefully alluring, she found it wasn't as easy as she'd hoped to take this next step out of her comfort zone. "I thought maybe a nice skirt. . ."

"Trust me. A cute necklace and earrings, maybe some white canvas espadrilles, and you'll be the belle of the ball." Kathy herded Sailor toward the dressing room. "And I expect you to model for me. I'll be checking out those silk blouses."

In the privacy of the dressing room, Sailor held up the pants and top and cast a doubtful gaze at her reflection. Quite a change from the usual conservative styles in humdrum colors that comprised the bulk of her wardrobe.

But where had conservative and humdrum gotten her? Absolutely nowhere.

"And where, exactly, do you want to be?"

The thought took her by surprise—a voice soothingly familiar and yet one she hadn't been paying much attention to lately. Her throat tightened. She sank onto the narrow bench beneath a chrome hook. Where *did* she want to be?

Not so much where, as with whom. She wanted to be with someone who saw her perfectly and loved her unconditionally, just like those couples in the romance novels. Someone who cared what she thought, who listened when she spoke, who looked at her as if no one else mattered in the world.

"And you think Chandler Michaels is that someone?"

Only a man who knew how to touch a woman's heart could write stories like those. Before the voices of doubt grew any louder, she slipped out of her jeans and into the chic new outfit she hoped would magically transform her into the woman Chandler Michaels would want to spend the rest of his life with.

Chapter 12

Parker straightened the combs and brushes lining his styling- tools drawer then did the same with an array of gels, mousses, and hair sprays on the shelf opposite the mirror. He checked his watch—4:27. He'd rushed his last two afternoon appointments through so there'd be no chance of running over into the time he'd set aside for Sailor.

His visit with Grams last night had left him only slightly more hopeful about his chances with Sailor. After he'd explained the idea Kathy Richmond had come up with—using Chandler's romance book as the perfect guide to how *not* to romance a woman—Grams had reminded Parker he already owned the best romance guidebook ever written: the Holy Bible itself, God's love letter to His children.

"And if you *really* want to get down to pure romance," Grams had said, "just turn to the Song of Songs. Never were more romantic words penned than Solomon's poems about his beautiful lover."

Home in his apartment last night, he'd opened his Bible to the Song of Songs. The elegant poetry in simile and metaphor carried him places in his heart he'd never allowed himself to imagine. To love someone so purely, so deeply, so openly, so reverently—to experience a love that so beautifully mirrored God's own love for His children—Parker's longing to personally experience such love became a gnawing hunger.

And he felt more certain than ever that he wanted it with Sailor Kern.

"Hi, Parker."

At the sound of her voice, the can of hair spray he'd been holding clattered to the tile floor. He sucked in a breath and forced a grin. "Hey, right on time."

Sailor glanced at the hair spray can rolling around between their feet. "Good thing that wasn't glass."

"No kidding." If he needed any further convincing of his total head over heels attraction to Sailor, his terminal klutziness in her presence ought to be plenty.

Time to focus, Parker. She expected him to be the consummate professional, and that's what he had to be. . .for now.

❧

By the time she left the shop, Sailor once again felt like Cinderella transformed. Pamela had touched up her manicure, Sandra had done her makeup, and Parker had styled her hair in a glamorous side-swept 'do that would show off the aqua hoop earrings Kathy had urged her to buy to match her outfit.

At home she slipped quietly in the back door. No way Uncle Ed could miss the changes in her appearance this time.

"That you, Sailor?" he called from the living room.

"I only have a few minutes to change for the dinner party." She scurried down the hall to her bedroom.

Closing the door, she took a few slow breaths. She had nothing to feel guilty about. She was an adult, after all, a red-blooded, passionate, thirty-two-year-old woman. A woman who was tired of looking mousy or—even worse—invisible. A woman who was ready to break out of her shell and start living.

She'd showered before leaving the Y, so all she had to do was slip into her new clothes. Careful not to muss her hair or manicure, she changed into the white crop pants and aqua-print blouse. The flowing fabric draped across her shoulders in a flattering line, with a self-tie that cinched her waist. Translucent sleeves angled to a point below her elbows. When she added the beaded necklace and bracelet, hoop earrings, and the white espadrilles, she stood before the mirror and gasped at the attractive woman gazing back at her.

At a few minutes after six she slipped down the hall and out through the kitchen before Uncle Ed could catch a glimpse of her. Any criticism from him would mar the wonderful evening she'd been dreaming of ever since she learned of Chandler's early return to Birkenstock.

"I'm leaving, Uncle Ed," she called from the back door. "Last night's leftovers are in the fridge. You can warm them up when you're ready."

"You mind your manners at that party, young lady. Remember who you are."

"Yes, sir." How many times had she been issued that warning? "Remember who you are" actually meant "Remember who your uncle and parents are, and don't embarrass or shame us."

She had no intention of doing either. She only wanted to be seen and loved for who she truly was, not as some goody-two-shoes phony.

Ten minutes later she arrived at the Biltmores'. Cars already lined the street, and she had to park three houses down from the posh brick two-story. She didn't see Kathy's car yet—but then Parker might be driving. The thought of them together caused a tiny pinch under her rib cage, which she quickly shook off as she marched up the sidewalk. Chandler Michaels, the man of her dreams, waited somewhere beyond the Biltmores' beveled-glass front door.

She reached for the bell with nervous fingers while her other hand clamped down on the new white woven clutch that matched her shoes. *Get a grip, Sailor. This is the moment you've been waiting for.*

Allan Biltmore greeted her with a gallant smile. "Welcome, Sailor! Come in, come in." He looked beyond her shoulder. "What, no date? I thought sure a young lady as lovely as you—"

"Nope, I'm by myself." With a steadying breath she marshaled what confidence she could and strode into the marble-tiled entry hall.

"I'm sure you're anxious to meet our guest of honor. He's in the living room."

Sailor's heart stammered out an erratic staccato as she followed Allan Biltmore through a broad archway. In the living room a gaggle of committee members and guests surrounded someone seated near the fireplace. The way everyone oohed and aahed and generally fawned over everything the person said, it could only be Chandler.

Allan took Sailor's elbow and pushed forward through the group of admirers. "Here she is, Chandler, the young lady who's arranging your personal appearances during your stay. May I introduce Sailor Kern."

The crowd parted, and Allan stepped aside. Sailor's eager gaze fell upon a complete stranger—a stoop-shouldered, gray-haired man who looked nothing like the book jacket photo she'd been swooning over.

The man extended a shaky hand. "Nice to meet you, Miss Kern. Call me Chandler or Charles or Chuck—whichever you prefer. I'll answer to just about anything these days."

A hiccup of a breath caught in her throat. She blinked and stared at his outstretched hand then looked into his face again—a nice enough face, a smile she realized wasn't entirely unfamiliar, eyes that carried a hint of sadness. Her gaze slid downward, now taking in the wheelchair in which he sat—and Allan's mention of Chandler's "special requirements" took on a new meaning. She'd been imagining things like chauffeuring, secretarial help, more of those unfamiliar Polish menu preferences.

Something was wrong with this picture—very, very wrong.

❧

Kathy squeezed Parker's arm. "Do you see Sailor anywhere? I know she's here. I saw her car down the street."

"Not so far—wait, that's her over by the fireplace." A blaze ignited in Parker's chest. "Wow!"

"I'll say. Love what you did with her hair. She looks like a model."

An appreciative sigh slid between Parker's lips. "Definitely the prettiest girl here."

Kathy elbowed him in the ribs. "Hey, buster, *I'm* your date tonight, remember."

A server paused before them with a tray of hors d'oeuvres. Kathy took a napkin and helped herself, but Parker's stomach was already in knots—for more reasons than he cared to count. Seeing Sailor looking so gorgeous, confronting Chuck Michalicek, wishing he didn't have to pretend to be Kathy's date. . .

"Who's the guy Sailor's talking to?"

Parker followed Kathy's gaze. "The guy in the wheelchair? I don't—" An invisible fist slammed him in the solar plexus. "I think it's Chuck."

Kathy gasped. "*That's* Chandler Michaels?"

Before Parker could react, Allan Biltmore stepped in front of them. "Good evening, Kathy. And Parker, how nice you could join us. Do come over and say hello to our guest of honor."

While Allan made the introductions, Parker shared a glance with Sailor, who smiled up at him with deer-in-the-headlights surprise. Clearly this wasn't the Chandler Michaels she—or any of them—had been expecting.

"Parker Travis. You were just a kid the last time I saw you." Chuck offered a trembling hand.

Reluctantly Parker accepted the handshake, weak but sincere. "How are you, Chuck?" Immediately his face burned at the inanity of the question. The guy was in a wheelchair, for crying out loud.

"I was just explaining to my new friend Sailor why I don't exactly look like my book jacket photo. It was taken several years ago, before I was diagnosed with multiple sclerosis."

"I–I'm sorry." Parker gave an awkward shrug and stuffed his hands into his pockets. He was truly sorry Chuck had multiple sclerosis, but it didn't change the past. And would this vulnerable version of Chandler Michaels leave Sailor even more susceptible to his charms?

"The prognosis isn't great, but I'm learning to make the best of things." Chuck extended one arm in a gesture that took in the roomful of dinner guests. "It's just so good to be home again."

"And we're all very proud of you, Charles." Allan Biltmore stepped beside Chuck. "I see my wife signaling that dinner is served. Shall we, everyone?"

Sailor fell in alongside Chuck's motorized wheelchair, already fawning over him as Parker feared she might. All he could do was continue the pretense of escorting Kathy as they merged into the buffet line.

"Well, that was quite a stunner." Kathy picked up a plate and served herself a small helping of thick, meaty stew from a stainless, gold-accented chafing dish. "He sure doesn't seem like the playboy type."

"Maybe not, but he sure has Sailor's sympathies." Parker watched Sailor carry her own and Chuck's plates out to the patio.

He and Kathy found seats in the living room, and he remembered all over again why he avoided such gatherings. Balancing a plate of food on his lap, avoiding kicking over the glass of tea by his feet, making sure not to dribble gravy down his shirt—definitely *not* his favorite form of socializing.

Halfway through the meal, he looked up to see Sailor crossing the room, a mug of something hot and steamy clutched between her hands. The evening breeze had tugged loose a few strands of her hair, but she still looked fabulous.

Kathy made room on the sofa for her. "You look like an icicle, Sailor."

She scooted in close to Kathy and shivered. "Chandler asked if we could eat outside. With the MS, he doesn't function as well when he gets too hot. Then the sun went behind the trees and the breeze picked up, and I told him I was sorry but I needed to warm up." She leaned forward. "Oh, and Parker, he asked if you'd come out and talk awhile."

"Me?" Parker grabbed his plate before it slid sideways off his knees.

Kathy nudged him. "Yeah, here's your chance to hobnob with a celebrity."

Celebrity or not, maybe it was time to clear the air with ol' Chuck. Parker deposited his plate on the kitchen counter and filled a mug with coffee before finding his way outside.

"Good, you got my message." Chuck directed Parker to the empty patio chair next to him.

"I thought you'd be surrounded by admiring fans. Where's your entourage?"

Chuck gave a helpless laugh. "They all deserted me after the sun went down."

"Sailor mentioned you don't handle heat well." Thankful he hadn't removed his tan blazer, Parker sipped his coffee.

"I've had a lot of adjustments to make as a result of my illness." Chuck angled his wheelchair toward Parker. "Until now I've worked hard to hide my condition. Several months ago, when I could no longer get around without the wheelchair, I ceased all public appearances. Then Donna DuPont contacted me about the Bards of Birkenstock award, and—"

"And you couldn't pass up the chance to let the hometown folks see what a raging success you've become." Parker didn't intend to sound so cynical, but he couldn't help himself.

Chuck closed his eyes briefly. "I—I came home hoping to redeem myself in the eyes of the people who knew me way back when. I hope you know how sorry I am for the pain I caused your family."

Parker stiffened. "I'm not the one who's owed an apology."

"I've already asked Ruthy for forgiveness, which she has very graciously given."

"You've been in touch with my aunt?"

"Years ago." Chuck folded his hands. "When I first got the diagnosis, I was a wreck. It seemed like the end of my career, the end of my life, the end of everything that mattered. I started to wonder if it was God's punishment for all the people—all the women—I'd hurt over the years."

Parker huffed. "I may not like you much, but I can tell you right now, that's not the way God works."

"Even so, I felt an urgency to make amends, and I knew I'd hurt Ruthy worst of all. Receiving her forgiveness made me even hungrier to know God. It may sound corny to say my illness helped me find Jesus, but it did. I'm not the same man I was when I left Birkenstock."

A tiny crack split the shell of Parker's resentment—but just for a moment, just long enough for him to recall the chapter he'd read last night in *Romance by the Book*: "How to Play the Field without Getting Caught."

He plopped his coffee mug onto the glass table and scooted to the edge of his chair. "If you really know Jesus, maybe you can explain to me how you could write—"

Across the patio, the french doors burst open and Allan Biltmore strode out. "There you are, Charles. I've opened a window in the living room, so you should be comfortable inside now. Do come in, and enjoy dessert and coffee with the other guests."

Chuck cast Parker a regretful glance and allowed Allan to help him over the sill and through the door. Coffee mug in hand, Parker stood on the threshold and watched as several guests quickly surrounded the esteemed Chandler Michaels.

And Sailor was right in the middle of them.

Chapter 13

Hair still damp from her Saturday-morning swim class, Sailor tapped on the YMCA director's open door. "Mrs. Slaughter, can I talk to you a minute?"

The slim woman looked up from her computer. "What can I do for you, Sailor?"

"I wanted to ask about lightening my schedule for the next few weeks." After the initial shock had worn off and she talked more with Chandler last night, she realized how necessary her assistance would be. Her romantic illusions might be shattered, but even with his physical limitations, Chandler couldn't be more charming.

Mrs. Slaughter toyed with a ballpoint. "You know you've become practically indispensable around here. Who'll cover your classes?"

"Josh offered to fill in with the swimming lessons, and Gloria said she could take over some of my office work. I'd still come in to teach my water aerobics classes."

"As long as it's only temporary." Mrs. Slaughter swiveled toward her computer screen and then shot Sailor a wink. "I just better not lose you to that hotsy-totsy romance writer."

Her face steaming, Sailor thanked the director and fled from the office.

She showered and changed then headed straight over to the Biltmores', where she and Chandler planned to have lunch and discuss the agenda for his stay. When his first request was to accompany her to a Sunday worship service, she asked what church he'd attended before he left Birkenstock.

"I. . .didn't," he answered with a sheepish frown. "Where do you worship, Sailor?"

She stabbed a chunk of chicken salad. "I've belonged to Mission Hills Bible Church practically my whole life. But lately worship seems—I don't know—not as fresh and alive to me. Last Sunday I visited Rejoice Fellowship, and I really liked it."

"Then let's go there."

It had been hard enough keeping her thoughts on God last Sunday after discovering Parker Travis played flute in Rejoice's praise band. Attending with Chandler Michaels? *Lord, help!*

Except now she could prove to Kathy once and for all that Chuck Michalicek had changed. This man seemed light-years removed from the womanizing prankster Josh Fanning had described and nothing like the shallow literary snob Kathy predicted.

At church on Sunday he sang and prayed with a fervor that raised goose bumps on Sailor's arms. There was nothing phony about his show of faith, and she longed to be kindled with that same spiritual fire. Throughout the days ahead, as she escorted him to service club meetings, book club discussions, and library readings, he talked more with her about how his faith had changed him, how the Lord had brought comfort and assurance as he dealt with the debilitating aspects of multiple sclerosis. Upon reflection Sailor realized even his most recent novels carried a subtle faith message. . .perhaps accounting for some of the gentle nudges toward God she'd been sensing lately.

Still, it tore at her heart to see the way he struggled to hold a knife and fork steady to eat a meal—not to mention the painstaking effort to scrawl his signature across the title page of one of his novels for an excited fan.

On their way to the Biltmores' following the Thursday-noon Lions Club meeting, Sailor marshaled her courage to suggest an idea that had been nagging at her all week. "Have you ever tried water aerobics?"

"Haven't been much of a swimmer since my days on the Birkenstock High School swim team." Chandler gave a low chuckle. "You mentioned your friendship with Josh Fanning. I'm sure he's told you I got booted for disciplinary problems."

"He. . .mentioned an incident." Sailor steered the rented handicap-accessible van into the Biltmores' circlular driveway, where she'd left her car. "It's just that I was thinking how much more freely you could move in the water. I've read it could be good therapy for MS."

"Doing your homework, eh?"

"Isn't it worth a try if it could help?" She hurried around to the side door, released the safety latches on Chandler's wheelchair, and extended the ramp. "I'm teaching classes at the Y this afternoon. Why don't you come with me?"

"Sounds like fun, but I'm exhausted." Chandler steered his chair down the ramp. "If I don't catch up on some rest this afternoon, I'll be a zombie for the Methodist ladies' book club tomorrow morning."

"Maybe another time then."

Mrs. Biltmore met them at the door, and Sailor said good-bye and went to her car. She'd just pulled into the YMCA parking lot when her cell phone rang. She answered it on the way into the building.

"Hi, Kathy, what's up?"

"I was about to ask you the same question. We've hardly talked all week. Is Chuck keeping you that busy?"

"*Chandler* has had engagements every day and most evenings." She waved at Gloria on her way to the ladies' locker room. "I hope Donna wasn't too miffed that I didn't make the Tuesday committee meeting, but Chandler had an appointment with the chamber of commerce board to talk about the parade plans."

"Right, he's going to be the grand marshal." Kathy's tone mellowed. "Have I told you how proud I am of you? I knew it would be a stretch, but you've gone far beyond the call of duty."

Warmth filled Sailor's chest. She hung her purse on a hook inside her locker and laid out her towel and swimsuit. "I'm having a wonderful time getting to know Chandler. He's amazing."

"Nothing like what any of us were expecting, huh?"

"Nothing like." Sailor sighed. "I hope you see now what a great person he is. He's thoughtful, wise, incredibly kind. I can talk to him about anything."

"That's great, Sailor. So. . .no more romantic infatuation?"

"I wish you'd quit saying things like that."

"Before you met Chuck in person, you *were* hoping for something more than mere friendship—don't deny it."

"I won't, but—" Sailor sank onto the narrow wooden bench in front of the locker bay. How could she explain to her best friend the confusing mix of elation and discouragement now filling her? Chandler made her feel so special—important, needed, appreciated. He seemed to truly care about her thoughts and opinions. And when he talked about God, his words brought warmth and light to the deep places of her heart. She could honestly say she was growing to love Chandler, love him as a friend and mentor and spiritual confidant.

Yet a part of her still yearned for something more, for the romantic love of a man who only had eyes for her.

"Sailor, are you there?"

She sniffed. "Sorry, Kath. I've got to get ready for my class. Call you later, okay?"

She flipped the phone shut and stuffed it into her purse before changing into her swimsuit. Then once more she sank onto the bench. Leaning forward, she covered her face with her hands.

Dear God, I'm really out of practice in the prayer department, and I'm sorry we've been so out of touch. Help me find my way back to You. Help me trust that You really are in control of my life—including the romantic parts.

She started to rise then quickly added, *Oh, and please help me not to be jealous of Kathy and Parker. I only want them both to be happy. Amen.*

❧

For the second Sunday in a row, Parker looked out from the Rejoice Fellowship chancel to see Sailor escorting Chuck Michalicek up the aisle. She had a bounce in her step, a perky self-confidence he'd only witnessed when she taught her classes at the Y. He should be glad—for more reasons than simply because he no longer had to worry about her being swept away by the Chandler Michaels persona.

Except he couldn't stop thinking about that stupid book. After he and Chuck were interrupted at the Biltmores' dinner, he'd never had another chance to corner the guy and ask him what possessed him—a professed *Christian!*—to write that piece of chauvinistic drivel.

Maybe today, if he could peel Chuck away from Sailor long enough. After the closing song, he gave his flute a cursory swab, packed it into its case, and hurried out front. "Hi, Sailor, Chuck. Nice to see you back at Rejoice."

"Oh hi, Parker. Loved the music today." Sailor's hair swung around her shoulders as she turned to face him.

His fingers tingled with the memory of touching those silky tresses. It was all he could do to keep his hands at his sides. "Chuck, I was hoping for another chance to talk. Do you have lunch plans?"

"Sorry, Parker, but as soon as Sailor returns me to the Biltmores', Allan is driving me to the airport."

Parker lifted a brow and tried to keep the hopefulness out of his voice. "You're leaving already?"

"No, we're picking up my stepson." An edgy look flickered across Chuck's face before he covered it with a crooked smile. "Quentin has been my writing assistant for a few years now. Don't know what I'd have done without him, especially after his mother—my wife—passed away two years ago."

"I'm sorry. I didn't know you'd ever married." Parker stuffed his hands into his pockets.

"Irene was a nurse I met during one of my hospital stays. She gets most of the credit for turning my life around and leading me to Christ."

Sailor checked her watch. "We'd better get going, Chandler. It was good to see you again, Parker. Sorry I haven't been available for those extra coaching sessions I promised you. Maybe after. . ."

He shrugged and nodded. "See you Tuesday, though?"

"You bet." Sailor followed Chuck's wheelchair toward the exit, and they were soon swallowed up in the crowd.

"Hey, son." Mom touched Parker's arm. "Was that who I think it was?"

Parker grimaced. "In the flesh."

She made a tsk-tsk sound. "I should have told you a long time ago that he apologized to Ruthy."

"So you knew?"

"She was already married to your uncle Jim by then, and she didn't want anyone making a big deal of it. It was enough for her to know Chuck finally got his act together."

But had he? Parker still couldn't reconcile the repentant, soft-spoken man in the wheelchair with the cocky, self-serving author of *Romance by the Book*.

❧

As Sailor parked the minivan in the Biltmores' driveway, Allan hurried over to open her door. "You should come with us to the airport, dear. I thought we'd stop for lunch in Springfield before picking up Quentin."

Chandler cleared his throat. "I'm sure Sailor has more exciting plans for her Sunday afternoon than making an airport run."

"Actually, no." Sailor shot Chandler a teasing grin. "Unless you have a copy of your next book I could curl up with for the afternoon."

"It. . .could be awhile before another Chandler Michaels romance is released." He angled his gaze toward the floorboard.

"Join us, Sailor. I'm sure you're as anxious as we are to meet Charles's stepson." Allan slid open the left rear door for his wife.

Mrs. Biltmore climbed in and settled into the rear seat. "Plenty of room. Come on back, Sailor."

"Well. . .if you're sure it's okay." Leaving the driver's seat for Allan, Sailor buckled in next to the silver-haired Mrs. Biltmore. While Allan rechecked the tie-downs on Chandler's wheelchair, Sailor made a quick call to Uncle Ed to let him know her plans.

On the drive to Springfield, Sailor couldn't help noticing how subdued Chandler seemed. He'd been so full of life and energy at church that morning —at least until Parker caught up with them. Maybe being reminded of his wife again had him down. . .or possibly whatever Parker had wanted to talk with him about. Sailor couldn't shake the feeling that there was some kind of history between Parker and the Chuck Michalicek of the past. Why couldn't Parker—and everyone else who knew Chandler before—see him as he was now?

Arriving in Springfield, Allan stopped for lunch at a steak house. Sailor and Chandler both ordered grilled chicken salads, but Chandler barely touched his. With the few bites he attempted, his hands shook so horribly that he almost couldn't get the fork to his mouth. Sailor ached to help him, but he'd already rebuffed Allan's offer; she feared more attention would only embarrass him. He finally gave up, saying he wasn't so hungry after all.

At the airport Allan parked in the short-term lot. "You're looking tired, Charles. Why don't you wait in the van?"

Chandler nodded and sighed. "Thanks, I think I will."

Mrs. Biltmore patted Sailor's arm. "I'll stay with Charles if you want to go in with Allan. They may need an extra hand with the luggage."

Sailor trotted to keep up with Allan's long strides on their way to the baggage-claim area. "Do you know what he looks like?"

"I've only seen a photograph, but Charles said we wouldn't have any trouble recognizing him."

Passengers were already retrieving their luggage when Sailor and Allan arrived at the carousel. Sailor scanned the crowd and wondered how exactly she was supposed to recognize a man she'd never seen before—until her glance landed on the handsomest face she'd ever laid eyes on. He had Matt Damon's rakish haircut, Hugh Jackman's seductive smile, Matthew McConaughey's sensitive gaze—

A shriek sounded to Sailor's left. "Oh my goodness, you're *him*! I just *love* your novels, Mr. Michaels. I'm reading *Love's Sweet Song* right now." The woman thrust a book at the tall, grinning man. "Would you sign it for me? Make it 'to Cheryl, my most adoring fan.' "

Sailor watched in stunned shock as the man accepted the book and scrawled something on the cover page—*as if he were Chandler Michaels himself!*

And then she realized that's exactly who he looked like. The debonair man in the leather jacket and open-collar shirt could have stepped right out of Chandler's book-jacket photo. Her breath snagged. Her heart ker-thumped. The image she'd clung to all these years, the Chandler Michaels of her dreams, now stood close enough that she could reach out and touch him.

Allan squeezed Sailor's elbow. "I think we've found Quentin."

❧

"I think we've got problems."

Parker held his cell phone to his ear and nudged the car door shut with his hip. "Kathy? What are you talking about?"

"Quentin Easley."

"Quentin *who*?" Impatience gnawed Parker's gut. His knees ached like he'd climbed Mount Everest, and his shoulder felt like a T. rex had taken a bite out of it. He'd just finished one of his busiest Wednesdays on record—six haircuts, two highlights, three full colors, and a perm—all for women who were dying to make a lasting impression on the famed Chandler Michaels. Going public with his real identity *and* his multiple sclerosis only seemed to endear him to his loyal Birkenstock fans even more.

If they only knew.

Kathy gave an exasperated huff. "Haven't you heard? Chuck's stepson. He came to town last Sunday, and he is major trouble."

Parker trudged up the stairs to his apartment and let himself inside. "I've got half an hour before I have to be at church for a band rehearsal that I'm too tired to go to, thanks to Chuck's untimely arrival. Tell me why I should be worried about Quentin what's-his-name."

"Because Quentin Easley is everything we were afraid Chandler Michaels would be. And Sailor is falling for him."

"You've got to be kidding." Parker flopped onto the sofa. Now he could add a screaming headache to his growing list of complaints.

"Quentin came with Sailor to the Bards of Birkenstock meeting last night. Everybody was expecting 'Chandler Michaels,' and they weren't disappointed. Seems Quentin has been standing in for his stepfather in public venues for months."

"Chuck said something at church Sunday about his stepson being his assistant."

"Assistant? More like his clone. Quentin claims he's here only for Chandler's sake and assured the committee he wouldn't be any added expense, but there's something about him that makes me very worried about Sailor."

Parker rubbed his eyes and struggled for perspective. "Give her some credit, will you? She's smart, sensible—"

"And extremely vulnerable. And Quentin really knows how to play on her affections."

"You've met him—what? One time? How do you know he's all that bad?"

"There's a big signing event tomorrow evening at Dale & Dean's Book Corner. Come with me, and judge for yourself."

Parker reluctantly agreed to go, but as he threw a sandwich together for a quick meal before praise-band practice, he hoped Kathy was wrong. Sailor had seemed so vibrant yesterday—even more so than normal as she skillfully and confidently coached his water aerobics class. If this was the result of spending time with Chandler Michaels—the real one or this new Quentin Easley version—what right did Parker have to interfere?

Lord, I only want what's best for her. If it means stepping aside for another man, give me the strength to do it. But if You've chosen Sailor for me, then help me do whatever it takes to win her heart.

Chapter 14

Sailor scooped a spoonful of leftover couscous into a plastic container. As usual, Uncle Ed had turned up his nose at the healthy recipe she'd tried. "Can I leave you with the dishes? If I don't hurry, I'll be late for Chandler's book signing."

Uncle Ed poked around in the refrigerator and came out with a jar of peanut butter. "That book writer fella has you hoppin' faster than a toad on a hot sidewalk. You've been dressing to the nines and out gallivanting nearly every night for the past two weeks."

"A couple more weeks and it'll be over." And probably so would her chances for romance. Quentin Easley had swept her off her feet the moment he took her hand at the airport baggage claim. He was everything she'd expected the real Chandler Michaels to be and more.

She pulled into the parking lot in front of Dale & Dean's Book Corner only moments before the Biltmores arrived. Quentin hurried to help Chandler out of the van. He looked up when Sailor approached and shot her a megawatt smile. "Hey, gorgeous. I've been waiting all day to see you again."

Her heart did a tiny flutter dance. She straightened her shoulders and tried to concentrate on business. "I stopped by this morning to check on the arrangements. Dean ordered an ample supply of all your titles, Chandler, and Dale situated the signing table just like you asked."

"Thank you, Sailor." He reached for her hand and gave it a feeble squeeze.

She noted the fatigue lines creasing the corners of his eyes and again felt thankful Quentin had come along to help. His assistance at Monday's book discussion group then fielding reporters' questions at yesterday's mayor's breakfast seemed to take much of the pressure off Chandler.

Within a few minutes of seating Chandler at his table, Sailor looked toward the front of the bookstore to see a steady stream of customers, all heading for the display featuring Chandler's books. A couple of younger shoppers spotted Quentin and rushed over, mistaking him for Chandler and gushing like the fan at the airport.

"Oh, Mr. Michaels, will you sign my copy of *The Heart's True Song*?" A brunette with a pixie haircut hugged the book to her bosom. "It's my absolute favorite."

Sailor stepped forward, ready to direct them to the real Chandler Michaels, but Chandler caught her arm. "It's all right; let them think he's me."

"But Chandler—"

"Quentin's doing me a favor, actually. Let's face it; a guy in a wheelchair who can barely hold a pen is *not* the dashing romance writer they want signing their books."

She chewed her lip, torn between wanting Chandler to have the recognition he deserved and her growing admiration for Quentin. He must really love and respect Chandler to work so hard at sparing him unnecessary awkwardness about his condition.

A poster of *Love's Sweet Song* stood on an easel near the table. Sailor's glance fell to the inset at the bottom right corner, Chandler Michaels's publicity photo. Or was it Quentin? Honestly she couldn't tell. She sank onto the folding chair next to Chandler. "I know you're not really related, but it's amazing how much he looks like. . .well, like I'd always pictured you."

"He does resemble me—the younger me—and of course he plays up that fact for the fans." Chandler's mouth flattened. "You're attracted to him, aren't you?"

She ducked her head. "What girl wouldn't be?"

"Appearances aren't everything, Sailor."

"You must think I'm really shallow." Her lips quirked in an embarrassed smile. "It's more than his looks. I've never met anyone so charming, so fascinating. He makes me feel. . ." She couldn't bring herself to say the word *beautiful*.

The autograph seekers quickly gathered, ending their conversation. Later, as the line thinned, a tall woman in a navy pantsuit approached the table. "Hi, Chandler. Goodness, it sure feels weird to call you that. I'm Gina Williams—but you knew me as Gina Young. We sat next to each other in Mr. Ochoa's algebra class."

Chandler offered a warm smile. "Gina, of course. Don't tell me our class valedictorian reads romance novels?"

"Are you kidding? I love your books—and they're even more special since I realized you're my old classmate! Will you sign my copy?"

"Happy to." Chandler fumbled with the pen, and Sailor reached over to help him find the title page. He took a couple of shivery breaths that gave her a moment of concern, and then he looked up and said, "Spell your name for me, please?"

"G-I-N-A." The woman gave an awkward laugh. "I'm surprised you have to ask, considering all those mash notes you used to pass to me when Mr. Ochoa's back was turned."

He shook his head as if clearing it. "Sorry, I meet so many people on these book tours."

"Understandable." Gina glanced toward Quentin, still chatting it up with Chandler's younger admirers. "That guy definitely knows how to work a crowd."

Sailor stood. "That's Chandler's assistant, Quentin Easley. He's been a tremendous help."

"I'm sure." Gina nodded toward the wheelchair. "I read your interview last week in the *Birkenstock Times*. I'm so sorry about the MS."

Chandler cleared his throat. "Sailor, would you mind getting me another bottle of water?"

She hesitated to leave Chandler alone at the table—he seemed a little unsteady this evening—but there was no one else around to ask. "Sure. Be right back."

Dale, the younger of the bookstore's co-owners, had just set out a tray of cookies in the lounge area when Sailor caught up with him and asked about the water. While Dale went to get another bottle, Sailor paced the long row of bookshelves, keeping one eye on Chandler and the other on the rear passageway from which Dale would emerge.

"There you are, beautiful."

She spun around, caught her new sling-back stiletto on a tear in the carpet, and fell headlong into Quentin's outstretched arms.

"Whoa, baby! I wasn't expecting such an enthusiastic greeting."

Extracting herself from his embrace, Sailor straightened her skirt and smoothed her hair. Heat singed her cheeks. Her pulse stammered. "I—I was just waiting for Dale. Chandler needed some water—"

"He's fine—visiting with another old flame from his high school days. Which works out perfectly for me. I've been waiting to catch you alone so I could give you something." He reached into the inner pocket of his blazer and withdrew a foil-wrapped box topped with a miniature silver bow.

"Quentin—"

He silenced her with a finger to her lips, his touch like red-hot metal. "Just open it. I can't wait to see your face."

Lightness filled her chest, an excitement she almost felt guilty for giving in to—her first gift from a—well, she couldn't exactly call Quentin a boyfriend, at least not yet. With trembling fingers she pried off the lid and lifted out a tiny velveteen drawstring bag. Quentin held the box while she loosened the strings and emptied the contents into her palm—a gold charm in the shape of a human hand with thumb, index finger, and pinky extended.

"It's sign language for 'I love you.'" Quentin moved closer. "It might be a little soon, but I saw it in the window of a jewelry shop yesterday, and I immediately thought of you. You're special, Sailor. You're someone I think I could actually say those words to someday."

Her heart hammered out a frightening rhythm as Quentin's face moved closer, hovering above hers. His lips parted. His eyelids lowered. If not for his hand circling around and pressing against her back, she might have swooned—just like the heroine in *Love's Eternal Melody*.

"Oh, Quentin. . ."

❧

"Aw, Sailor. . ." Defeat and rage and despair tied a tangled knot in Parker's belly. He and Kathy had arrived at the bookstore five minutes ago, and not finding Sailor with Chuck, they'd browsed the aisles until they spotted her—

just in time to see Quentin hand her the little silver box.

Bile rose in Parker's throat when he glimpsed the sparkly little charm, a trinket straight out of *Romance by the Book*. He remembered it from the chapter on "What Women Want": *"More than anything, a woman wants to believe you love her, and nothing says love to a woman like jewelry. A pearl necklace, a pair of heart-shaped earrings, an I-love-you charm—if you play your cards right, you'll have her right where you want her without having to spring for that diamond ring."*

Kathy punched him in the arm. "Now do you believe me?"

He turned away before the inevitable kiss. He couldn't bear to watch. "I think I'm going to be sick."

"I'm going to extract Sailor from this little tête-à-tête before things get any steamier." Kathy started down the aisle.

Parker grabbed her wrist. "Don't. . .embarrass her, okay?"

Kathy's shoulders sagged. "I'll make up some excuse about needing to talk to her about committee stuff."

With a groan Parker turned his attention to Chuck, still signing autographs at a table draped with a scarlet cloth. Chuck's hand suddenly jerked, and the pen toppled from his grip and clattered to the floor. Mouthing an apology to the waiting fan, he rolled his wheelchair back and bent to find the pen.

Parker could see the frustration growing in Chuck's face. He hurried over. "Here, I've got it."

Chuck looked up with a grateful half smile. "Thanks. Bad case of writer's cramp."

"Maybe you should take a break."

"Yes. My assistant's around here somewhere. . . ." A confused look wrinkled Chuck's forehead.

The customer tapped her book on the table. "What about my autograph?"

Dean from the bookstore stepped forward. "Folks, we're going to take a short intermission. We have coffee, juice, fruit, and cookies over in the lounge area. Please help yourselves."

While the bearded bookstore owner herded disgruntled fans away from the table, Parker guided Chuck over to a quiet area at the far end of the oak veneer checkout counter. "Are you okay? You look a little out of it."

"I'd forgotten how exhausting these events are." Chuck rubbed his eyes and then fixed Parker with a slowly clearing gaze. "Guess I should thank you for rescuing me."

Parker gave a huff. "I thought your stepson-slash-assistant was supposed to be helping you, not making time with your local PR person."

Chuck's eyes widened. "Quentin's with Sailor? Oh no. . ."

"Oh, *yes*. And worming his way into her innocent heart with guerilla romance tactics from *your* tacky little book."

Chuck grimaced. His Adam's apple made a painful-looking trail up and down his throat. "You know about the book?"

"My friendly neighborhood librarian—who happens to be Sailor's best friend—loaned me her advance copy." Parker ran his hands through his hair. "I don't get it, man. Since your return to Birkenstock, everyone, including you, had me convinced you're a changed man. I've even been told your romance novels are all sweetness and chivalry. What possessed you to write such a boatload of garbage and call it a romance guide?"

"I didn't." Chuck tipped his head and squeezed his eyes shut. "Quentin wrote it."

"Quentin? *He* wrote *Romance by the Book*?"

"It's a long story." Chuck let out a ragged sigh and explained how he'd at first been flattered when Quentin took such an avid interest in becoming his writing assistant. As the multiple sclerosis progressed, Quentin helped by doing research, taking dictation, and typing manuscript pages. When Chuck had bad days and wasn't up to writing at all, he sometimes allowed Quentin to try his hand at fleshing out the scenes.

"He really mastered my style, and he has genuine writing talent. Then last year at a book signing, someone thought he was me. It occurred to me that if I dropped out of sight for a while and then let him take over my public appearances, no one need ever know about the MS. Eventually, when the time comes that I can no longer write the books myself, he will carry on the Chandler Michaels name."

Parker smirked. "So he really is your clone."

"It seemed like the perfect solution to keep my faithful fans happy for many years to come. . .until Quentin came up with the idea for *Romance by the Book*."

"And you let him?"

"He wouldn't show me the draft, said he wanted to surprise me. I didn't see the actual contents until the page proofs arrived a few weeks ago—and wouldn't have seen them then except the editor accidentally e-mailed them to my address instead of Quentin's."

"But you're still letting it go to press."

"The legal steps to transfer my 'Chandler Michaels' identity to Quentin are already set in motion. If I stop publication now, I'm afraid it would mean public humiliation for both of us. So many people have read and loved my books. I can't let the Chandler Michaels name be tarnished with scandal."

Parker snorted. "I'm not sure having your name on the cover of that piece of trash is much better."

"There's always the hope readers will think it was written tongue in cheek." Chuck's clenched jaw indicated he believed no such thing.

❧

"There you are, Chandler." Sailor stepped forward and twisted the cap off a water bottle. She hoped her makeup camouflaged the blush warming her face. How much had Kathy seen before practically ripping her out of Quentin's arms?

Chandler looked even more fatigued than when she'd left him at the signing table. He thanked her for the water and took a sip. "Where's Quentin?"

"Mingling with the customers. Several were getting impatient." Sailor cast a worried glance at Parker. "Is everything okay here?"

Parker stood. "I think Chuck's had about all the public exposure he can handle for one evening. You should get him home to the Biltmores' ASAP."

"I'm fine, really." Chandler set the water bottle on the end of the counter and steered himself toward the signing table. His hand slid off the control, and he muttered a curse.

Sailor rushed over. "You've been running around like crazy the past couple of weeks. People will understand. Quentin can cover for you."

He heaved a pained sigh and tugged his hand into his lap. "Silly me. With Quentin here, no one will even notice the old guy in the wheelchair is gone."

The tone of his voice chilled Sailor. "Don't talk like that, Chandler. Think of all the people who've come especially to see the man they remembered from before."

"Exactly." Chandler pounded his thigh. "They all wanted to gawk at poor old Chuck Michalicek, erstwhile troublemaker and class clown, now a crippled has-been."

"That's not true." Sailor knelt in front of the wheelchair and covered his fist with her hands. "Your books have touched so many hearts. Your stories have made people believe in the power of love."

His gaze found hers, and the hard lines around his mouth softened into a tender smile. "Sailor, Sailor. Such an innocent, always ready to see the good in everyone."

Innocent? She was so tired of being seen as naive little Sailor Kern, the missionaries' kid. Tired of everyone thinking they had to protect her from the world. At least Quentin didn't treat her like a child. He made her feel beautiful, desirable, more womanly than any man ever had, except for. . .

She pushed to her feet, her glance shifting to where Parker stood next to Kathy. The meaningful looks passing between the two of them were unreadable. Probably they couldn't wait until they could make polite excuses and get away together. The thought left a sour taste in Sailor's mouth, and she mentally chided herself for her misplaced jealousy.

Allan Biltmore strode over, a stack of books balanced on one arm. He set them by the cash register and turned to Chandler. "For my three granddaughters. They'll love them. I won't ask you to sign them tonight, though."

Sailor stepped in front of Allan, keeping her voice low. "I think you should take Chandler home. He doesn't seem well."

Allan's bushy white eyebrows drew together. "I wondered earlier if he was having difficulty. I'll fetch Nelda, and we'll get him straight home. Would you mind dropping Quentin off later?"

"Of course—"

Parker shouldered his way up to the counter. "I'll be happy to give Quentin a lift. There's no reason for Sailor to stay."

She spun around, fresh indignation filling her. "Excuse me? I can't just leave. I'm the one who arranged this event."

Taking a half step back, Parker lowered his gaze. "I thought since Kathy's here. . .if you wanted to get home early. . ."

Kathy tucked her hand beneath Parker's arm in a possessive gesture that made Sailor's stomach twist. "Never mind, Sailor. We can see you've got everything under control. Tell Quentin good-bye for us, will you? Come on, Parker, you promised me a decaf latte at Logan's Bistro. And I'm dying for one of their blueberry scones."

Kathy hurried Parker out the door before Sailor could apologize for snapping at him. Good grief, her emotions were in knots lately. She turned to see Allan and his wife helping Chandler gather up his jacket and briefcase. Moments later they said their good-byes, leaving Sailor to close out the book signing with Quentin.

Older fans filtered out shortly after Chandler left, but the younger crowd remained enthralled by Quentin and didn't dissipate until nearly nine. Sailor's feet ached from standing so long in heels, and her cheek muscles felt frozen into a permanent smile. She could hardly wait to get home, kick off her shoes, and slip into her comfy cotton pajamas.

When the last customer headed out the door, Quentin whistled out a relieved sigh and draped his arm around Sailor. Pulling her close, he planted a kiss on her temple. "Thanks, babe. Couldn't have done it without you."

While Dale, Dean, and a couple of their clerks started clearing the table and straightening the book displays, Quentin helped Sailor on with her sweater. "How about you and I go somewhere quiet and relax for a while? It's been a long night."

"I shouldn't. Tomorrow's going to be another busy day." She tried to focus on anything but the flames Quentin's fingers ignited as he stroked her cheek. A bizarre mixture of anticipation and fear squeezed her heart. Hadn't she always dreamed of having a man treat her this way? Hadn't she always dreamed it would be Chandler Michaels. . .or at least the closest thing to him?

Thinking of Chandler, she stiffened. "Anyway, we should check on Chandler. He didn't look at all well when they left. I'm worried about him."

"That's what I love about you—always thinking of someone else." Quentin drew her under his arm and escorted her toward the exit. "Poor guy, the MS seems to get worse every day. I told him this trip wasn't such a good idea, but he insisted. I'll be surprised if he makes it to the festival."

Chapter 15

When Parker didn't see Sailor and Chandler in church the following Sunday, he hoped it only meant they were visiting elsewhere. On the other hand, it didn't surprise him in the least not to see them arrive with Quentin Easley in tow. Parker doubted the creep had ever so much as set foot inside a church.

After spending Monday morning doing the ladies' hair at the Willow Tree Assisted-Living Center then a busier-than-normal Tuesday at the salon, Parker was more than ready for his water aerobics class that afternoon.

As he prepared to blow-dry a client's hair, Carla buzzed him on the intercom. "Call on line 2. A lady from the Y."

Parker's nerves sang. *Sailor?* He snatched up the phone and tried to keep his voice level. "This is Parker."

An unfamiliar female voice responded. "Hi, it's Gloria from the Y. Sorry to call at the last minute, but Sailor had to cancel her classes this afternoon due to a personal emergency."

"I. . .see." Only he didn't. Nausea churned beneath his belt buckle. If Quentin Easley had anything to do with this—

"Sailor usually offers a makeup lesson whenever she has to cancel. I'm sure she'll be in touch. Plan on next week as usual unless you hear otherwise."

"Right. Thanks." He hung up and switched the hair dryer on, the *whir* masking his spinning thoughts.

Since he was free for the rest of the afternoon anyway, Parker left shortly after his last client. He headed straight for the library, hoping Kathy might know what was going on with Sailor.

"I don't know much." Kathy motioned him to the end of the checkout desk. "I heard Chuck had a rough weekend and had to cancel most of his appearances."

"He wasn't looking good Thursday night, that's for sure." Parker absently jangled the coins in his pocket. "Have you talked to Sailor since then?"

"Briefly. She's very worried about Chuck. Apparently they've formed a real connection since he came to town."

Parker snorted. "Better him than his stepson. I don't trust that guy farther than I can throw him."

When another librarian approached their end of the desk with a stack of books, Kathy reached under the counter for her purse. "I'll be back in ten, Zoe."

She led Parker to the elevator, and they rode it downstairs to the snack bar. Seated at a corner table, Kathy pulled out her cell phone. "I'll call Sailor right now and find out what's going on."

"Don't mention I'm here. Might give her the wrong idea."

"What, that we're checking up on her?" Kathy flicked one hand at him while flipping open her cell phone with the other. "Oh, hi, Sailor. I didn't expect you'd actually answer. Isn't this your class time?"

Smooth. Very smooth. Parker leaned back and folded his arms while listening to Kathy's side of the conversation. It sounded as if Chuck had taken a serious turn for the worse and was returning to New York.

"That's awful, Sailor. Give him my best, will you? And call me when you get home from the airport." Kathy pressed the DISCONNECT button and shoved the phone into her purse.

Parker sat forward. "Chuck's leaving Birkenstock?"

"It's kind of a good-news/bad-news thing." Kathy ran a knuckle along her jaw. "The good news is Chuck's setback is treatable, but he wants to see his own doctor. They're on the way to Springfield right now so Quentin can fly him home."

"And the bad news?"

"Quentin's catching a return flight on Thursday so he can fill in at the rest of Chuck's scheduled appearances, including the book festival."

Parker pressed his thumbs into his eye sockets. "Without Chuck here to keep Sailor busy and deflect Quentin's overtures, she'll be an easier target than ever."

"Which means you need to step up your game plan, Mr. Romance Man."

He lowered his hands and glared at her, his eyes mere slits. "*My* game plan? As I recall, this anti-*Romance by the Book* gambit was all your idea."

Kathy hunched her shoulders and propped her forearms on the table. "I'm still in shock after you told me Quentin wrote that stupid book. Makes me even more furious watching Sailor fall for a complete phony."

"And of course there's nothing phony about you and me pretending interest in each other so I can be your date at all these literary functions."

"How else could I get you to the events so you could keep an eye on Sailor? You want to save her from herself as much as I do."

Kathy's words jabbed like a knife. Parker clenched one fist atop the table. "Save her from herself? No, that isn't what I want at all. I want her to *be* herself. I want her to be true to the person God created her to be." *Whether that includes me in her life or not.*

Kathy straightened, her gaze as intense as his. "I think we can agree God didn't create Sailor to be arm candy for Quentin Easley. And until she figures that out for herself, I refuse to apologize for manipulating circumstances until she does."

❧

Sailor barely made it home from Springfield in time for the Tuesday-evening committee meeting and drove straight to the library in the rented van. When she plunked into her chair next to Allan Biltmore, he apologized again for not being available to take Chandler and Quentin to the airport himself. "But of course we couldn't reschedule Nelda's appointment with her cardiologist."

"It's fine." Sailor flicked her breeze-tossed hair off her shoulder. "I was glad to get the chance to tell Chandler good-bye, but I'm very disappointed he has to miss his own awards ceremony."

Allan sighed. "At least Quentin can fill in for him. What a dedicated young man."

"Yes, Chandler's fortunate to have him." She opened her folder of notes and pretended to study them while the memory of Quentin's almost kiss behind the bookshelves last week played havoc with her concentration. If not for Kathy's timely appearance. . .

Since the book signing, she'd used every means possible to avoid being alone with Quentin. Even so, his subtle touches—caressing her cheek, stroking the back of her hand, nudging her toe under restaurant tables—suggested he'd like to be much more physical. Flattered as she was, she was also secretly terrified. When it came to relationships, *inexperienced* hardly began to describe her. How could a shy, small-town YMCA instructor ever live up to the expectations of a sophisticated, jet-setting New Yorker? It would take a lot more than designer outfits, spa treatments, and expensive haircuts to turn this missionaries' kid into a woman of the world.

"Sailor? *Ahem*, Sailor!" Donna DuPont's piercing tone finally captured Sailor's attention. "We're ready for your report, dear."

"Right." The meeting had started already? Emerging from her brain fog, Sailor fumbled through her notes as she explained about Chandler's unexpected departure. A collective moan filled the boardroom, until she added that Quentin would return to fulfill Chandler's festival commitments.

"Oh my, that's so good of him." Donna splayed her fingers across her throat. "What a blessing he must be to Chandler."

A muted growl sounded on Sailor's right. She shifted her gaze to see Kathy's tight grip on the chair arm. Obviously Kathy had transferred her negative assessment of Chandler's character to Quentin, and Sailor could only hope it was equally misplaced.

With the festival just over a week away, the meeting ran much longer than usual. It was after eleven when Sailor gathered up her things with a yawn and started out to the parking lot.

"Sailor, wait up!" Kathy cornered her next to the statue of a child sitting cross-legged with a book in his lap. "Want to have lunch tomorrow? We haven't shared any decent girl talk since Chandler came to town."

"I'm way behind on my desk work at the Y." She fanned away a cluster of bugs attracted to the streetlight above her. "Besides, wouldn't you rather see if Parker's free for lunch?"

"Parker? Oh, um. . ." Kathy shuffled her feet. "He's probably got appointments."

"Then why don't you take him lunch at the salon?"

Kathy shrugged. "We'll see. But if you change your mind, let me know."

Truth be told, Sailor would much rather have lunch with Kathy than catch up on paperwork at the Y. She'd never expected serving on the Bards of Birkenstock committee would turn out to be so involved.

Forcing a cheery good-bye, she marched across the empty parking lot to the rental van and slid into the driver's seat. By the time she picked up her own car at the Biltmores' and let herself into the darkened kitchen at home, exhaustion overwhelmed her. Uncle Ed had probably gone to bed hours ago. At least she'd have one full day of "normal" before Quentin returned and the prefestival activities resumed at breakneck pace.

She closed the bedroom door and sank into her desk chair to see if her parents had e-mailed. Moments after her poky old computer struggled back to life, the Skype chime sounded. She clicked the ANSWER icon.

"Hey, Sailor-girl!" A grainy video showed her father's smiling face.

"Daddy!"

"Your SKYPE button lit up, so I thought I'd catch you while I could. We haven't talked in ages." He squinted toward his Webcam. "Is it the transmission, or are those dark circles under your eyes?"

"It's been a long day." She briefly described her unexpected trip to the Springfield airport. "How are you? How's Mom?"

"Your mother's still incommunicado while she oversees that new health clinic. It'll probably be her last one. The years are catching up with us."

"Oh, Dad." Sailor's stomach twisted. The worst part of having older parents—even worse than having them overseas most of her life—was realizing the time might soon come when she wouldn't have them at all.

And these days she needed a mother's advice more than ever.

They chatted a few minutes longer, until Sailor's father commented on her frequent yawns and told her to get to bed.

With sleep creeping in almost faster than she could change into her nightgown and brush her teeth, Sailor didn't waste any time. Lying there in the darkness, though, she felt an unexpected urgency to pray. She propped her pillow against the headboard, drew her knees up to her chest, and clasped her hands.

Dear Lord, please take care of my parents. I miss them and need them so much. And please help me know what to do about Quentin. His touch, his voice—he makes me feel things I never expected to feel. Yet I don't know whether I can trust my heart or not.

Especially when her heart kept whispering someone else's name. . .a name that slid through her lips on a sigh.

"Parker."

❧

"Have a seat, Gina. We're doing color and highlights today, right?" Parker flipped through his client file to verify the mix. Moonlit Mink #16, one of his favorites.

"I noticed my roots showing as I was getting dressed to go see Chuck—sorry, *Chandler Michaels*—at the book signing last week. Did you go?"

"Got there just before he left." He fastened the cape around Gina's neck and ran a brush through her hair. "The cut we did for you last time really suits you."

"Love it—so many compliments. You probably saw that tall, good-looking guy at the signing, the one who looks more like Chuck's book-jacket photo than he does?"

Parker took a slow, deep breath while he measured out the color and developer. "Quentin Easley. He's Chuck's assistant."

"He sure had the younger fans drooling. If I were single and ten years younger—"

Carla, the receptionist, skidded around the cubicle wall on the toes of her ballet flats. "Message for you, Parker."

"Thanks." He took the yellow slip from Carla and scanned the cryptic note: *Sailor working through lunch at Y. Think about it. Kathy.*

Carla folded her arms and shot him a knowing smirk. "Any response?"

"Uh, no. But you can do a couple of things for me. First, make sure I don't have any appointments over the lunch hour."

Carla's smirk morphed into a grin. "I already checked. You're free between eleven forty-five and one thirty."

She was too good. He'd have to give her a raise. "Then please call in an order to Audra's Café for. . ." He scanned his memory banks. "Make it two Asian salads with grilled salmon." Another memory flashed through his brain. "No wontons. And dressing on the side."

As he returned to his color mixing, he caught Gina's questioning look through the mirror. She wiggled an eyebrow. "Sounds like someone has a hot lunch date."

He simply smiled and retrieved his coloring brush. The more deeply he let himself fall in love with Sailor, the more uncomfortable he'd become with trying to manipulate her emotions. Bad enough having to watch Quentin playing on her heartstrings. Why should Parker risk confusing her with his own unimpressive attempts at romanticism?

Yet here he was, jumping at the chance to take her favorite salad over to her for lunch. He couldn't help himself. The idea of spending even a few minutes in her company bulldozed all reason from his usually logical brain.

He finished Gina's color and cut then hurried through two more styling appointments and a new-client consultation before he finally broke free shortly after eleven thirty. With two salads from Audra's Café in hand, plus chilled bottles of spring water, he strolled through the Y's sliding glass doors at five minutes before twelve.

The blond receptionist looked up from the front desk. "Can I help you?"

In the cubicle behind her he glimpsed a familiar blue-jeaned leg beneath a computer desk. The foot at the end of that leg tapped out a staccato rhythm—Sailor's typical show of frustration.

"I. . .uh. . ." His tongue stuck to the roof of his mouth.

"Mmm, I smell something from Audra's." The receptionist peered over the counter. "Did someone call in an order—oh wait, you're not from Audra's. You're the stylist from Par Excellence. Sailor's water aerobics student, right?"

The toe stopped tapping. Parker's heart thumped harder. A split second later Sailor stepped through the opening. A bemused smile creased her cheeks.

"Hi, Parker. What are you doing here?"

He lifted the bag and grinned like a lovesick schoolboy. "I brought lunch."

❧

Pinpricks zinged up and down Sailor's limbs as she showed Parker to the Y's break room. She pulled out chairs at a round table next to the soft drink machine and moved aside the napkin holder. "This is so sweet of you."

"Couldn't stand the thought of you stuck here working through lunch." Parker set out the clear plastic take-out boxes and fished two utensil packets from the bottom of the bag.

"My favorite salad—I can't believe you remembered!" Sailor opened the container—no wontons. A thousand hummingbird wings fluttered in her chest. She started to thank Parker and then froze. "Wait. Aren't you supposed to be having lunch with Kathy?"

"What?" The confused quirk of his eyebrows suggested the idea hadn't even been discussed.

She studied him through narrowed eyes. Now that the initial surprise had worn off and her brain cogs had reengaged, nothing about Parker's unexpected arrival made sense. "And how did you even know I'd be here over lunch? The only person who could have told you is—"

Kathy!

She pushed her salad aside and draped one arm along the edge of the table. "Okay, Parker, what's *really* going on here?"

His lips mashed together in a crooked frown before he whooshed out a long breath. "Kathy left me a message this morning, saying you'd be working through lunch. The rest was all my idea."

"So. . .what's Kathy doing for lunch?"

"She didn't say." He cut his eyes sideways and then seized his plastic knife and began slicing through a hunk of salmon. "This is really good dressing. I like the spiciness. Is that the ginger?"

"Yes, ginger." Sailor popped the cap off the small dressing container—wait, dressing on the side? Yet another of her preferences Parker had remembered. And he'd made a special trip to bring her lunch when he could just as easily have done the same for Kathy. If he was here with her, and not with Kathy. . .

The thought that not one but two men had eyes for her sent her pulse rate skittering—and after all these years of thinking herself plain and unattractive. Once again a prayer rose in her thoughts. *Father, You know how long I've dreamed of meeting Mr. Right and being swept off my feet. Well, I've been swept—twice!—and now I don't know which way to fall. Don't let me make a mistake.*

The quiver beneath her breastbone made her wonder if Mr. Right might be sitting right in front of her.

Chapter 16

Allan Biltmore insisted on picking up Quentin at the airport on Thursday, which brought Sailor no end of relief. For one thing, she couldn't afford to cancel any more of her water aerobics classes. And for another, whenever she spent time with Quentin, she began to doubt her own good judgment.

The phone rang Thursday evening as she brushed a lemon-teriyaki glaze over two chicken breasts for her and Uncle Ed's supper. Uncle Ed picked up and called her to the hallway phone. When he passed her the receiver, Quentin's mellow tones caressed her eardrum like a warm breeze.

"Hi, beautiful. I missed you. I can almost smell your perfume through the phone lines."

Something like an electric shock zapped her fingertips. She cast Uncle Ed a forced smile and motioned for him to set the chicken in the oven. Moving farther down the hall, she murmured into the phone, "I don't wear perfume."

"Then I'll have to do something about that. Hmm, roses? Jasmine? Citrus?"

"Quentin—"

"Jasmine, I think. Not too floral, not too spicy. Just like you."

Jasmine. . .like the heroine wore in *Love's Eternal Melody*. Sailor's breath snagged. Quentin sure knew all the right romantic buttons to push. Except. . .

"Really. I don't wear perfume. Gloria at the Y is allergic to scents, and it would wash away in the pool anyway, and—"

He chided her with a gentle *tsk-tsk*. "But you'd wear it for me, wouldn't you. . . when we're alone together? Sailor, I can't wait to see you again."

The sound of her name on his lips sent her stomach on a roller-coaster ride. She could almost feel his breath on her cheek. "I'm looking forward to seeing you again, too." And at that moment she meant it.

"How about tonight? I'm locked in to dinner with the Biltmores, but we could go somewhere later for a nightcap."

"Quentin, I don't drink."

"Coffee then. A malt. A root beer float."

Laughter bubbled from her throat. His charm was quickly dissolving her defenses. "I can't. I already had one late night this week, and if I don't get my eight hours—"

"Don't you dare say you need your beauty sleep. I can't imagine you looking anything but drop-dead gorgeous."

"Then don't stop by the Y after one of my classes."

"Now you've got me curious. Don't be surprised if I show up tomorrow afternoon."

"Please don't." She covered her eyes with one hand, already cringing with embarrassment.

"Hey, I might need to sign up for one of your classes myself, just to see you in a swimsuit."

"Now, Quentin—"

Sailor felt a tug on her elbow and turned to see Uncle Ed standing behind her. "I don't know what to do with the vegetables."

"Be right there," she mouthed. Into the phone she said, "I have to go, Quentin. But I'll see you tomorrow evening. We have tickets to the Branson show, remember?"

"Oh yeah, Frankie what's-his-name. Jazz isn't my thing, but if that's what it takes to spend time with you. . ."

They said their good-byes, and Sailor's thoughts returned to Chandler. He'd been thrilled to learn the committee had arranged for him to see a Frankie Verona show. "I grew up listening to his albums," Chandler had said. "When I'm writing a romantic scene, nothing inspires me like one of Frankie's slow, sultry love ballads."

While she finished getting supper on the table, Sailor found herself humming one of the songs from Frankie's show last month. She pictured Parker onstage, lost in the soulful music of his flute. As she settled into her chair, a shiver jolted her.

Uncle Ed looked up from stirring sugar into his iced tea. "You catching a chill?"

"No, I'm fine." She smiled and unfolded her napkin.

"Well, it wouldn't surprise me, the way you've been dressing lately." Uncle Ed harrumphed and sliced off a bite of chicken.

"Just because I'm dressing a little more stylishly doesn't mean—"

"Pains me to think what your parents would say if they could see how you're flaunting yourself in front of that romance writer person."

"I am not flaunting myself, and there is absolutely nothing improper about my new clothes *or* my behavior." Her cheek muscles bunched. Uncle Ed seemed more out of touch all the time. "Shall I say grace?"

❧

"Hey, Grams, not doing so hot today?" Parker leaned over his grandmother's recliner and dropped a kiss on her forehead. She had to be feeling bad to miss one of Mom's weekend performances with Frankie.

"Must be a front coming through. I'm stiff as an old leather boot." Grams reached up a gnarled hand to pat Parker's cheek. "But you didn't have to waste a perfectly good Saturday evening to come sit with me. Shouldn't you be making time with that sweet little water aerobics instructor?"

Parker rolled his eyes and plopped onto the sofa, wincing as his back muscle went into spasm. He stretched his left hand around to massage the sore spot.

If that "sweet little water aerobics instructor" didn't work him in for another practice session soon, he might have to move into Willow Tree with Grams.

"You know she was at Frankie's show last night." Grams adjusted the heating pad beneath her hips. "Would you hand me that afghan, please?"

Parker spread the pink and brown throw across her knees. "I heard the Bards of Birkenstock committee had reserved a block of seats. Kathy Richmond invited me as her guest, but I had to work late." Besides, he couldn't stomach yet another evening watching Quentin Easley cast his lecherous looks upon Sailor.

"It was not a pretty sight, let me tell you."

"What—Frankie's show?" Parker snatched a magazine from the coffee table. "I read this article on Billy Graham last week. Interesting."

"No, not Frankie's show, and don't change the subject. You know perfectly well what I'm talking about. I can't believe you're going to let some dude from New York City sweep that sweet little—"

"Grams, I get it. And I love you for caring so much." He tossed the magazine to the other end of the sofa and slid to his knees at the foot of her chair. Cradling one of her hands between his own, he stroked the swollen knuckles. These same hands once danced effortlessly up and down the keys of a flute, and it broke his heart to see how cruelly rheumatoid arthritis had abused them.

A sigh whispered between Grams's lips. "I only want you to be happy, son. You deserve to know a love like I had for your grandpa, like your mother and father shared." With a finger under his chin, she raised his head until their gazes met. "I know you feel a responsibility to look after your mother and me, but you have your own life to live. Besides, we're both pretty strong women, in case you haven't noticed."

"Headstrong, anyway." Parker released a chuckle.

"And planning to stay that way for a good long time." Grams's cheeks crinkled with laughter. "So stop wasting time. The Bible teaches us to 'number our days, that we may gain a heart of wisdom.' And God's wisdom tells us our lives are in His hands—every single part of our lives."

"I know, Grams, and I'm trying my best to trust the Lord." He pressed a kiss to the back of her hand and scooted onto the sofa. "But I can't force Sailor's affections. She has to choose for herself."

"Yes, but if you don't give her a reason to choose you. . ."

"I'm doing everything I can, but I can only be myself." Romance-meister or not, he couldn't change who he was to please Sailor any more than he'd expect her to change for him.

The problem was, Quentin Easley seemed all too persuasive in molding her into the woman *he* wanted her to be. And if he succeeded, the Sailor Kern Parker had fallen in love with might disappear forever.

❧

"I feel like I'm disappearing." Sailor stood before the mirror in the ladies' dressing room of Mabry's Department Store on Monday evening. A slinky black sequined cocktail dress clung to her slim figure.

Kathy stood behind her, two more dresses draped across her arm. "Don't talk like that. You look gorgeous."

"It's just. . .not me." Frustration choked her as she struggled to shimmy out of the tight-fitting garment.

"Hang on before you rip something." Kathy hung the other dresses on a hook and helped Sailor extract herself. Before Sailor could pull on her sweater top, Kathy grabbed the teal jersey calf-length dress and thrust it at her. "Oh no you don't. Like it or not, you've got to pick something for the gala. It's only five days away, or have you forgotten?"

"How could I?" With a groan Sailor stepped into the dress and slid her arms through the narrow sleeves. The higher neckline and longer hem made her feel less exposed, but the fabric hugged her curves—what few she had—almost as snugly as a swimsuit.

Kathy zipped up the back and peered over Sailor's shoulder. "The color's perfect, and I love the way the skirt flows out—makes you look like a ballerina. This is my favorite so far."

"You realize what all this shopping is doing to my budget. Why didn't you warn me being on your committee would be so expensive?"

The financial aspect was only the half of it. The closer they came to the Bards of Birkenstock Festival, the more she wondered what—*whom*—this whole experience was turning her into. While she enjoyed the new level of confidence gained from arranging first Chandler's and now Quentin's public appearances, she missed the predictable routine of her days at the Y. She missed the relaxing, if rather dull, evenings at home with Uncle Ed.

Most of all, she missed dressing in T-shirt and jeans, swooping her hair up into a ponytail instead of worrying about blow-drying it correctly, and going bare-faced in public without feeling underdressed.

"I'm so sorry, Sailor." Kathy sank onto the narrow bench opposite the clothing hook. "I got you into this mess. It's all my fault."

Something in Kathy's voice snagged Sailor's attention. She sank down next to her friend. "No, *I'm* sorry. Here I am complaining when you handed me the opportunity of a lifetime." She squeezed Kathy's hand. "I got to meet Chandler Michaels in person!"

Kathy tipped her head in a sheepish grin. "He turned out to be a pretty neat guy, huh? I felt awful when I realized he had MS."

"His courage is inspiring. And his faith—he taught me so much in the short time he was here."

"I thought I sensed a change in you. What happened?"

Sailor's gaze swept the ceiling. "Nothing I can pinpoint. But when I saw how important his faith was to him, how fervently he worshipped, I realized what I'd been missing. More and more I've felt God's gentle nudges. It's like He's been with me all along, but I didn't want to let Him in, and now I do."

"That's great, Sailor." Kathy drew her into a one-arm hug. "I think I'm going to cry."

"Oh, you!" Sailor pulled away and stood. "All right, Shopping Queen, is this *the* dress or not? It's nearly seven, and I still need to make a few calls tonight about Quentin's speaking engagements."

Kathy rose and studied Sailor from various angles. "Yes. Yes, this is the one. And you can wear those black stilettos you wore at the book signing the other night."

The mention of the book signing made Sailor's stomach roll. She pressed a hand to her abdomen and squeezed her eyes shut—a mistake, since the image behind her eyelids was that of Quentin's face looming above hers, his lips parted, his breath warm and tangy with breath-mint sweetness.

"Sailor? If you're worried about how much the dress costs—"

"It's not that." Sailor cast her friend a desperate frown. "Oh Kathy, I'm so confused. I wanted to fall head over heels in love with Chandler Michaels—or at least the man I imagined him to be. When I met him in person, I realized how childish I'd been. I was all ready to let go of those fantasies, until—"

"Until you met Quentin Easley." Kathy crossed her arms. "He's a hunk, no denying it, but. . ." She glanced to one side as if weighing her words.

"You can say it, Kathy. I know he's way out of my league." She pivoted. "Would you unzip me, please? I've really got to get home and make those calls."

"The truth is, *you* are way out of Quentin's league. He doesn't deserve you." Kathy exhaled sharply and slid the zipper pull down Sailor's back. "But there is someone who does."

Sailor squinted at Kathy from the corner of her eye. "What are you talking about?"

"I'm talking about the one man who's crazy for you, who's perfect for you, who loves you for who you are and not for who he could change you into."

A fizzy sensation swept from Sailor's knees to the top of her skull. She gazed into the mirror, seeing not the tiny dressing room at Mabry's but a black and jungle green cubicle at Par Excellence Salon—and behind her the face of a smiling Parker Travis.

Reality returned, and Parker's image dissolved into the face of her friend Kathy. "Stop fighting it, Sailor. You know exactly who I'm talking about."

Sailor forced a swallow over the knot in her throat and remembered Parker's unexpected arrival with lunch last week. She turned to confront her friend. "But—but weren't you and Parker—"

Kathy pressed her hands to her temples and whooshed out a sigh. "All a sham. When Parker told me he had feelings for you, I started inviting him to be my 'date' at Chandler's functions so he could keep an eye on you and hopefully prevent you from falling for Chandler's romantic come-ons. Only now we're trying to protect you from Quentin instead."

Sailor didn't know whether to laugh out loud or storm from the dressing room in righteous indignation. Probably the latter, except here she stood with her dress unzipped and slipping down her shoulders. With a huff she squirmed out of the dress and snatched up her street clothes.

"Sailor—"

"Don't talk to me right now." She thrust her legs into her jeans and ripped the sweater top over her head while shoving her feet into her sneakers. *Protect me indeed!* Like she was a socially inept child without the skills to make her own character assessments.

Okay, so maybe the *socially inept* part was true, but hadn't everyone else been wrong about Chandler? Couldn't they be just as wrong about Quentin?

Oh God, help!

She started out the dressing room door then whirled around to grab the teal cocktail dress. Kathy was right—it set off her features perfectly, the ideal dress to make a knockout impression on the man of her dreams.

If only she could get it straight once and for all just who that man was!

❧

"We have to talk." Kathy stood at the entrance to Parker's station, arms folded and a worried frown creasing her mouth.

"I'm a little busy here, Kathy." He parted off a section of his client's damp hair, combed it straight up, and snipped. Something must have happened for Kathy to show up at the salon unannounced. The pinch in his gut told him it couldn't be good.

"I told her. Last night it all came out. All but the book, that is. I was ready to tell her about that, too, but she was so angry that she left before I had the chance."

Parker swallowed and tried to maintain his composure. He wasn't about to have this discussion in front of his church council treasurer. Neither could he leave his client stewing while he whisked Kathy to the break room for a private chat. "So. . .she knows you and I aren't. . ."

"Exactly."

The pinch turned into an all-out stomach cramp. He couldn't blame Sailor for being upset. The game playing had to stop. "Maybe I can talk to her. I have my class this afternoon."

"Good luck."

Parker made a point of arriving a few minutes early for his water aerobics class. If only Sailor would give him a chance to explain. He scanned the pool, where the three high school teachers and Miranda Wright were already warming up. He didn't see Sailor anywhere.

He knew this would be an even crazier week for her, what with the festival kicking off this weekend. Friday evening began with the Birkenstock Public Library hosting a reception and speaker panel featuring several prominent Missouri authors. On Saturday Quentin would stand in for Chandler Michaels as grand marshal of the annual festival parade through downtown. Parker had been hearing the Birkenstock High School band practicing its routine almost daily for two weeks now. Just about every school, club, service organization, and civic group in town would either march or decorate and ride on a float vying for the coveted Best in Show trophy.

Another book signing at Dale & Dean's followed in the afternoon, with all the guest authors autographing their books. Then the big event Saturday night—the gala dinner, silent auction, and awards ceremony.

Parker could hardly wait for the madness to end, but he worried how the sudden return to normalcy would affect Sailor. In the spotlight ever since Chandler's arrival, her confidence apparently at an all-time high and looking as if she just stepped out of the pages of *Harper's Bazaar*, would she come crashing down to earth when Quentin Easley flew off into the sunset?

Okay, so the sun set in the west and Quentin would be headed up east to New York. The end result would be the same. Parker couldn't picture Sailor ditching her small-town roots for big-city glitz and glamour to trail after the likes of Quentin Easley. And he couldn't picture Quentin staying faithful for long to a woman as pure and innocent and genuine as Sailor. Now or later, Quentin was bound to break her heart.

Parker only hoped he'd be around to pick up the pieces. . .if Sailor would let him.

Chirpy voices sounded behind him. He turned to see the Douglas twins sashay across the deck. *Wow*. He hadn't seen them in two weeks, and they'd slimmed down noticeably. No doubt they'd worked in the practice sessions he hadn't managed to. He smiled a greeting. "Hello, ladies."

"Hello yourself, stranger." Lorraine—at least he was pretty sure it was Lorraine—clutched his elbow. "Lucille and I were hoping to get appointments with you before the big doings this weekend. But I suppose you're booked up weeks ahead."

He hid a grimace. His schedule was already squeezed to the limit, but he hated to turn anyone away, especially ladies like the Douglas twins who reminded him of Grams and her Willow Tree friends. Besides, the chlorine had really done a number on their perms, and he had a conditioning treatment he knew would help.

Rubbing his jaw, he mentally reviewed his calendar. He could easily work in a few evening appointments if he cancelled out on escorting Kathy to the rest of Quentin's prefestival appearances. Not much point in showing up for those anyway, now that Sailor knew the truth. And he wouldn't insult her with a big-brother-looking-over-her-shoulder routine.

With another quick look around the pool area, he turned to Lucille and Lorraine. "I just remembered I have a couple of cancellations. How about Wednesday or Thursday around six thirty?"

Lucille gave a squeal. "Oh, fabulous! Wednesday is choir practice, but Thursday would be *wonderful*!"

"Thank you *so much*, Parker!" Lorraine grabbed Lucille's hand and danced a little jig.

"My pleasure." He turned to follow them to the pool steps and found himself face-to-face with Sailor.

"That was nice of you." She tugged on the ends of the towel draped around her neck. "I guess that means you won't be at the library Thursday night. Quentin will be reading from Chandler's latest novel."

He rubbed the back of his head. "After what Kathy told me awhile ago, I figured you'd just as soon I didn't show up. Sailor, I'm sorry—"

"Apology accepted." She paused while the Douglas twins moved out of earshot. "I know you meant well. I just wish both of you would give me a little credit for being able to make my own decisions." Speaking so softly that Parker almost didn't hear her, she added, "You might even be surprised."

Chapter 17

With hardly a moment to herself all week, Sailor felt as if her head would explode. The pressure of constantly being "on" drained her both emotionally and physically. And to think, only a few weeks ago she'd been avidly looking forward to this weekend.

But that was before she met the real Chandler Michaels.

Before she met Quentin Easley.

Before she found herself torn between Quentin and Parker, the two most romantic men imaginable.

Although she doubted Parker Travis would consider himself the least bit romantic, much less on a par with Quentin. If only he knew how his soft-spoken ways and thoughtful attentiveness touched her heart.

Standing in front of the bathroom mirror, she manhandled a stubborn lock of hair around the styling brush and blasted it with the blow-dryer. Knowing Parker must have a full appointment list already—and especially after Kathy's confession Monday night—she hadn't felt comfortable asking for Parker's help getting ready for tonight's gala. Not that there would have been time. The autograph party at Dale & Dean's finally broke up around four, and the festival committee had been asked to be at the community center to oversee the setup arrangements no later than five.

Sailor checked her watch—nearly four thirty already! With a gasp she tossed aside the dryer and brushed her uncooperative hair into a ponytail. Parker had told her once how pretty she looked with her hair up. The memory evoked a tremor, but she couldn't afford to let her thoughts go there, not while this evening belonged to Quentin.

No, it really belonged to Chandler, and she would not let herself forget that.

She pulled the ponytail higher, coaxed it into a few tendrils with hair spray and the styling brush, and fluffed her bangs. It would have to do.

In the bedroom she slithered into the teal blue cocktail dress and struggled to get it zipped. Then came the dreaded stilettos. She'd need foot surgery after wearing them for six or seven hours straight. Maybe she could find a few moments later to—

The doorbell chimed in the hallway. Surely not Quentin—they'd already agreed to meet later at the community center. Cracking her door a couple of inches, she listened for Uncle Ed to answer the door.

"Well, I'll be!" Uncle Ed let out a hearty laugh. "Ogden Kern, you are a sight for sore eyes!"

Sailor's stomach flip-flopped. *Dad?*

"Where's our girl, Ed?" Mom's voice. "Ogden's been a little concerned since he talked to her a few days ago, so once I got the clinic up and running, we decided it was time to come home for a while."

"Thank goodness, Hazel. I can't keep up with that girl anymore. She's in her room, getting gussied up for that big writer thing at the community center."

Oh no! What had she said to worry her dad that much? Sailor started out the door then remembered how she was dressed.

Too late. Mom's footsteps echoed in the hallway. "Sailor? Sailor, honey?"

She pasted on her most welcoming smile. "Hi, Mom! I can't believe you're here!"

Her mother froze. "Sailor Kern—that dress! And so much makeup!"

She felt five years old again, shamed into submission beneath her mother's disapproving frown. "I'm. . .going out. It's an important event."

"We've read all your e-mails about this literary festival you were helping with, but you never said a word about—about—" Mom sniffed, her hands fluttering up and down the front of her blue chambray shirtdress. "Thank heavens we came home when we did."

Sailor's father joined them in the hall, towering over them both. "Lectures can wait, Hazel. We haven't hugged our daughter in over two years. Come here, Sailor-girl."

Relieved, she moved into her father's open arms. His plaid shirt smelled of Old Spice and hours sitting on a plane.

"I wish you'd let me know you were coming. I have to be at the community center in half an hour."

Her mother shrugged her purse up her arm and offered Sailor a belated hug. "Of course we're glad to see you. But I never expected—"

"Please, Mom." She needed to placate her parents quickly and hope she could still get to the gala on time.

She drew her mother through the bedroom door and signaled her father to follow. Closing the door behind them, she pulled out the bench beneath her vanity while her parents seated themselves at the foot of the bed. "I'm dressed up because tonight is a huge formal event. But surely you know I'd never do anything to embarrass you."

"And what about yourself? Or the uncle who raised you all these years?" Mom straightened her shoulders. "Why, you're made up like a painted woman. And after all we tried to teach you about conforming to Christ's standards, not the world's."

Painted woman? Sailor closed her eyes briefly. Her foot tapped a frantic beat against the faded beige carpet. "You and Dad have spent most of the last forty years in third world countries. Uncle Ed stopped living when Aunt Trina died and keeps his nose buried in biographies about people who lived centuries ago."

She spread her hands and gave a helpless shrug. "But this is the twenty-first century. And this is the way people dress when they're going to a gala awards dinner."

"Perhaps we are out of touch with modern society," her father said, his brows drawn together, "but in our minds you're still our little girl. The more we read your e-mails about spending so much time with this author person, and then your looking so tired and frazzled on the Webcam the other day, well, we're worried about you. The idea of your keeping company with a man who might want to take advantage—and you being so young and innocent—"

"Daddy, I'm not a child anymore." She reached for his hand, the sudden urge to cry tightening her throat. "I'm a thirty-two-year-old woman who's never even had a boyfriend. All I've dreamed about my whole adult life is to be seen as beautiful and special by a good man who loves me and wants to spend his life with me."

"Oh, Sailor, Sailor, honey." Mom rose and scooted onto the narrow bench next to her, pulling her against her side. "We want that for you, too. Your happiness is all we've ever wanted."

"It's why we left you in the States with Ed and Trina after you reached school age." Her father sighed and pushed his glasses up his nose. "They were younger, more stable. We thought they could give you a more normal life than you would have had traipsing to the farthest corners of the world with us."

"I know you did what you thought was best for me." A shaky sob tore through Sailor's throat. She rested her head on her mother's plump shoulder. "But I've missed you so much."

Mom patted Sailor's arm, her own voice choked with emotion. "Maybe it would've been better if we'd kept you with us after Trina died. You were at such a vulnerable age then."

"Now, Hazel, no use second-guessing ourselves. Sailor's got to get to her dinner. We can finish talking this out later." Dad stood and drew Sailor to her feet. "Let me get a better look at this fancy frock of yours. Why, the color's almost the same shade as your eyes. Mighty pretty, mighty pretty indeed."

Her father's compliment filled her with warmth. She cast a hopeful glance toward her mother.

Mom sighed. "You do look especially nice in that color, sweetheart. It's a lovely dress, very becoming." She used the side of her thumb to brush a tear from Sailor's cheek. "You'd best go fix your face, though. And all this hugging has mussed your hair."

Beaming, she gave her parents quick kisses and hurried to the bathroom. As she touched up her hair and makeup, she paused to thank God for giving her parents the grace of understanding. Halfway down the hall she stopped again, her heart brimming with unspeakable gratitude.

And thank You for loving me enough to bring my parents home exactly when I most needed them.

She couldn't wait for tonight to be over so she could introduce them to the man of her dreams—the man she realized she was falling a little more in love with every day.

❧

Parker hadn't worn a tuxedo since he'd stood up as best man in Andy Mendoza's wedding. The stiff collar chafed his neck, and those tiny studs that passed for buttons and cuff links gave him fits as he tried to manipulate them through their respective holes. But tie a bow tie? Forget it. With Mom down in Branson for Frankie's Saturday shows, he couldn't even ask her help.

He showed up on Kathy's doorstep ten minutes before five and held out the offending piece of black silk. "I should have opted for a clip-on, but the rental guy convinced me the real deal is classier."

"He's right." Kathy took the tie and ushered him into her living room, the full skirt of her black and silver waltz-length dress making soft swishing sounds. An aura of sandalwood surrounded her as she deftly worked the tie under his collar and shaped it into a proper bow.

Parker checked his reflection in the framed mirror hanging over the mantel. "Thanks. You look very nice, by the way."

"And may I say you look dashingly handsome, yourself. I'm glad you decided to go as my escort after all." Kathy scooped up a lacy black shawl and satin evening bag. "I guess in a weird way we've kind of bonded over this Chandler Michaels thing. And tonight it'll finally be over. . .one way or the other."

Parker knew exactly which way he wanted it to end. He didn't want to think about the alternative—one more reason he'd convinced himself to attend the gala with Kathy. He had a feeling Quentin Easley would be pulling out all the stops tonight, the night when Sailor would be most beautiful. . .and most vulnerable.

The community center bustled with activity—technicians checking the sound system, caterers from Audra's Café carrying in chafing dishes and massive serving platters, wait staff arranging table settings, committee members checking the silent auction tables or adding last-minute touches to the decorations.

Kathy showed Parker to one of two large, round tables reserved for committee members, front and center below the dais. "Sailor will be at the head table with Quentin and the other celebrity authors and their guests. But at least you'll be close enough to keep an eye on her."

While Kathy hurried off to help as needed, Parker settled into a chair and strove for an air of nonchalance. A couple of other committee members left their spouses at the table, which meant Parker had to engage in the requisite small talk.

A bored-looking husband sat down next to Parker. "My wife's the literary member of the family. Give me a good baseball game on TV any day." He used his index finger to poke at the ice cubes in his water glass. "You a Cardinals fan?"

"I catch their games when I can." Parker watched the entrance for Sailor's arrival, while a distant part of his brain processed his companion's words. Parker had seen the affectionate kiss the man's wife had given him before she left to help with arrangements. They may have different interests, but the love between them was obvious.

I want that, Lord. I want it with Sailor.

Voices to his right made him look toward the dais. Quentin and several others in formal attire laughed and chatted as they found their place cards at the head table. Quentin sat down almost directly above Parker, an empty chair between him and the person to his left, a small, blond woman with an exuberant smile—probably another author.

Still no Sailor. Worry niggled the back of Parker's brain. He was about to go find Kathy when he saw Sailor scurrying between the tables. Intent on Quentin, she didn't even notice Parker, which gave him time to stare in silent admiration. The teal dress accented her slim figure to perfection, and the ponytail—simplicity at its best. The only jewelry she wore was a pair of teardrop rhinestone earrings. Anything more, especially on Sailor, would have been overkill.

As she took the chair between Quentin and the blond woman, Sailor's glance caught Parker's. She gave him a quick smile, ducking her head when Quentin slid his arm around her shoulders and drew her close for a kiss on the temple.

Parker did a slow burn. He reached for his water glass and hoped a cool drink would put out the fire long enough for him to get through the evening.

❧

"You look gorgeous, baby." Quentin's hot breath against Sailor's ear sent chills down her spine. "With you beside me, I'm the envy of every guy here."

The compliment made her heart sing. She cast Quentin a timid smile and tried not to look in Parker's direction. Knowing he and Kathy had only pretended to be dating, she hadn't expected he'd be here tonight. Truthfully she'd hoped he wouldn't. The thought of having Quentin lavish her with affection while Parker watched their every move made her feel like one giant blush.

At six o'clock sharp Donna DuPont stepped to the microphone and gave her welcome speech then invited the pastor from Rejoice Fellowship to come up and offer a blessing. Returning to the microphone, Donna added, "Don't forget, the silent auction tables will be open until seven thirty, and we've had some outstanding donations this year. Keep those bids coming, because every cent goes to support literacy and the literary arts for our fair city."

The wait staff began serving dinner, and Sailor turned her attention to the sumptuous meal of rosemary chicken with artichoke hearts, prosciutto-wrapped asparagus, and rice pilaf. The chefs at Audra's Café had outdone themselves, and for once Sailor tried not to obsess too much about watching her diet.

When a server whisked away Quentin's empty plate, he crumpled his napkin and stood. He laid a possessive hand on Sailor's shoulder. "I need to step out for a bit. Care to join me?"

The thought of being alone with him made her stomach somersault. "No, thank you. I'm not finished with my dinner yet, and I see they're already bringing out dessert."

He bent closer, his fingers caressing the base of her throat. "Chocolate cake isn't exactly the dessert I've been hungry for." He started to leave then snatched up his wine glass. "Back in a few."

Sailor had barely a moment to stifle the tingles Quentin's touch had evoked before the blond woman to her left—an inspirational romance novelist from the authors' panel last night—nudged her arm. "That Quentin is a doll, almost as cute as my honey." She nodded toward the man at her left. "But what a shame Chandler Michaels couldn't be here. I was sure looking forward to meeting him. I love his books almost as much as my all-time favorite, *Gone with the Wind*."

"Yes, it's very disappointing." Reminded of Chandler, Sailor's heart dipped. She prayed he was doing better now that he'd returned home. Earlier, when she'd asked Quentin if he'd heard anything, she'd been slightly miffed to learn he hadn't made time to call and check.

Quentin still hadn't returned by the time Donna DuPont announced the silent auction had closed. "And it looks like you've all done a great job of running up those bids. Our auction judges have given me a rough estimate of the total, and I'm thrilled to report we've surpassed our goal by at least three thousand dollars."

When the applause died down, Donna gave instructions on how the winning bidders should pay for and claim their items. "And now the moment we've all been waiting for—the Bards of Birkenstock Annual 'Best of Missouri' Author Recognition Awards. It's my pleasure to welcome committee member Kathy Richmond to begin the presentations."

While Kathy made her way up the dais steps, Sailor scanned the room for any sign of Quentin. Chandler's award wouldn't be presented until the very end, but it wouldn't look good for him to wander back to his seat halfway through the ceremony. She breathed a sigh of relief when she spotted him hurrying along the side wall. He slid into his chair as Kathy stepped behind the microphone.

Quentin scooted closer to Sailor and draped his arm across her shoulders. "Didn't mean to cut it so close. Wouldn't want to miss my—uh, Chandler's award."

She felt the heat through the fabric of his tux sleeve and wondered what he'd been doing all this time. "Is everything okay?"

"You reminded me how neglectful I'd been. I decided to give Chandler a call and see how he's doing." With a reassuring smile he grazed her cheek with a spearmint-scented kiss then turned to listen as Kathy announced the recipient of the Best Missouri Playwright Award.

Sailor forced herself to wait patiently while a short, bespectacled man approached the podium from the other end of the dais and gave a rambling acceptance speech. As he returned to his seat, Sailor angled her head to whisper in Quentin's ear, "How is he?"

Quentin cast her a confused frown. "Who?"

"Chandler. You said you called him."

"Right. He's better. Glad to be home and out from under all this pressure. Said to tell you hi and to stay in touch."

They sat through several more awards and speeches, until Kathy announced, "And now it's time for the moment we've all been waiting for, the introduction of this year's recipient of the Birkenstock Arts and Letters Association's Award for Outstanding Literary Achievement by a Missouri Author. Doing the honors is my very best friend and the newest member of the Bards of Birkenstock Committee, Sailor Kern."

As Kathy stepped aside, Sailor palmed the index card containing her speaking notes and stood, thankful her calf-length dress covered her trembling knees. Grinning, Quentin squeezed her hand and winked. Her pulse thundered in her ears as she moved to the podium. The microphone, set for Kathy, was about six inches too high for her. When she adjusted it, a loud, scraping sound blasted through the speakers. An embarrassed flush crept up her cheeks.

Discreetly clearing her throat, she set her notes before her and clamped her fingers around the edges of the podium. *"It's all about the persona. Act confident and you'll feel confident."* Such was the advice Josh Fanning had given her a few days ago. She spotted him and Deb a few tables away, and his reassuring smile helped calm her.

"G–Good evening, ladies and gentlemen. I can't tell you what a thrill it has been for me to spend time this past month with the recipient of this coveted award." Sailor glanced briefly at her notes, but as the words poured from her heart, she found she didn't need them. "Getting to know Chandler Michaels as a person, not merely a handsome face on the back of a book cover, has been an amazing experience. He taught me about courage, perseverance, and especially about faith through difficult circumstances. Meeting him made me realize that—literally—you can't judge a book by its cover. More importantly, we mustn't judge people by outward appearances, because what comes from the heart is what really makes us who we are."

The hall rang with applause, and Sailor took a few steadying breaths while she waited for silence. "That's why it gives me such great pleasure to present this year's award to Birkenstock's own Chandler Michaels—or, as many of you know him, Charles Michalicek."

More applause, accompanied with loud cheers as several in the audience rose in a standing ovation. When the applause subsided, Sailor went on, "Sadly, Chandler had to cut his visit short due to health problems. Accepting the award on Chandler's behalf is his assistant, Quentin Easley."

Kathy waited at Sailor's right with the engraved plaque, which Quentin stepped forward to accept. "This is truly an honor!" he said as he tilted the microphone to his level. "It broke Chandler's heart that he wasn't able to accept this award in person, but I know he's with us in spirit. Many of you know of his battle with MS, a battle he seems to be losing." Quentin gave a sniff and drew his hand across his mouth. "But I want you to know, the Chandler Michaels legacy will go on. His head is still brimming with story ideas, and I intend to do everything in my power to ensure that there'll be many more Chandler Michaels romances to come. I—"

Quentin stifled a choking sound with a fist to his lips. He gasped a few quick breaths and then lifted the plaque high, his gaze fixed on a distant spot in the rafters. "This is for you, Chandler."

As the hall once again filled with applause and cheers, Quentin turned to Sailor with a teary-eyed smile. "This got to me more than I thought it would," he whispered. "I need to get some air. Will you step outside with me?"

This time she couldn't refuse. His touching display of respect and affection for Chandler stirred something deep inside her and made her question her feelings for him all over again. She reached for the plaque and laid it on Quentin's chair. "There's a courtyard with some benches behind the building. I'll show you the way."

While Donna DuPont returned to the podium to close out the evening, Sailor and Quentin slipped out a side door. Pink-tinged streetlamps illuminated the path leading around the community center to the small park area. They found a white wrought iron bench beneath a stately oak. Nearby, a fountain burbled amid beds of deep purple irises and fragrant roses.

Quentin undid the button of his tux coat and tugged Sailor onto the bench beside him. "It means so much that I could share this evening with you, Sailor. Getting to know you these past three weeks—I hate to see it end."

She stared down at his hand entwined in hers, and her heart spiraled. Everything about Quentin oozed romance—the romance she'd always dreamed of. His sensuous glances, his silvery words, his seductive smile all conspired against her restraint. "I've enjoyed spending time with you, too, Quentin, but. . ." She slid her hand from his and inched away. "As flattered as I am by your attention, I've realized how little we have in common. And besides, you're flying back to New York tomorrow."

"All the more reason to make the most of tonight. I've never felt this way about a woman before. Sailor, you do things to me." He reached for her hand and placed it against his chest. "Feel that?"

His heartbeat thudded against her palm, sending shivers up her arm. Her own heart raced. She jerked her hand away. *Dear God, help me! I want this. . . and I don't!*

"What is it, Sailor? Are you afraid?" He chuckled softly and ran his fingers up and down her cheek. "You poor little girl, so naive, so inexperienced. I could teach you so much, if you'd only let me."

"Maybe we should go inside—" The words came out in a breathless gasp. She stood abruptly.

Quentin rose and swept her into his arms. "Not yet, baby. Not until I get what I came out here for."

"Quentin—" She struggled against him, sudden panic freezing the air in her lungs. His steamy breath on her face nearly choked her—the spearmint no longer camouflaging what she now realized was the smell of alcohol—something much stronger than a glass of dinner wine! The words from her own speech paraded across her thoughts: *"We mustn't judge people by outward appearances, because what comes from the heart is what really makes us who we are."*

And she now saw with painful clarity exactly the kind of man Quentin Easley was.

Cocking her elbows, she braced her hands against his chest and gave a mighty shove. "You're drunk! How could you, tonight of all nights?"

He spread his hands and shrugged. "How else was I supposed to get through those cheesy acceptance speeches?"

"The emotion you showed earlier—it was all fake, wasn't it?" She crossed her arms and huffed. "I didn't want to admit it, but the evidence has been in front of me all along. All those fans mistaking you for him, the way you bask in the attention while you autograph his books—you want Chandler's fame and glory for yourself."

"It was his idea. You can't blame me for taking advantage of the opportunity"—he stepped closer, a leering grin contorting his face—"or the perks that go with it."

Her fists knotted. She backed away. "Why you–you're not half the man Chandler is."

"You've got it wrong, baby. Admit it, I'm everything you dreamed *he* would be, everything you ever wanted in a man." His face hardened. "Come on, quit fighting it. You've been flirting with me ever since we met."

Flirt? She didn't even know how! "You're so full of yourself, you wouldn't recognize true romance if it bit you on the nose." Outraged, she started toward the building.

He lunged for her, snagging her skirt as she swiveled out of his reach. She yanked it out of his hand and tried to run, but he seized her arm. A strange, manic hunger lit a flame behind his eyes. His mouth loomed over hers.

"No!" She reached up with her free arm and landed a resounding slap against his cheek. When he flinched in surprise, she stomped on his instep with the heel of her stiletto.

He stumbled backward with a yelp. Darting down the path, she heard a splash and glanced over her shoulder to see Quentin sprawled in the fountain. While he sputtered and fumed and tried to extract himself, she kept running, her only thought a constantly repeated prayer: *Help me, Father! Help me!*

She ran headlong into a firm chest and sheltering arms and collapsed in weak relief.

❧

"You're okay, Sailor. You're safe now." Parker smoothed her mussed hair off her face and ran a soothing hand up and down her back while she struggled to catch her breath. The moment he'd seen Quentin hurry Sailor out of the banquet, his protective instincts had kicked in. He'd searched the lobby and anterooms until a guest said he'd seen the couple exit the building. Following the sounds of raised voices, Parker came upon the path to the courtyard, arriving in time to see Sailor break free from Quentin.

Her slim fingers clutched his lapels like talons. Something between terror and rage blazed in her eyes. "I should have known better. I'm such an idiot!"

"No, Sailor, Quentin's the idiot." Parker's own heart hammered with the urge to break a few of Quentin's bones. If he'd hurt Sailor, if he'd so much as—Parker couldn't even let himself imagine. *Thank You, God, for protecting her.* "Go on inside. Find Kathy and tell her what happened."

Quentin staggered toward them, his wet tuxedo plastered to his frame. "I don't know what she told you, but *nothing* happened." He scraped a hand through his dripping hair and released an ugly laugh. "See, that's the whole problem. Nothing ever would have happened. Sailor Kern is nothing more than a scaredy-cat little tease."

Hot rage exploded in Parker's chest. He gripped Sailor's shoulders and moved her behind him before stepping toe-to-toe with Quentin. "You couldn't be more wrong. Sailor is the purest, sweetest, most unpretentious woman I've ever met." Punching a finger at Quentin's breastbone, he went on, "You, on the other hand, are nothing more than a big phony, riding on the coattails of the real thing. You're a disgrace to Chandler Michaels, a disgrace to the literary world, a disgrace to the male gender."

"This, from Birkenstock's perennial-bachelor hairstylist?" Quentin's mouth spread in snide laughter. "I bet the whole town wonders why you haven't settled down with the right woman yet—or maybe they know you're just not man enough to handle a real woman."

Parker let the insult slide. The creep wasn't worth it. Clamping his lips together, he turned to take Sailor inside. "I think you should report this to the cops. He assaulted you."

"No, wait." An unreadable smile flickered across her lips as she gazed briefly into his eyes. Then she marched up to Quentin. "What you said earlier about my being inexperienced and naive—you're right, of course. I expected romance to be tender and pure, just like in Chandler's novels, and I wrongly assumed you'd be that kind of man."

She took a step back and slid her hand into Parker's, her gaze filled with warmth as their eyes met. "I should have realized that man was right here all the time."

Parker's breath lodged somewhere around his Adam's apple. He figured he must be grinning like a fool. "Just get out of here, Easley, or I really will call the cops."

Squishy footsteps confirmed Quentin's hasty departure, and Parker heaved a thankful sigh as he found himself alone—finally—with the woman he'd fallen in love with weeks ago.

He pulled her into his arms. "Are you okay?"

"I am now." She sucked in a shivery breath. "Did you mean what you said about me?"

"I did. Did you mean what *you* said about me?"

"Every word."

"Sailor, I—" He drew her closer, his gaze sweeping the curve of her brow, the shape of her lips. "I don't think I can stand waiting a moment longer. Will you let me kiss you?"

❧

Sailor gulped and nodded. When his lips found hers in sweet, sweet ecstasy, she melted into his embrace. Her arms crept around him as the kiss warmed and deepened. A delightful languor spread from her core to the tips of her fingers and toes. It was everything she'd ever dreamed a first kiss could be—tender, sweet, gentle, insistent. How could she not have known, not have seen how much Parker cared for her? *Thank You, Lord, for saving me for this moment!*

Parker drew back with a shudder. "That was definitely worth the wait." He caressed the curve of her jaw, the corners of his mouth turning downward in a look of urgency. "I hope you know I'd never, ever hurt you. I love you, Sailor."

Her heart soared. She could scarcely find her voice. "I love you, too, Parker. I only wish I'd—"

As her hand slid down his tux coat, something protruding from his back pocket caught her wrist. Curious, she pulled the object from his pocket and held it to the light. *Romance by the Book: Tips and Tricks to Win Her Heart*—and the author was Chandler Michaels? Noticing the words *Advance Review Copy* bordering the front cover, she shot Parker a confused stare. "What are you doing with this?"

"Ammunition. Which, thankfully, I no longer need." He snatched the book from her hands and tossed it into the bushes.

"But wait—Chandler wrote that?"

"Not Chandler. Quentin." An exasperated breath whistled between his lips. "It's a long story."

Sailor shrugged and gave a half laugh. "Why do I have the feeling I really don't want to know?"

"There's only one thing you need to know: I'm crazy, wildly, madly in love with you." Parker swept her into his arms again and buried his face in her hair. "I may not be the most romantic guy on the planet, but I promise you, Sailor—if you'll let me, I'll spend the rest of my life learning how to make you happy."

"You already do." She snuggled against him and breathed in the crisp, starched scent of his dress shirt. "You already do."

Epilogue

"Thanks for arranging for these tickets, Sailor." Chandler Michaels reached across the arm of his wheelchair and patted her hand.

She smiled from her seat in the handicap-accessible row. "Having connections with Frankie Verona's show musicians has its advantages."

Deb Fanning, seated on Sailor's other side with Josh and two of their sons, leaned forward and arched an eyebrow. "Something tells me those connections could get a whole lot stronger in the near future."

"Now, Deb!" Sailor crossed her arms and fixed her attention on the maroon velvet stage curtains at Frankie Verona's Moonlight over Missouri Theater. Knowing Parker was once again filling in for the flutist this weekend, she'd thought it the perfect time to bring Chandler to a show.

As if falling more in love with Parker every day weren't enough, Sailor could hardly believe her favorite author had moved back to Birkenstock over the summer —*and* hired her as his part-time assistant! Learning of the incident with Sailor following the awards dinner, Chandler immediately halted all plans to transfer his authorial identity to Quentin. He could no longer deny the truth—Quentin was a manipulative womanizer, out to use Chandler's fame for his own gain. Surprisingly, with Quentin out of the picture, Chandler's health seemed to stabilize, making him suspect the stress of trying to rein in Quentin's behavior had taken more of a toll than he realized.

The other good news was that Sailor's parents planned to retire at the end of the year and settle back in Birkenstock. Could her life be any more wonderful?

The familiar timpani fanfare preceded the announcer's voice: "Ladies and gentlemen, welcome to Frankie Verona's Moonlight over Missouri Theater!" Sailor held her breath as the curtains parted and the music began. Spotting Parker, she beamed him a happy smile, her chest filling with pride as she watched him sway to the syncopated rhythms. She shifted her glance to Laura Travis standing with the backup singers and wiggled her fingers in silent gratitude for obtaining their tickets.

Each song seemed better than the last, and it warmed Sailor's heart to see how much Chandler enjoyed the show. Tilting her head toward him, she started to share an interesting detail about one of the band members when Frankie stepped to the front of the stage.

"And now, friends," Frankie began, "I have a very special song for you, one I recently cowrote with tonight's guest flutist, Parker Travis."

Deb nudged Sailor's arm. "How cool! Did you know about this?"

Sailor blinked. "I'm as surprised as you are."

Frankie motioned for Parker to join him at center stage. "You all know how I love romantic ballads, and this one, entitled 'With One Glance of

Your Eyes,' is quickly becoming a favorite. It's inspired by Solomon's Song of Songs, the most romantic book ever written."

With a brief nod in Sailor's direction, Parker lifted his flute to his lips, and the whispery, evocative tones filled the theater. Chills danced up and down Sailor's arms when Frankie's mellow baritone joined in, creating a rhapsody of emotion in words and music. The song told of blossoming romance, hearts joined in harmony, God's love reflected in human eyes. When the song ended, silence blanketed the theater for a long moment before wild applause broke out. Sailor found herself swept to her feet with everyone else for a standing ovation.

"Thank you, thank you, ladies and gentlemen." Frankie bowed several times, as did Parker, until Frankie finally raised his hands to quiet the crowd. "House lights, please?" His gaze sought out Sailor, and he winked. "Miss Kern, would you join us onstage?"

The next thing she knew, two ushers were escorting her to the nearest steps. Frankie took her hand and bent to kiss it before leading her across the stage to where Parker stood. If Sailor didn't already know something was up, her suspicions were confirmed when Parker traded his flute for Frankie's microphone.

As Frankie sidled away, Parker dropped to one knee and reached for Sailor's hand. "'Fair as the moon, bright as the sun, majestic as the stars in procession'—with one glance of your eyes, you've stolen my heart, Sailor Kern. I bless the day God sent you into my life. Will you marry me?"

Speechless at first, Sailor suddenly burst out laughing. "And you say you're not romantic!" She tugged on his hand until he stood, her gaze drinking him in while her heart soared far above the stage lights. A happy sob tore from her throat. "I can't imagine anything more wonderful than becoming your wife. Yes, I'll marry you!"

They shared a kiss beneath the spotlight, while a prayer of thanks rose in Sailor's heart. Over the past several months God had shown His love for her in so many ways, but none so beautiful as knowing one special man loved her just as she was.

WHERE THE DOGWOODS BLOOM

Dedication

For Mary Connealy, with gratitude for your friendship and inspiration. You're the reason this book exists!

Many thanks to my critique partner, Carla Stewart, for keeping me on track with both her writing advice and nursing experience, and also to law enforcement professional and author Steven Hunt for letting me pick his brain about police procedure. Any errors are my own.

And, as always, I pray a special blessing upon my husband and our gorgeous daughters, the best cheerleaders a writer could have!

Chapter 1

Broken! It can't be broken." Jilly Gardner squinted toward the light box where three X-rays of her left ankle glowed in haunting shades of gray. "Take another look, Doc. Maybe it's just a smudge on your glasses."

"I know what I'm looking at, Miss Gardner." The petite ER doctor's tone sizzled.

Okay, maybe she'd insulted the woman's intelligence a teensy bit. Besides, the doctor's bloodshot eyes and stooped shoulders suggested she'd been on duty all night. "Sorry. It's just. . .this is horrible timing. Are you absolutely positive?"

"Your X-rays clearly indicate a lateral malleolus fracture. Not bad enough to require surgery, but you'll be in a cast with limited weight bearing on that leg for a full six weeks."

Jilly winced as she scooted to the edge of the exam table. She refused to look down at the lower limb swollen to nearly twice its size. "But I've got bills to pay. I can't work with a broken ankle."

"Why not? You drive a standard?" The doctor scribbled something on a chart.

"What does my car have to do with anyth—Ow!" Standing up? Big mistake. She jerked the injured leg toward her chest and chomped down on the inside of her lip.

The doctor scowled over her wire rims. "Not a good idea to put weight on that foot."

"Yeah, I get that." Jilly eased back to the center of the table and allowed a nurse in lollypop-print scrubs to arrange an ice pack around her ankle. She squeezed her eyes shut, forcing out the tears that had begun to pool. *Oh God, this cannot be happening. Not now.*

"Hang in there, Miss Gardner. You're young and fit. It's not the end of the world."

With a loud sniff, she shot her gaze toward the ceiling. A deluge threatened behind her eyes. "I just hope it's not the end of my career."

She ignored the cynical voice in her head that taunted, *What career?*

The nurse patted her arm. "You'll get used to the crutches in no time."

Yeah, right. Kind of hard to swing a tennis racquet while balancing on one foot and two skinny aluminum sticks. Not exactly the perfect summer season Jilly had counted on.

Two hours later, she reclined on the sofa in her garage apartment, the ankle swathed in an ice pack and propped up on pillows. The swelling should go down in a couple of days, and she had an appointment with an orthopedist Monday afternoon to get a cast. In the meantime, pain pills had taken the edge off, and Jilly's world was mellowing fast.

"You need anything else, sweetie?" Her landlady, Denise Moran, set a tall glass of diet cola on the coffee table next to the current issue of *Tennis*.

"Just a new ankle." Jilly scraped a hank of straight, limp hair off her forehead. She desperately needed a shower and shampoo. Not gonna happen today. "Thanks for helping me home from the ER."

"After all you did for me when I had the flu last winter, it's the least I can do." The sixty-something widow plopped down in a Danish-style recliner. "Okay, young lady, tell me how in the world you managed to break your ankle."

"It was freaky. Totally freaky." Jilly poked around in her benumbed brain, trying to put the pieces together. One minute she'd been on a stepladder in the pro shop, retrieving the Becker 11 an adolescent Andy Roddick-wannabe insisted on trying out. She could have told him he wasn't ready for such a high-caliber racquet, but no. It was the Becker or nothing.

Then something in the air tickled her nose—probably the cheap aftershave the kid had slapped on after his shower. Scents and Jilly did not get along. She'd sneezed violently. The stepladder shook and she lost her balance. Then somehow a display of tennis balls got knocked to the floor, and her left foot came down hard on one of the canisters. The ankle gave a violent twist, and she'd yelped in agony.

If she didn't know better, she'd think. . . No, it was her stupid allergies, not an evil plot by an overachiever kid. Acne-faced, outgrowing his own skin, morning breath that could knock an elephant off its feet. And too cocky for his own good. Several of Paul Edgar's students had attitude problems—as did Paul himself these days. Despite her long-standing friendship with the other tennis pro at Modesto's new Silverheels Country Club, Jilly and her girls usually kept their distance.

"Freaky how, honey?" Denise patted Jilly's uninjured leg.

Oops, must have zoned out for a few seconds. Jilly reached for her cola. "I fell off a stepladder when I sneezed."

"They say accidents are most likely to happen when we're doing something ordinary. My mother fell and cracked her pelvis getting out of the bathtub last year. She's in her eighties, so it was quite a scare. You're young, though. You'll heal quickly."

"So I'm told."

But it wouldn't be soon enough. This summer might be her last chance ever to qualify for a major tournament, and now she faced weeks off the competition circuit. A long swallow of ice-cold diet cola did little to soothe the resentment burning the back side of her sternum. *Young* was a relative term in professional tennis, and at twenty-seven, she was way too close to being "over the hill."

❧

Cameron Lane stepped out of his Mercury Mariner hybrid and inhaled the clean scent of country air seasoned with a hint of wood smoke. Gray wisps curled skyward from the stone chimney atop rustic Dogwood Blossom Inn. It was a quiet Tuesday afternoon, a bit cool for this time of year. Tourist season hadn't officially kicked off yet, so the gravel parking area stood empty, save for Cam's SUV and a four-door Chevy pickup. Probably the Nelsons', who owned the inn.

It would be good to see Harvey and Alice again. He hadn't visited them nearly often enough since accepting the teaching position at Rehoboth Bible College four years ago. Creating lesson plans and grading papers didn't leave much time for keeping up with old friends. A mistake he hoped to correct this summer.

Along with a few others.

His chest throbbed with the sudden urgency to wrap his friends and mentors in a bear hug. He slammed the door of his SUV and took the split-log steps two at a time. He burst in the front door, his mouth stretching into a boyish grin.

The empty lobby squelched his eagerness. "Harvey? Alice? You around?"

Silence.

Must be working out back. They always had plenty to do before the onslaught of summer guests. Cam marched to the tall glass doors that opened upon an expansive view of Missouri's Lake of the Ozarks. The meandering lake stretched one lazy arm along the northeast edge of the Nelsons' property. How many summers had Cam spent casting his fishing pole alongside Harvey's from the little green boat that now lay upside down next to the weathered dock?

He stepped onto the redwood deck. "Harvey! Anybody home?"

A man's steel-gray head appeared in the doorway of a storage building next to the garage. "Glory be! Cameron Lane, is that you?"

"In the flesh." Cam bounded down the steps and met his old friend on the sloping lawn. Their chests thumped together in a manly hug that lifted Cam off his feet.

"Man, you are a welcome sight indeed." Harvey pounded Cam on the back with one hand while brushing something off his face with the other. A tear? Cam felt his own eyes well up.

"It's been way too long, Harvey. How are you? How's Alice? Is she around?"

The man's face clouded. He took a half step backward and shoved his hands into the pockets of his khaki work pants. "Alice is in the hospital. I was just wrapping some stuff up here, so I could pack a few things and stay in town with her."

Cam's stomach clenched. "What happened?"

"Some heart blockage, looks like. She's been ailing for a while, but you know Alice. Never one to burden others. Took us both by surprise when her cardiologist said she needed a quadruple bypass. The surgery's day after tomorrow."

"Sounds serious."

"Nothin' the good Lord can't handle." Harvey steered Cam toward the inn. "Come on inside and I'll fix us some coffee. Then you can catch me up on what all you've been up to. You'll come with me to the hospital, won't you?"

"Sure, Harvey. You bet."

Two cups of Harvey's stand-a-spoon-in-it coffee later, Cam aimed his SUV back the way he'd come. Concerned by Harvey's pallor and the deepening lines around his eyes, Cam had offered to drive him to the hospital. The old man could be headed for a heart attack himself if he didn't ease up.

"You never said what brought you up to Dogwood Blossom," Harvey said as Cam slowed to take a curve.

"I'm taking a break from teaching—a six-month sabbatical."

Harvey shot him an appreciative grin. "And you decided to spend some time with me and Alice?"

"That's part of it." The rest of his summer plans didn't seem so feasible now.

"I hear a 'but' in there somewhere. What else is going on?"

Leave it to Harvey. He could always read Cam like a large-print paperback. "As part of my sabbatical, I'm hosting a series of weekend prayer retreats for my church. I'd hoped to bring the groups up to the inn. But with Alice in the hospital—"

"No, it's fine. We've already got a good number of regulars coming back this summer, so I gotta keep the inn open. Can't afford not to, what with hospital bills piling up." Harvey sighed and let his head fall against the headrest. "God'll work things out, just like He always does."

Faith like a mustard seed? Harvey had faith like the Rock of Gibraltar. Cam's chest tightened. His own faith was in dire need of recharging. So how exactly had he expected to teach and inspire a bunch of church members on the finer points of prayer?

Maybe he should call off the retreats and help Harvey manage the inn instead.

He was about to open his mouth and make the offer when Harvey straightened abruptly. "Why, I know just who to call."

❧

Jilly's tiny apartment over Denise's garage would never qualify as handicapped-accessible. She'd gotten her boot cast yesterday and already lost count of how many times she'd rammed it into a door frame or chair leg. And turning around in the bathroom on crutches? Forget it!

She grew more stir-crazy every day, but the mere thought of trying to negotiate the stairs tied her stomach in knots. Denise had been kind enough to drive her to the orthopedist and also picked up some groceries and prepared a few meals, but if Jilly had to listen to much more of the dear lady's incessant chatter, her head would explode.

Work. She needed to work. And teaching tennis, the only thing she felt qualified to do, she couldn't. The pro shop manager said he'd try to work in a few shifts for her behind the counter, but he already had a full staff. Even if Jilly could manage coaching her advanced students from the sidelines, the beginning and intermediate players needed demonstrations and hands-on instruction.

One or two of her advanced kids might be willing to help, except the ones she'd consider asking had already told her they had summer jobs lined up to help pay for their lessons.

A ragged groan tore through Jilly's chest. *God, are You up there? This is so not fair!*

As she balanced on one crutch to retrieve the milk jug from the refrigerator, the phone rang. She set the jug back in the fridge and hopped on her right foot over to the counter. The caller ID registered a Missouri area code but no name. She couldn't think of a single person in Missouri she'd ever want to talk to again. Warily she lifted the receiver. "Hello?"

"Jillian? Is this Jillian Gardner?"

The male voice had a familiar cadence, but no one had called her Jillian since she was a kid. "Who is this?"

"This is Cameron Lane. I knew you when you were Harvey and Alice Nelson's foster child."

Cam Lane? The four chocolate sandwich cookies Jilly had just eaten chose that moment to do a square dance in her stomach. His mention of the Nelsons, however, had her struggling to keep her voice even. "I remember. You used to hang out at the inn."

"I know this call is coming out of nowhere, but Harvey asked me to get in touch with you. Alice is in the hospital, scheduled for quadruple bypass day after tomorrow."

Jilly squeezed her eyes shut. She didn't want to care, but she couldn't help herself. If only the past didn't still hurt so much. "I'm sorry. I'll send a card or something."

"Actually, Harvey was hoping for some help."

"Help? I don't understand."

"He'll have his hands full taking care of Alice while she recovers. He needs someone to manage the inn for several weeks this summer."

"And that involves me how?" *Please don't ask me what I think you're asking.*

"According to Harvey, you know almost as much about running the inn as he and Alice. He said you pretty much took over the summer they won that Alaskan cruise and were gone for two weeks."

"I was barely seventeen. And I had a lot of help from the staff."

Cameron chuckled. "You might remember, the staff back then was already ancient. Harvey's current staff hasn't been there long enough to know the inn business like you do. Besides, he really needs someone he trusts, someone who cares about the inn as much as he and Alice."

She may have a few fond memories of her years at Dogwood Blossom Inn, but still. . . "Did it ever occur to Harvey that I already have a job?" *Sort of.*

The line went silent for several seconds. "I guess not. I'll let Harvey know you're not available. He'll understand."

A torrent of emotions churned beneath Jilly's heart. She pictured Harvey's tender, compassionate gaze, Alice's bubbly smile. A part of her still loved that sweet couple, the ones who'd opened their hearts and home to her after she'd worn out her welcome with at least four previous families. The Nelsons were her last foster parents.

She'd hoped for something more. They'd promised more.

It hadn't happened.

"I won't keep you, then," Cameron said. "I'll tell Harvey—"

"Wait." The air rushed from Jilly's lungs. "I'm kind of on leave from my job. I could help for a while, I guess."

"Are you sure?"

Why not? Managing the inn might be just the thing to distract her from everything she'd be missing out on if she stayed in Modesto for the summer. "One small problem. The reason I'm free right now is because I broke my ankle. I'd have to delegate a lot of the physical work."

"Sorry about the ankle, but the staff will be there to help. Harvey just needs someone to oversee things and manage the office. I'll be staying at the inn off and on, myself, so you can put me to work any way you need to."

"Great."

"Harvey will be thrilled. Alice, too."

"Okay, I'll let you know as soon as I've made arrangements." After jotting down his number, she said good-bye, then crumpled against the kitchen counter, jamming her bent left knee against the lower cupboard door.

Great timing, God. If this was Your plan all along with this ankle thing, all I can say is, "You have a weird sense of humor." Notice I'm not laughing.

Though they'd kept in touch with Christmas and birthday cards, Jilly hadn't seen Harvey and Alice since they hugged her good-bye at the Kansas City airport the day she left for Stanford University, nearly a decade ago. Excuses, always excuses. At college it was a test to cram for, a research paper to complete, tennis practice and tournaments. After graduation came the competition circuit, training camps, her coaching schedule.

She should forgive the Nelsons, try to understand.

Maybe in another ten years.

She'd almost decided to call Cameron back and tell him she'd changed her mind when the phone jangled again. Startled, she staggered backward and would have landed on her rear if her kitchen had been any wider and the fridge hadn't broken her fall.

Catching her breath along with her balance, she glanced at the caller ID. Anonymous. Probably a telemarketer. She lifted the receiver and prepared to give her usual brush-off.

Before she could even say hello, static filled her ear, then a rasping voice: "Better forget what you saw, or next time it could be worse." The line went dead.

A *threat*? Jilly's chest felt like it had been hit with a backhand smash. Her pulse accelerated well past training rate, and she hadn't even broken a sweat.

Chapter 2

Cam, honey, are you still at the hospital? It's Friday. Did you forget we have dinner plans?"

"Aw, man. I'm sorry, Liz." Cam stood in the parking lot outside Blossom Hills General, cell phone pressed to his ear, right hip braced against the fender of his Mariner. A playful May breeze tossed a scrap of paper across the toe of his sneaker. "I have to pick up someone at the Kansas City airport and drive her up to Dogwood Blossom Inn."

"Her?" Liz's voice took on a suspicious edge.

"Harvey and Alice Nelson's former foster child. She's coming to manage the inn for a few weeks."

"But you'll be back in town for Sammy's ball game tomorrow morning, won't you? He'll be heartbroken if you aren't there."

The image of Liz MacIntosh's wide-eyed eight-year-old son tugged at Cam's heart. So much like Terrance at that age. Innocent. Trusting. Full of big-boy dreams.

He scrubbed a hand over his eyes and wrestled his thoughts back to the present. "You know I wouldn't miss Sammy's game for anything. See you in the morning, okay?"

He pressed the End button and checked the time. If he left right now, he should arrive at the Kansas City airport around the time Jillian—make that Jilly, at her insistence—retrieved her luggage from the baggage carousel.

Heading north toward I-70, he hoped he'd recognize Jillian Gardner after all these years. He still pictured a lanky kid with a thick, coffee-brown ponytail. All arms and legs, and a spitfire temper that matched her skill on the tennis court. The last of the Nelsons' dozen or more foster children to grow up and leave their nurturing home, she was the one they talked about—and clearly missed—the most. Harvey and Alice deserved sainthood for all they'd done for Jilly. He only hoped she appreciated it.

But considering the distance she'd put between herself and the Nelsons, he had to wonder. Not that he'd been much better about visiting, and he lived less than twenty-five miles from his friends. He owed Harvey and Alice an equal amount of gratitude for helping him through the most painful time of his life, a time when his parents were too wrapped up in their own grief to even acknowledge his existence.

"Enough, Lane." He slapped the steering wheel with an open palm and focused on the freeway signs. Time to let go of the past and move on.

❧

You've got to let go of the past, Jilly Gardner.

And good luck with that. The past was about to confront her with all the power of a Venus Williams serve.

As she eased the bulky blue boot cast to a more comfortable position under the seat in front of her, the flight attendant announced over the speaker that they were beginning their final descent into Kansas City. A confusing mixture of dread and homesickness tied knots around Jilly's chest. She pressed her forehead against the cool window and gazed toward the far eastern horizon. She imagined she could make out the nearest arms of the sprawling Lake of the Ozarks as it coiled around the hills like a multi-limbed dragon. If she could only see far enough, she might even glimpse the ribbon of road leading to Dogwood Blossom Inn.

It was a road she once vowed never to travel again. A road that would lead her back to the closest thing to a real home she'd ever known, into the arms of the couple who'd destroyed that dream forever.

Get over it, Jilly. What's done is done, and there's no going back.

The plane shuddered through a burst of turbulence. Nausea threatening, Jilly turned away from the window and fixed her gaze on the lavatory sign at the far end of the aisle. Too late to leave her seat. A red *X* slashed through the restroom symbol.

A more recent memory nudged aside the queasiness: last Saturday, the corridor outside the country club locker room. After three straight hours of teaching tennis classes during which she'd downed two tall bottles of water, she'd been in a hurry to get to the restroom. Not paying attention, she'd shoved through the men's door before she realized it, obviously interrupting a heated discussion between Paul Edgar and one of his muscle-bound protégés. They both spun around and glared at her, the boy quickly shoving something into the pocket of his warm-up jacket.

Muttering an embarrassed "Excuse me, my mistake," she'd scuttled backward, tugging on the door faster than its hydraulic closer wanted to allow. The urgency that brought her there in the first place hadn't given her time to process what she'd seen inside the men's room.

Then, not even an hour later, the misstep off the ladder and a torturous ride to the ER in the pro shop manager's cramped VW. Preoccupied with her broken ankle and then Cameron Lane's unexpected phone call a few days later, she hadn't given the men's room incident further thought until this moment.

Could it have anything to do with the weird voice on the phone, telling her to forget what she'd seen? After hanging up she'd tried to put the call out of her mind, convincing herself it must have been a wrong number. Now she wasn't so sure.

Although Blossom Hills, Missouri, might not be her first choice of destinations, getting out of Modesto sounded like a better idea all the time.

If she could only figure out what she'd walked in on in the men's room.

Drugs? Gambling? Blackmail?

No, despite Paul's moodiness lately, she couldn't believe he'd be involved in anything shady. He was too much of a pro.

When the plane landed twenty minutes later, she'd all but given up trying to figure it out. She retrieved her crutches from the flight attendant and hobbled up the jet bridge. At baggage claim, she chose the least crowded spot around the carousel and tried to figure out how to balance on crutches while snagging a moving fifty-pound suitcase. Sure, she worked out—or at least she had until the accident—but her training didn't include airport gymnastics.

A buzzer sounded, a red light flashed, and the metal luggage monster started spitting out suitcases. Jilly spotted her two battered blue bags tumbling onto the carousel behind a dented cardboard crate. While her suitcases traveled the circuit, she fortified herself with a deep breath, then shifted both crutches to her left side, freeing her right arm. With one less "leg" to stand on, she suddenly felt too wobbly to maneuver.

And there went her luggage.

Frustration gnawed on what was left of the airplane pretzels rumbling around in her stomach. She readjusted her crutches and glanced around in search of a sympathetic face, but most of the other passengers had already claimed their bags and left. If someone didn't come to her rescue soon, she could be watching those two blue suitcases circle the carousel all night long.

Just as they came around again, a muscular arm reached past her. A tall guy with thick, ash-brown hair hefted both pieces from the carousel and plopped them on the floor beside her. "These yours?"

"Thanks. How'd you—" Then Jilly looked up into her rescuer's hazel eyes. "Cam?"

He thrust out his hand. "Hi, Jillian—I mean Jilly. I'd have recognized you anywhere, even without that cast."

She studied the contours of the man's face. Beneath a few worry lines and the merest touch of gray at his temples, she glimpsed the young, lean, and roguishly handsome Cameron Lane she remembered. When she first met him, he'd been a happy-go-lucky fifteen-year-old. A prankster who drew perverse pleasure from tugging on her ponytail or dropping creepy-crawly things down the back of her shirt.

Then a couple of years later, Cam's younger brother died unexpectedly, and Cam had turned quiet, introspective. He and Harvey went on long hikes through the hills or spent hours together on the lake in Harvey's little green fishing boat. By then, Jilly had become too wrapped up in school and tennis lessons to give much thought to the changes in Cam. But as a blossoming young woman she'd definitely missed his attention, annoying as it could be.

A sudden shiver raised gooseflesh on her arms. She felt twelve years old again and wished she still had a ponytail.

"My car's just a short walk. Can you make it?" At Jilly's nod, Cam unzipped the flaps at the top of each suitcase and yanked the handles up. Towing the baggage behind him, he led the way. Jilly struggled to keep up while reminding herself she wasn't a kid anymore.

And neither was Cameron Lane.

But he seemed as quiet as ever as he helped her settle into the passenger seat of his SUV. Just as well. With her thoughts bouncing between her growing suspicions about Paul and his tennis student, her apprehension about seeing Harvey and Alice again, and now these girlish feelings fizzing around in her belly, Jilly had plenty to occupy her mind on the drive to Dogwood Blossom Inn.

❧

Not much of a talker, was she? Just as well. Guilt still plagued Cam for breaking his date with Liz tonight. And he sure didn't want to miss Sammy's game. If everything went okay getting Jilly situated at the inn, he should make it.

A heaving breath sounded from the passenger side. Cam glanced over as Jilly shifted and stretched her left leg. "If you need more room, you can slide the seat back."

"I'm fine. Just haven't gotten used to this cast yet." She turned toward the window.

Several more minutes passed, then another sigh. Cam blew out a long breath of his own. He could at least be polite and try to get reacquainted. "So you're in Modesto now. How do you like California?"

"It was actually pretty good, until. . ." Jilly shrugged and nodded toward her ankle.

Cam angled her a sympathetic smile. He checked his side mirror and pressed his turn signal before changing lanes to pass a pickup pulling a boat trailer. "It sure took a load off Harvey's mind when you agreed to come help at the inn."

Another shrug. "Actually, the timing worked out pretty good for me, too."

"You didn't sound so certain when I called you the other day." In fact, the subdued woman next to him barely resembled the energetic, single-minded adolescent he remembered.

"Let's just say it turned out to be a good time to put some space between me and Silverheels Country Club."

"Problems at work?"

"Wish I knew." Jilly tucked a strand of chin-length hair behind her ear. The ponytail was long gone. "Mind if we change the subject? How's Alice? No complications after the surgery?"

"Not so far. I thought you'd want to stop by and see them at the hospital before we head up to the inn. We have plenty of time."

His sideways glance caught her left fist curling around the edge of the seat. She stared straight ahead. "I think I'd rather settle in first."

"Sure, if you—" His cell phone chirped. Retrieving it from the center console, he checked the caller ID—Liz. "Excuse me, I should take this." He hooked his headset over his ear and pressed the CONNECT button.

"Hey, hon," came Liz's sultry voice. Country-western music played in the background, barely drowning out the sounds of little boys' laughter. She must be on her way home from picking up Sammy and his friends at school. "I felt bad about being so whiny earlier and just called to apologize. Forgive me?"

"I'm sorry, too. Didn't mean to cut you off, but I had to get to the airport. I'm on my way to the inn with Jilly Gardner."

"Jilly Gardner, the tennis player? *She's* the Nelsons' grown-up foster child?"

Cam cut his eyes toward Jilly. "Yeah, you've heard of her?"

"I used to date one of the guys on the University of Missouri tennis team. I remember seeing her in a few tournaments when Mizzou competed against Stanford. She was really good, the next Steffi Graf, people said. Then she kind of faded away." Liz's car radio snapped off. "What's she up to these days? Is she still single?"

The back of Cam's neck prickled. Liz's jealous side was showing itself again. Not one of her more appealing attributes. "As far as I know. Haven't seen her in ten years or so. We're just catching up."

A pause. "Don't forget, Sammy and I really miss you. I love you, sweetie."

"I. . .miss you, too. Give Sambo a hug for me." He clicked off and tossed the headset onto the console.

Love. Why'd she have to use that word? Like he didn't already feel guilty enough. He cared for Liz, enjoyed her company. And he loved spending time with Sammy. But he couldn't bring himself to commit to anything deeper with Liz than exclusive dating.

And he wasn't entirely sure why. Liz was thoughtful, attractive, attentive. Didn't complain *too* much about the long hours he devoted to his students and class assignments. One thing nagged at him, though. She claimed to be a Christian, but all too frequently she offered up excuses why she couldn't attend church with him. They were out too late the night before. She had a headache. The weather was too rainy/cold/snowy/hot.

At least she didn't mind Cam's taking Sammy to Sunday school. Every minute spent with that little boy nudged a little more of Cam's self-reproach aside.

He stifled a rueful laugh. As if anything could ever make up for failing his brother. Failing his family.

Failing God.

Chapter 3

Nothing had changed at the inn. Not even Jilly's old room in the family quarters behind the office. High school tennis trophies lined a shelf over her four-poster bed still covered in the pastel-striped quilt Alice had given Jilly for her fourteenth birthday—a big-girl bedspread to replace the Strawberry Shortcake coverlet Jilly had inherited from one of the Nelsons' previous foster kids.

Ice water flowed through her veins. Much as she wanted to hate the Nelsons, she couldn't.

Easing around to take in the rest of the room, Jilly caught the tip of her crutch on a pink fuzzy throw rug. She teetered forward with a gasp at the same moment Cam arrived with her luggage. The suitcases toppled to the hardwood floor, and Cam rushed over to grab Jilly's arm. Moving the crutches out of the way, he helped her onto the side of the bed.

"I'm okay, I'm okay." Grimacing, Jilly waved away his attentions. Shockingly aware of the heat of his touch, she gave a small cough to cover her uneasiness. "Haven't had a lot of practice time on these sticks yet. I warned you I wouldn't be much use."

"And I told you I'd be around to help." Cam retrieved the fallen suitcases and rolled them over to a bench near the bathroom door.

"I don't need babying, okay?" She checked her resentful tone and tried again. "Anyway, I heard your side of that phone call earlier. Sounds like somebody's anxiously waiting for you back in town. Who's Sambo? Your son?"

"Sammy's the son of my. . .friend." Cam's back muscles strained against his polo shirt as he lifted the larger of Jilly's suitcases onto the bench. "And they're not expecting me till tomorrow morning, so I'm at your beck and call. You want me to help you unpack? You can tell me where to put stuff."

The thought of Cameron Lane going through her suitcase, touching her things, sent a crazy shiver up her spine. She reached for the crutches Cam had laid across the foot of the bed. "That's okay, I can take care of it."

And when did her voice turn so squeaky?

Cam must have noticed. He grinned over his shoulder. "Got something in here I shouldn't see?"

"Just. . .undies and such." She stifled a sneeze. Didn't take her Missouri allergies long to find her. As if she didn't have enough to deal with. She'd better jot herself a reminder to refill her prescription soon.

Gingerly she positioned the crutches against her already sore rib cage and stood. "I'm starving. How about we go see what Harvey's got in the kitchen?"

❧

The next morning, Jilly scooted onto the rolling chair behind Harvey's massive oak desk and propped her crutches against the credenza. Time to catch up on what had been happening at the inn over the past ten years. . .and, more important, what Harvey had lined up for the summer. Last evening, Cam had introduced Jilly to perky, spaghetti-thin Heather McNealy, the Nelsons' new cook, who'd whipped up an amazing five-course meal for them. Earlier today she'd met Ralph Davenport, the retired Kansas City bus driver Harvey had hired as part-time groundskeeper and handyman.

After helping Jilly get settled, Cam had stayed the night in one of the guest rooms. He'd joined her for Heather's gourmet breakfast of whole-wheat french toast stuffed with cream cheese and strawberries and then hit the road. He explained he needed to stop by the hospital with a few items Harvey had asked for before meeting his friend Liz for her son's baseball game. He promised to return on Wednesday, and in the meantime Jilly could call on Ralph, Heather, or one of the housekeepers if she needed help.

She fingered Cam's notes about the weekend prayer retreats he'd scheduled. The first one began next Thursday evening, with six couples in attendance. They'd need seven guest rooms in all, plus the small second-floor conference room overlooking the lake. Three meals a day, coffee break setups, an evening snack bar.

Sounded easy enough—especially after sampling Heather's cuisine. With culinary talents to rival any New York chef, why the girl chose to work at such an out-of-the-way location blew Jilly's mind.

The desk phone jangled. She punched the blinking button and lifted the receiver. "Dogwood Blossom Inn."

"Jillian." Harvey's raspy baritone, rich with emotion. "Hi, sweetheart, how are you?"

Her heart played marimba on the inside of her rib cage. "Hi, Harvey."

"Meant to check on you last night, but Alice had a minor setback, and I got a bit distracted. You settle in okay?"

"Everything's fine here." She swallowed, squeezed her eyes shut. "Just like I remembered."

"Good, good. Cam's here. Says you met Heather and Ralph. They'll take good care of you till I can break away from the hospital."

Jilly fingered the phone cord. "How's Alice this morning?"

"She's having atrial fibrillation. They're keeping a close eye on her, trying to get her heart rhythm to—what did they call it? Convert. Say a few prayers, will you?"

"Sure." If she could remember how. *God, help!* and *Why me?* seemed the best she could do these days.

Silence stretched between them. "Honey, I can't tell you how much it means that you came. But it's like the good Lord whispered your name in my ear.

I'm hoping once Alice is better, we can all be together again. Make up for lost time. We've missed you something fierce."

"I. . .um. . .Harvey, I'm going over the reservations schedule and need to ask you some questions."

❧

Cam kissed Alice's forehead and signaled to Harvey he needed to go. On his way to the parking lot, he recalled Jilly's sudden stiffening when he'd suggested stopping at the hospital. What had caused Jilly's coolness toward the Nelsons? Couldn't be anything they'd done. Harvey and Alice had to be the sweetest, most caring people Cam had ever known. Whatever had come between them and Jillian Gardner, it had to be something *she'd* done.

And if he ever found out what it was, he'd give her a huge piece of his mind.

In the meantime, he had a ball game to get to.

He arrived at the ballpark as the second inning began. Spotting Liz in the bleachers, he waved and picked his way up the weathered steps.

"Just in time." Liz scooted over to make room. "Sammy's next at bat."

As he edged in beside her, the crowd exploded in an ear-splitting roar and surged to its feet. Cam sprang up to see Sammy toss the bat aside, his short legs propelling him toward first base, then second, all the way to third before the right fielder zinged the ball to the pitcher.

Cam pumped his fist. "All right, Sam!"

"Way to go, Sammy-boy!" Liz gave a piercing whistle, then looped her arm around Cam's neck and pulled him toward her until their lips met in a celebratory kiss.

At least that's all it meant to Cam. Liz returned her attention to the game, shouting encouragement to her son when the next batter hit a line drive that brought Sammy home. Cam found himself staring at Liz's profile, long blond waves sweeping across her shoulder. . .and feeling nothing.

When the game ended, Liz invited Cam to join her and Sammy and a couple of his teammates for lunch at Riley's Pharmacy—her treat, since she got an employee discount. The old-fashioned drugstore soda fountain served up the best chili dogs in town. Afterward, Liz and Sammy shared a double-fudge banana split while Cam nursed a root beer float.

Liz reached across the table and touched his hand. "You're awfully quiet today. Still worried about Alice?"

"A little, yeah." He stared at the swirls of melted ice cream in his frosty mug.

"Bypass surgery is so common now, it's practically the same as getting your tonsils out. She'll be fine."

Cam gave an irritated snort. "Not quite that simple. Alice isn't out of the woods yet."

"I just meant—"

"Mom, can I go play an arcade game with Elliot?" Sammy scooted out of the booth.

Liz rolled her eyes and reached for her purse. After digging around in her wallet, she brought her hands out empty. "Oops, all out of quarters."

Cam fished a handful of change from his pocket. "Here, I've got a few. Knock yourselves out."

"You spoil him." Liz flicked a straw wrapper across the table toward Cam.

Grinning, he flicked it right back. "I love him."

"I know you do. I wish. . ."

A boulder settled atop his chest. His breath hitched. Easy to say he loved that feisty little guy who reminded him so much of Terrance at that age. Why couldn't Cam love Sammy's mother?

He finished off his float and stuffed his napkin into the empty mug. "I should go. Still have some prep work to finish before my first prayer retreat. I'm leading an introductory session during Sunday school hour tomorrow."

"For Pete's sake, Cam, you're supposed to be on sabbatical." Liz sat back with a huff. "I thought we'd get to spend *more* time together, not less."

"A sabbatical isn't just an extended vacation. It's supposed to be a time for reevaluating your life and career, getting a new perspective, learning and growing."

"But why prayer retreats? Why don't you write a book? Go rafting on the Black River? Climb Taum Sauk Mountain?"

"I don't want to write a book, I prefer my water sports in a quiet lake, and I'm not a mountain climber." Cam slid from the booth and fished his keys from his pocket. "I decided to lead the prayer retreats because helping others explore prayer seemed like the best way for me to get closer to God, myself. And that's what I need most right now."

Liz stood and tucked her arms beneath his. "More than this? More than me?"

The warmth of her cheek against his shoulder made him want to do anything but pray. Which meant he needed to more than ever. He eased out of her embrace. "I'll call you later." With a quick good-bye to Sammy, he left.

❧

A blanket of quiet lay over Dogwood Blossom Inn. Jilly roamed the expansive log cabin-style facility, the hardwood floors echoing under her feet—make that *foot*. Step-*thunk*, step-*thunk*. Ralph and Heather had the day off, and since Jilly couldn't stomach the idea of showing up at New Hope Fellowship and facing all the Nelsons' old friends, spending a lazy Sunday at the inn seemed like the best plan.

Years before Jilly came to live with them, the Nelsons had added a small chapel onto the northwest corner of the inn. A peaked roof arched above rows of lacquered pine benches inside the chapel. Floor-to-ceiling windows behind the altar looked out upon stately oaks and hickory trees marching up the hillside, the occasional dogwood peeking through the canopy for a glimpse of sunshine. A few weeks ago the forest would have been awash in white blossoms and the woodsy fragrance of dogwoods.

Jilly had forgotten how soothing this special place could be. She edged onto a bench and let the spectacular view wash over her.

"I'm still not sure about this, God." She allowed her gaze to settle on the hand-carved wooden cross suspended above the altar. "How many times have I told You? I can't forgive Harvey and Alice for letting me down. Is bringing me back here Your way of forcing me to do the impossible?"

"All things are possible with God."

"But not with me, Lord. I'm only human."

She sat in silence for a long time, then finally rose with a sigh and headed to the kitchen for a ham sandwich. Spreading mayonnaise across a slice of wheat bread, she decided she'd already been spoiled by Heather's incredible cooking. She'd have to find some way to work out if she expected to stay in shape over the summer.

As she hobbled over to the fridge to put away her sandwich makings, the phone rang. It took another three rings before she could grab the kitchen extension. "Dogwood Blossom Inn. This is Jilly."

"Hi, it's Cam. How's it going?"

Her heart chose that moment to try a syncopated rhythm. She took a second to let it normalize. "Oh, just peachy. Having a sandwich, getting ready to tackle the summer reservations schedule again."

"So no problems, huh? I'm at the hospital. Harvey asked me to call and check."

She stretched her mouth in a phony smile, hoping it would leach into her voice. "Tell him I've got things under control."

"Alice is still in A-fib."

Jilly hunched over, an imaginary eggbeater churning inside her stomach. Surely she could have mustered the compassion to ask about Alice. But no. Self-Centered-R-Us. "I'm so sorry. Please tell her I'm praying for her."

And she would. Starting right now.

Cam offered what little he knew about Alice's condition, saying the doctors were monitoring her and that Harvey planned to stay in town until Alice was on the mend. "In the meantime," Cam went on, "I was thinking I'd come on out to the inn this afternoon."

Jilly swiveled toward the window. Out by the lake, the afternoon sun polished the silver-green keel of Harvey's old rowboat. "I thought you weren't coming until midweek."

"Decided I could use a few extra days of peace and quiet to get ready for my first prayer retreat. And Harvey reminded me Ralph and Heather had already asked for the day off, so I could be there to help with whatever you need." A pause. "You don't mind, do you?"

"No, that's fine." There went her crazy heartbeat again.

"Great. See you in a bit."

"Could you maybe pick up a pizza or something? Since Heather's off, I mean."

"You bet. I'll bring a movie, too."

"Great." As Jilly hung up, a shiver of déjà vu rippled up her spine. Pizza,

Cam Lane, and *Braveheart*. Even though it was R-rated, many of her school friends had seen it and told her what a fantastic movie it was. Anything with Mel Gibson had to be good, but Jilly had seen the previews and knew she'd never be able to sit through all the blood and guts.

Then one rainy Saturday, Cam got permission from the Nelsons to bring the video up to the inn. Unfortunately, he also brought Terrance, his annoying younger brother, for whom the term *bully* had been coined. Alice stuck two frozen pizzas in the oven, and they all sprawled on the sofas in the lounge to watch the movie on the inn's big-screen TV.

Determined to stick it out, Jilly held her breath and squeezed her eyes shut whenever the scenes became too intense. Terrance kept sticking his pimply face in Jilly's, mimicking a fraidycat whimper and punching her in the shoulder until her arm went numb. Neither Alice's stern glares nor Harvey's quiet warnings had much effect on the boy's behavior.

Finally Cam had come to Jilly's rescue. Without a word, he grabbed Terrance by the scruff of the neck and plunked him down in a chair across the room. Joining Jilly on the sofa, he tucked her under his arm, shielding her eyes during the scary parts and telling her when it was safe to look.

She'd harbored a secret crush on him ever since.

❧

Cam placed the pizza order, then stepped next door and browsed the video shop while he waited. What movie would interest a girl like Jilly? He had to keep reminding himself she wasn't a kid anymore. Jillian Gardner was all grown up.

Maybe she'd prefer something athletic, like *Wimbledon*. Or action/adventure—*Indiana Jones* or *Pirates of the Caribbean*. For all he knew, she might be into romantic comedies, but Cam didn't want to go there. Not this weekend.

He decided on *Ratatouille*, a clever animated feature Sammy had enjoyed and Cam wouldn't mind seeing again. If it didn't appeal to her, he'd just excuse himself and settle in with one of the books on prayer he needed to study.

Heading to the checkout counter, Cam took a shortcut and found himself on the aisle displaying classic dramas. A familiar title caught his eye—*Braveheart*—and in the space of a nanosecond his thoughts traveled fourteen years back in time. He forced his mind past the memory of Terrance's misbehavior, actions that should have clued him in from the start.

Instead, he concentrated on the first time he'd noticed—really noticed—the Nelsons' precocious foster child. He could still feel her shivering against his rib cage, still hear her tiny, scared voice: *"Is it over yet? Tell me when I can look."*

When the video ended, she'd released this huge, noisy, lung-collapsing sigh. Knees drawn up to her chest, she smiled up at him and squeezed his hand. Their eyes met for a brief instant before two bright spots of pink flamed on her cheeks. Abruptly she bolted from the room, swinging that ponytail he took such delight in tugging on.

That was the moment he realized what a beauty Jillian Gardner would grow up to be.

The moment he wished she wasn't four years too young for him.

Chapter 4

Well, the grown-up Jilly Gardner wasn't too young for him now.

Cam slid the extra-large pepperoni-mushroom-black olive pizza onto the counter, his gaze fixed on the way Jilly's coffee-colored bob formed a comma around her left ear. Balanced on her crutches, she bent over the oven controls. "You think two-fifty is hot enough?"

He cleared his throat. Why did his T-shirt neckband suddenly feel too tight? "That should keep it warm till we're ready to eat."

Jilly pulled open the oven door so Cam could set the pizza box inside. "I saw some colas in the fridge. Help yourself." She hobbled over to the counter, where Cam had laid the DVD. "*Ratatouille*. Fun."

"Seen it?" Cam popped the top on a lemon-lime soda can. Maybe an ice-cold drink would cool him off. He tried to call up an image of Liz in his mind's eye. He should be thinking about her, not the woman who'd brought the Nelsons so much heartache.

"No, but I remember the trailers." She flipped the DVD box over and studied the blurb on the back. "You should have brought that little boy you've been talking about. I bet he'd like this movie."

"Sam. We already watched it together. He loved it."

"Did you make it to his ball game okay?"

"Great game. Sammy's team won by three runs. He even hit a homer in the sixth inning."

"Sounds like he's really special to you." Jilly started for the door, then glanced over her shoulder with a wry grin. "Or is it his mom who's so special?"

Soda fizzed up the back of Cam's throat. For a second he couldn't get any words out. "Liz is just a friend."

"Ooookay." Jilly's wide-eyed stare suggested maybe his response had come out a bit too forcefully. "Keep telling yourself that, big guy." She cut through the dining room and headed toward the lounge.

Cam took another swig of soda, then drew his shirtsleeve across his lips. Maybe he should be using some of his sabbatical time to figure out what he really wanted in a relationship. Liz obviously wanted more than he felt ready to give.

❧

Same lounge, same extra-long wraparound sofa. New upholstery, new DVD player, new widescreen HDTV.

And definitely a new and improved Cameron Lane. Her cast cradled by a throw pillow atop the coffee table, Jilly scooted deeper into the brown velour cushions and admired Cam's lean, muscled frame as he set up the DVD. How did a Bible college professor stay in such great physical shape? And she liked the way he smelled. Cologne-free, just a clean, manly scent.

Cam tossed her the remote and dropped onto the sofa beside her. "You're in charge of the TV. I'll be the pizza-and-cola gofer."

"Sounds like a plan." She scrolled through the menu options and pressed PLAY MOVIE. Much safer to watch an animated rat who loved to cook than dwell on long-forgotten feelings for a man who already had a girlfriend and probably couldn't care less about the kid he once rescued from his bullying brother. Besides, Jilly didn't plan to stick around Blossom Hills, Missouri, any longer than necessary.

Half an hour into the movie, she found herself dozing. Her mind flitted through a parade of crazy images—Heather with a rat nose, cooking for a snobby food critic who bore an uncanny resemblance to Mel Gibson. Cam galloping through the inn on a white steed. Terrance the bully's acne-pitted face staring over Paul Edgar's shoulder in the country club men's room.

A tap on the arm stirred her from her dreams. She blinked and tried to focus on the man with the half grin gazing down at her. "Was I asleep?"

"I'd say so. A bit jet-lagged, are we?"

Fists pressed into the sofa cushions, she pushed herself upright and tried to read the numbers on the digital clock over the TV—7:23. "Remember, it's two hours later here. My body's still on California time."

"You'll adjust in a couple of days." Cam chuckled when a loud rumble emanated from somewhere beneath her waistband. "Sounds like you're ready for some pizza."

While Cam went to the kitchen, Jilly finger-combed her hair and rearranged herself into a somewhat more dignified position. She only hoped she hadn't drooled during her nap. Not exactly Sleeping Beauty material.

The TV displayed a freeze-frame of Remy the rat balanced on the rim of a stockpot. The image sent Jilly's mind spinning back through her jumbled dreams. *Terrance in the Silverheels men's room?* What was *that* all about?

And then it dawned on her. The reason those students of Paul's bugged her so much was because they reminded her of Terrance Lane. Bad attitude, bad complexion, and, oh yeah, even the bad breath.

Cam returned with the pizza box, paper plates, and napkins. "Be back in a sec with the drinks."

"Cam," Jilly called as he turned to go, "tonight got me remembering your brother. I don't know if I ever told you how sorry I was about his death."

He halted in the doorway, his chest collapsing. "Thanks. It's still hard to think about."

"It was the year you graduated from high school, wasn't it?"

"Yep." He straightened. "Better get those drinks."

❧

In the kitchen, Cam stalled long enough to lean over the sink and splash water on his face. Why did Jilly have to bring up Terrance tonight? As if Cam's mind didn't dwell on the tragedy every waking moment of his life since the day his mother found her second son collapsed in the basement next to the weight machine.

At the sound of Jilly's crutches creaking through the dining room, Cam snatched a paper towel from the roll by the sink and blotted his face. By the time she entered the kitchen, he'd tossed the towel in the trash and had filled two tumblers with ice.

He shot a forced grin over his shoulder. "What are you doing up? You're useless in here, remember?"

"I needed to stretch." She pursed her lips. "And I wanted to apologize if bringing up Terrance upset you."

"Forget it." Cam opened the refrigerator and tried not to think about the pitying stare she must be leveling at his back just now. "Cola? Lemon-lime? Root beer? Name your poison."

"Better make it something with caffeine, or I'll never get through the rest of the movie."

"Cola it is." Cam tucked two cans under his arm and grabbed the tumblers off the counter. He glared at Jilly and nodded toward the door. "Get a move on, girl, before my armpit goes numb."

She rolled her eyes. "Try crutches for a few days, and you'll come to appreciate numb armpits."

A welcome lightness warmed Cam's chest. This was the Jillian Gardner he'd always liked best. Spunky, sassy, spirited. He'd focus on those qualities instead of the memories her mention of Terrance had dredged up.

Although he might be wiser to keep the grown-up Jilly at arm's length. A few hours in her company and he had the sense she could easily send him careening down the fast track toward an emotional train wreck.

❧

By Tuesday morning, Jilly had the inn routine firmly in hand. The inn had occasional guests year-round, but the summer season officially launched with Memorial Day weekend, which also happened to be Cam's first prayer retreat. Yesterday she'd gone over menus with Heather and placed the food order with their supplier. The housekeeping staff would resume full-time duty starting Wednesday. Ralph had the grounds looking spiffy and had set aside today to take care of some minor repairs to the boat dock and gazebo.

Seated at Harvey's desk, Jilly gazed out the broad picture window overlooking the lake. To her left, the redwood deck stretched across the back of the inn. She glimpsed Cam reclining in an Adirondack chair, a pile of books on a side table and a legal pad propped on one thigh.

A raspy breath slid between her lips. If she'd known how quickly her youthful crush would come rushing back, she might have given more serious thought to her decision to return to Dogwood Blossom Inn. She'd better shake it off in a hurry, though, because the guy was spoken for. As they resumed the movie Sunday night, all Cam would talk about was Liz and her little boy.

Just a friend. Right. "Methinks Mr. Lane doth protest too much."

Rubber soles squeaked on the floorboards outside the office. Heather stepped into the room, her white chef's apron covered in chocolate-brown speckles. She waved a slim silver cell phone. "Hey, Jilly, this yours?"

"Did I leave that in the kitchen again? Sorry."

"No prob." Heather dropped the phone into Jilly's outstretched hand. "It started buzzing. I think you have a voice mail."

"Thanks." Jilly thumbed a key to scroll through recent calls. One from her landlady, Denise. Another from Silverheels Country Club. Probably Therese Fessler, her boss.

"Gotta get back to my dessert. A new twist I came up with for buttermilk pie. If you and Cam like it, I'll serve it this weekend."

Groaning, Jilly patted her stomach. "I bet I've already gained five pounds eating your cooking. Soon as I return these calls, I'm headed to the exercise room."

After which she planned to strangle the Dogwood Blossom chef. No one who sampled her own creations with Heather's gusto deserved to stay that skinny.

Alone in the office again, Jilly listened to her messages. The first one was from Denise. "You told me to check your mail for bills. I've forwarded a couple to you."

Bills. Couldn't travel far enough to escape those. She never thought to ask if Harvey planned to pay her for managing the inn. If he offered, fine. If not, at least she was getting a little help from Worker's Comp.

Her nose tickled and she reached for a tissue. Drat these allergies. She had enough pills to last another two or three weeks at most. She'd need to place a refill order soon.

The next message was from Paul. "Hey, Jilly, hope your ankle's okay. Therese said you'd be out of town for a while. She's got me doubling up on classes and working my tail off." A pause. "Give me a call, will ya? Got something to ask you about."

Hmmm. Maybe something to do with that little episode in the men's room?

A third message began. For the first few seconds Jilly heard only static. Then a sandpapery voice: "You talked to the cops, didn't you? Bad idea." *Click.*

"You have no more messages. To save your messages, press—"

With shaking fingers Jilly hit the END button. Talked to the cops? Did the caller mean the nice guy in the Modesto PD uniform who'd helped her into the ER the day she broke her ankle? About all she'd managed to say to him was a pained thank-you.

Clearly, someone believed she knew something and wanted to make sure she didn't tell.

"You look like you ate some bad sushi. Everything okay?"

She looked up to see Cam standing in the doorway. "I'm not sure."

"About the sushi, or about being okay?" He smiled, but concern filled his eyes.

Her shoulders drooped. "How are you in the advice department, professor?"

❧

"So you have no idea what you walked in on." Cam propped his elbows on the deck rail behind him and studied Jilly's face. The usual impish sparkle in her eyes had vanished.

Seated in one of the adirondack chairs, she hugged her rib cage. "Not a clue."

"And you think it has something to do with your accident?"

"It sounds crazy, but yes. The kid I showed the racquet to wasn't the one from the men's room, but I've seen them hanging out together."

"You also had a voice mail from this Paul guy? No indication of what he wanted to talk to you about?"

"Paul's an old friend. If he's involved in something shady"—Jilly shuddered—"I'm almost afraid to find out."

"Call him back. At least find out what he has to say." Cam pulled a chair next to Jilly's. "Put it on speaker. Maybe I can pick up on something."

Casting him a skeptical frown, Jilly tugged her phone from her pocket. She pressed several keys and then hit the SPEAKER button.

"Jilly. I was hoping you'd get back to me."

She glanced at Cam, who gave her a reassuring nod. "Hi, Paul. Got your message. What's up?"

"Thought I should touch base with you before the Memorial Day weekend tournament. I see you have three of your girls entered."

"Oh man, I forgot all about that. Are you working with them?"

"Yeah, but it's hard to keep up. Like I said, Therese gave me all your students on top of mine." A sharp sigh. "I told her it wasn't a good idea, but she said I didn't have a choice. Silverheels is trying to watch expenses, so they're not hiring a replacement for you while you're on leave."

The guy sounded stressed, but Cam hadn't heard anything to suggest a threat or illegal involvement. Maybe Jilly had an overactive imagination. She'd replayed the last message for him. *"You talked to the cops, didn't you? Bad idea."* Maybe it was just someone on the country club staff who was afraid she'd sue over her accident.

He caught her looking at him, a question mark in her eyes. He shrugged and signaled her to keep talking.

"I appreciate your help with my kids. I know they can learn a lot from you."

"It's just. . .you know my guys. They take the game seriously, both on and off the courts. You've got a good bunch of kids. I wouldn't want there to be any trouble."

Nothing in the man's tone had changed. Cam rolled the words around in his brain, inspecting them for hidden meaning. He cocked an eyebrow at Jilly and shook his head.

She released a controlled breath. "My kids have good heads on their shoulders. They'll be fine. Anything I can tell you to help get them ready for the tournament?"

The conversation turned to things like racquet tension, backhand technique, and other tennis stuff beyond Cam's understanding. When Jilly took the phone off speaker to continue her discussion, he rose and strode to the railing.

If only Terrance had had somebody with a "good head on his shoulders" looking out for him when his athletic ambitions led him down the wrong path. It should have been Cam.

It wasn't.

Chapter 5

Here you go, Mr. and Mrs. Hartford. Room 207, top of the stairs, third door on the left." Jilly handed the elderly couple their keys and tried not to inhale. An overpowering gardenia scent played havoc with her sinuses.

Mrs. Hartford leaned on a three-footed cane. "I don't get around like I used to. Do you have an elevator?"

"Just past the stairs and around the corner." Jilly pressed a tissue to her nose. "Need help with your luggage?"

Cam came in from the deck, notebook under his arm. "I'll get it for you, Ruth. How was the drive up, Ivan?"

"Gorgeous. Been looking forward to this retreat ever since we saw it in the church bulletin."

Before Cam and the Hartfords had left the lobby, two more seventy-something couples arrived for the prayer retreat. By five o'clock everyone had checked in. Apparently Cam's first group consisted solely of senior citizens. Jilly decided she'd better remind Heather to go easy on the spices. The inn's selection of emergency toiletries didn't include antacids.

As she came around the front desk on her crutches, Mr. and Mrs. Hartford appeared from the direction of the elevator.

"I declare, you're worse off than I am." Scooting forward with her cane, Mrs. Hartford cast Jilly a sympathetic frown. "What happened, honey?"

"A minor mishap with a stepladder."

Mr. Hartford harrumphed. "Couldn't have been minor with a cast that big. We'll say some prayers for you."

"Thanks." Jilly gave a self-conscious nod. "Dinner will be served in the dining room at six thirty. Feel free to explore the grounds while you're waiting."

Mrs. Hartford edged closer. At least some of the gardenia scent had dissipated. "I was telling Cameron earlier that you look so familiar. He says you grew up here."

"That's right." The old resentments tied knots in Jilly's stomach. With effort she kept her expression neutral. "The Nelsons were my foster parents."

"Then we should know you," Mr. Hartford said. "We used to attend New Hope Fellowship with the Nelsons before we moved across town."

Jilly shrugged. "I've been away almost ten years."

"You're not. . ." Ivan Hartford squinted. "My word, Ruth, it is! It's little Jillian, the tennis player."

Mrs. Hartford gasped, her mouth spreading into a happy grin. "Jillian, of course! Harvey and Alice were always so proud of you, the daughter they never had. Haven't you grown into a lovely young lady!"

Heat crept up Jilly's neck. She flicked her gaze toward the kitchen and hoped for a quick escape.

"What, and no ring on that finger? Oh my, and our handsome Cameron being single and all." Mrs. Hartford tugged on her husband's sleeve. "We must get these two together, Ivan."

Please, Lord, get me out of this. "I believe Cam is seeing someone."

He would pick that moment to jog down the stairs—and looking svelte in slim-fitting black jeans and a V-neck cotton pullover with the sleeves pushed up. He sidled between the elderly couple. "Ivan, Ruth. Just the folks I was looking for. Get settled in okay?"

"Room's excellent." Mr. Hartford clapped Cam on the shoulder. "And what a view of the lake."

Mrs. Hartford linked her arm with Cam's. "We were just telling Jillian—"

"She prefers Jilly." Cam winked.

Jilly felt her blush deepen. "I need to get to the kitchen and check on dinner preparations. Will you excuse me?"

She did her best imitation of a graceful pivot on crutches and hurried from the lobby. Good thing Cam's girlfriend wasn't around to see him flirting like that.

Oh, get over yourself, Gardner. Of course Cam wasn't flirting, just being cute for his friends on the retreat.

Which, frankly, caused her even greater chagrin. She'd never be more to him than the gangly youngster with tennis on the brain and a brick where her heart should be.

❧

His back pressed against the rough trunk of a dogwood tree, Cam smiled at the six elderly couples seated in lawn chairs around him. The first morning of the retreat had gone well. "Before we go inside for lunch, I'd like to close our session with a reading from the Psalms."

He thumbed through the pages of his well-worn Bible until he found Psalm 17. "'I call on you, my God, for you will answer me; turn your ear to me and hear my prayer. Show me the wonders of your great love, you who save by your right hand those who take refuge in you from their foes.'"

Cam's voice trailed off, and he allowed the psalmist's words to resonate in his thoughts. He wanted to believe God heard his prayers. This morning he'd invited the couples to share any personal experiences of answered prayer, and some of their stories bordered on the miraculous. Protection during a restaurant robbery. Healing from a supposedly terminal illness. The birth of a healthy child after they'd been told they could never conceive.

How much of a miracle would it take for Cam to finally have peace?

"Good job, son." Ivan Hartford stood over him, offering a hand up. "This retreat is already filling up my spiritual well."

Cam dusted off the seat of his jeans as he ducked from beneath the tree. The Hartfords, sadly, hadn't received the miracle they'd prayed for. "You've had a tough year, haven't you, Ivan?"

"Not easy losing a child. Ruth took it even harder. Madeline's cancer was the toughest thing we've ever had to face." Ivan released a noisy breath. "Guess your family knows all about loss, though. I remember how broken up your folks were after Terrance died. They sure are blessed to have you."

The old wounds throbbed. Cam's fingers tightened around his Bible. He couldn't say what he really thought. Instead he said, "They've retired to Arizona, you know."

"So we heard. Be sure and give them our best next time you're in touch." Ivan took Ruth's arm and supported her as they followed the other retreat participants into the inn.

On the way through the lobby, Cam stopped at the front desk, where he found Jilly seated on a barstool behind the counter. He leaned across the counter to see Ralph, the groundskeeper, arranging a footrest for Jilly's cast.

Ralph straightened and dusted his hands. "There, that ought to be more comfortable for you."

Jilly tested the footrest. "Much better. Thanks."

Ralph swiveled toward Cam. "Got everything all ready for your evening campfire by the lake. Should be a beautiful night for it."

"Sounds good. Thanks."

Jilly flicked her hair behind her ear, a gesture Cam grew more and more fascinated with. He stared at her earlobe and wondered how it would feel to comb his fingers through the thick hair at her nape.

"Cam? Earth to Cameron." Jilly waved a hand in front of his eyes.

He jerked backward, his face burning. "What?"

"I just asked if everything's going okay with your group."

"Oh. Yeah. Fine."

She nodded toward the dining room. "Better join them for lunch. Heather's serving manicotti and homemade sourdough bread. The marinara is to die for."

"You've eaten already?" Why the thought should fill him with such disappointment he had no idea. *What is wrong with you, Lane? Jillian Gardner is trouble on two—make that* one *leg.*

Jilly dropped some envelopes into the out-box on the end of the counter. "I ate with Ralph in the kitchen. We needed to talk over some inn business."

Ralph propped an elbow on the counter and tipped his head toward Jilly. "This gal's on top of things. Harvey did good having her come fill in for him."

The hesitant smile curling Jilly's lips drew Cam's gaze. He coaxed his eyes upward to meet the brown ones looking back at him. "I'm glad it's working out."

Ralph shook his head. "You realize this gal hasn't even seen the Nelsons since she got to town? I offered to cover the desk so she could visit them at the hospital, but she won't hear of it."

"Really, it's okay." Jilly waved a hand. "There's too much going on here. I'll have plenty of time to see them next week."

And what excuse would she come up with then? Anger bristled where moments before Cam had once again been fighting the attraction he should rightly be feeling for Liz. What was it about Jilly Gardner that so thoroughly messed with his head?

❧

"You like him, don't you?" Ralph shot Jilly a crooked grin.

"Cam? Please." Ignoring the pinpricks tickling her neck, Jilly straightened a stack of blank registration cards. "He's a nice guy. Like a brother. I'm sure he thinks of me the same way."

Ralph hooted. "Doubt that!"

"You know what I mean. And anyway, he has a girlfriend. Sounds like they're getting serious."

"Liz MacIntosh? Pshaw. Those two are oil and water. Sunshine and rain. Porterhouse and frankfurters."

"You know what they say. Opposites attract." Jilly found a letter opener and sliced open one of the bills that had come in the morning mail. The momentum of her forceful stroke swung the opener within inches of Ralph's chin.

He flinched. "Careful there, girl."

"Sorry!" She dropped the letter opener onto the counter, her fingers darting to her forehead. She smoothed back her hair and groaned. *What is wrong with me?*

"My fault. Got you all riled up with my teasing. Can't help it. You remind me of my granddaughter."

Jilly couldn't resist a smirk. "Oh, and I suppose your granddaughter appreciates Grandpa meddling in her love life."

"Not in the least. But since her dad died a few years ago, I'm her only father figure, so I do my part to make sure she stays on the straight and narrow. Career, love life, whatever." Ralph chuckled. "Meddling is my middle name."

Jilly's throat tightened. She ducked her head and swallowed. "She's lucky to have you."

"I'm lucky to have her. The Lord blessed me mightily when He nudged Heather to return to Blossom Hills."

"Heather? The chef?" Jilly brought her chin up in surprise. "She's your granddaughter?"

"You didn't know?" Ralph furrowed his brow. "But then why would you unless somebody told you? She's never called me Grandpa, always Ralph."

"So Heather's mom is. . ."

"My daughter. She got a job in Joplin after her husband died. Not long afterward, Heather finished chef's training at this fancy school in Paris. She didn't want to be too far from her mom, so when I learned the Nelsons needed a new cook—excuse me, *chef*—she took the job."

Jilly quirked a brow. "I wondered how someone with her talents wound up in Blossom Hills."

Ralph crossed his forearms atop the counter. "You're a local girl, too. How's it feel to be back?"

"Weird. Very weird." A gnawing sensation scraped across Jilly's stomach. She picked up the bill she'd just opened and studied the figures.

"Well, I know for a fact you're a blessing to Harvey and Alice." He turned to go, then shot her a pointed look over his shoulder. "And you best get yourself into town to see them right quick, or I'll pack you into my pickup and haul you up there myself."

Jilly huffed. Apparently Ralph's meddling didn't stop with Heather. If one more person told her she needed to go see the Nelsons, she'd throw her crutches at him.

Chapter 6

"You need to go see the Nelsons." Cam leaned in the office doorway, one eye narrowed in an accusatory glare. "The retreat is over. You have three days of quiet before the next group gets here. No more excuses."

Jilly's chest collapsed. Since Harvey couldn't break away from the hospital, Cam had decided to stay at the inn most of the week. Helpful intentions or not, he'd become a major thorn in Jilly's side. Giving a huff, she clicked the PLACE ORDER button on the mail-order pharmacy website and turned away from the computer. "You won't give me any peace until I do, will you?"

"Nope." Cam stepped into the room and kicked the door shut behind him. "Whatever you did to create this wall between you and the Nelsons, I know they're more than willing to forgive—"

"*They're* willing to forgive?" Jilly shoved to her feet, wincing when the injured ankle took her weight. She quickly shifted to her right foot and braced one hand on the desk. "I'm the one who needs to do the forgiving. I'm the one who was wronged."

"You?" Cam spread his hands, a confused look etching his face. "You're the one who left. You stayed away for ten long years. Do you have any idea what that did to them, how much they've missed you?"

"Do you have any idea how they hurt me?" A vise tightened around Jilly's throat. Her eyes burned. She sank into the chair and tried to focus on the invoices spread out before her. "Don't even presume to barge in here and tell me how to run my life."

She held her breath waiting for Cam's retort. When only silence answered, she cut her eyes toward him moments before the door slammed shut in his wake.

Sick and angry, she rolled the chair away from the desk and slumped forward. *I shouldn't have come here, God. No one understands. Especially not You. If You cared at all, You never would have let things end this way.*

She straightened with a groan and brushed the wetness from her cheeks. How many times had she told herself to stop dwelling on might-have-beens? Nothing could change the past.

Her gaze drifted around the pine-paneled room, sliding past photographs of Dogwood Blossom Inn's more prestigious guests—Harvey shaking hands with a famous Missouri-born actor, Alice accepting a kiss on the cheek from the St. Louis Cardinals manager, a group of state representatives and their spouses picnicking by the lake.

Then, next to the door, the embroidered sampler Alice had hung there years before, a verse from Psalm 68: A FATHER TO THE FATHERLESS, A DEFENDER OF WIDOWS, IS GOD IN HIS HOLY DWELLING. GOD SETS THE LONELY IN FAMILIES, HE LEADS OUT THE PRISONERS WITH SINGING.

Once, long ago, Jilly had believed those words. No longer.

Her cell phone vibrated in the pocket of her khaki bermudas. Grateful for the distraction, she tugged out the phone, then suffered a moment of panic before reading the caller ID. Silverheels. Good. The harassing calls had all registered anonymous. "Hello?"

"Jilly, it's Therese. Thought you'd like to know your girls did really well in the tournament."

"Super. I tried to call Paul a few times over the weekend, but his voice mail kept picking up."

Therese's long exhalation whispered in Jilly's ear. "That's the other thing I wanted to let you know. Paul's been suspended."

The news slammed Jilly against the back of the chair. "What? Why?"

"Accusations were made by a couple of his students."

"Accusations?" Jilly raked her fingers through her hair. She thought again about the strange encounter in the men's room. Her stomach curled around itself.

"Let me just ask you, friend to friend." Therese's tone became secretive. "Have you ever seen Paul physically abusive with any of his students?"

"Abusive? As in, hit them?"

"Mm-hmm."

"Never. I've known Paul for years, and that's not like him at all." Even the men's room incident hadn't raised any suspicions about violence. The guys just seemed. . .intense.

"Okay, forget I said anything. Anyway, how much longer do you expect to be out of commission?"

Jilly stared down at her foot. "I've got this cast on for at least another month. I'll probably need a few weeks of physical therapy before I can compete again, but by midsummer I should be able to coach."

"Good. We need you."

"I promise, I'll be back in Modesto as soon as I possibly can."

❧

"How long do you think we can keep Jillian here?"

Cam cast Harvey a doubtful frown. "Probably not any longer than it takes for her ankle to heal. She still has a tennis coaching job waiting for her back in Modesto."

Harvey stared at the closed door to Alice's hospital room, worry deepening the furrows across his forehead. The doctor's latest report had not been encouraging. "I wish Jillian would come and see us. Alice won't stop asking about her. I know it would help if she could see her again."

Cam's jaw clenched. He'd tried again this morning to talk Jilly into coming to the hospital with him, but she'd refused. That girl could create more busywork than a stressed-out college professor. And Cam should know.

He thumped a knotted fist against his thigh. "Sometimes I could strangle that girl. How can she be so calloused?"

"Don't be so hard on her, Cam." Harvey trudged to a bench on the opposite wall and sank down.

"Don't be so hard on her? After how she's treated you and Alice?"

"She came out to help, didn't she? She didn't have to."

"And wouldn't have, if not for her broken ankle and being temporarily unemployed." Cam plopped onto the bench next to Harvey. "You're too forgiving. She doesn't deserve it."

Harvey shifted to stare at Cam, his face contorted. "Cameron Lane. I can't believe that came out of your mouth. You know better."

Remorse stabbed Cam's gut. He lowered his head. "I do know better. But it kills me to see you and Alice hurt like this."

"I'm pretty sure you wouldn't be judging Jillian so harshly if you weren't still hurting, yourself." Harvey patted Cam's arm. "Son, you've got to let go of the guilt. What happened to Terrance was not your fault."

"My head knows you're right." Cam huffed out a pained breath. "My heart doesn't agree."

"Then do whatever it takes to convince it otherwise."

A nurse exited Alice's room, and Harvey rose. "Any change? Can I see her now?"

She gave him a weary smile. "She's resting comfortably. Go on in. The doctor should be making rounds in another hour or so. He'll be able to tell you more."

Cam looked in on Alice for a moment before excusing himself to take care of some errands. He needed to pick up a few things from home and make sure the neighbor hadn't forgotten to feed Bart, Cam's gray tabby. Not that missing a meal or two would hurt the obese feline, but by now the litter pan contents could probably be classified hazardous waste.

On the drive across town, Cam couldn't get Alice's pale, haggard face out of his mind. Her atrial fibrillation was under control, but now she'd developed an infection. Cam didn't know what Harvey would do if he lost his beloved wife.

Again Cam wondered whether he should cancel the rest of his prayer retreats. He'd said as much to Harvey this morning, but the man wouldn't hear of it. Said Alice would rest better knowing business at the inn went on as usual.

Which of course sent Cam's thoughts careening back to Jilly Gardner. No more arguments, no more excuses. She would come into town to see Harvey and Alice this afternoon if Cam had to hog-tie her to the roof rack of his SUV.

❧

Jilly balanced on her crutches in the middle of the lobby, Cam on her left, Ralph on her right. Talk about double-teaming. Perspiration slid down her temples, as much from the stress of being cornered as from the modified weight training routine she'd just completed in the exercise room. "Okay, okay, I'll go see them.

Give me time to shower and change."

She swiveled toward the family quarters and clunked to her room. The guys were right. She'd have to face Harvey and Alice eventually. Might as well get it over with.

Her left foot ensconced in a waterproof cast protector, Jilly clambered over the side of the claw-foot bathtub. She drew the curtain closed and eased onto the plastic patio chair Ralph had scrounged from among the inn's cast-off deck furnishings. With the shower spray pounding her shoulders, she pondered the latest reports about Alice's condition.

"Oh, God, please don't let her die."

The sudden surge of emotion stole Jilly's breath. She couldn't help herself—she loved the Nelsons, loved them dearly. And that was the root of her problem. They were supposed to be her forever family. They had promised. Talked to lawyers about adopting her. Gotten her hopes up. For three wonderful years she waited, prayed, grew to love Harvey and Alice as the father and mother she'd always longed for.

And then nothing. Three months after her seventeenth birthday, they told her it couldn't be worked out. No explanation, just apology after tearful apology. She'd given up trying to understand. Easier to focus on surviving her senior year and then leave the Nelsons—and the memories—behind when she headed off to college.

Salty wetness flowed down Jilly's face along with the shower stream. She turned off the water and flung back the curtain. Snagging a towel off the rack, she buried her face in its fresh-air softness. Alice always kept the family linens separate from the inn's. An old-fashioned clothesline and clean Ozark air imparted a fragrance no commercial laundry could duplicate.

A fragrance Jilly had come to associate with family and love.

She tossed the towel over the edge of the tub and hobbled out to her closet. Not much to choose from. She opted for an old pair of jeans she'd split partway up the left leg so her cast would fit through. A pink plaid shirt over a fuchsia tank top completed her attempt at casual chic. Wouldn't want the Nelsons to get the idea she'd dressed up for this visit.

Back in the lobby, it appeared Cam had won the coin toss for who'd be driving Jilly to town. She could have driven herself, and said as much, but both Cam and Ralph made it clear they didn't trust her to actually make it to the hospital.

At Blossom Hills General, Cam parked under the covered drop-off area and helped Jilly out of the Mariner. "I'll park and meet you inside."

She quirked her lips and glared. "I can find my own way to Alice's room. You don't have to babysit me."

"I should hope not." Cam slammed the driver's-side door and drove away.

A tremor snaked up Jilly's spine. With one look, Cam could make her feel twelve years old again and starving for his approval. Well, she didn't need it. His or anyone else's.

So why had she let him coerce her into this hospital visit?

"Because it's the right thing to do."

"Right for whom, God? You, me, or the Nelsons?" She tipped her head and stared at the underside of the roof. Her gaze settled on a moth caught in a spider's web. Exactly how she felt.

The electronic doors whispered open, and she limped inside. The atrium-like reception area glimmered under a ceiling of skylights. Ficus plants with braided trunks shed their dead leaves in massive clay planters. Bromeliads with spiky pink and orange flowers added a touch of color.

Jilly's one athletic shoe contributed its annoying squeak to the sound of her crutches tap-tapping across the marble floor. At the reception desk she waited for the white-haired volunteer to acknowledge her. "Can you direct me to Alice Nelson's room, please?"

The woman beamed a surprised smile and rose. Her abrupt motion sent the rolling office chair careening toward the lateral file behind her. "Oh my gracious. You're Jillian!"

Jilly gulped. "Yes."

"Well, aren't you a sight for sore eyes!" The elderly woman, whose nametag read MARGIE ALBERT, reached across the counter and clutched Jilly's hand. "It's been so long you probably don't recognize me. I'm Alice's cousin."

"Margie. How are you?" And how many more blasts from the painful past would Jilly have to endure? She glanced at the gnarled, age-spotted hands gripping hers and recalled the feisty, formerly raven-haired woman who used to toss tennis balls to her out behind the garage so she could practice her backhand. Dear Margie, yet another member of the family Jilly should have had.

"Why, I'm just fine, sweetie. Oh, it's so good to see you again!"

"You, too, Margie." She forced a smile. "Alice's room number?"

Margie gave her directions, and Jilly made her way to the bank of elevators, hoping she could get upstairs before Cam made it inside from the parking lot. The smaller her audience for this dreaded reunion, the better.

Chapter 7

At the sight of the tired-looking man with steel-gray hair, Jilly's heart stuttered. Harvey stood at the nurses' station, deep in conversation with a tall man in green scrubs. She edged toward them, wishing her crutches didn't creak so much.

Harvey stopped in midsentence and glanced over his shoulder. "Jillian."

"Hi, Harvey."

The fatigue drained from his face, and he seemed to grow three inches right before her eyes. He covered the distance between them in three long strides, reached out to hug her, then stopped short and cradled her face in his hands. Wetness pooled in the hollows alongside his nose. "Aw, sweetie, it's good to see you. You're as pretty as ever."

Jilly wobbled, her arms aching and tired after her weight workout earlier. "Mind if we sit down somewhere? I've been on my feet for a while—make that *foot*—and these crutches are killing me."

"There's a bench outside Alice's room. We can talk for a bit before you go in to see her." One hand hovering near her elbow, Harvey showed her the way.

"Cam told me the latest about Alice. I'm so sorry." Jilly lowered herself to the bench while Harvey propped her crutches against the wall.

"The docs are doing all they can." Harvey sighed and sat next to her. He reached for her hand, laced his fingers through hers, and squeezed. "I can't thank you enough for coming."

His palm felt cool and dry. His slim gold wedding band pressed between her knuckles. Beyond the nurses' station she saw Cam step off the elevator. Catching her eye, he gave a slight nod, then turned in another direction.

She fought the urge to leap from the bench, run him down, and insist he drive her straight back to the inn. As if she could run anywhere. The blue cast at the end of her left leg mocked her. Her lungs deflated on a barely muted groan.

Over the panicked hum filling her ears she heard Harvey speaking. ". . .so they're going to try a different antibiotic, and if she responds, we'll probably move her to a rehab hospital for a few weeks since the inn is so far from town."

"I see." She extricated her hand from Harvey's on the pretext of scratching her nose, then curled her fingers around the front edge of the bench. She touched something sticky—gum?—and scrubbed her fingertips on the leg of her jeans. "Will you stay in town with Alice until she's able to come home?"

"For the time being anyway. Church friends said I could use their guest room, but I'm staying here as much as I can." Harvey rubbed his chin. "You'll probably need to get back to Modesto before Alice is back on her feet, but if you'd show Ralph how to manage the front desk, he could help me keep things running."

"Speaking of which. . ." Jilly retrieved her crutches and pushed herself to a standing position. "I have some office work to finish up, and Heather and I still need to go over next weekend's menu."

"I won't keep you, then. Let's just look in on Alice for a minute." Harvey crossed the corridor and eased open the door. Glancing over his shoulder, he nodded at Jilly. "She's awake."

The hospital smells intensified inside the small private room. The lyrics of a soothing hymn flowed from a CD player. Several floral arrangements clustered on the wide windowsill, their subtle fragrance tickling Jilly's nose. She maneuvered into a position at the foot of the bed and let her gaze travel the length of Alice's frail body. Rheumy eyes stared back at her from beneath drooping lids. Silver-gray curls formed a halo around the pallid face.

Alice's mouth twitched into a semblance of a smile, and she wiggled the fingers of one hand. "Jillian."

Jilly bit down hard to keep her chin from quivering. She sniffed and drew the back of her hand beneath her nose. "Sorry. Allergies."

Harvey yanked a tissue from the box on Alice's nightstand and passed it to Jilly. "Forgot how bad your hay fever used to be."

"My allergies are even worse in Modesto." Jilly choked out a laugh. "Can't get away from them, I guess." *Can't get away from Alice and Harvey either.*

She drew a noisy breath. "Alice, I just wanted to come by and see how you're doing. Harvey says they're taking real good care of you."

Alice nodded and flicked her gaze toward the side of the bed, a clear signal she wanted Jilly to sit next to her.

Please, Cam, come and rescue me. Now!

When no knight in tarnished armor came to her aid, she gave a shrug and worked her way around to Alice's side. Handing off her crutches to Harvey, she perched next to Alice's hip. A huge knot tightened around her windpipe as Alice's hand crept into hers. Old feelings, old longings pulsed with every beat of her heart.

Slowly, slowly, Alice's eyes fell shut. Her chest rose and fell with peaceful regularity. Yet her hand stayed locked around Jilly's.

"She'll sleep for a while now." Freeing Jilly's hand, Harvey eased Alice's arm under the covers. "I knew your visit would help."

"I should get back to the inn." The words came with difficulty, as if someone had stolen her voice away. Jilly retrieved her crutches from Harvey and worked her way to the door. If she stayed a moment longer, she'd shatter into a million pieces.

Harvey held the door for her, love and gratitude lighting his tired eyes. "You come back soon, okay? And if you need anything at all—"

"I know." She gave a crisp nod. "Good-bye, Harvey."

She found Cam on the bench outside the room. He looked up from a tattered *Newsweek* magazine and cast her a questioning smile. "Ready to go?"

❧

Cam had no idea a woman on crutches could move so fast. One moment Jilly was standing outside Alice's closed door, the next she'd plowed into Cam's chest.

And clearly not by accident.

The crutches fell away and would have crashed to the floor if Cam's reflexes had been any slower. While he snagged one with each hand, Jilly's arms wound around his neck, her face buried in his shoulder as her body shook with sobs.

"Hey, hey." He spoke gently while maneuvering both crutches to his left hand. He felt for the wall behind him and propped the crutches aside, then moved his hands up and down Jilly's back in a soothing rhythm. "Why the tears? Is Alice worse?"

"No, it's just—" A wet sniffle sounded in his ear. "Just get me out of here. Please."

"Okay, sure." He slid his index finger under her chin and raised her head until they made eye contact. With his thumb he smoothed away the wetness from one cheek. "Can you wait one minute? I'll say good-bye to Harvey and we'll be on our way."

Jilly nodded, and Cam swiveled her in a half turn until he could ease her onto the bench. With a quick glance over his shoulder, he slipped into Alice's room.

Harvey rose from the recliner by the window. "Is Jillian all right?"

"She's a little shook up. I'm taking her back to the inn." He wanted to ask what happened during Jilly's brief visit. He wanted to ask what happened ten years ago that still caused them all so much grief.

"You take good care of her, you hear?" Harvey wrapped his fingers around Cam's forearm and squeezed, then returned to the chair and reached for his Bible on the windowsill.

Cam cast a final glance at the sleeping Alice and edged out the door. Wordlessly he helped Jilly to her feet and took her downstairs. By the time he brought the car around, she seemed more in control but not ready to talk. They drove several miles in silence.

And in the silence Cam prayed. *Lord, there's obviously more to this situation than either Jilly or the Nelsons have shared with me so far. Show me how I can help.*

On the outskirts of Blossom Hills, Cam turned onto the winding road leading to the inn. The forest closed in around them, filtering the midday sun. Cam stole subtle glances at Jilly, but in the shadowy interior of the SUV, her features blurred. He had to pay attention to his driving anyway. The twists and curves mimicked his jumbled thoughts.

He couldn't deny his loyalty and respect for the Nelsons. Nor could he resist Jilly's tug on his emotions. He might not want to admit it, but as a kid she'd wormed her way deep into his heart, eliciting big-brother feelings that made him want to protect and look out for her.

Only in the brother department, he'd already proven himself useless.

And the feelings he had for her now were anything but brotherly.

He slammed his fist against the steering wheel. Jilly jumped, and he shot her an apologetic frown. "Sorry. Just thinking."

"Me, too." She blew out a gale-force sigh.

Up ahead, a painted wooden sign indicated the turnoff to Dogwood Blossom Inn. Cam swung the Mariner up the narrow lane and pulled into the staff parking area behind the building. As he helped Jilly from the car, his gaze drifted toward the lake and the upturned fishing boat.

He gave Jilly's sleeve a tug. "You up for a boat ride?"

"I have office work to do." She looked down at her leg with a sad-eyed smirk. "Besides, I'm not exactly seaworthy."

"I doubt your cast will sink us. Give me a head start and by the time you limp down to the dock, I'll have the boat in the water." He winked. "Come on, it'll be fun."

Her quirked brow implied her doubts, but she nodded. "Why not? It's too nice a day to spend behind a desk."

Cam ducked into the storage shed to look for a couple of life vests, all the while wondering what had prompted this sudden idea. Something told him he needed to get Jilly to open up, finally talk about whatever had caused the rift between her and the Nelsons. Maybe if he could help her face her problems, it would begin to make up for how badly he'd failed Terrance.

❧

A boat ride. Honestly.

Jilly made her way toward the lake with slow, mincing steps. No sense breaking her other ankle with a misstep on the uneven ground. She skirted the fire pit and didn't notice the crescendo of her thudding heart until she reached the gnarled old dogwood tree.

Oh no. Were they still there, the initials she'd carved in the trunk all those years ago, the day after the *Braveheart* movie? She hoped Cam had never found them. JG + CL. How corny could a girl get?

"You coming or not?" Cam stood on the dock, one hand gripping a rope tied to the prow of the little green boat.

"Cool it, will you? I'm at a slight disadvantage, in case you hadn't noticed."

By the time she reached the dock, her ribs ached from the pressure of the crutches, and she gladly handed them off to Cam. He took her by the elbow and helped her balance while he eased her arms into a life vest. Somehow he finagled her into the boat without tipping them into the drink.

Plying the oars, Cam aimed the prow toward an open area of the lake. A light breeze rippled the surface. It was one of those delicious late-spring days in the Ozarks that could be both chilly and warm at the same time. Jilly couldn't help smiling up at the vivid blue sky, puffy cotton-ball clouds playing hide-and-seek with the sun. The air tasted fresh and moist.

A couple hundred yards from shore, Cam stowed the oars. He blotted the perspiration from his forehead with his shirtsleeve and heaved an appreciative sigh as his gaze traveled the tree-lined horizon. "Nothing like nature to put everything else in perspective. God's amazing, isn't He?"

"It's gorgeous out here, I have to agree." A tremor caught in Jilly's throat. The emotions she'd been suppressing since leaving the hospital came surging back.

"Want to talk about it?" Cam's voice grew quietly persuasive.

"I'm not sure I can."

Cam reached across the space between them and laid her fingers in his palm. "Come on, Jilly. Isn't it about time you dealt with whatever came between you and the Nelsons? Is ten years of resentment doing you or them any good?"

She released a shuddering sigh. "Obviously not."

Clutching both her hands, he gave them a small shake. "Then get it out. Tell me what was bad enough to keep you and the Nelsons apart all these years."

Jilly closed her eyes and dropped her chin to her chest. Every breath felt like an effort. "It's stupid. *I'm* stupid. It's my own fault. I should never have gotten my hopes up."

"About what?"

She met his confused gaze. A sigh raked her lungs. "About being adopted. They promised me. Harvey and Alice were supposed to be my"—Jilly's voice faltered; she could hardly speak the childlike term—"my forever family."

Cam straightened and shook his head. "They were going to adopt you? What happened?"

"That's just it. I don't know." Jilly yanked her hands free of Cam's and twisted on the seat. Her cast banged one of the oars. She grabbed her shin with one hand and the side of the rocking boat with the other. The *splat-splat* of the water against the hull kept time with her anxious breaths. Life vest or not, she could see her cast dragging her to the lake bottom like a cement block.

"Steady, it'll settle down in a minute." Cam slid to the other side of his seat, counterbalancing her weight shift. He gave a soft chuckle. "Didn't think to ask if you were afraid of water."

"Not afraid." Jilly swallowed the last remnants of panic. "Just not feeling very competent on land or sea these days."

"Understandable. How about I take us back to shore?"

"Good idea."

Cam reached for the oars. "So tell me more about this adoption thing. I never realized they'd even applied."

"They said it would be better to keep it between us until it was official." Jilly fixed her eyes on the dock as the memories sifted through her mind. "Guess they already had their doubts and didn't want a lot of explaining to do if it fell through." She grimaced. "Make that *when* it fell through."

"But you never found out what happened?"

"Figured they decided a teenage daughter was too much trouble after all."

❧

Cam reached for the whistling kettle and poured hot water over the spiced-apple teabags in two ceramic mugs. "Sugar?"

Jilly flicked her hair behind her ear. "Not the real stuff. One of those yellow sweetener packets, please."

He brought the mugs to the table and settled into the chair next to hers. They sipped their tea in silence for several minutes, the warm kitchen and the hot drinks melting away the tightness in Cam's rowing muscles. He pondered Jilly's revelation—the Nelsons had planned to adopt her? He knew full well how much they loved her, how much they'd sacrificed so she could pursue her tennis dreams throughout junior high and high school. If the adoption fell through, it must have been as heartbreaking for Harvey and Alice as it was for Jilly.

Pushing his mug aside, Cam leaned forward and reached for Jilly's hand. "I'm sorry you had to go through such disappointment, but there has to be a valid explanation. Harvey and Alice wouldn't have given up so easily."

Jilly shrugged, her face a mask of cynicism. "If there is an explanation, they certainly never shared it with me."

"Did you ask?"

"Of course I did. I pleaded with them to tell me why. All they'd say was that they only wanted what was best for me. By the time I finished high school, it was like they couldn't ship me off to college fast enough."

"So you left Blossom Hills and never looked back."

Her voice quavered. "If they didn't care enough to fight for me, I didn't see any reason to stick around."

Cam stroked her hand and found himself wondering at its softness and yet its power. The calluses at the base of each finger. The hard places at the tips. These hands belonged to a woman of strength, determination, drive. Jilly knew how to go after what she wanted. Why, then—adoption or not—would she give up on the one part of her life that should mean the most, the love of two people who cared for her so deeply?

He met her teary gaze. "It's not too late, you know."

"Oh, please." She yanked her hand from his. "I made it this far without parents. I sure don't need them now."

Cam sat back and crossed his arms over his chest. "Why am I not convinced?"

She shot him a bemused stare, opened her mouth as if to speak, then snapped it shut. She drained the rest of her tea and fumbled for her crutches. "Think whatever you want. I have work to do."

Watching her hobble from the room, Cam fought the urge to go after her. He threaded his fingers through the handle of his mug and pressed it hard into his palm. If he couldn't undo his own mistakes, maybe he could at least do something to bring closure to Jilly and the Nelsons.

Chapter 8

Seated at Harvey's office computer, Jilly keyed in another prayer retreat registration and hit the ENTER key. This weekend Cam's participants were high-school students, which meant rooming girls with girls and boys with boys. Several of the seventeen registrants had specified a roommate. At least five had not. Now, was Lindsay Gibson a boy or a girl? And what about Devin Daley? Wouldn't do to accidentally mix genders. And Cam had said to assign the odd man out to share his room. What if the odd "man" turned out to be female?

"Aaack." Jilly shoved away from the desk and massaged her temples. She needed caffeine. Now.

"That bad, huh?" Heather sidled into the office and propped her hip on the corner of the desk.

"How do you feel about being overrun by teenagers?"

"Yeah, I heard." Heather's mouth drooped. "Figured they wouldn't appreciate tahini-glazed eggplant or gnocchi with truffle cream."

"Appreciate? I can't even spell that stuff!"

"Which is why we stocked up on pizza and burgers for the weekend." Heather pressed the back of her hand to her forehead. "Alas, my culinary talents will be wasted upon this horde of heathens."

Jilly checked her empty mug to see if she'd left even a drop of coffee in the bottom. No such luck. "Whip me up another cup of that orange mocha cappuccino you served at breakfast, and I'll appreciate you enough for a whole herd of teenagers."

"My pleasure." Heather slid off the desk. "Anything new about Alice?"

"Cam called from the hospital awhile ago. Said she's responding to the antibiotics." Stifling a rush of emotions, Jilly returned to the computer.

"That's encouraging. She's such a sweet lady. Back in a few with your 'ccino."

Heather's footsteps faded, and so did the words on the monitor. Jilly blinked away the blurriness and tried to concentrate on the next registration entry, but her mind kept spinning back to her conversation with Cam yesterday. He *had* to raise those haunting questions again, and just when she'd convinced herself she no longer cared.

Yeah, right.

Okay, so she did care. And always would, probably. But she didn't need Cam or anyone else constantly dredging up the past. Especially when her time at Dogwood Blossom Inn had already honed those feelings to razor sharpness.

And as if matters weren't difficult enough, now Jilly had to deal with the resurgence of her girlhood feelings for Cam. Why did she have to stumble straight from Alice's hospital room into his arms yesterday? Worse, why did he have to be so tender and sweet? Number one, he already had a serious relationship with that Liz person. Number two, even if he were available, Jilly would be returning to Modesto in a few weeks. It would be pointless to entertain anything more than friendship.

Pointless. She had to keep telling herself that.

❧

"This is pointless, Harvey." Cam wadded up his napkin and tossed it next to his empty pie plate. "Jilly has a right to know the truth about why you called off the adoption."

Harvey shifted sideways, his cafeteria chair creaking. "Playing tennis for Stanford was her dream. We couldn't take that away from her."

"I know, I know." Cam groaned at the irony of the whole situation. He'd finally extracted the full story from Harvey. Jilly had just missed out on receiving one of Stanford's full athletic scholarships, but the school had offered her a partial instead. Even so, the Nelsons could never have afforded to cover the rest and were almost out of options when they learned of a supplemental scholarship available only to foster children. If they'd adopted Jilly, she would have become ineligible.

"It about killed us pretending there were other reasons the adoption didn't work out." Harvey rubbed his eyes. "You know how much Jillian wanted a real family. If we'd told her the truth, she'd have chosen us over Stanford, and then we'd have carried that guilt the rest of our lives."

"It's time to tell her, Harvey."

"What if she hates us even more?"

"She doesn't hate you." Cam clasped his hands on the table. "Anybody with a brain can see Jilly still loves you and Alice more than she can admit even to herself. It isn't too late for the three of you to be a family again. But it won't happen without honesty."

Harvey rubbed his eyes. "Guess you're right. Alice is doing a little better this afternoon. I could probably leave for a bit, drive out to the inn and talk to Jillian, if you think she'll listen."

"I'm betting she will." Cam gave a soft chuckle. "But you might score some extra points if you drop the 'Jillian' and just call her Jilly."

Laughter rumbled up through Harvey's chest. "Jilly, huh? Guess it does sound a bit sportier. I'll give it a try, but she'll always be my precious little Jillian."

Later, at his apartment, Cam sorted through some of the materials he planned to use for the youth prayer retreat. It was slow going, what with Bart padding across his lap and Cam's mind continually returning to his conversation with Harvey. *"Precious little Jillian"?* Cam snickered. What alternate universe had Harvey been living in? Jilly Gardner had always been a handful—stubborn, opinionated, determined—

He winced, and not from Bart's claws digging into his thigh. Nope, the truth hurt. The truth that those qualities were exactly what endeared Jilly to him. Exactly the reasons he found himself thinking about her more and more.

And less and less about Liz.

❧

Jilly had just sat down to supper with Heather and Ralph in the kitchen when the front door chime echoed over the intercom. "Who in the world could that be? Cam said he wouldn't be back until tomorrow morning."

Ralph rose. "You stay put. I'll go see."

"Don't be long," Heather called after him. "Lamb tagine tastes better when it's hot."

"These flavors are interesting, Heather. Tastes kind of—" Jilly's last bite of lamb lodged in her throat. At the sight of Harvey standing in the doorway, a sudden surge of panic stole her breath. "Oh no—is it Alice?"

"No, no, Alice is doing much better. Didn't mean to alarm you." Harvey ambled into the room and tucked his thumbs into his front pants pockets. "Thought maybe we could visit for a bit if you wouldn't mind."

Heather jumped up. "Have you eaten? I'll set another place."

"Smells mighty good." Harvey pulled out the empty chair across from Jilly. "Looks like you've outdone yourself again, Heather."

While Ralph and Heather took their seats, Jilly gave her anxious feelings a moment to subside. If Alice's condition had improved, then Jilly would soon be able to return to Modesto and get her life back on track. Surprisingly, the thought didn't give her the rush of anticipation she'd expected.

She tried to join in the dinnertime conversation but the edgy tone in Harvey's voice distracted her. He seemed nervous about something, pushing his food around his plate despite frequent compliments to the chef.

"You two aren't eating much." Heather rose to clear the serving dishes. "No baklava for you if you don't clean your plates."

Baklava. Jilly's lips creased at the mere thought of all that syrupy sweetness. "Save mine for later. Maybe I'll have it for a bedtime snack with a cup of that fantastic decaf Kona we had last night."

"You have Kona?" The anxiety briefly vanished from Harvey's eyes. "I'd love a cup."

"Great." Heather reached for the coffee carafe. "I'll start it brewing right now."

Ralph crumpled his napkin beside his empty plate. "Harvey, you got time to look at what I've done in the planter boxes out back?"

"Maybe later, Ralph. I need to talk about some stuff with Jillian." Harvey slid his gaze toward her. "I mean Jilly."

A strange letdown smothered Jilly's heart, for no reason she could explain except for Harvey's unexpected use of the nickname she'd been going by since her freshman year in college. Jilly was her grown-up name, her tennis persona. Suddenly—at least in Harvey's eyes—she only wanted to be Jillian.

Heather scooped coffee beans into the grinder. "If you two want to visit out on the deck, I'll bring the coffee as soon as it's ready."

"Sounds good." Jilly pushed up from the table and glanced around for her crutches. Ralph brought them over from where they'd been leaning against the pantry door. Irritated at her own helplessness, she closed her eyes for a second and breathed deeply. "Thanks."

Accepting help from others had always been hard for her, especially after she left the Nelsons behind and began the uphill struggle to make a name for herself in the tennis world. Yet even though she'd dedicated every spare moment and ounce of energy to the pursuit of tennis, her heart had gone out of it the day Harvey and Alice told her the adoption was off. From that time forward, she'd only been going through the motions. The trophies and accolades she'd hoped would fill her empty heart gradually meant less and less.

The sun had disappeared behind the hills by the time Jilly and Harvey settled into Adirondack chairs on the deck. Stifling a shiver, Jilly forced a smile. "So what is it you needed to talk about?"

"Jillian—Jilly—" Harvey sat forward, his hand inches from hers. A sigh rasped between his tight lips. "It's time I explained why Alice and I called off the adoption."

"Called off the adoption." The words sliced upward through Jilly's chest. Harvey had never used that exact phrasing before. He and Alice had always talked around the subject with words like *"It just didn't work out,"* or *"You'll understand someday."*

Apparently, someday was today. Jilly stared into the half light and tried to follow the meandering trail of a lightning bug. "I'm listening."

"It was the scholarship. That and nothing more." With halting words, Harvey poured out the whole story of how they'd realized adoption would make her ineligible for the supplemental scholarship for foster children. "It was the hardest decision we ever had to make, but we couldn't take your dream away, even if it meant you'd hate us forever."

Jilly's breath froze in her lungs. She could hardly believe what she was hearing. Slowly, painfully, she shifted her gaze to meet Harvey's. His tortured expression surely matched her own.

"But don't ever, ever think we didn't want you," he went on, "didn't love you as our very own daughter. Don't love you still. Alice and I cherish you like—"

"Stop. Don't say it!" She couldn't bear to hear another word. *Take her dream away?* He just didn't get it, did he?

She sprang to her feet, crying out as her injured ankle took her weight. She seized her crutches, fumbled to position them, dropped one. She nearly tripped over it as she lurched across the deck. The steps daunted her but only for a moment. She had to get away before she imploded.

She grabbed the handrail. Balancing on one foot, she lowered the lone crutch to the first step. She stepped off, teetered, then landed hard on her left foot. Pain ripped through her. As if watching a movie frame by frame she saw herself falling, falling, each wooden step pummeling another part of her body, until finally she lay sprawled on the grass, her world a white, pulsing scream of agony.

Chapter 9

At the sound of the doorbell, Cam tore his mind away from the Richard Foster book he'd been reading and checked the digital clock on his cable box. After seven. Who'd be dropping by this time of night?

"Move it, Bart. We've got company." He pushed the fat old cat off his lap and strode to the door.

"Hey, stranger." Liz stood on his front porch. "I come bearing pizza."

The aromas of cheese, pepperoni, and crispy garlic crust reminded him he hadn't eaten since lunch. On the other hand, Liz's untimely appearance stole away whatever appetite the pizza smells had conjured up.

"Wow. This is a surprise." What could he do but invite her in? He stepped aside and opened the door wider.

"I know I should have called first, but you'd have told me not to come."

Good guess. He noticed she was alone. "Where's Sammy?"

"Playing at a friend's. I don't have to pick him up until nine." She crossed in front of Cam and carried the pizza box and a weighty-looking plastic grocery bag into the breakfast nook. Her skintight jeans accentuated every curve. Her hips swayed with a deliberateness clearly meant to assault Cam's masculine sensibilities.

He drew up short and leaned against one side of the kitchen archway. "What are you doing, Liz?"

"Bringing you supper. What does it look like?" She cast him an innocent smile before going to the cupboard for plates and napkins. "Want to pour us some drinks? I brought diet cola for me and root beer for you. The caffeine-free kind." Another smile, this time with a wink. "See, I remembered."

Frustration rolled through Cam's chest. He should be flattered, but all he felt was annoyance. He pulled a hand down his face and stepped closer. "Liz—"

"Want to eat at the table or on the sofa?" She snagged a metal turner from the utensil drawer and served them each two slices of pizza.

"Liz."

Her hand froze above the plate. "What is it, Cam? You look upset."

"I'm not upset. It's just. . ." How could he explain without hurting her? The feelings—if he'd ever really had any for her—were no longer there.

She faced him, her shoulders drooping. "I understand. Your mind's a million miles away on your retreat stuff or whatever. And I barged in without calling or even considering you might already have eaten or maybe weren't in the mood for pizza or—"

The kitchen extension shrilled. Grateful for the interruption, Cam shot Liz an apologetic frown and reached for the receiver.

"Cam, it's Harvey." His voice sounded strained, urgent. "Can you meet me at the hospital?"

Cam's heart plummeted. Alice must have taken another bad turn. "I can be there in twenty minutes. Are you there now?"

"No, I'm at the inn. The ambulance is about to leave with Jilly, and I'll be—"

"Wait. *Jilly?*" Harvey's words ping-ponged through Cam's skull. "What happened?"

"She took a bad spill off the deck. I'll tell you more when we get to the hospital."

"Okay then. Tell her—" The line went dead.

With numb fingers, Cam set the receiver on the base. He pressed his palms against the beveled edge of the counter and closed his eyes in prayer. *Father, please let Jilly be okay. Help her know how much You love and care for her. How much Harvey and Alice and I all—*

"Cam, honey?"

He jerked his head around. Liz stood right behind him. "I have to go to the hospital."

"I gathered that. Something happened to Jilly?"

"A fall. That's all I know." With a shrug he turned to face her. "Sorry about the pizza." *Sorry about everything.*

Liz tucked her hands against his sides. "Is it so important for you to be there? I mean, really, what can you do?"

"I don't know. But I need to go." He took her wrists and gently moved her aside, then grabbed his keys and wallet from the end of the counter. "Can you let yourself out?"

"Let me go with you, honey. I can see how worried you are." She snatched her purse off a kitchen chair.

The breath rushed from his lungs. The last thing he wanted was Liz at the hospital with him. He choked out a laugh and imbued his voice with forced lightness. "How quickly we forget. Don't you remember when Sammy cut his foot last spring? You had me take him to the ER because you were afraid you'd pass out."

A sick look flickered across Liz's face. "Okay, so I have a thing about blood. But will you call me? I could wait for you, keep the pizza warm."

Halfway through the door to the garage, Cam spun around and gripped Liz's shoulders. The confusion and disappointment clouding her expression made his heart ache. "Please go home, Liz. I have no idea how long I'll be. And you'll need to pick up Sammy soon anyway."

"But—"

"Please. I'll call you." He yanked the door closed behind him and punched the garage door opener. As the heavy door rumbled along its track, he climbed behind the wheel of his SUV and said another prayer.

Father, whether there's a chance for something between Jilly and me or not, I know I'm about to hurt Liz, and there's nothing I can do about it. Help me handle this with as much grace and compassion as I can.

❧

Slowly, unwillingly, as if being dragged down a long, echoing corridor, Jilly felt awareness return. Every sound seemed amplified—garbled voices, wheels rolling across a hard floor, the clatter of metal against metal.

And a sound she didn't recognize. Breathing? No, more like snoring.

Light filtered between her fluttering eyelids. She squinted against the streaks of sunlight cutting through the half-closed vertical blinds and struggled to remember where she was. When she tried to lift her arm, the tug of an IV tube answered her question.

Great. I'm in the hospital.

Her stomach heaved. She swallowed down the nausea as her mind retraced the events that had brought her here. Supper with Harvey. His confession about the Stanford scholarship. The rage and disbelief that propelled her across the deck and sent her tumbling down the steps.

The rasping snores deepened. She forced her thoughts to the present. Easing her head to the left in search of the source, she glimpsed Cam sprawled in a recliner.

A new emotion warmed her chest. Her breath hitched. She blinked several times and reached up to brush away a sudden spurt of tears. How long had he been sitting there? And why?

He stirred, opened his eyes, straightened. Grinned. "Hey, kiddo, when did you wake up?"

"Just a minute ago." Her throat felt raspy. She tried to cough.

"Here, the nurse said you could have ice chips." Cam reached for an insulated plastic container and offered her a spoonful of shaved ice.

The coolness soothed her dry mouth. "How long have I been out?"

"Pretty much since your surgery last night."

"Surgery?" More nausea, this time accompanied by raw panic. She did a quick mental survey of her body parts. Everything felt intact, if stiff and sore. Then she noticed the dull ache in her left leg and the bulge under the blanket where her broken ankle was propped up. She raised questioning eyes to Cam.

He eased onto the side of the bed and took her hand. "Jilly, you reinjured your ankle. It was pretty torn up. They had to put it back together with pins and I don't know what all."

"Terrific." She looked away, her breath coming in short, sharp gasps.

"Your doctor will be able to explain it better—how serious the break was, what your recovery will entail."

Every exhalation scraped against her wounded heart. "I don't need a doctor to tell me my tennis career is over."

Cam pressed her hand against his chest. She could feel his heartbeat beneath his nubby pullover. "Jilly, I want you to know I'll be here for you. I mean, Harvey and I both—"

"Please, don't!" She yanked her hand away and rolled her torso toward the window. As much as she could anyway, with her left leg pretty much useless and the rest of her feeling like she'd been trampled by a herd of wild horses.

With gentle firmness Cam took her by the shoulders and made her look at him. "I know about the scholarship. I know that's why Harvey and Alice called off your adoption. And I know you're angry and confused. But you have to believe they did it because they love you. They loved you too much to keep you from your dream."

"My dream?" Bitterness seared her throat. "My dream was to have a real family. A real home. A mom and dad who would always be mine."

"Do you think an adoption certificate would have made Harvey and Alice love you any more than they already do? They gave up their dream, too, in case you didn't notice. But that's what love is. Sacrificing your own happiness for someone else's."

"They gave up their dream, too." Jilly had never considered the Nelsons' disappointment might equal her own. An immense weight of shame and regret pressed down upon her. She'd wasted ten long years resenting the Nelsons for a decision they made out of the purest love.

"If they'd only told me why, if they'd only given me the choice. . ." Tears cascaded down her face. She couldn't bring herself to look at Cam. "I need to be alone now. I just need to be alone."

❧

Seated on a hard plastic chair in Alice's room, Cam stifled a yawn. He pressed his hands against his thighs. "I should get out to the inn soon. Those teenagers will start arriving in a few hours, and with Jilly out of commission, I told Ralph I'd help him at the front desk."

"After spending all night at the hospital?" Harvey tucked Alice's covers around her and tugged her pillow higher. "You're dead on your feet, son. Maybe you should cancel the retreat."

"We'll manage." Cam rose, exhaustion dragging on every muscle. "If I leave pretty quick, I can grab a nap before the kids start showing up."

Alice slapped away Harvey's fussing fingers and motioned Cam over. "Are you sure Jillian's going to be all right? Do you think she'll forgive us?"

"Give her some time to let it all sink in." He glanced at Harvey and saw the guilt and worry carved into his face. "Don't blame yourself for Jilly's fall. She needed to know the truth, no matter how much it hurt."

Harvey sighed and paced to the window. "Yeah, I know. And I know it's no good wondering if we should have handled things differently ten years ago. Got no choice now but to keep trusting the Lord to heal Jillian's heart and her body."

"He will. . .in time." Cam smiled down at Alice and smoothed one of her silver curls away from her face. "Just like He's healing you. Sure glad to know you're doing better."

"Oh, I'm coming along fine." She aimed a scowl at Harvey. "Which is why I'm sending this man back to the inn with you. He's nothing but a nuisance here, fussing around like an old tom turkey. Better he burns off his nervous energy helping you ride herd on those teens."

"Now, Alice," Harvey began.

"No argument. You two get on out of here so Cam has time to put his feet up for a bit." Alice aimed her index finger at Harvey's chest. "Wouldn't hurt you to sleep in a real bed for a change either, old man. One more night in that recliner and your body's going to petrify in a permanent S-shape."

Cam raised an eyebrow and started for the door. "Harvey, I think we'd better do as Alice says. She's looking almost fit enough to leap out of that bed and wallop us good if we don't."

He and Harvey shared a laugh on the way to the parking lot. It felt good to relieve some of the tension shrouding them both. At the inn, Cam went straight up to his room and stretched out on the bed without even turning back the quilt. He fell asleep in minutes.

❧

Jilly jerked awake. She'd been dozing off and on for two days, as if her body couldn't quite purge itself of the anesthesia. At least the nausea had subsided.

But the tears had not. When a nurse came in to check on her and saw the dampness on Jilly's pillow, she jammed a thermometer between Jilly's lips to make sure she wasn't running a fever. Noticing Jilly's tears, she handed her a tissue. "You had a really bad break, and it's scary, I know. Would you like to talk to someone? The chaplain, or maybe a psychologist?"

Talking was the last thing Jilly felt like doing. It was too soon. She gave her head a shake and willed away the grogginess. Finding the bed control, she pressed the button to raise her head. "Just tell me when I can get out of here."

The nurse checked Jilly's chart. "The doctor's still concerned about a possible concussion and those rib contusions. He wants you to stay one more night for observation. If everything looks good tomorrow, we'll get a new cast on that ankle and you can go home."

Home. Where was home anymore? Most likely she didn't have a tennis career to go back to. And even if the ankle strengthened enough to allow her to coach again, no way could she expect Therese to hold her job indefinitely.

The nurse opened the door to leave and suddenly halted. Turning to Jilly, she said, "You have a couple of visitors, honey." She stepped out of the way as Harvey pushed Alice's wheelchair into the room.

"Oh, my baby Jillian!" The smile on Alice's face stretched wide. Her eyes crinkled at the corners, and tears seeped out. She reached up to slap Harvey's hand. "Come on, you old coot. You can move faster than that. I need to hug my girl!"

Harvey rolled the wheelchair close enough that Alice could lean up and plant a kiss on Jilly's cheek. "She wouldn't wait a minute longer," Harvey said. "I've been looking in on you, but you seemed to need sleep more'n you needed company."

A tumble of emotions sent Jilly's heart thudding. The tears she'd been fighting for two days burst forth anew. "I'm sorry," she said. "I'm so, so sorry."

Harvey rushed around to the other side of the bed and carefully pulled her into his arms. "We're the ones who are sorry, darlin'. Can you ever forgive us?"

One arm tucked against Harvey's warm chest, her other hand snuggled into Alice's amazingly firm grip, Jilly felt the last remnants of resentment drain out of her. Oh, how she loved these people! How she needed them! All the words she longed to say jammed against one another and couldn't escape. A phrase from Alice's sampler filled her mind: *"God sets the lonely in families. . . ."*

She could only smile through the flood of tears and hope Harvey and Alice could read the love in her eyes. *Please, God, forgive me. Help me somehow make up for all the lost years we could have had together. The Nelsons are my family and always will be.*

Chapter 10

Cam stepped behind the lectern on the chapel dais to close the Sunday-morning worship segment of his teen retreat. "Let's take a few minutes now for personal prayer requests." He jotted notes as the group called out special concerns. When the room grew silent, he asked everyone to bow their heads. As he lifted up each concern, he drew on scripture to claim God's promise of healing, hope, strength, and salvation.

"Finally, Father," he said, hands clasped atop his notes, "heal and comfort my friend Jilly. Help her to know Your love. Show her that You can always be counted on, no matter what difficulties or disappointments she faces. In Christ's name, amen."

A murmur of amens whispered through the chapel, and Cam dismissed the group for lunch. By the time he gathered up his notes and Bible, the teens had moved into the dining room. Crossing the quiet lounge, he heard Ralph call his name and detoured to the lobby.

"Thought you'd want to greet our arrival." Ralph stood at the inn's double entry doors, one pulled wide as Harvey wheeled Jilly through. Her left leg rested on a wheelchair extension supporting her ankle cast.

Jilly grinned at him. "Sorry I left you in the lurch. You surviving all those wild and crazy teenagers?"

Cam couldn't explain the sudden elation swelling his chest. Where moments ago he'd been fighting a midday slump, renewed energy surged. He loped across the floor and halted at Jilly's side. He reached out and tousled her hair, and the feel of it under his fingers brought back memories of a thick brown ponytail. "You'll do anything to get out of work. Even throw yourself down a flight of steps."

Jilly gave a wry smile. "Not a technique I would recommend."

"Didn't think so." Cam shot a questioning glance at Harvey, whose eyes sparkled with happiness. Apparently Jilly and the Nelsons were working out their differences.

"Just in time for lunch," Ralph said. "Heather's whipped up some gourmet burgers and seasoned oven fries you have to taste to believe."

Fatigue lengthened Jilly's face. She cast Ralph a regretful look. "Maybe you could have her save me some?"

"Sure thing. You coming, Cam?"

Sounds of laughter and noisy conversation filtered from the dining room. Right now, it was the last place Cam wanted to be. "Would you tell the kids

I'll be there in a few minutes? I'll help Harvey get Jilly settled."

Ralph shot him a knowing wink. "Take your time, bud."

As Harvey wheeled Jilly into the family quarters, Cam got the doors and made sure no obstacles barred their path. In Jilly's room, he helped Harvey lift her onto the bed. While Cam propped pillows behind her back and under her ankle, Harvey excused himself to get the rest of Jilly's things from the car. He returned with a small overnight bag and a walker.

Jilly took one look at the aluminum contraption and groaned. "As if crutches weren't bad enough, now I have to shuffle around like a little old lady."

Cam couldn't resist a chuckle. "Glad my digital camera has movie mode. That's gonna go over big on YouTube."

"Try it and I'll dig up those snaps I took of you with your mullet."

"Hey!" Cam gave her a playful slap on the arm. "I was a doofus teenager at the time."

Harvey stepped between them. "That's enough, you two, or I'll pull out a few incriminating photographs of my own." He bent to kiss Jilly's forehead. "I'll make sure things are running smoothly out front before I head back to town. You sure you're gonna be okay?"

Love shone in her eyes. She squeezed his hand. "I'll be fine, Harvey. And tell Alice to keep getting better so she can come home, too."

"I'll be back to check on you in a sec," Cam told her, following Harvey out. In the lobby he pulled Harvey aside. "Haven't seen you this happy in a long time. Jilly either, for that matter. Are things as good between you as they look?"

"We're getting there." Harvey nodded, his mouth curving in a satisfied smile. Then his expression turned grim. "I'm more worried about how she's going to handle giving up tennis. She's putting up a brave front, but it's gotta be breaking her heart."

Cam shook his head. "I keep praying there's still a chance she can play again."

"You'll keep a close eye on her this weekend?"

"You betcha."

While Harvey headed for the office, Cam made a quick trip to the kitchen, where he had Heather prepare a burger and fries for Jilly. He filled a glass with iced tea, then carried the tray to Jilly's room.

She looked up in surprise. "Aw, Cam, you didn't need to do that."

"My pleasure, m'lady." He waited while she laid a pillow across her lap, then set the tray on top of the pillow. "Missing anything?"

She checked the hamburger trimmings. "Looks perfect. You even remembered I don't like mayo."

"There's a lot I remember about you." Cam stuffed his hands into his back pockets, boyish shyness warming his face. At her curious glance, he went on, "Like, I remember you could never do your homework without the TV on in the background. And your favorite color is red. And you don't want an anchovy within ten miles of your pizza, but you like them in your caesar salad."

Jilly grinned. "Wow. Didn't know you were paying attention."

"You were a hard girl to ignore."

"Were?"

"Still are." He stared at the toes of his sneakers and hoped she couldn't detect the throb of his pulse beneath his jaw.

She cleared her throat. "Shouldn't you be getting back to your retreat kids?"

"Oh. Yeah, I guess so." He spotted her purse on the end of the bed and moved it within reach. "Is your cell phone on? I've got mine on vibrate. If you need anything at all, just give me a buzz. If I'm tied up, I'll send Ralph or Heather right away."

Jilly sighed and gave a meaningful eye roll. "Please. I've got my walker, lunch, and the TV remote. What more could a girl need?"

"Okay, if you're sure. . ." Cam edged toward the door. Halfway into the hall, he stopped. Turned. Shot her a squint-eyed stare. "You really have a picture of me with my mullet?"

❧

The moment Jilly heard the outer door close behind Cam, she set the lunch tray aside. Easing onto her right hip, she reached to open the nightstand drawer. It slid out with the familiar squeaks and moans from her childhood. With a practiced motion she lifted the entire drawer onto her lap and tipped it until she could run her searching fingers along the bottom.

Seconds later she secured her prey, a thin manila envelope taped to the underside of the drawer. She moved the drawer to the other side of the bed and emptied the envelope contents onto her lap, a giggle erupting as adolescent memories tumbled through her thoughts along with the color snapshots that now lay before her—every single one of them a picture of Cam.

She found the one she'd been looking for—Cameron Lane, age sixteen, thin and lanky and solemn-faced. He wore Levi's 501 jeans and a brown T-shirt bearing a sketch of Jesus with outstretched arms and the words SEE HIS NAIL-SCARRED HANDS.

"Ah, yes, the year of the mullet." Jilly shook her head and laughed at the image of Cam with super-short hair all over his head except for the long fringe around the nape. Blackmail material indeed.

Except back then Jilly had thought him the handsomest, coolest guy on the face of the planet.

Her stomach did a roller-coaster loop-the-loop. The mullet was history, but Cam Lane remained as handsome as ever. She shivered at the memory of his fingers ruffling her hair. Could he ever think of her as anything but the pesky kid she used to be?

Did she want him to?

She plopped her head against the pillow and released a long, slow sigh.

She did. She definitely did.

❧

On Monday morning, Jilly determined to get back to work. She sat sideways at the desk in Harvey's office, her left leg propped on a cushioned footstool. With Ralph's help, she'd rearranged the computer setup to make it easier to reach the keyboard from this awkward position.

She'd been hard at it for two hours now, and the entries in the financial software program blurred before her eyes. With a groan, she pushed the keyboard aside and pressed her palms into her eye sockets.

"You don't have to do this, you know."

At the sound of Cam's voice, her hands fell to her lap. She offered him a weak but grateful smile. "I felt useless lying around watching TV all weekend while everybody else looked after your teen group."

"We managed fine." Cam pulled over a chair and straddled it, resting his forearms on the back. "At least take a book out to the deck and enjoy some fresh air. It's too gorgeous a day to be cooped up in front of a computer screen."

The view of the sun-dappled deck and the lake beyond did look tempting. Jilly frowned, then shook her head. "Work is better for me right now."

As she reached for another invoice from the stack, Cam laid his hand on her arm. "Harvey said he'd be home later to help catch up. Come outside with me."

The warmth of his hand penetrated her thin T-shirt sleeve. She didn't know which was worse—facing the possible end of her tennis career or confronting her growing attraction to a man who was completely unavailable. "No boat rides, okay?"

"No boat rides." He stood and set her walker in front of her, steadying it as she pulled herself upright.

"So what are you still doing here?" she asked on the way through the lobby. "Don't you have a life beyond the prayer retreats?"

He chuckled and held the door for her. "Me, a life? You've got to be kidding!"

Something in his voice tugged at her senses. She eased into one of the Adirondack chairs and allowed Cam to lift her cast onto the matching wooden ottoman. Choosing her words with care, she asked, "Don't you miss that little boy? And his mom?"

A pained look settled around Cam's eyes. He sighed through his nose. "Can we talk about something else?"

"Okay." She'd hit a nerve, obviously. She'd suspected all along his feelings for the woman and her son were stronger than he wanted to admit. A heavy emptiness pressed down on her. Guess she really was still just a kid in Cam's eyes. The extra attention he'd been lavishing on her all weekend had been that of a concerned big brother, nothing more.

"Sorry, Jilly, didn't mean to snap at you." Cam sank onto the edge of the ottoman, facing at a slight angle from her. He locked his clenched hands between his knees. "It's just. . .Liz and I need to have a serious talk soon. She's pushing for more than I'm ready for."

Jilly's heart did a slow roll. This emotional seesaw ride just never seemed to end. "I see." *Not.*

He squared his shoulders and met her gaze. "Enough about me. What's going on with you? And don't pretend everything's okay. You've had more trauma in one weekend than most people face in a lifetime."

She shrugged, the breath rushing out of her lungs. "I'm a washed-up, out-of-work tennis pro with no clue what happens next. What do you want me to say?"

"I want you to say how it makes you feel. Yell. Scream. Cry. Whatever it takes."

In spite of the ache in her soul, she wanted to laugh. "You're a guy. Guys don't usually want to deal with feelings, much less the screaming and crying."

"Yeah, well, I thought you might appreciate seeing my sensitive side." He took her hand, and all rational thought flew from her mind.

What were we talking about?

Oh, yeah. Her emotional state. Just a wee bit haywire at the moment. Must be the new pain meds she'd been on since the surgery.

"Jilly?"

She widened her eyes in a vain attempt to clear both her vision and her brain. Cam, pain medication, and the sunshine warming her shoulders made for a dangerous combination. His hand still held hers, and it felt so nice. "Cam, really, you don't need to worry about me. I'll be okay."

"You always were too independent for your own good." Resignation darkened his eyes. "But just know I'm here for you if you ever feel like talking."

Talking? Cam's nearness pulled all moisture from her mouth. She swallowed. Her gaze slid to his lips. "I, uh. . .sure."

❧

Cam tossed his razor and toothbrush into his travel kit and zipped it shut. He should have hit the road hours ago, before Jilly's plucky resilience tunneled any deeper into his heart. That languid look in her eyes as they sat on the deck nearly undid him. But he didn't dare deal with his growing feelings for Jilly until he broke things off with Liz.

Lord, help me do it right.

He hadn't driven halfway back to town when his cell phone chirped. When he read Liz's name and number on the caller ID, his pulse ramped up. He took a steadying breath before answering and struggled for a nonchalant tone. "Hi, Liz. What's up?"

"Where are you, honey?" She sounded peeved.

"Just now heading home from the retreat."

"I knew you wouldn't want to be bothered during your prayer thing, but I've been worried." A pause. "You never called to let me know what happened at the hospital."

Cam's stomach clenched. "Guess I got busy and forgot." He saw a turnout up ahead and pulled over. No sense risking an accident. This conversation had already proved too distracting.

"Well? Is that all you have to say?" Her voice shook. "Do I mean so little to you that you can't spare two minutes to let me know what's going on?"

"I didn't mean to ignore you. I'm sorry." Cam released his seat belt buckle and rested his forehead on the steering wheel. Shame and regret curdled his insides. Whatever his feelings for Liz—or lack thereof—she deserved better than this.

And he called himself a Christian.

He hauled in another deep breath. "Where are you calling from? Can we meet somewhere?"

"I'm at Riley's. My shift ends at two thirty. I'll have an hour before I have to pick up Sammy from school."

Cam mentally ran through Liz's route from the pharmacy to Sammy's school. Halfway between was the Something's Brewing Café. He checked his watch. Not quite two. Still time to drop his things at home and check on Bart. "What if I meet you at Something's Brewing around two forty-five?"

"I. . .guess that would be okay." The pout in her tone chafed his nerves.

All the more reason to bring this relationship to a timely end.

Chapter 11

At least with the walker, Jilly didn't have the problem of sore ribs from the crutches, but even though she'd tried to keep up a modified workout routine, bearing weight with her arms grew tiring after a while. As she contemplated another trek from her room to the front desk, the wheelchair looked mighty tempting.

Nope, not ready to settle for invalid status. She gritted her teeth and reached for the walker.

Harvey met her in the hallway. He'd taken to sleeping in his own bed the past couple of nights, now that Alice had been moved to the rehab hospital. "'Mornin', sleepyhead. On your way to breakfast?"

"Already ate. Just came back to brush my teeth." Jilly inched the walker forward and slid-hopped her right foot along behind it. She stopped long enough to press one finger under her nose before a sneeze erupted, then dug a tissue from the pocket of her shorts.

"You taking anything for those allergies?"

"My prescription meds usually help a lot, but I got distracted when I ordered my refill and forgot to give this address. I'm trying to stretch out my doses until my landlady forwards the package." She continued down the hall, and Harvey edged around her to open the door into the lobby.

"I'm heading into town to sit with Alice awhile," he said. "Want to come along?"

Jilly eyed the overflowing in-box on the front counter. "I'd love to, but it's Wednesday already. I should catch up on more paperwork before things get busy with Cam's next retreat."

"Aw, this looks like mostly junk mail." Harvey riffled through the stack and tossed several items into the recycle bin beneath the counter. "Besides, you've been working way too hard for somebody who's just had surgery."

"I'd rather work than sit around twiddling my thumbs." Jilly eased onto the barstool behind the counter and set her cast on the footrest. She didn't add that keeping busy kept her mind off other things. Like the end of her career. Like losing ten years with the two people who loved her most. Like falling for a guy who probably still thought of her as a selfish, spoiled kid.

After all, Cam hadn't so much as called since he left the inn Monday afternoon.

She sneezed and grabbed a tissue from the box next to the phone. "You go on, Harvey. Give Alice a big hug for me. I promise I'll visit her in a few days."

"All right, have it your way. But don't feel like you have to do it all. I'll be back this afternoon, and I'll be in and out all weekend, too."

When the back door closed behind Harvey, Jilly let the breath whoosh from her lungs. She'd tried, really tried to stay upbeat for his sake. He carried too much blame already for the lost years, and now for her fall and new injuries. She couldn't let him see the panic lurking just beneath the surface, the stark dread of an empty, meaningless future.

She knotted a fist and hammered the countertop. There *must* be some way to get back to tennis. If she found a topnotch orthopedist, worked hard at physical therapy—it *couldn't* be the end of the line for her. *Oh please, God!*

❧

Beneath the greenery in the rehab hospital atrium a fountain burbled, its gentle sounds muting the conversations going on around Cam and Alice. He'd stopped by for a visit this morning, his first since she'd been moved. "Nice place. Are they treating you okay?"

"Never a dull moment. They'll have me fit for a marathon in no time." Alice touched his shoulder. "You look down today, Cam. Something bothering you?"

His breath seeped out through tight lips. "I broke it off with Liz."

"Oh, honey, I'm sorry. Did something happen between you?"

"More a case of what *wasn't* happening." Cam shifted on the window seat next to Alice's tropical-print lounge and stretched one leg out. "I'm not sure I ever had feelings for her. If not for Sammy, we might never have gotten together in the first place."

Alice chuckled. "I remember when you first started tutoring that little boy as part of your church's afterschool program. You bragged on him like crazy."

"He's one great kid." Cam massaged the back of his neck. "But I can't base a relationship with Liz strictly on the fact that I've gotten attached to her son."

"That's true. It wouldn't be fair to either of them, or to you."

"I could probably continue tutoring Sam, but I'm not sure it's a good idea." He glanced at Alice, hoping she'd tell him otherwise.

She didn't, of course. "I know you'll miss him. And you'll both grieve for a while. But you'll both be fine, in time."

Footsteps echoed on the tile floor. Cam looked up to see Harvey striding their way. Lifting his hand in greeting, he scooted sideways so that Harvey could sit next to Alice.

"There's my beauty queen." Harvey dropped a kiss on Alice's cheek before joining Cam on the window seat. "The nurses told me you were off gallivanting with some handsome young man."

"Well, since there weren't any handsome *old* men to escort me, I didn't have much choice." Alice wedged her hand into Harvey's, and they shared a loving glance.

Cam's heart warmed. If only he could hope for a lasting relationship of his own someday.

"Our Cam's had a difficult few days," Alice said. "He and Liz are no longer together."

Harvey swiveled to face Cam. "Is that true?"

Cam gave a halfhearted shrug. "We had a long talk Monday afternoon. I told her I couldn't see a future between us."

"How'd she take it?"

"Hard. Typical Liz." Cam lowered his head, fingers laced between his knees. The hateful words she'd spewed—most of them about Jilly—still burned his ears. "I always knew she had a jealous streak. It came out in spades when I told her it was over."

"Honestly, son, I can't say I'm sorry. Liz just never seemed your type." Harvey patted Cam's leg. "God has someone special in mind for you. For Liz, too, if she'd ever open her heart to receive Him."

"That was probably our biggest problem. She claimed to believe in God, but her life never evidenced any level of faith."

Alice made a *tsk-tsk* sound. "All you can do for a person like her is to keep praying. And I will."

Just one more reason Cam loved the Nelsons so much. A half smile quirked his lips. "Alice, with you praying for her, Liz's salvation is as good as secured."

"There's somebody else we should all be praying for." Harvey looked from Alice to Cam. "I'm worried about Jillian. And I'm not talking about her broken ankle."

❧

Jilly sprawled on the sofa in the Nelsons' cozy den, her cell phone pressed to her ear. "Hi, Therese, how's it going?"

"Jilly, I'm glad you called. How much longer before you can be back on the courts?"

Jilly clamped her teeth together. She couldn't make her circumstances sound too dire, or Therese would ask for her resignation on the spot. "I've had some complications with my ankle. It's going to take a little longer to heal than I expected."

"Oh, man." Therese drew out the words with a groan. "We are really hurting here. Paul is nowhere to be found, the sub we hired can never seem to get to work on time, and with summer here we've got a two-page waiting list of new students."

It felt great to be needed, but Jilly couldn't see any way to resolve Therese's dilemma. At least not in the foreseeable future. She focused on the first part of her boss's statement. "What happened with Paul?"

"I told you we had to suspend him because of those accusations." Therese huffed. "Now the cops want to question him, but it looks like he's skipped town."

"The cops? Why?"

"We're keeping a tight lid on it because we don't want the club's rep to suffer." Therese lowered her voice. "Jilly, they're saying Paul's kids were doing steroids, and the cops want to know if he was involved."

Jilly choked on a breath. "Steroids! Last time we talked, you said Paul had been accused of physical abuse."

"That's what we all thought at first. Then the cops dug deeper and ended up questioning three or four of Paul's students. Those families have since cancelled their club memberships, and I heard the kids have been permanently banned from their high-school tennis teams." Therese's voice dropped another notch. "Did you ever see *anything* suspicious, either on or off the courts?"

A sick feeling churned in Jilly's gut. The men's room. Her fall from the stepladder. The threatening phone calls.

A knock sounded on the outer door. "Jilly, you there?" Ralph's voice.

"Hold on a second, Therese." Jilly's brain felt like mush. She didn't need one more thing. "It's open, Ralph."

He appeared in the den doorway. "Sorry to interrupt, but you've got a visitor from Modesto."

While Jilly scrambled to process this information, a blond head appeared over Ralph's shoulder.

Paul!

She looked from the former Silverheels tennis coach to the cell phone in her left hand. Everything Therese had just told her raced through her mind. Paul missing. . .the cops. . .steroids. Half of her wanted to snap the phone shut and immediately dial 911. The other half remembered the one-time mixed-doubles partner who'd tracked her down two years ago to let her know about a women's tennis-pro opening at a new country club in Modesto.

She could believe Therese, or she could trust her instincts about her friend.

Or she could pray.

She squeezed her eyes shut. *Jesus, tell me what to do.*

She lifted the phone to her ear. "Therese, I'll have to call you back."

❧

The outer door clicked shut behind Ralph, and Jilly glared at the slump-shouldered man frowning back at her. "What are you doing here, and how did you know where to find me?"

"Therese suspended me. The cops are all over me. I didn't know where else to turn." Paul crossed the den and sank onto the edge of Harvey's sagging brown recliner. "You're the only person I could think of who knows beyond a doubt that I'd never use steroids, let alone push them on my students."

Jilly tapped her fingertips on her crossed arms. "Okay, that answered the first part of my question."

"I, uh, stalked your mailbox. Saw your landlady picking up your mail and readdressing it to forward."

"Paul—" Jilly started to chew him out about invasion of privacy until a new concern pricked her nerves. If Paul could so easily track her down—and if he really was innocent in the steroid scandal—then whoever had placed those threatening phone calls could locate her just as easily.

She reached for a glass of ice water on the end table and sipped slowly, trying to sort out her thoughts. "Okay," she began on a long exhalation, "tell me everything. Including what I walked in on in the men's room the day I broke my ankle."

Paul scraped a hand down his face. "I'd been suspicious for a couple of months that some of the boys were juicing. After class that day I followed them into the men's room, where I saw my prime suspect, Alex, doing some kind of deal with this other kid, Ted. Ted gave Alex some cash, and Alex handed Ted something that looked like a medicine vial. After Ted left, I confronted Alex, and that's when you walked in."

"Ted." Jilly released a whistling breath. "He's the guy who insisted I show him the Becker racquet."

"I'm so, so sorry, Jilly." He stared at her injured ankle and shook his head. "If I'd come forward sooner, I might have kept this from happening."

Images flashed through Jilly's thoughts—the men's room, the stepladder, the acne-faced kid. She raked her fingers through her hair in a vain attempt to untangle the confusion beneath her skull. "Why didn't you tell someone? Me. Therese. The cops. Why did you keep your suspicions to yourself?"

Paul lowered his chin to his chest. "Because of something else I didn't want anyone to find out about—especially you."

"Paul, we've been friends for years. What could be so bad that you didn't think you could tell me? So bad that you wouldn't report activity you *knew* was illegal?"

"Because I'm almost as guilty myself, and Alex knew about it." His voice fell to barely a whisper. "I'm fighting an addiction to pain pills."

A coldness seeped into Jilly's bones. Her gaze shifted sideways to the bottle of prescription pain relievers next to her water glass. "How? When?"

"Remember when I tore a shoulder muscle during our mixed-doubles game in the US Open qualifying round?"

Jilly nodded. "We were one game away from taking the match."

"Even after surgery and PT, the pain wouldn't go away. The doc tried to get me to wean off the pills, but hard as I've tried—more times than I can count—I haven't been able to kick them completely."

"So you've been getting them illegally?"

Paul's jaw muscles tensed. He flicked his gaze toward the floor. "Not *exactly*. I mean, I got legitimate doctors' prescriptions, but. . ." He gave a helpless shrug. "I won't bore you with the details."

Jilly had an overpowering urge to lunge off the sofa and pummel some sense into Paul's twisted brain. Only the bulky cast on her leg prevented it. She hugged her rib cage and took slow, deep breaths until she felt calm enough to speak. "Okay. What's done is done. But now you have to do the right thing. First, tell the cops everything you know about the steroids. Second, get yourself off those pain pills even if it means checking into rehab."

The macho tennis jock Jilly had known since college days vanished beneath

Paul's shame-faced expression. He sent her a timid half smile. "That's why I came looking for you, Jilly. I knew I could count on my best friend to hold me accountable."

"Oh, believe me, now that you've hauled me kicking and screaming into the middle of this mess, I certainly will."

❧

On Thursday morning Cam scanned the church library shelves in search of the Tozer book he planned to refer to during his next prayer retreat. "Evelyn," he called to the librarian, "I can't find *The Pursuit of God*."

"Sounds like a spiritual problem to me." The plump redhead chuckled as she tapped her computer keyboard.

"Hah. Leave the jokes to the pastor."

Evelyn, who also happened to be the pastor's wife, rolled her eyes. "Who do you think supplies his sermon material?"

Cam sauntered over to the desk and peered at Evelyn's computer monitor. She ran a finger down the onscreen list. "Sorry, Cam, the Tozer book is out on loan. Not due back for another week."

"Rats. The Bible college library didn't have any copies in either. Would you put my name on a waiting list and call me when it's returned?"

"Sure thing."

On his way to the parking lot, a lightness invaded Cam's steps. Hard as it had been to end things with Liz, he felt better about the decision with each passing day. And now, with nothing keeping him in town except a fat cat with litter box issues, he'd decided to return to the inn a day early for the next prayer retreat. Okay, so his reasons didn't entirely hinge upon enjoying the peaceful surroundings while he finished his preparations. Truth be told, he couldn't wait to see Jilly again.

And not simply out of concern for her state of mind.

No, ever since he'd picked her up at the Kansas City airport, she'd been inching her way into his heart. Or maybe expanding the portion he'd kept reserved for her all these years without even realizing it. A lot had happened in both their lives since they were kids. Unpredictable circumstances had sent them down vastly different paths. And yet here they were, together again and surely not by coincidence. Cam had to believe God had a hand in bringing Jilly back to Blossom Hills. And now, more than ever, he prayed he could help Jilly come to terms with her past and her future—and, God willing, convince her that her future could be right here with Cam.

Arriving at the inn, he parked the Mariner near the front entrance. He scooped up his soft-sided briefcase full of books and notes, looped his arm through the handle of a sack of bakery goodies, and grabbed his travel bag from the backseat. He jogged up the porch steps and peered through the beveled-glass doors, hoping Jilly wouldn't be at the front desk this time of day. She didn't expect him until tomorrow, and he wanted to surprise her.

No sign of her in the lobby. He slipped inside and listened. Voices drifted down the broad staircase—probably the housecleaning crew. The door to Harvey's office was open, and a quick glance told Cam Jilly wasn't working there either. If she obeyed doctor's orders—not to mention Harvey's and Cam's—she should be in the family quarters taking it easy.

He dropped his briefcase and travel bag by the front desk and started down the short corridor with the bag of baked goods. As he lifted his hand to knock on the door, a peal of laughter burst from the inn kitchen. He'd know Jilly's bubbly laugh anywhere, and the sound of it made his heart zing. He reversed direction and headed across the lobby.

As he neared the door to the kitchen, an unfamiliar male voice drew him up short. "And remember the time you backpedaled to go for that overhand smash and fell smack on top of the ball boy?"

"Poor kid was probably scarred for life." Jilly's voice shook with mirth.

"No kidding." The guy again. "Hey, are there any more of these macadamia nut cookies? They're great."

"The tall canister on the counter."

"Can I bring you anything?"

"Anything but those. You know me and macadamia nuts. How about a chocolate-chip from the other cookie jar?"

Cam peered around the door frame to see Jilly and a muscled blond guy nibbling on giant cookies. When the guy reached across the table to flick a crumb from Jilly's chin, Cam's stomach bottomed out.

He glanced down at the bag he carried. It contained a half-dozen apple fritters, the thick, doughy kind Jilly used to gorge herself on as a kid. His gut twisted. Suddenly Liz's bouts of jealousy seemed downright tame.

Chapter 12

Jilly slapped Paul's hand away from her chin. As she reached for a napkin, she glimpsed Cam standing in the doorway, and her breath snagged. Her mouth spread into a surprised grin. "Hey, guy! Guess we were talking and laughing so much that I didn't hear the door chime. What are you doing here? Did I get my days mixed up?"

"Decided to come out a day early." His voice carried an unpleasant edge. The look on his face made Jilly's stomach tighten.

Paul rose and stepped around the table. "Just a wild guess. You must be Cameron Lane." He thrust out his hand. "I'm Paul Edgar. Jilly's been talking about you ever since I got here."

"Paul. Jilly's told me about you, too." Cam stared at Paul's outstretched hand a microsecond longer than seemed polite. When he finally took it, his jaw knotted. He glanced toward Jilly, confusion narrowing his eyes.

Of course. Unless Cam had talked to Harvey since last night, he'd be wondering why Paul had shown up here, especially after Jilly had shared her suspicions about the men's room incident and the threatening calls. And if he'd been standing there very long, he had to have heard them laughing together as if nothing was wrong.

She positioned the walker in front of her and pushed off the chair. "Finish your cookie, Paul. I'll just go get Cam checked in."

Cam waved stiff fingers. "No rush."

"It's okay. I could use the walker practice." She started for the door. As she passed Cam, a whiff of something sweet and delicious filled her nostrils. Childhood memories burst upon her brain like a bite into a tender, juicy baked apple.

Fritters! She flipped her head around and spied the small white bag Cam carried, definitely the source of the tantalizing aroma. She grinned at Cam, then nodded toward the bag. "Anything in there for me?"

"As a matter of fact." The rigid lines around his mouth slowly eased. "I was driving by Ruth Hartford's bakery and out of the blue it came to me that you used to love apple fritters."

"Still do. Ruth Hartford, the lady from your first retreat?"

"Yep. Her daughter runs the bakery now. You remember Ruth?"

Jilly grimaced. "Hard to forget someone who kept trying to. . ." *Okay, let's stop right there.* No sense embarrassing herself further with reference to the Hartfords' utterly unsubtle attempts at matchmaking.

She edged behind the front desk and scooted onto the barstool, then shoved the walker aside and reached for a registration card. "One deluxe suite for Mr. Lane."

Cam chuckled. "Since when do I rate the deluxe suite?"

"Since you brought me apple fritters, naturally." Jilly handed him a room key and smiled up expectantly.

He slid the bag toward her with a lopsided grin that turned her insides doughy. "All yours, Miss Gardner."

Glancing toward the kitchen, Jilly remembered Paul. Her smile faded as she looked up at Cam. "I guess you're wondering what Paul's doing here."

He leaned his elbows on the counter and tipped his head in the direction of the kitchen. His face hardened again. "So what's the deal?"

Jilly slid a fritter out of the bag and broke it in half. "Here, share this with me and I'll explain."

❧

Steroids. Cam's gut clenched. The three bites of apple fritter he'd swallowed rose on a wave of bile. He wanted to feel relief that Paul Edgar was only a friend, not a serious romantic interest for Jilly. He wanted to thank God for saving Jilly from anything more serious than a broken ankle because of Paul's stupidity and cowardice.

But all he could think about was Terrance. All he could see was Terrance's swollen, acne-pitted face. All he could hear were his mother's terrified sobs when she discovered her younger son dead in their basement rec room, the result of a steroid-induced heart attack.

And Jilly was taking Paul Edgar's side. She'd given him a room here at the inn. She'd sat there in the kitchen, laughing with him and eating cookies as if Paul's turning a blind eye to steroid use and abusing oxycodone were no big deal.

"Cam?" Jilly's concerned voice sliced through his angry thoughts. "Cam, you look furious. What's wrong?"

"What's *wrong*?" His knotted fist beat a slow rhythm on the countertop. He slid his gaze toward the kitchen, then whipped it back to Jilly. "What's wrong is you're harboring a criminal and acting like it's perfectly fine."

Jilly stiffened. "It is *not* perfectly fine. And for the record, Paul is not a criminal. He's a friend, and I'm trying to help him. Harvey gave me the name of a lawyer who can get Paul straight with the Modesto police. And in the meantime," she continued with a huff, "I was hoping my other friend—namely you—might have some professional contacts who could help Paul get off the drugs."

Her pointed words bled off some of Cam's anger. He scrubbed the back of his head. "Sorry, I overreacted."

"No, you didn't. I know where you're coming from." She dipped her chin. Her voice dropped a notch. "Last night Harvey told me about Terrance. Cam, I'm so sorry. I never realized his death was due to steroid abuse."

"My parents did their best to keep it quiet. Not many people knew." *But I should have. I was his big brother, closer to him than anyone. If only I'd recognized the signs, I could have done something.*

Jilly's tone softened even more. She reached across the counter to touch his elbow. "Harvey says you've never really gotten over it."

The feel of her fingertips drew his entire focus. His lungs refused to function. He didn't want to think about Terrance or Paul or the prayer retreat. "Jilly, I—"

"Hey, y'all." Paul.

Great timing. Cam jerked his arm off the counter and turned to face the blond tennis jock. He struggled for an impassive expression.

"Sorry, didn't mean to interrupt." Paul stuffed his hands into his jeans pockets. "There's a delivery guy at the kitchen entrance asking where to put stuff."

"Oh, boy." Jilly hopped off the barstool and grabbed her walker. "That's the food for this weekend. And Heather left early today because of a dentist appointment."

Cam pulled himself together and started for the kitchen. "I can get there faster than you. What do I tell the guy?"

"Cold stuff in the fridge, everything else on the table. I'm right behind you to help put it all away."

"I can help, too." Paul jogged up beside Cam. "Might as well make myself useful."

Cam cut him a sidelong glance. Behind them, Cam heard the chimes as someone entered through the front door. He paused to see a young couple breeze in with luggage in tow. They approached Jilly just as she rounded the front desk.

"Oh, you must be the Wyatts. Your room's all ready." Jilly waved Cam on. "Be there in a few minutes. I need to get these folks checked in."

Cam nodded and continued to the kitchen. He showed the deliveryman where to put things, then got started sorting the groceries. Paul pitched in, doing a fair job of figuring out what went where, considering the muscle-bound, drug-addicted jerk probably knew his way around a tennis court way better than a kitchen.

Get a grip, Lane. Give the guy the benefit of the doubt, why don't you? For Jilly's sake if for no other reason.

Paul shifted a ten-pound bag of rice from one hand to the other. "I take it Jilly filled you in on my situation?"

"Yep." Cam studied the label on a jar of Kalamata olives. *"Serving size, 5 olives. Calories per serving, 45." Might need to know that someday.*

"I never meant to get her involved. It's just. . .I didn't know where else to go."

"Right. Since you're friends and all." Garbanzo beans. *"Total carbs, 45 grams. Dietary fiber, 12 grams." Important stuff on product labels.*

"I just want you to know, I'm gonna get clean and get this mess straightened out."

"Good." Cam tucked several jars and cans between his forearms and chest and stalked to the pantry.

"She's crazy about you, by the way."

Four cans of garbanzo beans hit the tile floor with an ear-splitting crash.

❧

"What on earth is going on in here?" Jilly hobbled over to where Cam stood amid a tumble of dented vegetable cans.

"I. . .uh. . ."

"Dropped something. Yeah, I noticed." She tried to read the look on his face. He seemed a lot more shook up than he should be after dropping a few bean cans. "You okay?"

"Here, let me." Paul rushed over and started grabbing up cans. "Didn't drop any on your foot, did you? That would hurt."

"No. No, I'm fine." Cam stepped over a can and shoved an olive jar onto the pantry shelf. He turned and stared at Jilly as if he wanted to say something but couldn't figure out how.

Paul ducked past Cam and set the cans in the pantry. "I should go give that lawyer another call. Hopefully he's talked to the Modesto police by now." Seconds later he vanished in the direction of the lobby.

A kitchen chair sat nearby. Jilly scooted toward it and plopped down with a groan. "Cam, if you're going to give me another chewing-out about trusting Paul—"

"That's not it." Cam lifted his hands in a helpless gesture before sinking onto the chair facing her. He sighed. Laced and unlaced his fingers.

Jilly tried to be patient and let him find whatever words he searched for, but his edginess had her worried. Did he have something else to get off his chest, maybe something more about how his brother died? She couldn't believe she'd never known Terrance had OD'd on steroids. Poor Cam, carrying that grief all these years, and then to be confronted with the issue all over again when Paul showed up—

"Did Harvey say anything to you about Liz and me?"

The question blew through her brain like a sudden gust of wind. "What?"

"I said, did Harvey—"

"I heard the question. I'm just trying to change gears here." Jilly rubbed her temple. As his words penetrated, her stomach somersaulted, then plummeted to her toes. Cam and Liz were getting married. What else could it be? He'd thought things through, gotten over his commitment phobia, and popped the question.

Disappointment assaulted her. Disappointment she had no right to feel.

She willed her mouth into some semblance of a smile and blinked away a sudden spurt of tears. "Oh, Cam, I'm so happy for you. Sorry, these allergies. . ." She groped for a tissue in her pocket and blew her nose. "Have you set the date? I bet that little boy is so excited to be getting a new dad."

It slowly dawned on her that Cam was staring open-mouthed, one eyebrow arched as if she'd grown two heads. He straightened, his lips twisting into a crooked grin. "What are you talking about?"

"You and Liz. Isn't that what—" His bemused expression told her they'd experienced a major disconnect. She wadded the tissue and dabbed away the trickle beneath her left eye. "You and Liz, you're not engaged?"

"How many ways do I have to tell you? There is nothing between Liz and me." He took her hand in his and inched closer. His tone mellowed. "I thought Harvey might have told you already. Liz and I are no longer seeing each other. It's over."

His touch seared her palm. Her voice squeaked out. "Over?"

"As much as anything that never really amounted to much can be called *over*." His thumb raked across her knuckles. He kept his eyes lowered. "Jilly, I'm feeling like there could be something between you and me. Am I crazy?"

Surely he could hear her thudding heart, feel the pulse throbbing beneath his fingertips. Words log-jammed in her throat. Any second now her chest would explode.

He lifted hazel eyes full of questions. "Jilly?"

He'd spoken the words she'd imagined hearing from his lips almost since the day he hefted her luggage off the carousel at the Kansas City airport—since she was a string-bean preteen with a king-size crush, if truth be told. A fizzy, fuzzy sensation swirled around her head. "I feel something for you, too, Cam. I just didn't think we had a chance."

"Because of Liz?"

"Liz. . .and a whole lot of other things." Like the fact that she hadn't planned on sticking around Blossom Hills indefinitely. Like the fact that she couldn't let go of the hope of rehabilitating her ankle and resuming her tennis career, or at least coaching if she never made it back on the pro circuit.

"I know I've kind of sprung this on you." Cam's knee brushed hers. "But I was hoping we could see where things go."

She sighed. Maybe she should stop worrying about the future and enjoy the possibilities of *now*. "Yeah. I think I'd like that."

❧

He'd like to cancel the prayer retreat this weekend and spend some time alone with Jilly. Unfortunately, five couples from the young marrieds Sunday school class would show up in less than four hours.

Last night had been interesting. The couple who'd arrived at the same time as the grocery delivery turned out to be newlyweds on their honeymoon trip. As the inn's only midweek guests, they earned special attention, including a candlelight dinner served by Heather, followed by dessert and coffee on the deck as the sun set behind the hills. They concluded their evening with a moonlight row across the lake, courtesy of Ralph wearing a cheesy black-and-white-striped gondolier's outfit.

Cam and Jilly had secretly watched from the office window until Harvey arrived and chided them for spying. His harangue held little bite, however.

The glint in his eye suggested he rather liked the idea of Cam and Jilly sharing the romantic view.

Cam rather liked it himself.

And he liked the view before him this morning. Jilly sat on her barstool behind the front desk, a half-eaten apple in one hand, a ballpoint pen flicking back and forth in the other. She bent over a checklist of some sort, probably something to do with the retreat guests. A pretty pout pushed out her lower lip. Her tongue flicked out to catch a dribble of apple juice.

She looked up suddenly and smiled. "How long have you been standing there?"

"Long enough to wish I could break free from the group this evening and borrow Ralph's gondolier shirt."

"Oh? And why's that?"

"So I could row you across the lake, and we could watch the stars together."

A sultry laugh burbled from Jilly's throat. Using the end of the pen, she tucked that curvy lock of hair behind her ear. "Mr. Lane. You've been spending too much time around our honeymooners."

"Since they're staying through the weekend, I was thinking about inviting them to join the retreat. What do you think?"

She arched an eyebrow. "I hope you're kidding."

"What, you don't think they'd go for the idea?" He feigned a disbelieving frown.

The couple in question strolled in the back door. Jilly shot Cam a warning glance before greeting the newlyweds. "How was your hike? Did you find the waterfall I told you about?"

"It was gorgeous," the new Mrs. Wyatt answered. "We considered getting lost up there, but James was too worried about missing lunch." She flicked a starry-eyed, if somewhat frustrated, glance at her groom.

"That chef of yours is amazing." James's face seemed to have frozen in the permanent grin of a typical honeymooner. He gazed lovingly at his wife. "Allison, maybe you could ask Heather for some pointers."

The remark earned him a slug to the solar plexus. Forget the prayer retreat—this couple might be better served by some preemptive marriage counseling.

"Don't worry, you're back in plenty of time for lunch." Jilly reached for a note by the phone. "Oh, and I confirmed your dinner theater reservation for this evening. Doors open at seven, so you'll want to leave here no later than six fifteen."

"Great, thanks." James slid his arm around Allison's waist. "How long until lunch?"

Jilly checked her watch. "At least forty-five minutes. In the meantime, there's fresh iced tea and appetizers around the corner in the lounge."

The Wyatts smiled and excused themselves. Cam noticed they bypassed the lounge entrance and went straight upstairs.

Yep, honeymooners.

He stole a glance at Jilly. Could she ever love him like that? Did she wonder, as he did, if their mutual attraction could someday lead to a lifetime commitment?

Chapter 13

At the sound of voices, Jilly looked up from the office computer to see Cam leading his retreat group through the lobby. They'd just finished lunch, and for their afternoon session Ralph had set up extra chairs on the deck. Two of the wives were visibly pregnant, which meant sprawling on blankets under the trees was out of the question. Not to mention the necessity of a ladies' room nearby.

Jilly chuckled, but as she heard them step through the back door onto the deck, a subtle urging tugged at her heart. Cam had told her several times she was welcome to sit in on any of his sessions, but until now she'd resisted. She and God still had a few issues to work out.

Fingertips fidgeting on the computer keyboard, she watched the couples find seats around the circle. The fathers-to-be took the less comfortable plastic deck chairs, helping their wives into the adirondacks. A couple of the other guys sparred good-naturedly for a mesh lounge. The huskier of the two finally won out. Jilly hoped the mesh would hold him.

Cam started speaking, his words muffled by the window glass. The tug in Jilly's spirit grew stronger. She hopped around to the other side of the desk and eased open the sash.

". . .so what I'd like to focus on this afternoon," Cam was saying, "is how our prayer life is directly affected by how we see God. If you think of Him as judge or lawgiver, your approach in prayer is going to be much different from the person who looks to God as a loving Father."

"I know what you're saying," one of the wives said. "My dad died when I was very young, so I didn't grow up with a strong father figure. It took years before I could think of God as a Father who loved me unconditionally."

Jilly scooted onto the corner of the desk. Yeah, she could relate. She had no idea who her real father was. Her birth certificate listed him as "unknown," and information she'd gleaned from case workers suggested any one of her mother's several male acquaintances could have been her father, none of whom seemed worthy of the title.

As for her mother, she'd never managed to stay off the booze long enough to figure out this whole parenting thing. Eventually a social worker convinced her to terminate her parental rights.

Jilly returned her attention to the conversation outside as one of the husbands said, "I didn't become a Christian until a couple of years ago. Not really, anyway. My parents always took me to church, but the preacher was one of those fire-and-brimstone types. Scared me so bad, I wanted nothing to do with Christianity." He draped an arm around his pregnant wife's shoulders.

"At least until Kathy got hold of me and helped me see God in a new light."

Jilly could thank Harvey and Alice for showing her what genuine parental love really was. And for teaching her about the love of God. A pained sigh rippled through her chest. If only she'd trusted them. If only she'd trusted God. She might have spared herself and the Nelsons a decade of heartache.

Paul sidled into the office. "Hey, Jilly, you busy?"

"Just checking on the group outside." She closed the window and swiveled to face him. "What's up?"

"Needed somebody to talk to." He collapsed into a chair, hands knotted between his knees. His futile efforts to stifle the withdrawal tremors tore at Jilly's heart.

She edged around the desk and settled into her chair. "You staying off the pain meds?"

"Yeah, but it's tough. Man, I don't know if I can do this." He exhaled sharply. His glance moved to the pill bottle next to Jilly's water glass. A hungry look flattened his lips. "Be careful with those, that's all I can say."

"Believe me, I am." She'd already cut back on the dose as much as she could bear. Enduring a little discomfort now seemed far preferable to fighting addiction later. She slid her hand toward the pill bottle and swept it into the desk drawer. Out of sight, out of mind. *Maybe.* "Try to hang in there until Monday. Cam promised he'd take you to get help."

"Yeah. So talk to me. Please." Paul inched lower in the chair, nervous fingers drumming on his thighs. Sweat beaded his upper lip. "Tell me more about this Cam guy. He seems cool."

"Like I told you, he's an old friend from when I grew up here."

"That line didn't fool me the first time you used it, and I'm not buying it today. You two have a whole lot more than friendship going on."

Jilly snatched up a pen and doodled on a scratch pad. "Maybe. But we're taking time to get to know each other again."

Paul sprang from the chair and paced between the desk and a row of filing cabinets. "What's he gonna do when you go back to Modesto? Long-distance relationships are the pits."

An imaginary knife blade carved a hole in Jilly's midsection. Since her fall down the deck steps she'd been trying not to think too far ahead. Part of her desperately hoped a few months of rehabilitation would put her back on the tennis courts, at least in some capacity. Another part—a part that grew stronger each day—made her want to wrap her arms around Cameron Lane and never let go.

Couldn't she have it both ways? *God, are You listening?*

Paul halted in front of her and jammed his hands into his pockets. He nodded toward the window. "So what's with all this prayer stuff? You think it does any good?"

Jilly's head popped up. *Did she?* "I'd like to believe it does."

"Cam seems like a smart guy." Paul began pacing again. He drew the back of his hand across his mouth. "He told me last night I should ask God to help me through this. So after I went up to my room, I sorta prayed. At least I think I was praying. Never really tried it before."

A funny, tickly feeling started under Jilly's breastbone—a twinge of conviction mixed with exhilaration. She pulled her walker closer and stood. "You know, I'm a bit rusty in the prayer department, too. How about we go sit in on Cam's afternoon session?"

❧

"Before we move on, does anyone else—" Cam twisted his head around at the sound of footsteps and the unmistakable *clunk-creak* of Jilly's walker.

"Sorry to interrupt." Jilly cast him a sheepish grin. "Paul and I thought we'd join you if it's okay."

"Sure." Cam stood to enlarge the circle and drew up a couple more chairs. He made sure Jilly took the one immediately to his left, although when his pulse kicked into a higher gear, he gave serious thought to the wisdom of having her so close.

He cleared his throat and took his seat. "Everyone, you remember Jilly. She's the gal who checked you in yesterday. And this is her friend Paul Edgar."

"Hi again, Jilly," said Roy, the man on Cam's right. "How long have you and Cam been married?"

The turkey wrap Cam had for lunch sprouted feathers and wings. A quick glance in Jilly's direction revealed a blush creeping up her neck.

One of the pregnant ladies caught Cam's eye and winked. "Obviously Roy and Cheryl are new at Covenant. Cam is a confirmed bachelor."

"Yikes, my bad." Roy grimaced. "I just assumed from the way you two were making eyes at each other at dinner last night. . ."

His wife nudged him. "Honey, you're embarrassing them."

"A*hem*." Cam doused the flames heating his own face with a swig from his water bottle. He plopped open his Bible. "Let's get back on topic, shall we?"

Doing so proved more challenging than he'd expected. . .or maybe not. While he attempted to steer the discussion toward various forms of prayer, he found himself continually distracted by Paul's fidgeting. The poor guy would cross one leg, then the other, twiddle his thumbs, rake fingers through his hair. The other couples grew more and more unfocused, as well.

Finally Jilly reached over and rested a hand on Paul's arm, holding it there until he stilled. "Maybe this wasn't such a good idea," she whispered. "Cam, I'm sorry. We shouldn't have intruded."

A still, small voice told Cam otherwise. "No, stay. I'm glad you joined us. Paul, would you mind if I tell the group a little more about you?" With his eyes he tried to convey his intention to be tactful.

Paul's knees jumped up and down. "Okay, I guess."

Addressing the group, Cam said, "Without going into details, let me just say Paul is struggling with a substance abuse problem. I only met him a couple of days ago, so we really don't know each other. What I do know is that he came here because he knew he could count on his friend Jilly for help, which plays right into the whole subject of prayer. Christ is the one true friend we can always turn to, whatever problems we face."

A chorus of murmured responses sounded throughout the circle: "Amen." "So true."

"And just as we approach our heavenly Father in various ways—through the Psalms, intercessory prayer, thanksgiving, worship—we need to be open to the different ways He comes to us. One very tangible way is through other human beings, imperfect as they are." Cam shifted his gaze to Jilly and offered a gentle smile. "Sometimes the answer to a prayer is as near as the friend sitting next to us."

❧

By the time the session ended, Jilly couldn't wait to get back inside. Despite the pleasant warmth of the afternoon sun, something in the air had completely blocked her sinuses and turned her eyelids into sandpaper. The package with her allergy prescription had yet to arrive, and every time she thought to call Denise to ask about it, something else distracted her.

While Paul went to the kitchen for a caffeine hit, she hurried to her room—as much of a hurry as she could manage with the walker—and pawed through her purse in search of her cell phone. She carried it across the hall to the den and sank into Harvey's recliner, then flipped open the phone and scrolled for Denise's number.

Moments later her landlady answered. "Jilly! Are you still in Missouri? How are you?"

"A little worse for wear. I hurt my ankle again and had to have surgery."

"Oh, honey, how'd you do that?"

"Long story. I'll tell you later." Jilly reached for a tissue and dabbed her drippy nose. "What I really need is my allergy meds. Did they ever come?"

"I found the package on your doorstep just yesterday. I took it straight to the UPS store to have it forwarded."

"Thank goodness!" Jilly whooshed out a thankful breath.

"Looks like it got lost in transit somewhere. The box was pretty beat-up."

"At least it's on its way. Everything else okay there?"

"Finally got my new sprinkler system installed. Oh, and I'm thinking about getting a burglar alarm. The neighborhood watch committee sent out a flyer the other day about possible prowlers."

An unexplained niggling started at the base of Jilly's neck. Then she remembered Paul had found out where Jilly was by watching her mailbox. She'd have to rag him about getting her neighbors all riled up. With a casual laugh, she said, "Our neighborhood has always been very safe. I'm sure they're just being overly cautious."

"Maybe. But Stanley next door told me he's seen suspicious-looking vehicles cruising the block. As single women we can't be too careful."

"I guess not." No point in saying anything about Paul. His mailbox snooping may have been unlawful but no real harm had been done.

"So when do you think you'll be home, honey?"

Jilly squeezed her itchy eyes shut and exhaled through tense lips. "I don't know how to tell you this, Denise, but I'm not even sure I'm coming back to Modesto. At least not to stay."

Denise gasped. "Why ever not?"

As Jilly explained about her fall down the deck steps and the depressing prognosis concerning her future in tennis, her eyes brimmed with tears. "It was the job at Silverheels that brought me to Modesto in the first place. If I can't continue coaching, I'm seriously considering staying here in Blossom Hills."

"I know you have family there and all, but I'd sure miss you."

Family. Yes indeed, Jilly had family here, and the reminder brought renewed comfort. *Thank You, Lord.* "I'd miss you, too, Denise. You've been a great friend and a wonderful landlady." She sucked in a quick breath. "But nothing's settled yet. By summer's end I should have a better idea about my plans."

"All right then. I'll keep forwarding your mail. Do stay in touch, though."

"I will, I promise."

As they said their good-byes, a knock sounded on the outer door. Jilly clicked her phone shut. "It's open. Come on in."

The squeak of rubber-soled sneakers sounded in the hall, followed by Cam's appearance in the den doorway. "You okay? I could tell your allergies were kicking in big-time out there."

"I'm out of meds. My landlady finally forwarded my prescription yesterday, but of course it'll be a few more days before it gets here."

Cam propped a hip against the door frame. "Isn't there anything over the counter you can take?"

"Nothing works as well as my prescription."

"Why don't you call your doctor and have him phone in something to a pharmacy here? Harvey could pick it up on his way home from visiting Alice."

Jilly brightened momentarily, then her shoulders drooped. "It's Saturday. The doctor's office won't even be open."

"He has a service, doesn't he? When you explain your situation, I'm sure they can get a prescription called in."

Jilly reached for her cell phone again. "I'll need to give them a pharmacy number. Got any recommendations?"

A frown flickered across Cam's face. He shrugged. "I always use Riley's. One of the pharmacists there goes to my church. And it would be on Harvey's way from the rehab hospital."

"Okay, I'm desperate enough to try anything." She sniffled and blew her nose while Cam jotted the number on the back of a magazine she handed him. Interesting that he knew a pharmacy number so well he didn't have to look it up. Cam didn't look the type to have that many health problems.

The doctor's answering service promised to have someone return her call within the hour. She cradled the phone in her lap and smiled up at Cam. "Wish I'd thought of this days ago. With any luck I'll be breathing again by evening."

"Great. Breathing is always a good thing." His eyes softened, and Jilly's heart rate kicked up a notch.

She crumpled her damp tissue. "Don't you need to get back to your retreat?"

"We're taking a thirty-minute break. I was worried about you."

"I'm fine. I'm just going to sit here with my feet up for a while and maybe try a cool washcloth on these allergy eyes." Wow. She must look really appealing with her drippy nose and swollen lids.

"Here, let me." Cam scurried to the bathroom and returned with a damp cloth. "Want a pillow under your ankle? Need some water? A soda?"

"Please, I'm not an—" She started to say *invalid*. All right, so she basically was one. She gave a self-conscious laugh and allowed herself to wallow in the attention as Cam helped her get settled. "Careful there, you could spoil a girl with this kind of treatment."

He grinned. "I aim to please."

Chapter 14

Of all the weekends Cam had to schedule a prayer retreat, why did it have to be this one? Surrounded by all these happily married young couples gushing over each other, all he could think about was Jilly. When he'd left her earlier, with that cast on her ankle, her eyes practically swollen shut, and a red nose to rival Rudolph's, she'd looked so enticingly vulnerable. He'd like to send the retreat couples packing—or maybe up to their rooms for some married R & R—and spend the rest of the weekend taking care of Jilly.

The last session of the afternoon finally wrapped up, and Cam followed the couples down the broad staircase from the second-floor conference room. As he crossed the lobby, Harvey swept in through the back door.

"Hey, Cam, how's our girl? I picked up the meds from Riley's."

Cam signaled his group into the dining room, where spicy garlic and tomato aromas beckoned. *Hope the couples packed mouthwash.* "Last time I checked, Jilly was taking a nap in your recliner. Probably the best thing for her right now."

"Poor thing. Always did have a terrible time with hay fever. I'd hoped—"

The front door burst open, and a UPS delivery person strode to the front desk. "Got an overnight package for a Ms. Jillian Gardner, care of the Dogwood Blossom Inn."

Harvey set the pharmacy bag on the desk and stepped forward. "That's my daughter. I'll take it."

Admiration warmed Cam's chest. Harvey hadn't hesitated for even a second. Jilly *was* his daughter in every way that counted.

The UPS man handed Harvey a small box, tapped some keys on his handheld tracking computer, and scurried out.

Cam peered over Harvey's shoulder at the shipping label. "Denise Moran from Modesto—that's Jilly's landlady, isn't it? Maybe it's the prescription Jilly was waiting on. She didn't think it would get here before next week."

Harvey chuckled. "Good, then she ought to be well stocked for a while. That Liz gal at Riley's personally made sure the prescription was ready and waiting when I got there."

Cam's stomach clenched. "Liz was working today?"

"Said she recognized Jillian's name when the doctor's call came in." Harvey tucked both packages under his arm. "Best get these to Jillian. The sooner she gets her medicine down, the faster she'll start feeling better."

Watching Harvey disappear through the door to the family quarters, Cam could only imagine Liz's awkwardness at having to handle Jilly's prescription. He still felt horrible for the pain he caused Liz with the breakup. She was a good person, a good mother, and she didn't deserve to be hurt. But neither did she—nor Sammy—deserve the false hope of a future that simply wasn't going to happen.

❧

On Monday morning, Jilly stood before the bathroom mirror and inhaled through a completely clear nose. Man, it felt good to breathe again! She glanced at the two prescription bottles sitting side by side on the counter. That Denise—what an angel for going to the trouble and expense of overnight shipping. Jilly had noted the cost on the shipping label, and first thing Sunday morning she wrote out a check and a heartfelt thank-you note to mail to her landlady.

"Jillian, you up?"

"'Morning, Harvey. Come on in."

"Thought I heard you stirring around." Harvey leaned in the bathroom doorway and grinned at her reflection in the mirror. "Cam's in the lobby with Paul. They're ready to head to town anytime. You still planning on going along?"

"I'll be ready in a sec. And once we get Paul set up with a rehab counselor, I'd like to visit Alice."

"She'll be so glad to see you. Tell her I'll be by later this afternoon."

Jilly ran a comb through her hair and applied some lip gloss, then grabbed her walker and followed Harvey out to the lobby.

"Hey, gorgeous." Cam ambled over and tucked a strand of her hair behind her ear, his touch raising goose bumps on her neck. "I can actually see those big brown eyes of yours this morning."

Jilly snickered. "And I can actually see out of them."

"I parked near the front steps. Are you sure you can manage them okay with that contraption?"

"Are you kidding? I'm getting to be an old pro." She wouldn't admit that the hardest part of going anywhere was maneuvering the stupid walker. But what choice did she have, other than plopping her rear into a wheelchair and allowing someone else to chauffeur her around? The walker may be cumbersome, but at least it spared her bruised ribs while giving her a semblance of independence.

Although, when she looked into Cam's warm gaze, independence seemed slightly overrated. Which was why she didn't argue when he suggested they bring the wheelchair along "just in case."

Within the hour, they sat with Paul in the waiting room of New Life Addiction Recovery Center. Jilly didn't like what she saw in Paul's face. Even though the lawyer had gotten Paul off the hook with the Modesto police, four days off the pain pills had left him shaky and pale. He edged lower in the gray tweed chair and leaned his head against the wall.

Jilly reached across the magazine-strewn side table and touched his arm. "It's going to be okay. Hang in there."

Paul slid bloodshot eyes in her direction and gave a weak nod.

An inner door opened and a stocky, bearded man stepped through. "Come on back, Paul. I'm Ed Huttar. I'll be your counselor."

A glimmer of panic widened Paul's eyes. He stood and groped for Jilly's hand. "Keep saying those prayers for me, okay? That's all that's holding me together right now."

"You bet." Jilly pulled herself up with her walker and gave Paul a reassuring smile before he trudged through the door with the counselor.

Cam tucked an arm around her shoulder. "I've known Ed for years. Paul couldn't be in better hands."

"It just hurts to see Paul go through this. I've known him for years, too."

"Like he said, we'll keep praying for him." He gave her shoulder a squeeze and started for the exit. "You ready to visit Alice?"

She blew out a noisy breath and pushed the walker forward. "Let's go."

❧

Jilly and Cam arrived at the rehab hospital in time to watch Alice complete the cooldown portion of her cardiac exercise class. Her face glowed with renewed health as she grinned at them from the treadmill. A nurse beckoned Alice over to a chair and gave her a few minutes to rest before taking a blood pressure reading.

"Looking good, Mrs. Nelson. You're free until after lunch." The nurse turned to a computer to type in some information.

Rising, Alice gave an exaggerated sigh. "*Free* is a relative term around here. Real freedom is when you let me go home."

The nurse laughed. "At the rate you're improving, I'm sure that'll be very soon."

Alice reached for a towel and patted the beads of perspiration from her forehead as she worked her way between the rows of treadmills and exercise bikes to reach Jilly and Cam. "Aren't you two a welcome sight? Want to join me for some fruit juice?"

"Love to." Waves of warmth bathed Jilly's limbs as she leaned across the walker to receive Alice's hug. How she'd missed the firm grip of those arms, the caress of a mother's cheek.

Her throat tightened on a choked sob. She sniffed back unexpected tears.

"Honey?" Alice drew back, brows knitted. "What is it?"

Jilly thumbed away the wetness beneath her eyes. "Nothing, nothing at all."

Her gaze still on Jilly, Alice tucked her arm beneath Cam's. "Cam, the snack bar is just down the hall. Would you be a sweetie and go fetch us some drinks?"

Cam shot Jilly a worried look of his own. "Sure, Alice, glad to. What would you like?"

"I could go for a cranberry juice. How about you, Jilly?"

She shrugged. "Sounds fine."

Alice pointed Cam in the direction of the snack bar and said they'd meet him in the atrium. As they started toward the corridor, she murmured something else to Cam that Jilly couldn't hear.

Falling into step beside Alice, she matched the older woman's shuffling pace—not difficult to do with the cumbersome walker. "Care to tell me what that was all about?"

Alice cast her an achingly familiar smile of understanding. "Just told him to take his time. Thought maybe you could use some woman-to-woman talk."

A shiver started in Jilly's belly. It wasn't merely woman-to-woman conversation she needed. What she craved was motherly advice.

In the atrium they found a quiet corner near a potted palm. Jilly sank onto a bamboo love seat with hibiscus-print cushions and shoved the walker to one side.

Alice nudged a footstool over for Jilly's ankle, then settled next to her, tucking one leg under the other in a girlish pose. "Now tell me, how's my girl? How are you *really* doing, honey?"

"Oh, Alice, I'm confused about so many things. My whole life is one big mess."

Alice enfolded Jilly's hand in her own. "I know Harvey and I had a lot to do with your confusion. I'm so terribly sorry for the pain we've caused you."

"Now that I know the truth about why you didn't adopt me, I. . .well, I'm doing my best to understand."

"And do you understand that you truly are our daughter? Always have been and always will be?" Alice's grip tightened. Her voice grew firm with resolve. "No judge's decree or adoption certificate could make us love you any more than we already do."

"I know that now. I guess I've always known it deep inside—in here." Jilly touched her breastbone and blinked back tears.

Alice flicked away a trickle from her own cheek. "Then you forgive us?"

"Of course I do." A ragged sigh tore through Jilly's throat. "I'm just so sorry for the lost years."

They shared a long, healing hug, then chuckled at each other's weepiness. Jilly composed herself with a slow, deep breath. "Wow, I haven't cried this much in I don't know how long."

"You never were one to give in to tears. Always so brave and stoic."

"Yeah, and look where that got me." Jilly flicked her hair away from her face. "I think that's part of why I'm so confused lately. I don't know what to do with all these emotions."

Alice offered a shy smile. "And do any of these emotions have to do with a certain young man of our acquaintance?"

"If you mean Cam, then. . .yes." Jilly shuddered and tucked her hands between her knees. "Alice, I'm terrified. Even before a major tournament I was never this nervous."

"But what's to be afraid of? It's pretty clear he's smitten with you, too." Alice quirked a brow. "Has been since you were kids, if I'm any judge of true love."

At the word *love*, Jilly jerked her head around. "Do you think so?"

"I do."

"But I was so flaky then, a self-centered tennis brat."

Alice chuckled. "I'm pretty sure that isn't the way Cam saw you."

"Well, at least I'm not naive little Jillian Gardner anymore." Regret congested her throat. "I wanted so much to be someone different, so badly that after I left for college, I even quit going by the name Jillian."

"And I understand why." Alice patted her arm. "But who you are is not dependent on what name you're called. It's who you believe yourself to be. It's who God created you to be."

Thoughts of romance temporarily banished, Jilly stared at the cast on her ankle as her entire tennis career played out across the stage of her mind. Without tennis, who was she, really? A washed-up has-been. A nobody. How could this possibly be what God created her to be?

❧

Cam paused in the atrium entrance, his heart thudding at the sight of Jilly's forlorn expression. He glanced at the tray of drinks he carried and considered ducking down the corridor to give Jilly and Alice a few more minutes alone.

Then Alice caught his eye and signaled him over. Disguising his concern with a casual grin, he sauntered in and set the drink tray on a glass-top coffee table. "Cranberry juice for the ladies and a decaf for me."

"Why, thank you, Cam." Alice winked. "I hope you didn't get lost in the maze of hallways."

"Nope. Thought I'd take the scenic route." He perched on the edge of a chair across from them. Passing them their drinks, he cast Jilly a questioning look.

She quirked one corner of her mouth and shrugged before taking a sip of juice.

Alice tipped her head in Jilly's direction. "Our girl's a wee bit perplexed about what the future holds."

Cam had a few ideas of his own about Jilly's future. It took all his willpower not to claim her in his arms right now and tell her so. Instead, he scooted deeper into the chair and wrapped his hands around the warm cardboard sleeve of his coffee cup. "I could give you that trite saying about how we don't know what the future holds, but we can trust the One who holds our future—"

Jilly thrust out a hand. "I know, I know. And I'm trying to trust God. But if I can't play tennis again—"

"You'll find something else to do with your life. God won't leave you stranded."

"Cam knows what he's talking about, honey." Alice set her juice cup on the table, the corners of her eyes crinkling in a sad smile. "He was lost once, too."

The old regrets edged closer. Cam clenched his jaw against the sting of guilt and grief. If he wasn't careful he'd crush the coffee cup between his fists.

A soft murmur penetrated his thoughts—Jilly's voice.

"I think I have it bad because I might have to give up tennis. I can't even imagine losing a brother. How did you ever find your way after Terrance died?"

Cam's chest collapsed on a pained sigh. How could he reply, when he still groped for answers, for peace, for healing? Despite all his seminary studies, prayer retreats, and God-talk, he still fought to believe in Christ's love and forgiveness. But he *had* to believe. Most days, faith was the only thing that kept him going.

Dear Jesus, help me. I don't want to be a fraud any longer.

A favorite scripture passage from Jeremiah nudged its way into his thoughts. *"Because of the LORD's great love we are not consumed, for his compassions never fail. They are new every morning; great is your faithfulness."*

If he had any hope of encouraging Jilly through the difficult decisions she faced—if he nurtured even the smallest hope of sharing a future with her—he'd have to dive headfirst into the Lord. He'd have to claim the compassion of Christ for himself and live in it.

❧

What a week! Cam couldn't believe it was Thursday already. Unsure how long he could convince Jilly to stay in Blossom Hills once her ankle was better, he'd planned special outings with her every day. He figured the more time they spent together, the quicker she'd see they were meant for each other. Then maybe she'd forget all about returning to Modesto and decide life was pretty good right here.

After they'd said good-bye to Alice on Monday, Cam had convinced Jilly to swallow her pride and let him push her in the wheelchair along the sidewalks of Blossom Hills's quaint downtown area. Window boxes of cascading petunias graced storefronts. Several old-timers had their usual checkers tournament going in front of Max's Barbershop. A sidewalk sale at the neighborhood bookstore had Cam and Jilly sharing laughs over titles long out of print and horribly out of date.

On Tuesday Cam arranged a picnic lunch at a picturesque park, and on Wednesday they took a drive through the Ozarks. During one of their many conversations about their personal likes and dislikes, Jilly shyly revealed that ever since they'd watched *Braveheart* together all those many years ago, Mel Gibson had become her favorite actor.

So on Thursday morning, with his bags packed for the next prayer retreat, Cam stopped by the video store on his way to the inn and rented all the best Gibson movies in stock. As soon as he could drag Jilly away from working on inn business with Harvey, he parked her on the sofa in the lounge, popped *Forever Young* into the DVD player, and plied her with diet cola, buttered popcorn, and Heather's gourmet pizza.

By midnight they'd clutched each other's hands through *Ransom*, wept with each other through *The Patriot,* and chuckled through the animated feature *Pocahontas.*

"Enough! Enough already!" Laughing and bleary-eyed, Jilly wrestled the remote out of Cam's grip.

He pinned one of her arms and tried to grab the remote from her flailing hand. "Hey, we haven't even gotten to the Mad Max and Lethal Weapon movies."

"Oh, please! If it's possible to OD on Mel Gibson, I think we've just done it." She stuffed the remote between the sofa cushions, well out of Cam's reach. "Anyway, shouldn't you be studying for your retreat?"

"After leading three already, I'm as prepared as I'll ever be. Come on, how about one more serving of Mel before we call it a night?" Cam reached across her, one hand pawing under the cushions.

His opposite elbow jabbed her ribs. She yelped and gave him a shove. He jerked back, nearly sliding off the sofa before he caught himself. With a huff, he scooted onto the sofa, sliding in so close that his lips brushed her neck.

"Jilly. . .Jilly." His arm crept around her shoulders. His other hand caressed her face as he guided her lips to meet his.

The tender urgency of her response shot waves of heat down his limbs. She lifted a hand to his neck and wove her fingers through the hair at his nape. He shuddered, moaned, drew back. His gaze settled on hers, and he grinned. "Wow."

She grinned back, breathless. "My sentiments exactly."

Chapter 15

Jillian. Hey, Jilly!"

She shook herself and focused on Harvey's face. He leaned across the front desk, one unruly eyebrow slanted toward the ceiling. "Sorry, guess I was daydreaming."

"Must'a' been a mighty good one, judging from that sappy smile you were wearing." Harvey chuckled. "How you comin' on those room assignments?"

Uncomfortably aware of the heat creeping up her neck, Jilly studied the computer screen. Okay, obviously Mr. and Mrs. Kaye would not like sharing their room with the Russo sisters. How had that happened? Nothing to do with lingering over the memory of Cam's amazing kiss last night.

Riiiiiight.

And if the guy walked by the desk one more time with that come-hither look in his eyes, she would either have to put on blinders or switch to decaf for the rest of the day. One glance from Cam and her heart started dancing like Maria Sharapova setting up to return a serve.

She made the correction on the room list and hit the PRINT button. "That should do it, Harvey." A glance at her watch told her she'd finished none too soon. Cam's retreat guests would begin arriving any minute.

Harvey stepped around to Jilly's side of the counter. "How about I take over? You look like you could use a nap." He winked. "That mean ol' Cam's been running you all over the countryside and keeping you up till all hours of the night."

A nap sounded delightful, but it was true—she'd spent so much time with Cam all week that she'd fallen far behind on inn business. With Alice on the mend, Harvey had resumed many of his usual duties, but Jilly still managed most of the bookkeeping and scheduling—Alice's areas of expertise. She cringed at the thought of the unopened mail and paperwork screaming to her from the inner office.

On the other hand, as brainless as she felt right now, she would be risking the inn's financial ruin if she got anywhere near the accounts.

She swiveled on the barstool and reached for her walker. "Think I'll take you up on that offer, Harvey—"

The glass door to the deck whooshed open and Cam sauntered into the lobby. "Ralph's got the fire pit fueled and ready." His gaze skated past Harvey and settled on Jilly. One corner of his mouth lifted in a provocative smile. "The sky's clear as a bell. It's going to be a gorgeous night."

A gorgeous night in the company of nine retreat guests while she fought the urge to drag Cam behind the garage and drink up more of his delicious kisses? This weekend might prove to be the longest three days of her life.

❧

Cam felt as if he'd just struggled through the longest weekend of his life. The latest prayer retreat had been geared toward Sunday-school teachers and youth sponsors, so between sessions and late into the evening he found himself cornered with questions about practical application. Usually he thrived on digging deeper into theology and helping others expand their understanding. But when he'd planned the content and direction of these retreats, he never anticipated the distraction of falling deeper and deeper in love.

Much less having the object of his affection close enough to set his insides aflame every time he walked through the lobby.

By the time the last participant left on Sunday afternoon, Cam caved beneath the physical and mental exhaustion. He found Jilly in the office. After buzzing her cheek with a lazy kiss, he plopped into the chair next to the desk.

She nailed him with a doubtful smirk. "Is that the best you can do?"

"Give me a five-minute nap and I'll show you."

"Promises, promises." She returned to her paperwork with a one-shoulder shrug. "From the looks of you, I don't think five minutes is quite going to handle it."

"Okay, ten. Twenty, tops." He slid lower in the chair. Legs extended, hands folded across his abdomen, he faked a chest-rattling snore.

"Terrific. If that's what you sound like when you sleep, I pity your future wife."

Cam's pulse stammered. He slitted his eyes and lifted his head an inch. "Oh, yeah? And what if I'm look—"

The ringing phone cut him off. And none too soon, considering the mixture of panic and embarrassment he'd just observed dancing across Jilly's face. He used the armrests to push himself upright as she grabbed up the receiver.

"Paul, hi! How's it going?"

They talked for a few minutes, then Jilly covered the mouthpiece and whispered to Cam, "He's doing great. They said he could move to outpatient status."

After only one week in rehab, that was good news indeed.

Except it probably meant Paul would be back at the inn. Just a friend or not, Cam wasn't so sure he liked the idea of another eligible—and actually fairly good-looking—bachelor on the premises.

Jilly finished the call and turned toward Cam. "The drugs are out of Paul's system and he's determined to keep it that way." Her lips flattened. She tapped a pen on the desk. "There's just one small stipulation about releasing him."

A prickly sensation worked its way up Cam's spine. Why did he have the feeling he wasn't going to like what she said next? "And that would be. . .?"

"He's still going to need to see his counselor every day, so he really needs a place to stay in town."

"Oh. Then we need to find him a cheap apartment or hotel near the center."

"Um, not exactly." Jilly's breath whistled through her clenched teeth. "Paul's counselor won't release him unless he has someone to stay with. Someone to help keep him accountable."

The picture became clear. Cam straightened and crossed his arms. "I'm not exactly in the market for a housemate. Maybe it would be better for Paul to stay at the center awhile longer."

"They need his bed for someone with problems a lot worse than his. And anyway, you said you're friends with his counselor."

"Ed. Yeah."

"Would he okay something not in the best interests of his patient?"

Cam cringed. She had him there. Still, he hadn't counted on stepping in as accountability coach for a virtual stranger.

On the other hand, with Paul staying in town, Cam would have fewer worries about any possible rivalry for Jilly's affections.

He raised his hands, palms outward. "Okay, okay. I just hope he likes cats."

"Oh, thank you, thank you, thank you!" Jilly shoved herself out of the chair, spun on one foot, and landed on his lap. She threw her arms around his neck and pressed her cheek against his.

Suddenly he forgot all about that nap he'd been so sure he needed.

❧

The pungent odor of fish swirled around Cam's head as he dumped a can of tuna-mackerel mush into Bart's food dish. Before he drove over to the New Life Center to pick up Paul this morning, he'd better take another swipe at the litter box. Cats certainly made for very *aromatic* pets.

He'd started out back with a plastic bag of soiled litter when the doorbell rang. Great. The last time he had an unexpected visitor, he found Liz on his doorstep. Surely she hadn't come to ply more of her futile charm tactics?

The chiming became insistent. "Okay, I'm coming."

But not with this smelly bag of cat litter. Cam yanked open the patio door and tossed the bag behind a potted plant, then decided he should probably wash his hands before greeting whoever seemed so anxious to see him this early on a Monday morning.

Finally he made it to the front door, his hands still dripping. "Jilly. Harvey. What are you two doing here?"

Jilly huffed. "That's a real friendly greeting. Can we come in before my one good leg goes numb from standing on it so long?"

"Yeah, sure." Dumbfounded, Cam made room for Jilly and her walker to pass.

Harvey wiped his feet on the doormat. "Sorry if we took you by surprise. Jillian really wanted to go with you to get Paul, and since I was coming to town to visit Alice, I offered to drop her off here."

Jilly headed for the bench next to the coat tree and sank down with a groan. "This cast cannot come off soon enough—oh, hi kitty. You must be the infamous Bart."

Cam rushed over and swooped the old cat into his arms. "Hey, your allergies—should you even be inside my house?"

"It's okay, let me hold him. Cat dander is among the few things on earth I am *not* allergic to." She grinned. "Otherwise, as a cat owner you'd never have gotten within ten feet of me before my eyes swelled shut."

A welcome wave of relief surged through Cam. If it came down to a choice between Bart and Jilly. . .well, there was no choice. But he hesitated to think how painful it would have been if he had to find another home for Bart.

Jilly held out her arms and took the cat onto her lap. Bart's purring soon filled the entryway. "Wow, I think he likes me."

Cam knelt beside Jilly and smiled up at her. "What's not to like?"

"Oh, brother." Harvey heaved an exaggerated groan. "It's getting too deep in here for me. I'm off to see Alice. You two lovebirds stay out of trouble, you hear?"

Cam hardly glanced up as the door closed behind Harvey.

❧

"Um, maybe we ought to think about heading over to the rehab center." Jilly had long since forsaken the purring cat. Cupping Cam's face between her palms to savor his kisses was much more enjoyable. Except it was getting awfully hot in this tiny entryway.

Still kneeling, Cam shifted his weight to his heels. "Yeah, Harvey did tell us to stay out of trouble. And I'm gonna be in big trouble if you keep kissing me like that."

Jilly shook a finger in Cam's face. "Why, Mr. Lane, don't you dare put all the blame on me. If you weren't so incredibly handsome—"

"Please!" Cam thrust to his feet and pulled Jilly up with one hand while moving her walker closer with the other. "Let's go get Paul while I still have any willpower left."

The Paul who greeted them in the New Life waiting room looked light-years healthier than he had one week ago when they brought him in. His year-round tennis tan had faded slightly, but his eyes seemed brighter, his posture more erect.

Jilly scooted closer and wrapped him in a hug. "It's so good to see you looking like your old self again."

"Feels good, too. Thanks for coming to get me." Paul stepped back and nodded at Cam. "And thanks for giving me a place to stay, man."

"No prob." Cam shuffled closer, extending his right hand to shake Paul's. His other arm settled firmly around Jilly's shoulders—almost possessively if she were to hazard an opinion.

A shiver zinged through her. Things with Cam had moved at lightning speed this past week. She'd relished every moment of their time together, but if she allowed herself to fall any more in love with the guy, she could never bear to leave him. Modesto—or wherever her tennis career took her—would be too far away.

Her ankle cast suddenly dragged her leg down like a lead weight. *You keep forgetting, Gardner. Your tennis career could very well be history.*

"Jilly?"

She looked up to see Cam frowning at her, a worried look creasing his brow. "Sorry, just frustrated with this cast and walker. Paul, you ready to go?"

Back at Cam's house, Jilly made herself comfortable on the den sofa while Cam showed Paul to the guest room and helped him settle in. Cam's Bible lay on the end table, a devotion booklet beside it open to today's date. Cam must have been sitting in this very spot for his morning Bible study. Even hours later, Jilly imagined the plush ribbed velour still held the warmth from his body. Her eyes drifted shut for a moment. A yearning sigh escaped her lips.

Looking toward the front door, she glimpsed the bench by the coat rack, and immediately her lips tingled with the memory of Cam's kisses. There was so much to love about him. His tenderness. His faith. His generosity. She had the feeling she could ask anything of Cam and he'd go to the ends of the earth to please her.

But, if by God's grace, Jilly made it back on the tennis circuit—something she prayed for with all her heart—how could she ask Cam to come with her? To leave behind his home, his church, his professorship at Rehoboth Bible College?

Oh, Lord, I love him so. Don't make it a choice between Cam and my career.

Once again, her glance drifted to the Bible. She drew the weighty, leather-covered volume onto her lap and let the onion-skin pages fall open in the New Testament. Her gaze skimmed the verses for any perceived word from the Lord, until she found herself in the book of Philippians. Here, Cam had highlighted chapter 4, verse 6: "Do not be anxious about anything, but in every situation, by prayer and petition, with thanksgiving, present your requests to God."

Anxious. She'd been plenty anxious lately. About her career. About her relationship with Harvey and Alice. About Paul and the steroid scandal.

And most of all, about the possibility of a future with Cam.

Jesus, I'm trying to pray, trying to turn all this over to You.

A furry head nudged beneath Jilly's elbow. Bart must have grown bored trailing Cam and Paul on the house tour. Jilly ran her hand down the length of the cat's arching back, static electricity raising Bart's hair all the way down to his tail. He showed his appreciation with a noisy purr.

"Doesn't take much to make you happy, huh, fella?" Oh, for the simple life of a house cat.

Footsteps drifted from the hallway. Sliding the Bible onto the end table, Jilly looked up to see Cam striding toward her. "Did you get Paul moved in?"

"We rearranged some things in the closet and bathroom to give him some space." Cam crossed in front of her and opened the back door. "It's a gorgeous day. How about sandwiches on the patio?"

"Is it lunchtime already? I can help." Reaching for her walker, she pulled herself off the sofa.

"I can handle it. You go on outside." With scarcely a glance in her direction, Cam bustled to the kitchen.

Obviously with Paul in the house, Cam must be playing it cool. She knew as well as he did that if he dared get too close, they'd be in each other's arms in a matter of seconds. Okay, she'd play along. . .for now. She shuffled out the door and chose a padded swivel chair in the shade of the patio table umbrella.

Seconds later a putrid odor assaulted her nostrils. She wrinkled her nose. "Eeew! Hey, Cam, it smells like something died out here."

Cam darted out. "Oops. Forget about the cat litter. I'll run it out to the trash can."

"Please do." Jilly frowned at the cat, who had followed Cam and now wound through the legs of her walker. "Whoa, buddy, you are some stink machine."

Somewhere in the neighborhood a lawn mower rumbled. The breeze carried the scent of exhaust fumes and grass clippings. Jilly sneezed. And sneezed again. "Oh boy."

Digging a tissue out of her jeans pocket, she glimpsed Cam loping across the lawn. He stepped onto the patio as a third sneeze doubled her over. "You okay?"

"I'm late taking my allergy pill this morning. The bottle's in my purse. Would you mind bringing it to me with a glass of water?"

"Sure, right away."

On second thought, maybe she should go inside and stay there until the medication kicked in. Between sneezes she worked her way through the door, and in one motion shoved the walker aside and dropped onto the sofa cushions.

Cam rushed over with a glass of water and her pill bottle. "Guess fresh air wasn't such a good idea after all."

She sniffled as Cam shook a pill into her open palm. "My fault. I was supposed to take my pill at ten, and we got so busy with. . .other things. . .that I forgot."

He grinned knowingly as he capped the bottle and dropped it into her purse. "Next time remind me and I'll set a timer."

The pill slid down on a sip of water, and she rested her head on the back of the sofa. "I'll be okay in a few minutes."

"I'm in the kitchen making sandwiches. Holler if you need anything else."

She nodded and closed her eyes.

Minutes later she jerked upright. Something didn't feel right. Her chest hurt, as if the pill had gotten stuck on the way down. She swallowed the rising saliva and waited for the sensation to pass, but it only grew worse.

The roof of her mouth began to itch. Her lips tingled—and this time not pleasantly. Heat flamed up her chest, her neck, her face. She tried to cough, but it came out in a painful wheeze.

"Jilly?" Cam rushed from the kitchen. He leaned over her, one hand on her back. "Jilly!"

His voice sounded far away. A misty curtain slid over her eyes. Her head tipped backward. Her last conscious thought was that Cam really ought to paint that water stain on his ceiling.

❧

"Jilly. Jilly!" Cam eased her sideways onto the sofa while his panicked brain tried to make sense of the situation. You couldn't pass out from sneezing, could you? At least she was breathing—but like Darth Vader with a chest cold. "Jilly, can you hear me?"

God, what's happening here?

"Cam? Is everyth—" Paul skidded to a halt beside him. "Oh, man. This isn't good." He dropped on one knee and checked Jilly's pulse and airway. "Hang on, girl. Keep breathing."

Her eyes fluttered open. She groped for Paul's hand, her chest heaving with every grating breath.

"Do you know what's wrong with her?" Cam didn't recognize his own voice. And he barely recognized the woman lying on the sofa, her face ashen, her lips a hideous shade of blue. An angry rash mottled the skin around her mouth.

"Looks like anaphylactic shock. Where's her purse? She always carries an epinephrine injection."

"It's, uh—" Cam's mouth tasted like old pennies. He stood. Backed away. Clawed his hair. *Please, God, help her!*

Paul shot him an impatient glare. "Find her purse, man! And call 911."

Cam forced himself to swallow, to think. His gaze scoured the room until it fell upon Jilly's purse. He grabbed it and thrust it at Paul, then stumbled to the kitchen phone. While he explained Jilly's condition to the operator, he watched Paul snap open a tube-like container and jab it into Jilly's thigh, then massage the area roughly.

Even from the kitchen, Cam could hear the change in Jilly's breathing. The rhythm steadied, the sound grew less labored and raspy. Phone receiver cradled in his hands, he sank into the nearest chair and waited for the thudding of his own heart to subside.

As the wail of sirens neared, one thought pounded through Cam's brain: *You froze, man. When she needed you the most, you froze.*

Chapter 16

"I don't understand." Jilly had to force the words out over her raspy throat. She drew both hands through the hair at her temples and plopped her head against the mushy hospital pillow. "The only thing I react to that way is macadamia nuts. And I wasn't anywhere near nuts today."

The ER doctor checked her bedside monitor and jotted something on his clipboard. "What were you doing just before this happened?"

Jilly gave a hoarse laugh. "Taking my allergy pill."

"Do you have the pills with you?"

"They were in my purse, but. . ." She glanced over at Paul, who sat stiffly on a hard plastic chair.

"Your purse must still be at Cam's." Paul stood. "You want me to call him?"

A sick feeling churned through Jilly's stomach. Her mind locked on the image of Cam standing on his front porch as the EMTs wheeled her down the sidewalk to the ambulance. The anxious little-boy look on his face shredded her heart.

"Jilly?" Paul's soft reminder drew her attention.

She frowned at the doctor. "Do you really need to see the pills?"

"If that was the last thing you ingested, yes. We need to determine exactly what precipitated the anaphylaxis."

Paul sidled toward the opening in the privacy curtain. "I'll step out and call Cam. Be right back."

The doctor finished his exam and excused himself, leaving Jilly alone in the brightly lit cubicle. She stared at four and a half pale, wrinkled toes protruding from the ankle cast that had become the bane of her existence. "If not for you, you stupid thing, I'd still be in Modesto. I'd still have a job. I'd still have hopes of making it to the US Open.... Okay, so, maybe not. But I wouldn't be sitting here in a hospital bed, mooning over a guy with issues of his own."

"Talking to yourself?" Paul ducked through the curtain. "Not a good sign."

Jilly sniffed back tears that threatened to clog the plastic tubes feeding her oxygen. Good grief, she'd turned into a veritable fountain lately. "Did you reach Cam?"

"He's bringing your purse." Paul nudged his chair closer to the stretcher and plopped down. "What's the deal with him anyway? I thought he'd want to come with you to the hospital."

Jilly mashed her lips together to suppress a shudder. "When he gets here, don't be too hard on him, okay?"

"If you say so." Paul leaned back and crossed his arms. "He sure freaked, though. For a minute there, I was afraid I'd be scraping him off the floor."

"Seeing me like that, thinking I might be dying. . .it must have really scared him."

"Yeah, you told me about his brother. Losing someone you care so much about. . .I guess it's something you never completely get over."

"Anyway, have I thanked you for remembering my epinephrine?" She reached for Paul's hand. "You probably did save my life."

Paul screwed his mouth into a bashful grin. "Aw, shucks, ma'am, weren't nothin'."

An amazon of a nurse came in to take Jilly's vitals and check her IV. Before she finished, an aide appeared with Jilly's purse and set it in her lap. "A gentleman just left this for you at the desk."

Jilly's heart rate soared. She sat forward and tried to see past the aide through the slit in the curtain. "Is he still here?"

"Take it easy, ma'am. Breathe normally and relax." The nurse, in the middle of taking a blood pressure reading, poked a meaty fingertip to Jilly's breastbone and nudged her back against the pillow.

Jilly shot Paul a pleading gaze. He nodded and left the cubicle, only to return moments later to say Cam had already left. Jilly sagged under the weight of disappointment and quietly let the nurse finish her exam. Part of her sympathized with Cam's terror, but couldn't he at least look in on her to make sure she was all right?

Paul touched her arm. "Jilly, your pills. The doctor's waiting for them."

"Oh, right." Giving herself a mental shake, Jilly unzipped her purse and retrieved the vial of allergy pills. She shoved it into the nurse's outstretched hand. "I don't know what they expect to find. I've been taking this same prescription for three or four years now."

❧

After handing over Jilly's purse to an attendant at the ER desk, Cam wasted no time escaping the cloying hospital atmosphere. Five steps out the sliding glass doors, he zigged left and collapsed against a pillar. Across from him purple and red petunias overflowing a concrete planter mocked him with their cheerfulness.

Shame crawled through him like an ugly spider. What a coward! What a helpless, useless mass of nerves. If Paul hadn't been there—*Oh God!* It didn't bear thinking about.

But you didn't lose her. She's okay. And you're out here feeling sorry for yourself while she's in there probably wondering what kind of idiot professes his love and then chokes in a crisis.

For better or for worse? Oops, flubbed that one already. Good thing they were still a long way from the proposal stage.

Cam hauled in a shuddering breath. Time to buck up and be a man. He owed Jilly—and Paul—an apology.

The glass doors glided open, and Cam strode to the admitting desk. The same woman he'd handed Jilly's purse to looked up from her computer terminal. "Something else I can do for you, sir?"

"Can I see her? Jilly Gardner?"

"Are you family?"

"No, but—"

"Then I'm sorry, I can't help you."

Frustration deflated Cam's lungs. "Could you at least let her know I'm here?"

"Name, please?"

"Cam Lane."

The woman nodded to a silver-haired aide in a lavender smock. The aide disappeared down a corridor, and Cam stepped to one side.

Behind the desk, a doctor settled in at one of the work areas and began scrawling notes in a file. A tall, heavyset nurse approached and handed the doctor a pill bottle. "Miss Gardner found her prescription. Do you want me to send it down to the lab?"

At the mention of Jilly's name, Cam edged closer. The doctor took the vial and studied the label. One eyebrow lifted. "Hmmm, one of the more potent allergy meds, but I've never heard of it causing anaphylaxis." He uncapped the vial and peered inside. "There's some kind of powdery residue. That's not normal for this drug either. Yeah, send it down to the lab and have them put a rush on the results."

A tap on Cam's shoulder made him jump. He whirled around to see the aide in the lavender smock smiling up at him. "Miss Gardner wants to see you. I'll show you the way."

He hesitated. His first impulse was to snag that doctor and find out exactly what the guy thought was wrong with Jilly's pills. Before he could react, the doctor grabbed up another file and headed off in a different direction. Cam reined in his urgent need for answers and followed the aide down a corridor reeking of disinfectant and other smells he'd just as soon not identify. The aide peeled back a curtain to reveal Jilly gazing at him through shimmering eyes.

A sudden attack of shyness curbed his headlong rush to her side. He stopped at the foot of the stretcher. "Wow, you sure look better than the last time I saw you."

One side of her mouth curled up. "I could say the same for you."

Paul stood and edged past Cam. "Think I'll go find a coffee machine."

Without taking his eyes off Jilly, Cam tipped his head toward Paul. "Take your time."

Through the thin curtain, muted voices joined the squeak of rubber-soled footsteps and rattling wheels. Ignoring everything but the woman before him, Cam stepped to Jilly's side and took her hand. His glance fell to their clasped fingers. "Can you forgive me for abandoning you? I was just so scared."

"It's okay. I understand." She tugged him closer. "So quit apologizing and kiss me."

❧

Jilly angled an irritated glance at the nurse checking her blood pressure for what felt like the millionth time in the past three hours. "I'm feeling fine. Are they ever going to let me out of here?"

"Dr. Hayes won't release you until your heart rate, BP, and oxygen levels normalize. He's also waiting on confirmation from the lab about what brought on the anaphylaxis."

"Speaking of which. . ." The doctor breezed through the curtain, clipboard in hand.

Both Cam and Paul rose and stood next to Jilly, their eagerness for answers as palpable as her own. Cam spoke first. "What did you find, Doctor? Was it the pills?"

"The pills themselves are fine. But the lab found traces of macadamia nut powder in the vial and coating several of the pills."

Jilly's stomach somersaulted. "That's insane! How could my pills be contaminated with macadamia nuts?"

"I hate to even suggest this." Dr. Hayes's mouth spread into a grimace. "Is there anyone who would want to harm you—someone who knows about your allergy?"

She looked from Cam to Paul, her thoughts racing. "There was some trouble back in Modesto. In fact, I'm suspicious the fall that broke my ankle was no accident."

"She's right, Doc." Paul shoved his hands in his pockets. "A couple of guys on our country club tennis team were dealing steroids and thought Jilly might be on to them."

Jilly's mind flashed to the damaged packaging of her mail-order prescription. She explained what her landlady had told her and how the package was so late in showing up. "But still, how would any of those kids have known about my allergy?"

Paul grimaced. "Remember the Christmas party? I sent the boys to the bakery for cookies. And I specifically told them nothing with macadamia nuts because you were allergic."

The doctor checked his notes. "This happened in Modesto? But the vial you gave me had a Riley's Pharmacy label. That's right here in Blossom Hills."

At Cam's sudden intake of breath, Jilly swung her gaze toward him. "Oh, Cam, don't jump to conclusions. The Riley's prescription was only a couple of weeks' worth, so I topped it off with the mail-order pills and put the bigger bottle away for now."

"Without examining the other vial, we won't know which prescription is the actual source of the contamination." Dr. Hayes narrowed his gaze. "Miss Gardner, I strongly suggest you notify the police and let them conduct a full investigation. I don't think I have to tell you how serious this could have been if your friend hadn't injected the epinephrine so quickly."

Again she felt Cam cringe. She gripped his hand. "Okay, Doc, we get it.

Will you release me now?"

❧

Later that evening, as they turned onto Cam's street, Jilly glimpsed Harvey's truck parked in front of Cam's house. She sucked in her breath. "Oh no, did anyone think to let Harvey know what's going on?"

"I phoned him as soon as I knew you were okay." Cam hit the remote on his visor and waited for the garage door to open, then drove inside.

Harvey bustled through the kitchen door, ready to help Jilly out of the SUV. "Honey, honey! Thank the Lord you're all right."

"I'm fine, I promise." Leaning on Harvey's arm, Jilly hobbled up the single step into the house, where Paul had already moved her walker. She maneuvered to a kitchen chair and plopped down, more from relief than exhaustion. Three emergency trips to the hospital in the space of one month seemed a bit excessive.

The doorbell rang. Cam tossed his keys onto the kitchen counter. "Maybe that's Ralph."

"Ralph?" Harvey shifted his confused expression to Cam. "What's he doing here this late?"

As Cam headed for the door, Jilly said, "I called him. I needed him to bring something from the inn." She laid a hand on Harvey's arm. "Maybe you'd better sit down."

By the time Cam ushered Ralph into the kitchen, Jilly had explained about the contaminated prescription. Ralph dropped a brown paper grocery sack onto the table. "Found the packaging in your bathroom wastebasket, just like you said, Jilly. Got your bottle of pills, too."

"Thanks, Ralph." Jilly spread open the top of the bag and peered inside.

The doorbell chimed again. Cam pivoted. "And that'll be Keith Nelson."

Harvey gasped. "Oh my goodness, you called Keith?"

"Cam said he's the best." Jilly couldn't help but smile at the thought of seeing her almost-cousin again, a hot-tempered rookie on the Blossom Hills police force last time she saw him. She was pleasantly surprised when Cam told her Keith Nelson had matured into one of the sharpest detectives in the state.

Harvey slid a hand down his face and fell into the chair next to Jilly. "You really think this was deliberate? That someone intended to harm you, possibly even kill you?"

She'd had several hours to process the idea, but it still turned her insides to jelly. And when she glimpsed the solemn expression in Detective Keith Nelson's deep blue eyes, her mouth went too dry to speak.

❧

Cam braced one hip against the kitchen counter and listened in silence as Jilly and Paul gave Keith a detailed account of all the events leading up to today. His mind, however, spun out prayer after prayer that the investigation would clear Liz—for her and Sammy's sake as well as for Cam's peace of mind.

"Okay, I think I've got this all straight." Keith flipped his notebook shut and rose. "But I'm telling you, Jilly, next time you show up in town without calling me for a lunch date, I'll have no choice but to run you in for failure to appear."

She smirked. "Between Harvey and Cam, I've been staying pretty busy since I came home."

Keith extended his hand to Cam. "Good to see you again, man. Take care of this gal, you hear me? You, too, Uncle Harvey. Give my love to Aunt Alice, and tell her I'll try to get by to see her in a few days."

"Sure will, son." Harvey stood and walked Keith to the door.

Twenty minutes after Keith left, Cam had his duffel bag restocked with clean clothes for a return trip to the inn. No way was he letting Jilly out of his sight until the police got this mess straightened out. Planning to ride out with Harvey and Jilly, he gave Paul the keys to his house and car, along with instructions for looking after Bart—although Paul didn't look real keen on the litter box business.

"Look, you need to stay in town for your rehab sessions. I'll check in with you every chance I get, and I also asked my pastor to stop by. You've got Ed's number at the center and my cell if you need any help." Cam waited until Harvey and Jilly had started out to the pickup before continuing. "Besides, we both need to be sure nothing else happens to Jilly."

Paul rammed his fingers into his back pockets. "I hate this, man. If one of my kids did this to her—"

Cam left his own thoughts unspoken. His mind kept returning to the Riley's prescription bottle. . .and Liz. She'd been furious the day they broke up, but angry enough to hurt someone? The mere idea made his stomach cramp. No, Liz was a good woman, a devoted mother. Besides, how would she have known about Jilly's macadamia nut allergy? Cam hadn't even been aware of it until today.

Paul nudged his arm. "Better get moving or they'll leave without you."

"Yeah." Cam looked toward the door as a fresh wave of doubt assailed him. He'd do everything in his power to keep Jilly safe until the police nailed the culprit. But he wouldn't—couldn't—put his own heart on the line again.

Sorry, God, not even what little faith I have would be enough to get me through losing Jilly.

Chapter 17

Jilly looked up from the mail she'd been sorting and heaved a sigh. Across the lobby, Cam sat on a love seat facing away from her, apparently engrossed in some heavy reading. He'd barely spoken five words to her all morning. In fact, ever since they'd arrived at the inn yesterday, he'd hardly even made eye contact. And when he did, his expression revealed nothing. It was as if the man she'd begun to fall in love with had disappeared, leaving only a shell.

The front door swung open, setting off a chime. Cam tossed his book aside and lunged to his feet, waylaying Keith Nelson before he made it through the door. "Did you get the lab results? Do you know who did this?"

"Give the poor man some breathing room, Cam." Jilly maneuvered her walker around the front desk and scooted over to the seating area. "What is it, Keith? Did you find out anything?"

"I've got a few answers for you." Keith's face was all business. He tugged a notebook from the inside pocket of his navy blazer. "The prescription sent from Modesto is definitely the source of the contamination. The lab found macadamia nut powder not only inside the prescription vial but in minute traces under the tape used to reseal the original packaging."

"Then it must have been one of the kids dealing steroids. They stole it off my porch." Jilly sank into the nearest chair, not sure whether to feel relieved or even more terrified. She glanced up at Cam. His head fell forward. He covered his eyes with one hand before turning away.

Keith took the chair opposite Jilly and braced his elbows on his thighs. "I've been in touch with the investigating officer in the steroid case, and I'm forwarding all the evidence and lab reports directly to the Modesto Police Department."

Cam stepped closer, fists knotted at his sides. "Did you find any fingerprints? DNA? *Anything* you can use to nail these creeps to the wall?"

At the jagged edge in Cam's tone, Jilly cringed. She'd never seen him so angry.

Keith closed his notebook and shrugged. "We did find a partial print under the sealing tape, but it didn't have enough detail to match with prints on file."

"That's just great." Cam thrust one hand to the back of his neck. "For lack of solid evidence some street-smart dopehead could get away with attempted murder."

"I didn't say that, Cam." Keith's professional calm belied the concern Jilly read behind his eyes. "Now that the Modesto cops know what they're looking for, they'll be checking the suspects' homes, cars, and clothing for any trace of the contaminant."

Jilly cupped her palms around her temples. "So what happens next, Keith?"

"More than likely, you'll have to go back to Modesto to give statements and ID the suspects. You should be hearing from. . ." He consulted his notebook. "Detective Leigh Smith. She can fill you in on where the case stands and answer any questions about what will be expected of you."

"Wow, what a summer. I feel like I've been on a never-ending roller-coaster ride." Jilly shot a quick glance toward Cam, who stood with his back to them in the lounge doorway. What was still eating him? Shouldn't he be relieved to know the crime originated in Modesto, not the Blossom Hills pharmacy he'd suggested?

Keith pushed up from the chair. "I need to get back to town. But remember, I'm only a phone call away if you need anything."

Jilly pulled up on her walker and stretched to wrap an arm around Keith's neck. "Thanks, Keith. I'm sure glad we had you on this case."

"Glad I could help." He nodded in Cam's direction and lowered his voice. "Hang in there with him. He's scared, that's all. He'll come around."

"I hope you're right."

❧

Three days later, Ralph drove Jilly and Paul to the Kansas City airport. Though Detective Smith already had Paul's statement and had cleared him of any related charges, Paul was itching to return home and—if Therese would still have him—get back to work. His rehab counselor set up a referral to a Modesto facility so that Paul's recovery could continue uninterrupted.

Watching the Ozarks fade to shades of purple along the eastern horizon, Jilly sent up a silent prayer of thanks for Paul's amazing turnaround. Now, she could only pray Cam would come to his senses. Guilt over missing the signs of Terrance's steroid abuse, combined with his fears about what *could* have happened to Jilly as a result of teens using steroids, had grown into an impenetrable wall between Cam and everyone he cared about. Not even Harvey's homegrown wisdom or Alice's prayerful prodding seemed to have any effect.

At the Sacramento airport Jilly and Paul arranged for a shuttle to take them straight to the Modesto Police Department. Detective Leigh Smith ushered them to her desk, moving a box of files out of the way to give Jilly space to maneuver. Now that her ribs were healing, she'd ditched the cumbersome walker and had gone back to using crutches.

"I appreciate your coming straight here." The detective edged behind her desk and shuffled through some files. "We've had a break in the case since last time I talked to you."

"Really? That's great." Jilly sipped from a bottle of water she'd purchased at the airport.

"Alex, one of the boys dealing steroids, decided to talk." Smith narrowed her gaze over the rim of tortoiseshell reading glasses. "He fingered his cousin, a hospital tech named Frank Ford, as the supplier."

Paul ran a hand down his face. "I knew it had to be something like that. Those kids weren't smart enough or well-connected enough to be getting the drugs on their own."

"Exactly." Smith turned toward Jilly. "Alex admitted he and his friend Ted tried to scare you into silence because *they* were scared of Ford and didn't want him to find out their little enterprise may have been compromised. Then they heard at the country club that you'd left town, so they kept an eye on your apartment, watching for your return. When your prescription was delivered, they snatched it on a whim."

Jilly's lips flattened. "What about the macadamia nut powder?"

"The boys got worried that you'd left town to protect yourself because you were planning to turn them in, so they finally told Ford everything and gave him the package they'd stolen. When Ford saw it was a prescription, he figured you'd be needing it soon and thought they could use it somehow to get to you. That's when Alex remembered your macadamia nut allergy."

"So they contaminated my pills and then left the package back at my apartment. You can prove this, right?"

"Based on Alex's statement, we obtained a search warrant for Ford's apartment. Stuffed in the back of a closet we found a trash bag with an empty nut can and a pair of latex gloves with the powder clinging to them." The detective chuckled. "That tech should really think about taking out his trash more often."

Smith went on to explain that the crime lab matched prints found inside the gloves with those of the hospital tech. When questioned, Ford was all too ready to make a deal in exchange for a list of everyone he'd been supplying drugs to.

Cold fingers tightened around Jilly's midsection. "Exactly what kind of deal?"

"We prosecute for the lesser charge of aggravated assault instead of attempted murder. After all, he can claim his intent was only to scare you, not kill you."

"Aggravated assault?" Jilly sat forward, hands clamped around the armrests. "You realize I could have died?"

The detective lowered her gaze. "Of course I do, and I don't mean to play down the seriousness of what happened to you. But Alex and Ted did eventually cooperate and, being minors, the boys will most likely do their time in the juvenile justice system—always with the hope of rehabilitation. On the other hand, even on the lesser charge, Frank Ford can expect a pretty stiff sentence."

❧

The last thing on earth Cam felt like doing this weekend was leading another prayer retreat. He drove around behind the inn, shut off the engine, and leaned his head on the steering wheel. "Lord, give me strength."

A tap on the window glass brought him up with a jolt. Harvey pulled open the door. "Thought maybe something happened to you. A couple of your retreat folks have already checked in."

"Sorry." Cam heaved himself from the SUV and retrieved his duffel bag from the backseat. "I'll go see to them right now."

"No hurry. Ralph and Heather are keeping them entertained with coffee and conversation." Harvey matched Cam's slow pace toward the deck steps. "What's wrong, son? Missing Jillian?"

Like crazy. But he couldn't let himself even think about her. He kept his response noncommittal. "You heard if they got to Modesto okay?"

"She called about twenty minutes ago. Already met with the detective." Harvey filled Cam in on the details Jilly had learned.

Relief settled across Cam's shoulders. He elbowed his way through the glass door to the lobby. "Good. Now maybe she can put this mess behind her and get on with her life."

And maybe I can, too.

Harvey sighed as he stepped behind the front desk. "Sure hope so. She's gonna have an awful hard time adjusting to life without tennis, though, if it comes to that."

Cam dropped his duffel bag and rested his forearms on the counter. "You think it will?"

"Before she left, she got the name of a top-notch Modesto orthopedist and made an appointment to see him first thing Monday." Harvey shuffled through some registration cards. "Whatever he tells her will be the deciding factor."

A whirlwind of emotions twisted through Cam's gut. If Jilly couldn't play tennis again, would she return to Blossom Hills? And if she did, how could he bear having her so close? Yet if she went back on the tennis circuit, he might never see her again. Either option meant sheer torture.

❧

Paul, Therese, and Denise had each offered to take Jilly to her orthopedist appointment, but she insisted she could drive herself. If the prognosis came back as she feared it would—and prayed it wouldn't—she'd rather not have an audience.

After several X-rays and a CT scan of her ankle, the doctor didn't keep her in suspense. "Whoever did your surgery after the second fall did everything right. But even with intensive physical therapy, you'll never regain full range of motion, and there'll always be some weakness. You'll be good for most routine activities, even an occasional recreational tennis game. But to subject that ankle to the stresses of professional tennis would be risking permanent disability."

The tears she expected didn't come. Even two hours later, sitting alone in her apartment and staring at a blank TV screen while sipping diet cola, she felt nothing more than a vague emptiness.

So she couldn't play professional tennis anymore. She still had two good legs, or would as soon as this cast came off. She had a brain. And she had a family.

Thank You, Lord, for giving me back Harvey and Alice.

Her cell phone warbled. She retrieved it from her purse and checked the caller ID. Therese.

Acceptance sat upon her shoulders like a heavy blanket. She flipped open the phone and prepared to offer her official resignation as women's tennis instructor at Silverheels Country Club.

Therese was, of course, disappointed. At least she hadn't balked at reinstating Paul, and his return helped temper the loss of Jilly.

So now what? Without her job at Silverheels, she had no reason to stay in Modesto. Decisions about her future would be a lot easier if she knew for certain Cam was waiting for her back in Blossom Hills. But he hadn't called her once since she left. And she hadn't the nerve to call him and risk his not answering, or worse, his open rejection.

"God, I'm so confused! Help me know what to do."

The act of praying spurred her to search for her Bible. Unopened for months, if not years, it lay beneath a hodgepodge of pens, pencils, old receipts, and other odds and ends in an end-table drawer. She let it fall open to where a ribbon marked the Psalms—probably placed there when the book was manufactured. Hungry for sustenance, she let her gaze slide across the verses.

Words from Psalm 62 leaped from the page: "Truly he is my rock and my salvation; he is my fortress, I will not be shaken. My salvation and my honor depend on God; he is my mighty rock, my refuge."

Understanding seeped into her consciousness like a soothing cup of tea. Her life wasn't about tennis. Her life wasn't about Cam. Her life wasn't about the family she'd always felt deprived of and now cherished in Harvey and Alice.

God alone is my rock. God alone must be the source of my fulfillment and happiness.

He'd already proven He could restore lost dreams. Whatever her future held, she'd trust in the One whose love never failed.

Chapter 18

How he made it through another prayer retreat, Cam would never know. Okay, so he had a pretty good idea. It had to be all God, because Cam was running on empty.

Leading a group of Rehoboth Bible College students also helped a lot. All Cam had to do was throw out a discussion question and the participants took over. Nobody seemed to notice he didn't have much to say. He could only thank God it was over and pray he could get his mind in gear to prepare more thoroughly for next weekend—the final prayer retreat he'd scheduled and sure to be the most emotionally and spiritually challenging.

But first, he needed to restock his refrigerator. He steered his grocery cart along the frozen-food aisle and paused in front of a selection of microwavable dinners. Normally he took satisfaction in whipping up his own meals, but not today. He didn't want to think too hard about anything.

The open glass door quickly frosted over as he perused the shelves. Chicken teriyaki, chipotle burrito, and spinach ravioli dinners found their way into his cart. Oh well, the spinach part had to be healthy, didn't it? Better grab a bottle of antacid on the way out.

As he turned down the next aisle, he narrowly missed ramming his cart into another shopper. "Oops, sorry—"

He sucked in his breath. *Liz.*

"Hello, Cam." Her glacial stare rivaled the ice crystals forming on his frozen dinners.

At least Sammy wasn't with her to witness this first encounter since Cam broke it off. He swallowed. His hands clenched the cart handle. "Hi, Liz. How are you?"

"Oh, just peachy." She faked a smile. "I suppose you knew the cops would question me about Jilly's prescription."

Cam flinched. "Liz, I'm sorry. I hope they didn't cause you any trouble."

"More embarrassment than anything. They said it was just routine."

"Still, I hope you know I didn't—*couldn't* believe you had anything to do with it." He stepped to the side of the shopping cart and lowered his voice. "You're a good woman, Liz. And you deserve to be happy. You and Sammy both. I'm sorry it didn't work out between us, more sorry than you can ever know."

"Get over yourself, Lane. I'm sorry, too, but I'll survive." Her eyes softened. She gave her head a small shake. "You, on the other hand, I'm not so sure about."

He drew his chin back. "What's that supposed to mean?"

"It means where romance is concerned, you've always been your own worst enemy. If you ever stop wallowing in guilt over stuff you can't control, you'll make some lucky lady a fine husband." She whipped her cart in the opposite direction, then shot him a rueful frown. "Just wish it could have been me."

Her blue-jeaned hips taunted him until she turned down the next aisle.

Her words taunted him for hours afterward. *"Your own worst enemy. . . If you ever stop wallowing in guilt. . ."*

"But I *am* guilty," he shouted as he dished up a serving of chicken liver delight for Bart. The smell warred with what should have been the tempting aroma of a spicy burrito warming in the microwave.

The old cat obviously didn't care one way or the other about Cam's guilt. *Just feed me,* he seemed to say with his incessant purring and weaving around Cam's legs. Pets had to be the quintessential example of unconditional love—or in Bart's case, unconditional indifference.

❧

"I picked up some more boxes for you." Denise edged through Jilly's apartment door with an armload of flattened cardboard packing crates. "Caught the Safeway manager before he got rid of them."

"Wow, thanks, this should be plenty." Jilly wrapped another coffee mug in newsprint and found a space for it in the box at her feet.

Denise grabbed the packing tape and reassembled one of the boxes. "Wish I could talk you into staying. Surely Modesto has way more job opportunities than Blossom Hills."

"You're probably right. But even though I love you to death"—she hooked an arm around Denise's neck and squeezed—"I need to be with my family. I've already put too much time and distance between me and the Nelsons."

"They sound like real special people." Denise smacked a kiss on Jilly's cheek before they both resumed packing. "Of course this big hurry to move to Missouri has nothing to do with that fellow you told me about."

The mention of Cam put Jilly's insides on spin cycle. More than a week had elapsed since she last saw him. He'd been standing on the deck, arms crossed in stoic silence, as Harvey helped Jilly into the pickup for the drive to the airport. A strange mixture of sadness and relief had etched frown lines around his mouth and eyes.

She glanced at the tennis racquet–shaped clock over the dinette—nine twenty. This was Saturday, so if he followed his usual retreat schedule—which would make it eleven twenty in Missouri—the group should be camped out in the shade of the old dogwood tree. The one she'd carved their initials into so many years ago. She'd never told him. Had he ever noticed?

Dear God, I love him so much. Help him face whatever demons haunt him. Help him find his way back to me.

❧

"Dear God, I loved her so much." Roger Tennant's voice ripped through the morning air. The poor guy couldn't be much older than Cam, but he'd lost his wife to ovarian cancer four months ago.

Cam had to bite down on the inside of his lip to stem his own surge of emotion. Though the guests on this retreat were all widows and widowers, Cam hadn't intended this to be a grief workshop. When he posted the information in the church newsletter, he'd recommended it for people who had passed at least the one-year anniversary of their spouse's death.

Apparently Roger hadn't read that far. The man's raw anguish was affecting everyone.

Ralph, a widower himself, had arranged some time off from inn duties to sit in on Cam's retreat. He laid a hand on Roger's shoulder. "It's okay, man. We've all been there. And as you can see, we all survived."

Roger looked up with brimming eyes. "How? How'd you do it? I don't even want to go on without Pamela."

Ralph looked around the circle, a slow smile creeping across his lips. "I think I can answer for everyone here. And there's only one answer: God."

Nods of agreement met his words, and Cam sent up a silent prayer of gratitude for Ralph's wisdom. The simple statement helped Cam regain a measure of control and refocus his thoughts. "I think what Ralph is saying is that when our own strength fails, when it feels like we can't survive another day, God carries us." He turned to a passage he'd marked in his Bible. "In the book of Lamentations the prophet Jeremiah writes, 'Because of the Lord's great love we are not consumed, for his compassions never fail. They are new every morning; great is your faithfulness.' Every day, all over again, we can go to God for the strength to keep living."

A shudder raked through Roger. He swiped at the wetness on his face. "It's a good thing, because I'm all out of strength."

Cam closed the Bible. Obviously his planned agenda on prayer was out the window. Might as well go with the flow. "Maybe it would help if you shared some of your good memories of Pamela. I remember working with her on the evangelism committee a couple of years ago, but some of these people never had the chance to know her."

"Yeah. . .yeah." Roger gave a loud sniff and cleared his throat. "She was the greatest. Funny, smart, creative."

As he continued, Cam pushed himself up from the ground to ease his stiff knees while he recalled the lovely woman Roger described. The shakiness left Roger's voice. He even chuckled at some of the stories he told about his wife. And his love for her—the love they shared—resonated in every word.

Cam looked away, one hand pressed against the trunk of the dogwood tree. He squeezed his eyes shut. *Oh, God, if I could have a love like that someday!*

And then the thought hit him: *It's right in front of you, Cam. But you've got to be willing to step out in faith.*

When he opened his eyes, his breath caught. Not two inches from where his hand rested on the tree trunk, he made out a roughly carved shape.

The gnarled bark had partially obscured it, but the outline of a heart was unmistakable.

And inside it, the initials JG + CL.

When the thrumming in his ears subsided, the voices of the retreat guests filtered into his consciousness.

"Wish I'd known her."

"Your Pamela was a keeper, that's for sure."

"What sweet memories. Cherish those, Roger."

And Roger's voice again: "Thanks. Just talking about her like this has made me realize it was all worth it—even the mistakes I made. I'd rather endure this pain and regret than never have loved her at all."

"Are you listening, son?"

The impression on Cam's spirit couldn't be stronger. He tilted his head heavenward and inhaled the sweet, green scents of summer. As the midday sunshine sifted through the branches and lit a fire behind his eyelids, so did God's healing touch flame in his heart. *"You made mistakes, and you will make more. But I love you anyway, and you are forgiven. Now forgive yourself, as many times as necessary. Let yourself love and be loved."*

The conversation beneath the tree had subsided. Cam glanced at his watch—noon already. He swiveled toward the group, his gaze seeking out Ralph while he snapped his cell phone off his belt. "Can you show everyone inside for lunch? I need to make a phone call."

❧

Jilly poked out her lower lip to blow a damp strand of hair off her forehead. "I had no idea I'd collected this much stuff since I moved in."

"How are you planning to get it all to Missouri?" Denise tore off a piece of tape to seal the box she'd just filled.

"It sure won't fit in my car. Guess I'll have to either rent a trailer or have it shipped." She sank onto the nearest chair and took a long swallow from her water bottle. "I need a breather. How about some lunch?"

"It's that time, isn't it? Want me to go pick something up?"

Jilly's gaze swept across the array of boxes and general packing clutter. She rasped out an exhausted moan. "I'd rather get away from this mess for a bit. Just let me freshen up."

Ten minutes later she hobbled down the apartment steps behind Denise and climbed into the passenger seat of Denise's Camry. They opted for their favorite salad buffet, Jilly's treat.

Denise speared a mandarin orange with her fork. "I sure don't envy you that long, lonesome trip. How far is it, anyway?"

"I checked online the other day. Nearly two thousand miles." Just speaking the words made Jilly weak with fatigue and dread. She sank against the seat, her fork clattering to the table.

"Oh my. That's. . ." Denise tilted her head sideways and squinted, her fork drawing invisible figures in the air. She shot Jilly a worried frown. "Honey, with a trailer, that'll be a good four days on the road."

"It's not like I have much choice." She stiffened her spine. "Hey, I'm a big girl. I'll be fine."

"You're a big girl with a broken ankle. There's no way I'm letting you take off cross-country by yourself." Denise broke into a wide grin. "Why don't you let me go with you? I can keep you company and help with the driving."

"Oh, Denise, I couldn't ask you to do that."

"Come on, it'll be fun. Besides, I've always wanted to visit Missouri."

A four-day car trip with her chatty landlady? Jilly could only imagine! And yet the idea of having a friend along on the arduous drive somehow made it more palatable. She shrugged and reached for her wheat roll. "Why not? Let's do it. Can you be ready to leave by Tuesday? Harvey's usually booked solid at the inn over the Fourth of July, so I told him I'd try to be back by the weekend so I can help."

"Shouldn't be a problem. Just need to put a hold on my mail and newspaper and get Sally next door to water my plants. Do you have your cell phone with you? I can call her right now."

Jilly unzipped her purse and fished her phone from its depths. "Give me the number and—oh, rats. The battery's dead."

Chapter 19

Cam snapped his cell phone closed and plunked down on a chair in the lobby. It was the afternoon break, and the retreat guests were in the lounge, savoring slices of Heather's rhubarb pie. Delicious as it surely was, Cam had lost his appetite hours ago. He'd tried Jilly's cell three times since lunch but kept getting her voice mail. Just now he'd started to leave a message but got so tongue-tied, he had to hang up before he made a total fool of himself.

He could only imagine what would go through her mind when she finally retrieved the garbled message. *"Jilly? Hi, it's Cam. I, uh, wanted to tell you that. . . See, I found this thing on the tree and. . .I wondered if. . . Actually, I thought you should know—" Click.*

A hand clamped down on Cam's shoulder. He twisted to see Harvey standing above him, a questioning look in the older man's deep-set eyes. "Half your retreat folks are already upstairs in the conference room. You planning on joining them?"

"Yeah, guess I should get moving." He pushed up from the chair and started for the stairs, then pivoted. "Harvey, have you heard from Jilly recently?"

Harvey looked up from the stack of magazines he'd been arranging on an end table. "Not for a couple of days. I expect she's busy packing."

"Packing?"

"Haven't you heard?" Harvey broke into a wide grin. "She's moving back to Blossom Hills."

Electricity zinged through Cam. The best news ever for him, but it must mean Jilly's appointment with the orthopedist hadn't turned out the way she'd hoped. He sucked in a huge gulp of air and let it out slowly. "No, I hadn't heard. When do you expect her?"

"End of the week, most likely. She wants to make it back for the Fourth." Harvey tossed down a magazine and shot Cam an accusing frown. "I've been trying to keep my nose out of it, but I gotta ask. What's with you and Jilly? Up until the day she had that terrible allergic reaction, I'd have sworn things were really heating up between you. Now when we talk she'll hardly mention your name, and you've been moping around here like an abandoned puppy dog."

Cam combed his fingers through his hair and let them come to rest on the back of his neck. "I've been a little mixed up about things."

"Kinda gathered that. I've been praying for you."

"Thanks. I think it's working." Cam checked his watch. "And I'm very late for my session. If you hear from Jilly again, tell her I'm really glad she's coming home."

❧

Home. Jilly heaved a sigh as she closed the door of her garage apartment for the last time. Hard to believe in only a few days she'd once more be calling Dogwood Blossom Inn her home. With her cell phone recharged, she'd called Harvey on Sunday evening to update him about her travel plans, and as soon as she disconnected, her phone beeped with a voice mail notice—a full day after the fact, no thanks to her cellular provider. Her whole body atremble, she'd listened to Cam's bumbling message. Three times she'd almost called him back, only to decide what she had to tell him—and what she hoped and prayed he was trying to tell her—could only be said in person.

Now, if all went well, in three and a half days she'd be able to do just that.

Denise met her at the foot of the stairs. "Ready to go?"

"Ready as I'll ever be." She made her way to the rear of her Honda CRV and double-checked the hitch on the small trailer she'd rented. Even so, her belongings still jammed the backseat and cargo area almost to the roof. She slid her crutches into a gap behind the driver's seat, shoved the door closed, and climbed in behind the wheel.

Denise, already settled in the passenger seat, pumped her fist. "Road trip!"

Her now ex-landlady's enthusiasm was contagious. Jilly grinned and slipped on her sunglasses. She started the engine, plugged Denise's favorite Beach Boys CD into the stereo, and backed out of the driveway. "Blossom Hills, here we come!"

❧

Cam paced the length of the inn's front porch, pausing at the end of each trek to peer down the road. Four o'clock already and no sign of Jilly's car. Okay, so he didn't know what she drove and wouldn't recognize it anyway. It didn't help that every hour or so since noon another vehicle arrived with a family checking in for the holiday weekend.

"Cameron Lane, you are wearing a path in my porch." Alice strolled out and joined him at the railing. She'd been fluttering about the inn like a hummingbird ever since Harvey brought her home yesterday.

"I thought she'd be here by now. What time did she say they left Lincoln?"

"They were on the road by eight. Probably stopped for a long lunch. And remember, she's pulling a trailer." Alice tweaked Cam's ear. "Why you won't call her yourself is beyond me."

"I told you why." He shot her a smirk while rubbing his burning earlobe.

"Yes, and it's exactly the same reason she gave Harvey and me for why she won't call you." Alice clicked her tongue, but her eyes sparkled. "More stubborn sweethearts than you two I have never known."

"Admit it. You're loving every minute—" The low hum of a car engine rumbled through the trees. Cam's fingers tightened around the porch rail. He strained his gaze toward the bend in the road. Slanting sunlight cast a glare across the windshield of a dark blue car.

A car pulling a trailer!

"It's her!" Cam raced down the porch steps. His sneakers crunched across the gravel parking area as he ran to meet Jilly at the road.

By the time she pulled the car to a stop, his heart pounded so fiercely he thought his head would come off. His breath came in quick, noisy gasps. Every limb tingled with the anticipation of seeing her again, holding her again, kissing her again.

Then her door opened, and he froze. Took a step back. Slid trembling fingers into his back pockets.

She swung her casted ankle out of the car, then her other foot, clad in a scuffed brown driving moc. Long, tanned legs stretched upward to the hem of faded jean shorts. One hand on the door frame, the other on the steering wheel, Jilly raised her eyes to meet his.

A lazy grin spread across her mouth. "I've been stuck in this overstuffed vehicle for four days straight, and my backside is killing me. Are you just going to stand there looking goofy, or are you going to get a crowbar and pry me out of here?"

Everything around him faded into a blur. He edged forward, hands extended, reaching for the woman he loved. In one swift motion he hooked his arms under hers and pulled her to him. He sank the fingers of one hand into the thick mass of hair at her nape. With the other he pressed her closer, closer, until he felt the pounding of her heart against his own. His mouth searched out hers, and when their lips met, he tasted the salt of tears—his or Jilly's, he didn't know. He only knew he'd never let her go again.

❧

With the sun slipping behind the hills and the stars popping out one by one, Jilly folded her hands beneath her head and peered through the branches of the old dogwood tree. Her chest rose and fell with a contented sigh.

Seated Indian-style on the blanket next to her, Cam nudged her with his knee. "Better sit up. Ralph will be starting the fireworks soon."

She traced the length of his forearm with her index finger, enjoying the feel of his taut muscle. "The only fireworks I'm interested in are happening right here under this tree."

In the gathering darkness she couldn't make out his expression, but his throaty chuckle told her all she needed to know. He eased down beside her and drew her head into the hollow of his shoulder. "Why didn't you ever tell me you carved our initials into the tree?"

"Because you were a hunky high-school kid and I was a dorky tennis jock who wasn't even on your radar."

"Not true." He kissed her forehead. "I was never hunky."

She rose up on her elbows and glared at him. "Oh, so you agree I was a dorky tennis jock? Why, you—"

A shower of blue and gold sparks exploded over the lake, followed by a concussive *pop*. From the shoreline came the oohs and aahs of Dogwood Blossom Inn's Fourth-of-July guests. Memories of other glorious Fourths here with the Nelsons propelled Jilly to the edge of the blanket for a better view.

Cam scooted next to her, one arm curling around her shoulder. She leaned into him as another explosion of light and color filled the sky. "I never thought I'd say this, but it sure is good to be home."

"Do you mean that?" Cam's warm breath tickled her ear. "I mean, you've faced a lot of changes in a really short time. Are you sure you're okay about everything?"

For a brief moment, the chill of disappointment seeped back in. "If you mean, do I have any regrets about giving up tennis, then, yeah, of course I do. But it's like I heard you say in one of your prayer retreats. God uses everything in our lives to help us grow into the person He created us to be. And through all this, God has helped me realize that tennis is something I do—or did—not who I am."

"I was thinking. I've got an idea I wanted to run by you."

She shifted to get a better look at his face, lit briefly by another burst of fireworks. "What kind of idea?"

"Remember I told you about volunteering at my church's after-school program?"

Jilly tensed. "That's how you met Liz. Tutoring her little boy, Sam."

He squeezed her shoulder and pressed his head against hers, wordless reassurance that his relationship with Liz was completely over. "We also try to get the kids involved in something fun and active, and I was thinking they might enjoy learning a little tennis."

Jilly let the idea skitter through her brain. Could she stand the daily reminder of what she'd lost? Or would it be easier if she gave up tennis entirely? "I don't know. . . ."

"I could introduce you to the program director at church next Sunday. You could meet a few of our kids." Cam's lips brushed her cheek. "You don't have to decide anything until school starts, and even then you could do it on a trial basis."

Teaching kids the sport she loved, and without the pressure of competition. The more she thought about it, the better the idea sounded. *It's all in Your hands, Lord. I'm not making any decisions tonight—*

"I was thinking something else, too." Cam's voice had grown husky. His fingertips grazed the back of Jilly's hand, sending shivers up her arm.

A tremulous breath whispered through her lips. "Wh–what were you thinking?"

"I was thinking how much I love you, Jilly Gardner. I was thinking I'd really like to make you my wife."

Epilogue

Dogwood blossom time. The air pulsed with the heady scent. Four-petal white blossoms with yellow centers clustered along gnarled branches, adorning the hillside like a bride's train. Though the spring day held a chill, bright sunshine warmed the crown of Jilly's head beneath her tulle veil. Clutching a bouquet of dogwood blossoms and red roses, she smiled first at Alice, then Harvey, each walking beside her down the petal-strewn path.

Their destination: an ancient dogwood tree where a lovesick young girl once carved a heart, and inside it her initials next to those of the boy she secretly adored. JG + CL.

The boy himself—now a handsome man—watched her approach. Cam's beaming face seemed to light up the shadows cast by the tree's blossom-laden canopy. Scarcely aware of the guests who'd gathered on the lawn—Denise, Paul, Heather, Ralph, members of the Nelson clan, church friends, Cam's colleagues from Rehoboth Bible College, and Cam's parents, who'd flown in from Arizona—Jilly strode forward into the future she'd been dreaming about and planning for, ever since that night last summer under the fireworks.

The pastor smiled his welcome. "Who presents this woman to be wed?"

Harvey and Alice spoke in unison: "We, her parents, do."

Tears lodged in Jilly's throat. Harvey lifted the veil away from her face, his own eyes spilling over. She pulled the couple into her arms, love and gratitude so powerful within her that she could hardly breathe. Harvey patted her shoulder and nudged her forward, guiding her hand into Cam's. He gave their entwined fingers a squeeze, then took Alice's arm and helped her to their seats.

The rest of the ceremony went by in a blur. Jilly only knew she'd be spending the rest of her life with the man she loved. The man who completed her. The man who had helped her find her way back to God and family.

"Ladies and gentlemen, I present Mr. and Mrs. Cameron Lane." The pastor nodded at Cam. "Sir, you may kiss your bride."

"Thought you'd never ask." A twisted grin curled Cam's lips. He tugged Jilly into his arms, swooped her backward into a daring dip, and planted an earth-shattering kiss on her waiting mouth—to the whoops and applause of everyone in attendance.

"Wow!" Jilly gasped, coming up for air. "I'd say you aced that serve, Mr. Lane. I demand a rematch."

Before he could react, she whipped him around, dropped him across her bent knee, and kissed him with equal vigor. The guests cheered even louder.

Righting himself, Cam gave a whistle and grinned. "That's what I get for marrying an athlete. Everything's a competition, and she always has to win."

"And don't you forget it." Jilly edged into his arms, her tone mellowing. She spoke not just to Cam, but to everyone present. "The truth is, I've been a winner since the day my social worker told me I'd be living with the Nelsons." Her gaze sought out the only real parents she'd ever known, and she cast them a tender smile. "Harvey and Alice taught me what family, faith, and love are all about. If not for them, I wouldn't be the person I am today, and I thank God for them."

Cam kissed her again, this time slowly, deeply, gently. "And I thank God for bringing me you."

A Letter to Our Readers

Dear Readers:

In order that we might better contribute to your reading enjoyment, we would appreciate you taking a few minutes to respond to the following questions. When completed, please return to the following: Fiction Editor, Barbour Publishing, Inc., P.O. Box 719, Uhrichsville, OH 44683.

1. Did you enjoy reading *Gateway Weddings* by Myra Johnson?
   ❑ Very much. I would like to see more books like this.
   ❑ Moderately—I would have enjoyed it more if ______________

____

____

2. What influenced your decision to purchase this book? (Check those that apply.)
   ❑ Cover ❑ Back cover copy ❑ Title ❑ Price
   ❑ Friends ❑ Publicity ❑ Other

3. Which story was your favorite?
   ❑ *Autumn Rains* ❑ *Where the Dogwoods Bloom*
   ❑ *Romance by the Book*

4. Please check your age range:
   ❑ Under 18 ❑ 18–24 ❑ 25–34
   ❑ 35–45 ❑ 46–55 ❑ Over 55

5. How many hours per week do you read? ______________

Name ____

Occupation ____

Address ____

City__________________ State__________ Zip___________

E-mail ____